Songs by Honeybird

PETER MCDADE

Copyright ©2022 Peter McDade

All rights reserved. Worldwide softcover edition published in the United States of America by Wampus Multimedia, Winchester, Virginia. Copyright ©2022 Wampus Multimedia.

This is a work of fiction. Names, characters, places, and incidents are either the product of the author's imagination or are used fictitiously, and any resemblance to actual persons, living or dead, business establishments, events, or locales is entirely coincidental.

ISBN: 979-8-9850353-0-8
Library of Congress Control Number: 2022930684

Wampus Multimedia Catalog Number: WM-118

The companion album to this novel, *Songs by Honeybird: Original Soundtrack*, is available from online music retailers.

Photo by Vivian Alvarez.
Jacket design by Anne Richmond Boston.

www.peterjmcdade.com

For BLC

JANUARY

Excerpt from an interview with Harlan Honeybird. The Great Speckled Bird, *April 12-25, 1968.*

Great Speckled Bird: Let's talk about your songs. Because, man, the shit going down is unreal, right? It's almost like there's too much to write about.

Harlan Honeybird: Crazy, crazy time. The world is blowing up, no doubt.

GSB: So how do you decide what to say? Where do these songs come from?

HH: I just let my mind go, you know? Maybe pour myself a little something to drink, or find myself a little something to smoke? [Laughter] Then I pick up a guitar and see what happens. And, it's like, I need to forget everything else, you know? Stop worrying about opening everyone else's mind, and just deal with my own shit.

GSB: It sure sounds like you're writing about the South. About our crazy past, our fucked up present.

HH: For sure, for sure. Gotta see it for what it is before we can fix it, right? Try and make it what it can be?

GSB: And what can it be?

HH: Fuck if I know. [Laughter] I'm still trying to see it for what it is.

GSB: And what does your father think about his rock-and-roll son? You know, Hank Honeybird said some—

HH: Oh, man, we don't need to talk about him, do we?

1 | Sid

Nina stands in the middle of her studio apartment, surveying the wreckage. The amount of trash is impressive: a multi-colored assortment of take-out containers, crumpled Grubhub bags, randomly tossed clothes, wine bottles, and Yoo-hoo cans. Did she really buy a six-pack of Yoo-hoo? It's a snapshot from the life of someone who hit a rough patch two months ago, not two weeks. The morning light streaming in from the sliding glass doors behind her creates ominous, uneven shadows, as if promising that the worst is yet to come. At least this stage of her grief is a secret shared only with Sid, sound asleep on the bed she swore she would train him to stay off. She knows he won't tell anyone.

She tilts her head, as if changing the angle of her view can diminish the scale of the wreckage. Inhales, exhales. Stretches.

Last night she'd promised herself she would do one challenging task this morning, and she has narrowed her choices down to cleaning the apartment or calling her mother for the first time in two weeks. Nina calculates it will take less physical exertion to pick up her iPhone than it would to find trash bags, never mind fill them up.

Nina delivers the news as soon as her mother answers. "Ben and I broke up."

"That asshole. He hit you, didn't he?"

"Jesus, Mom, no. He never hit me."

"Men hit."

"Yes, men hit." She makes her way to the sliding glass doors, staring out into the parking lot behind her apartment building. "And dogs bite and cats scratch."

"Well, I don't know what that has to do with anything."

Nina sighs. "Just because someone can do something doesn't mean they do it."

"But—"

"He made me kill all the cockroaches, Mom. Ben never hit anybody in his life."

"Huh." Pause. "I don't think it's drugs or booze."

"You met him," Nina says, wondering if it's too late to hang up and clean the apartment instead. "Did he seem like someone who would hit me, or have an alcohol problem?"

"Just because I met him does not mean I know him. For that matter, just because you dated him does not mean you knew him, either. People have secret sides."

"I know, Mom. But trust me, Ben had no secret violent side. He couldn't even beat me in Scrabble."

"He was cheating?"

"At Scrabble?"

"You know what I mean."

Nina stares at Sid, still sleeping on the futon. Weren't dogs supposed to sense when their humans were upset and offer comfort? Of course, most dogs run to the door at the sound of your key in the lock, and that was not Sid's style, either. "That wasn't it, Mom."

Pause. "So why did you break up with him?"

Being too embarrassed to correct her mother and explain that Ben broke up with her makes Nina feel closer to thirteen than twenty-five. Her mother would ask why, though, and that's something Nina can never reveal. "Relationships end, right?"

"Yes, they do. And you know I was not his biggest fan. I'm just trying to understand how things changed so quickly. Usually that means someone fucked around or fucked up."

Nina wonders—and not for the first time—if she should leave Atlanta; maybe she and her mother have been in the same city for too long. "Does it matter? All that matters now is that I am alone again." An overt move for sympathy, an obvious attempt to focus attention on Nina's pain and interrupt her mother's imminent monologue on the evils of men, but it works.

"Remember, baby," her mother says, voice softening, "men may be like bad colds, but that also means there's always another one just around the corner."

"And there's no cure?"

"Sleep and food."

Nina closes her eyes, leans against the glass door, rubbing her forehead with her left hand. "Okay. I can do that."

"Of course you can."

For a moment there's silence. It's a rare occurrence in one of their phone calls, and exactly what Nina needs to hear. Just as she gives her mother credit for reading the situation correctly, the silence is broken.

"And a good vibrator. Cheaper than a man and a lot more reliable."

"Goodbye, Mom."

Nina moved into B-6, a studio apartment in an old building on 12th Street, four years ago.

She made the decision toward the end of one of those Atlanta Novembers when it never stops raining. She had just broken up with Michael Marone, a barback from Miller Union. Never intended to be anything more than a meaningless fling, one of those boys that never even met her friends, Michael missed the memo. It proved to be an uglier breakup than she'd prepared for. In the climactic scrum, held in the Krispy Kreme parking lot, he landed a solid punch with his line about her behaving like she was "afraid to live in the real world." Then he drove away, leaving her in front of the darkened *Hot Donuts Now* sign.

She woke up the next morning and realized she was still sleeping in the same bed she'd gotten for her fourth birthday. Nina had shared the same small house with her mother, and her mother's mother, since Nina's father died. If she didn't escape before they started collecting cats, she would never leave.

So she called her friend Denise. A year earlier Denise had asked her to split the cost of a cool two-bedroom apartment in Midtown, but Nina had worried about the money and about living with Denise, whose flakiness had threatened more than once to end their friendship. Denise had never found a roommate, and said she'd love for Nina to move in. The catch: she was in a studio, 400 square feet. "But Tony has a place in Buckhead," she explained, "and I'm there a lot."

"Oh," Nina said, energized enough to sit up in bed. She'd never heard the name Tony before, but Denise was rarely without a boyfriend. "So this could work."

"It could actually be great," Denise said. "You can watch Sid when I'm not here."

"Sid?"

"My dog. I know I told you."

Denise remembered a lot of conversations Nina was sure never happened, and she certainly would have remembered hearing about a dog. Denise was the least likely of any of her friends to keep a plant alive, never mind an animal. "A dog? In 400 square feet?"

"He's more like a cat, I promise."

Nina looked up at the Depeche Mode poster she'd hung on her wall in ninth grade, hoping to find an answer, but none of the band members were even looking at the camera. It was up to her to decide. "Okay," she said. "Let's do this."

She went down to breakfast and announced her plan. Her grandmother nodded silently, the way she did at any piece of news she received, large or small, but her mother was skeptical. "12th Street? It'd be nice to be close to the park, but Midtown has become a wasteland of Starbucks and expensive parking. How much is the rent?"

"My share's only $350 a month." She didn't add that it was so cheap because it was a studio apartment.

"350? Now I'm worried. Do you have to clean the lobby? And Denise? The lesbian?"

"No. That's Debbie."

"Oh." Her mother paused, and then shrugged. You could say many things about Marion Alexander, but you could never accuse her of lingering over decisions. "Just remember—they arrest you if there's weed in the apartment, even if it's not yours."

Nina packed that afternoon, and hit the buzzer for B-6 before dinner. Her mother was right: Midtown had more yuppies and fancy restaurants than Nina remembered seeing when she cut school to go to the High Museum on its free Thursday afternoons. Yet Denise's building, an old motel that had been converted into small apartments, looked as if it had not changed in decades. The exterior was stubbornly un-updated, its pale beige paint seeming to fade even as you looked at it. The interior was still dominated by the wonderfully flamboyant gay men who used to be the only people daring or desperate enough to live in this part of Atlanta.

The apartment itself did not feel as cramped as she'd feared. The large sliding glass doors along the exterior wall helped, letting in so much light that the room felt bigger. Denise quickly ran through the quirks for Nina: the toilet handle needs to be held down, and never flush before showering; don't put too much in the garbage disposal, which sucks, but a new one is on the way; and the guys in C-6, one floor above, are loud when they have sex, but it never lasts long.

Sid turned out to be a bichon poo—part bichon frise, part toy poodle. A gift from the boyfriend before Tony, an older man who'd been a huge Sex Pistols fan, Sid was fifteen pounds soaking wet, with big eyes, shaggy black hair that always looked like it needed a comb, and a tendency to walk a little sideways. His best trait, as far as Nina was concerned, was his demeanor. Instead of being one of those small, yippy dogs determined to deal with a too big world by shouting at everything it saw, Sid was almost catatonic, so quiet that Nina forgot all about him as she and her new roommate chattered away. After Denise caught a Lyft to Buckhead to stay with Tony, it was as if Nina was living by herself.

Perfect.

She put Stevie Wonder on shuffle, ordered some tacos, put fresh sheets on the futon, and then carved out a drawer of her own in Denise's dresser. It wasn't until she was getting ready for bed that she remembered Sid, staring at her from his spot in front of the glass doors. "Huh. You probably need to go out, right?" she wondered aloud. When she walked to the front door to get the leash he followed her, patiently sitting still as she slipped it over his neck.

She hadn't even taken her phone, planning to be out just long enough for Sid to do his business. The night was nicer than she had expected, though, and she discovered that the leisurely pace of a stroll with a small dog was enjoyable if you surrendered yourself to it. When they returned to the apartment, she was surprised to learn they'd been gone over an hour.

Denise only slept in B-6 half a dozen nights over the next two months, so it was not a surprise when she said she was going to live with Tony, who was tired of paying for her rides. Nina had landed a job at South City Kitchen by then, making enough to cover the rent, so she wasn't upset by the news—especially when Denise said she was leaving the futon, dresser, and bookcase behind.

But that dog.

"What do you mean, you're leaving him here?"

"Tony's allergic."

"But you keep talking about how much you love this dog," Nina said. "How can you leave him?"

"I love my futon, and you're happy I'm leaving that."

Nina turned to stare at Sid, who was watching them closely. He looked like a child listening to his parents fight about who would be stuck with custody—then leaned back and started licking himself. "So what am I supposed to do with him?"

"Feed him, walk him? You've been doing it already, right?"

"Oh, I don't know, Denise." She had grown to like the mandatory walks, Nina had to admit, but there was a difference between taking care of a friend's dog and having one of your own. Walking Sid felt like driving a rental car, because she knew if anything broke or got too dirty she wouldn't have to deal with it. She'd never owned a pet of any kind; the one time she'd asked if they could at least get a hamster, her mother told her no living creature should be kept against its will.

That's when Denise checked her watch, which is what she did when she was getting bored. "Fuck it. I have to pack up my stuff, and Tony really wants to see some Marvel movie. Put up with Sid for one more night, and I can take him to the pound? First thing in the morning?"

Nina began rearranging as soon as Denise left. She started in the corner next to the sliding glass doors, dragging the broken end table down to the trash bin, then pushing the low bookcase closer to the kitchen. Opening up the space made her imagine saving up enough to buy a decent electric piano, which could now fit there. She would play much more if she didn't have to go back home to do it.

It was early evening by the time she finished. She took Sid for a long walk, following the same route from the first night she moved in. Over the last two months, she'd learned where Sid liked to stop and sniff, and had figured out which trash cans were best for dropping little bags of poop. As she strolled the now-familiar blocks she felt at peace, as if she were no longer a visitor but at home. And why not, she asked herself, when she walked back into B-6 and took off Sid's leash. The apartment was now hers.

And so was Sid. When Denise inevitably called the next morning to say that something had come up, and she'd have to take Sid to the pound another day, Nina told her not to bother.

When Nina hangs up with her mother, she's surprised to see it's not even 9:30; she would have guessed it was almost noon. She leans against the sliding glass door and stares at the floor of her apartment. The clothes and trash are a minefield she must cross to make it to the small galley kitchen area, also known as the Land of Coffee. She decides the best strategy is to just look straight ahead and ignore the occasional crunching sound she makes as she walks. The noise wakes Sid, who catches her eyes long enough to shoot a look of annoyance.

The two grocery items she has made sure to keep on hand since the breakup are coffee and cream, a sign she hasn't completely lost her sanity. She measures the grounds and water and then stands right next to the coffee maker, so she can pour a cup as soon as it is done. She checks her phone while she waits, hoping to see a message from someone asking her to cover a lunch shift. Working is the one thing that has distracted her since Ben left, and word is out that Nina will take anyone's hours.

No messages, but one reminder: "First Day of Semester!" Had she really been excited enough to add an exclamation point? There's still enough time to make it to her 10 a.m. class, but she knows she's not going. Ben has a Monday/Wednesday/Friday schedule this semester, and the last thing she wants to do is run into him on campus. Last night she'd set up a walk with Troy, which sounds much more manageable than a trip to Georgia State.

When the coffee finishes, she fills her mug and drinks it standing at the kitchen sink. There's no window, so Ben insisted on hanging up a picture of *Water Lilies* from some museum catalog. He was right: it is much better than staring at a wall. A trip to Giverny, to visit the house where Monet once lived, had been on their fantasy list of Places to Visit, never written down but frequently added to.

She should probably stop thinking of all the things they had planned to do together.

Once she has finished her first mug and poured another she has the strength to head back into the living room. It's even brighter than it was a few minutes ago, the morning light throwing the mess into sharper relief. Why are there so many Chipotle bags? Has she really gotten delivery from there four, five—one more bag, under the futon—six times? Does she even like Chipotle?

Nina examines her current outfit—baggy sweat pants without any visible stains, oversized Led Zeppelin T-shirt—and decides it is good enough for a walk. She manages to get her shoes on, then heads back to the kitchen, pours the last of the coffee into a travel mug, and picks Sid's leash up off the dining table.

Nina had always heard that dogs woke you up in the morning, desperate to go for a walk, but Sid prefers to sleep as late as possible. "Oh, you're coming," she says to him. "And I don't want to hear a word of complaint." As she watches him hop down and slowly walk over to her, she feels her phone buzz in her sweatpants. Troy is texting to tell her that he and Carol, his chihuahua, are outside and waiting. If Troy's on time, she's late.

"Hurry it up," she says to Sid, rattling the leash again. "Your girlfriend is waiting for you."

2 | Harlan Honeybird

When Ben first started teaching his own sections of freshman history, he tried to earn a reputation as a hard-ass. He taught one class a semester as part of his Ph.D. funding, and wanted to be that teacher you were later glad you'd had since you learned so much. He assigned lots of writing, deployed the occasional pop quiz, and kept the classes for their fully scheduled time, even on the first day of the semester. Now that he's in his fifth year of the program and his third year of teaching, he's as anxious to get out as the students are. On opening day of the spring semester, he lets everyone leave after just twenty minutes and feels no guilt.

After class he heads to the eighth floor, home of the Georgia State history department. Across the hall from the department proper, with its secretaries and nice offices and tenured faculty, is the Cube Farm, the name graduate students have assigned the large double classroom subdivided into fifty cubicles. Each graduate research assistant gets a cheap desk, a chair that may or may not still be adjustable, and access to the department's spotty Wi-Fi, all separated by a system of half walls that looks as though it will collapse if examined too closely. In spite of its shabby quality, the Cube Farm has become the place that most feels like home to him since he moved to Atlanta. Only Nina's apartment felt more so, but he's never going back there.

Ben got lucky with his cube placement. He's far enough from the front door that he never has to answer random knocks and close enough to the small sitting area in the back corner to participate in endless debates with his fellow grad students. What does the continued popularity of reality TV say about the country? Which mainstream political party is less incompetent? What's the best burger in Atlanta? What were the true intentions of the writers of the Constitution, and should those intentions still be given consideration? These discussions improve Ben's ability to use the same basic facts as everyone else to create a more engaging story. History is told by more winners than losers, yes, but the most lasting accounts are those written by the better storytellers.

Just as Ben expected, Duncan is the only other person in the Cube Farm this early; they are the only two grad students who volunteer to teach the 8 a.m. freshman survey course. Duncan, whose cubicle is just across from Ben's, is two years ahead in the Ph.D. program, and has been a valuable guide. He's let Ben know which seminar teachers to seek out and which ones to avoid, and, most importantly, offered tips on how to minimize the time spent grading for forty-five students. Duncan also serves as a warning, though. He's already a year behind schedule and struggling to finish his dissertation on subversive medieval art. He received an extra round of funding for this year but has not yet heard anything about next year.

"Welcome to spring semester, Professor Stephens," Ben says, jealous of the large cup of coffee on Duncan's desk.

Duncan turns around, his chair smoothly rolling away from his desk. It's one of the best chairs in the Cube Farm, and he rightfully lives in constant fear of it getting swiped. "Same to you, Professor Davies," he says, narrowing his eyes. "And can I just say, you look like shit this morning."

"Thanks." Ben examines his day's wardrobe. It's his standard casual professor look: khakis, neutral button-down, dark suit jacket. No visible coffee stains or open fly, so the strain of the last few weeks must be visible in his eyes. "Always good to hear."

"Break was that good, or break was that bad?"

Ben shrugs. "Break was okay."

"Hmm. Your answer is vague, at best." Duncan picks up his coffee and takes a sip. "Something went down with the family in Seattle?"

"No, I kept it nice and light." Ben takes his MacBook out of his messenger bag and places it on his desk. "All the tension was wonderfully unspoken."

Another sip of coffee. "Your dead guitarist, then. Problems there?"

It drives Ben crazy to hear Harlan Honeybird called "his" guitarist, but he also knows it is undeniable that most grad students become protective, even possessive, of their research subjects. Now that it has happened to him, he understands it may be the only way to generate the stamina required to finish a dissertation. "Harlan had a quiet break," Ben says, "but I am optimistic about the spring."

Duncan puts down his coffee cup, claps his hands together. "Then there must be something going on with the girlfriend."

Ben opens the Mac, clicks the space bar to wake it up, and turns back to Duncan. "Nina and I broke up." He watches Duncan's face for a reaction, but all he gets is a slight eyebrow raise. Duncan had warned him about dating undergrads; how annoying that the warning proved prescient.

"I always find it interesting when someone says 'X and I' broke up," Duncan says, after a short pause. "It implies both parties agreed to the decision. Truth is, these things are rarely mutual." He takes a sip of coffee and continues. "Which means you're either using this grammatical construction to cover up for being dumped or because you feel guilty about dumping her."

Ben dramatically puts his hands to his chest, as if his feelings have been hurt. "Five years. You'd think that after five years I'd have found a more supportive friend."

"Oh, my middle name is supportive." Duncan says. "Supportive enough to demand the truth." He picks his coffee back up. "How long has it been?"

"Two weeks."

"Huh." Nod. "So it's really over?"

"Over."

"Done?"

Duncan's tone is colored with disbelief. For a moment Ben considers revealing the reason for the breakup, but that would lead to a much longer and more complicated conversation about what can and cannot be real, what is and is not sane. And he is not ready to have that conversation. "Done."

Duncan nods and turns back around. Ben sits down in his squeaky, slightly uneven chair, and disables the Wi-Fi. Nina's gone but the semester is here, and he needs to finish studying someone else's past so he can get on with his own future.

Ben hadn't planned on researching the short life of an obscure guitarist from the 1960s. Five years ago, when he arrived at GSU to start work on his Ph.D., he looked for a dissertation topic with roots in the Southeast. He first planned to examine the legacy of *The Great Speckled Bird*, an underground newspaper published from 1968 to 1976. The subject seemed especially timely given the current discussion of how information could—if at all—be presented without bias. The underground papers of that time period not only made no attempt to conceal their point of view, they reveled in it. Did that make them less trustworthy or just the opposite, since the reader knew the stories were filtered through a specific prism?

The underground newspapers of the Sixties had been written about more than he'd realized, though, so he began looking for a single story within the paper to focus on. He spent some time researching the garbage strike of 1968 in Atlanta; Martin Luther King Jr., had been in Memphis for a sanitation strike when he was assassinated, but Ben still thought these workers' struggles never got as much attention as they should, considering the way they encapsulated the connection between race and class. The other possibility he considered was *Stanley v. Georgia*, a Supreme Court case that tackled the right to own pornography. That the state tried to put someone away for having porn seemed impossible in the modern world, where pictures few in 1968 could ever imagine seeing were just a click of the mouse away.

The story Ben kept coming back to, though, was about Honeybird, a rock trio out of Macon, Georgia. There were many articles about bands in the *Bird*, most of them focused on skinny white boys with guitars and cigarettes, but Honeybird was different. Yes, there was a skinny white boy on guitar, but an accompanying band photo also revealed a white girl with frizzy red hair and a Black drummer with arms the size of small cannons. No one in the band looked older than twenty, and they had just released their second record.

The concept of a multiracial, multigender band based in Macon, ninety miles south of Atlanta, in 1968, was shocking. There was Sly & the Family Stone, of course, but a quick Google search showed that Sly's first hit didn't come until April of 1968, a year after the release of Honeybird's first record. Besides, Sly was from California, a continent and a few metaphorical decades away from Macon, which was still fairly segregated in the Sixties. The Allman Brothers were an integrated band with a deep connection to Macon, but their first record didn't arrive until 1969. Did that mean Honeybird actually helped pave the way for the Allmans?

The picture that caught Ben's attention accompanied a short interview with Harlan Honeybird, the white guy in the photo. He played guitar and sang, and the red-headed bass player was his sister. The next mention of the band was a few months later, and this time the photo was of a burned-out barn. A lone sheriff stood glumly in the ruins, hat in hand and head bowed as if in prayer. The barn had been Honeybird's practice space, and Harlan had died in the fire. The drummer was also presumed dead, but his body was not found, at least at the time of the photo. Tragic, Ben thought as he returned to the shot of the three young musicians looking so alive. There were no follow-up stories about the cause of the fire, but in the fall of 1969 the paper published an article about a posthumous live album's unexpected success.

Honeybird became the story Ben would work on when he wanted to avoid grading or prepping for a lecture. Learning more about them would take some dedicated research, given the band's short life and limited success. He settled for researching the Macon rock scene of the Sixties, which meant lots of time watching old Otis Redding clips.

By the start of his second year in the Ph.D. program Ben hadn't worked on the Bird in months and knew he needed to change topics. If he waited any longer he ran the risk of needing more than six years to finish and running out of funding. He broached the idea during his first meeting that semester with Dr. Barbara Reed, his advisor. Reed's research had dwindled off in the last few years, but her books on race and gender, *The Color of Our Colors* and *The Whites of Our Eyes*, were groundbreaking arguments when they were published in the eighties, and beautifully written. Her agreement to advise Ben had been a significant factor in his picking Georgia State. When he told her that he was beginning to wonder if *The Great Speckled Bird* was what he wanted to focus on, she did not look surprised.

"Yes," Reed said, her thick gray hair pulled into a single, chaotic ponytail. She tapped her fingers while a Miles Davis album played softly from a Bluetooth speaker hiding on her desk among the stacks of papers, half a dozen coffee cups, and four potted plants, at least two of which appeared to be dead. The floor was just as cluttered, with so many piles of haphazardly stacked books that getting to one of the chairs felt like running a maze. "I think you could find a more complicated subject."

He mentioned the garbage strike and the pornography court case as possible topics. Dr Reed nodded but did not seem overly excited. When he started talking about Honeybird, though, her eyes came to life.

"An integrated band in Macon? Pre-Allmans?"

"Yes."

"Fascinating."

"But could it work for a dissertation? They were around for less than five years."

"Of course. Race, rock and roll, and gender: three very interesting topics that become even more powerful when connected." She paused, tilted her head. "And the band's name is Honeybird?"

"Yes, after Harlan Honeybird, the guitarist and songwriter. His sister Darlene was in the band, too."

"Any connection to Hank Honeybird?"

"I haven't looked into their backstory that much yet, because—"

"With a name like that, it has to be—and that's your jackpot, Ben." Dr. Reed cut him off and grabbed the long walking stick she kept propped against her desk. She banged it twice against the wall before calling out loudly, "Kuperman! Kuperman! Get in here and earn your money."

A moment later, Dr. Carl Kuperman was standing in the doorway to her office, holding a half-eaten sub in his hand and wearing a stained "Margaritaville" shirt. He didn't say anything, just raised his bushy gray eyebrows.

"Hank Honeybird."

"Ha!" Kuperman took a bite of his sandwich, shaking his head as if appreciating a great punchline. "The Biscuit King of Macon, the poor man's Herman Talmadge. Ran a terrible campaign for Senate in 54? 58?" Pause, nod. "56." Shrug. "How many times have I threatened to write a book about him?"

"Ben here is looking into Hank Honeybird's son," Reed said.

Kuperman looked down at Ben. "Harlan? Died young, right? Fire?"

"That's him," Reed said. "More specifically, his band."

"Ha! Yes. The band." Kuperman looked at Reed again. "Kid could play guitar, is what I heard." With a wave of his hand he abruptly turned and headed back to his office.

As soon as Ben got back to his cube, he Googled Hank Honeybird. Reading about the awful Senate campaign of 1956, Ben realized he finally had his dissertation topic. The leader of one of the South's first interracial rock bands, if not the first, had a father who campaigned for office as a die-hard, race-baiting segregationist.

3 | Not the Live Together Kind

Troy is standing on the sidewalk with Carol, his Chihuahua, in his arms. Carol hops down, eager to head over and sniff Sid. Troy gives Nina a quick hug, and then stands back, hands on her shoulders, and examines her appearance. "Not awful," he says. "You going to shower today?"

"Yes," she says.

"Promise?"

"Yes, yes," she repeats. "Now, let's walk, before Carol's nose gets stuck in Sid's butt."

They move at a leisurely pace, both of them firm believers in letting the dogs stop and smell and pull as much as they want, only forcing the pace if it's cold or one of them has to be somewhere. These walks are one of the unexpected bonuses of having Sid; she used to think that all she and Troy had in common was the fact they were both friends of Connie's, but she's learned they have similarly tinged worldviews (borderline optimistic, with a heavy layer of protective cynicism) and senses of humor (deadpan).

"How many days?" Troy asks.

"Fourteen."

"You remember what I said when you first told me, right?"

Nina nods. "How could I forget? It was the perfect reaction. 'Men suck.'"

"Well, I am smart about these things."

"Sucking men?" She turns to look at him, pleased to see him blushing. "Oh, I got him with that one, America."

"Yes. But also, breakups. Unfortunately, I have been through many more than you have."

"So have you figured it out?" They have stopped so Sid and Carol can circle around a phone pole. She talked Troy through one big breakup—Edwin, the actor who decided he needed to play the role of a literal straight man. Once Troy found Trent, though, she knew she would never need to talk him through the end of another relationship. "Why do we put ourselves into pairs when the breaking up sucks so much?"

"What I said," Troy says, ignoring her questions as they resume walking, "was that you get two weeks. And then all of this . . ." He pauses, turning to her and dramatically pointing at her with the hand not holding Carol's leash. "All of this has to get its act together."

"Can I ask for an extension?"

Troy rubs his chin, as if carefully considering a critical request. "No," he says, shaking his head. "The boy had a decent body, and a kind of appealing intellectual look in his eyes, so he is worth two weeks of moping around. Not a moment more."

"Please, sir, I want some more." She raises her eyebrows and assumes her best lonely orphan look.

"Mooooooore?" he bellows. "Oliver Twist has asked for more?"

It is so unusual for Troy to raise his voice that Nina starts to laugh, and Sid and Carol both turn around to look. If starving orphans being denied more gruel can still make her laugh, maybe there is hope yet.

Troy then proclaims they cannot refer to Ben for the rest of the walk, and for thirty minutes she is happily distracted. "Eat Your Art Out," the podcast Troy has co-hosted for the last three years, has been slowly gaining popularity, which means his work stories are starting to feature occasional cameos by B-level celebrities. The episode they just taped featured a phone interview with that Food TV host who has spiky white hair, and Troy's impersonation of their discussion about the greasy diners the host would bring Oscar Wilde to makes her laugh. Two laughs in one walk: a good sign.

When she gets back to the lobby, Morris, the building manager, is ensconced at the large wooden desk he uses as an office. He is surrounded, as usual, by several much younger and buffer men, masses of muscle packed into tight shorts and holding phones; they all seem to adore the sixtyish (seventyish?) Morris, with his dyed hair and omnipresent silk scarf. She has never been able to figure out if he is dating one or all or none of them. For the last two weeks she has avoided him, but she decides to go ahead and do a second hard thing on the same day.

"Hey," she says, catching his eye.

"Well, hey hey," he answers, with his thick drawl and customarily confident smile. Missing several front teeth has not dimmed the man's bravado. "How are you, darling?"

"Fine, thanks." She takes a deep breath. Morris had let her have the first look at a bigger apartment that had opened up, but if Ben isn't moving in, she can't afford it. "Turns out I'm not gonna take D-14, after all. Can I just renew B-6?"

Morris immediately assumes a look of compassion. "Well, of course, of course," he says. "Things didn't work out with your young man?"

She shakes her head, determined not to cry, though she suspects there are worse places to break down in tears than in front of half a dozen gay men. "Nope. Turns out he's not the Live Together Kind."

Morris reaches across his desk to pat her arm, and one of the Muscle Shirts next to her says sympathetically, "Few of them are, baby. Few of them are."

She forces a smile and makes an appointment to sign the lease later that afternoon. When they walk through the door, Sid heads to his favorite morning sun spot in front of the glass doors. He stretches and gives what Nina thinks of as his "hold my calls look" before he sits down, so she knows he will probably not move again until lunchtime. She drops his leash on the small dining table, on top of a dirty pair of jeans and an empty shake cup from Five Guys. The short burst of energy from her walk with Troy is fading quickly, so she carries her phone over to the futon, still open as a bed, and scans her messages.

"So what now?"

"What now?" Nina drops the phone next to her, lies down, and closes her eyes. No work requests. "Sleep? Maybe I should just go back to sleep."

"That's my plan," Sid says, without turning his attention away from the glass doors. "But I expected more from you."

"Well, that's why expectations are dangerous." She lifts her head up slightly and opens her eyes to look at this dog she had never planned on having. Sid scratches the back of his head with his right paw and then stands up to pace in a small circle. "Maybe that should be my new motto: no expectations," Nina says as she watches him find the perfect spot and then collapse, forming a small, black ball of fur.

She closes her eyes again. Much better. As tired as she feels, she knows she should force herself to log into the GSU website and sign up for new classes. If she starts spending too much time in this studio apartment, just Nina Alexander & Her Amazing Talking Dog, she might be living in Crazy Town by the start of summer. If she's not already there.

4 | No One Ever Aims for Macon

By 11 a.m. the Cube Farm is more crowded and much louder. There's lot of standard opening day banter as the other grad students start to wander in, and Ben welcomes the distraction. He joins Duncan and Shelley on the couch to debate (again) whether future historians will identify smartphones as the savior or destroyer of civilization, a topic that somehow segues into Cheap Trick's eventual place in rock history. Shelley is in her second year, and everyone is excited to see how she is going to tie the women of the abolitionist movement to punk's strongest female icons. Ben was jealous when he heard that Shelley's advisor was the department's cutting edge new hire, Cherize Pollant, whose essay on post-post modernism made it into the *New York Review of Books*. Duncan says he's heard that Shelley has only actually met in person with Pollant once, news that makes Ben a little more grateful for Dr. Reed. She may be disorganized and slow to respond to email, but at least Reed seems to always be on campus.

Ben is interested to hear Shelley's defense of Joan Jett after Duncan lumps her in with artists who traded their credibility for easy radio hits, but he needs to go to the library. He's working his way through the *Macon Telegraph* from the years Honeybird was active, attempting to understand the world that molded the band when they came into existence.

He says his goodbyes and heads back down to the quad. Deserted when he showed up for class, it's now full of students with backpacks hanging lightly off their shoulders and phones held as security blankets. The start of a new semester always fills Ben with optimism. The academic world is once again a cleanly scrubbed slate, and there is no reason for anyone to imagine how wrong things might go.

Weaving through a sea of undergrads on his way to the best slice of pizza in walking distance, Ben thinks of Nina, who introduced him to Rosa's. Not that Nina turned out to be like other undergrads. She had a wonderfully sharp edge that revealed itself most clearly in her sense of humor. It could have been the result of her being a few years older than most undergrads, but her essays and comments in class made Ben suspect she had been sharpening that edge her whole life.

Ben didn't talk about his dissertation with her initially because he imagined there were few things more boring for a girlfriend than listening to her history geek boyfriend talk about his "work." There was something so off-putting about that possessive: "My work deals with blah, blah, blah," as if interpreting an event somehow gives you ownership of it. But the first night they sat on the floor of her studio eating takeout from Panang—something that became a Friday night tradition—she insisted he talk about it. They'd been dating a month or so at that point, which had already made it the longest relationship he'd had since undergrad.

"Now that's a good fucking story," she had said after he gave a quick summary of the rise and fall of Honeybird. "The whole lost great band angle, complete with a made-for-TV, tragic ending."

"Not to mention the body they couldn't find."

"Right? Harlan leading this band, with a racist dad, his little sister on bass, his Black best friend on drums, all in Macon in the sixties? From what I've seen of Macon, I wouldn't be surprised if some locals set the fire on purpose."

"You've been to Macon?"

"Once or twice, when our family was on the way to Florida. Wasn't like we aimed for it." She assumed a serious face. "No one ever aims for Macon."

"I went once to walk around."

"And what did you think?"

"Kind of a sad ghost town, though you can feel some sections of the city trying to come back to life. I wonder what it was like fifty years ago."

"Well, it may have had more people wandering around then, but they would probably not have been happy to see a Yankee historian like yourself show up."

"I'm not a Yankee."

"Washington State." She tapped her finger on her chin, as if deep in thought. "I forget. Is that north or south of the Mason-Dixon Line?"

"West."

"And north, College Boy. I mean, bonus points for not beating us in the War of Northern Aggression and all, but it's still north."

"Maybe you should come with me next time?"

"I would love to serve as your bodyguard."

She flexed her arms comedically, still holding her chopsticks, but Ben was impressed. The ultimate Nina metaphor: arms stronger than most people would ever suspect. "You're hired."

"To be honest, though, I still can't believe this can be a serious topic for a dissertation. No offense."

"Well, there will be lots of people who agree with you. That's part of why I'm so worried about finding some big insights, or lessons the Harlan

Honeybird story reveals. Why the previous 200 pages or so are important. Blah blah."

"Okay, then." She pointed at him with her chopsticks. "What's your angle?"

"You got a lot of it already, I think. Integrated band in Macon, fifty years ago? And I keep the story focused on Harlan, the songwriter attempting to overcome the sins of his father—the sins of the previous generation, really." He was disappointed to find all the green beans gone, so he snatched one off her plate with his chopsticks. "Died before he could finish his journey, but paved the way for those who followed. That makes his story just the kind historians look for—someone previously unnoticed who had a big effect. I just need to collect enough evidence. It's one thing to say it, and another to build a credible argument."

She used her chopsticks to take a dumpling off his plate. "Okay, but were they any good?"

"Yes," Ben said. "I was relieved at how good they were. That some of the stronger songs stand up so well helps my argument."

"When do I get to hear them?"

"Well, next time we hang out."

"Next time, huh?"

"Yup," he said. When they first started dating they made the tenuous nature of their relationship a running gag, future plans made with the proviso, "If we're still going out." It was one of the reasons he suspected the relationship would last. "So now there has to be a next time."

"What about the fire?" Nina said. "Is there something there?"

He watched her chopsticks move toward his plate again, but this time he blocked with his. "What do you mean?"

"Like, some secret or something? Does it seem suspicious? I wasn't kidding about locals sending a message."

Ben shook his head. "Not officially ruled arson, at least. Harlan smoked a lot. And drank. It's certainly believable that those two habits could start a fire."

"But they never found Nate's body?"

"Nope. Hank Honeybird was convinced Nate started the fire and left town. They could never find him, though, and Nate's family was convinced he'd been with Harlan at the time, so he was dead, too."

She raised her eyebrows dramatically. "What do you think? Could he still be alive?"

"It's possible, I guess? I mean, I could see him wanting to get the hell out of town—everyone would blame the Black guy, right? And there's a small universe of Honeybird obsessives who are convinced that's the case."

"Oh! Maybe you can find him. There's a damn book, right?"

Ben had daydreamed about being the one to find Nate, alive and well and ready to tell his story. "Oh, it would be a helluva book," he said. "But the boring, simple explanation is usually the right one."

"History? Boring? Doesn't sound like the teacher I had," she'd said with a flirtatious tone, stretching out her leg and draping it comfortably over his. Her ease with casual physical contact had been an unexpected bonus of their time together. His most serious girlfriend had been Amy McIntosh from junior year, and as much fun as she could be, she was not inclined to touch him so consistently.

He'd been dating Nina for almost a year when she told him her lease was up for renewal. The building manager had let her know there was a bigger apartment available, and she could afford it with a roommate. He felt completely like himself around her; she was the first girlfriend with whom he hadn't needed to act like the boyfriend he thought he was expected to be. Still, he hesitated, even though he already slept at her place several nights a week. In a year and a half he'd be done at Georgia State and looking for a job that would most likely require him to move. So they'd live together for a year or so, and then he'd wind up roaming the country as an itinerant history post-doc.

Nina talked him into doing it anyway. "So you'd give up what could be a good year because that might be all we have?"

"But what if it's hard to leave? I mean—"

"If it's hard to leave, then we've been having a good time. Live in the moment, right?"

He wondered if losing her father at a young age made her less uptight than he was most of the time. Did a tragedy like that help internalize the idea that life is fleeting? Maybe he was just making excuses because he'd never lived with a girlfriend before. Was he afraid to let someone see him at his morning worst, all smelly breath and impossible hair?

So he said yes to the idea of living together for one great year. After spending his whole life as the younger, less charismatic Davies brother, he had a funny, smart, good-looking girlfriend. What could go wrong?

And then she told him about her talking dog.

Her reincarnated talking dog.

When he gets to Rosa's, he is still thinking of Nina. She changed her order every time, and thought it was hilarious that he always got the same thing. "One slice with green peppers and sausage," he says. As he waits, he can't decide if he should call or text Nina to see how she is, or just stay focused on sticking to his usual routine, because that's the easiest path to take.

5 | Whistles and Jockstraps

Her mother had enough internal aging hippie left to support Nina taking a gap year before college. High school had been torture, and the last thing she wanted was to immediately enter a larger version of that world, with more cliques and crowded hallways and teachers who rarely noticed her.

Nina had done well enough to qualify for Georgia's Zell Miller Scholarship, though, which meant an almost free ride with the state universities. When she decided to do something besides bounce around waitressing jobs and hang out with Connie and Troy, she started taking one course a semester at Georgia State. She approached college as if it was a casual hobby—something she could tell people she was doing, to appear as though she had more of a life plan than she really did.

She avoided taking the required world history course until her fifth semester. High school history had been the fiefdom of the football coach, a grumpy old man in a fading windbreaker who made students memorize dates for multiple-choice quizzes, or pretend to read old issues of *US News & World Report* while he surfed his phone. None of the English courses she wanted synced up with her schedule, though, and anything was better than College Algebra.

Ben was not a football coach or grumpy. He was funny and engaging when he lectured, promised no dates would need to be memorized, and seemed genuinely interested in hearing what his students had to say. It was the first time she'd had a crush on a teacher since fourth grade, when Mr. Jayson's deep laugh made her feel like she was smiling too much every time she heard it. Nina drove Connie crazy with her regular debriefings about Mr. Davies' class—the way his hands moved when he talked, the way he made sarcastic comments so subtle that most of the class missed them, and yes, the way his pants hugged his legs—but she couldn't stop herself. As the semester progressed she became convinced that he looked forward to seeing her as much as she looked forward to seeing him. Two weeks after the semester ended she emailed about her grade, pretending she couldn't access it because of some hang-up with financial aid. It only took a few days of exchanging bantering notes for him to finally ask her to meet for coffee.

"Thank God," Connie said when Nina told her. "If this went on any longer I was going to email him myself and pay him to take you out."

Before the next semester started she'd met him three times for coffee and they were texting frequently. He'd almost convinced her that school could be more than a hobby, that she could actually finish her degree.

She wrote him after she signed up for a spring class. *Finally registered. Hablas español?*

His response was immediate. *Only one?*

She groaned loud enough for Sid, curled up on the floor, to raise his head and stare at her. *Knew I shouldn't have told you*, she wrote back. *You professors are drug dealers always pushing one more hit.*

But it will take so long unless you take more?

What's the rush? Not like the world needs another English major wandering around, looking for shelter and food.

The world needs you out there.

She'd been so touched by that last message that she had looked for another class to take. If she scheduled them back to back in the morning, she could still work the lunch shift at South City. When they met up the next day in the quad she wanted to hug him hello but wasn't sure they had reached the "Hug Hello" stage. Instead she held up her fingers in a peace sign and said, "Two classes, baby."

"Excellent idea," he said.

"You'd better be right," she said. "Because now I'm taking Speech & Communication."

"Okay," he said, reaching out to lightly touch her shoulder, "if you have to suffer through that, the least I can do is buy you dinner tonight."

Before the semester ended she'd gone to the registrar for a printout of all the classes she still needed in order to graduate, so she could begin to plan what she took more carefully. She went from thinking she would never finish to thinking she could actually finish in three more years. Maybe.

Nina wakes up early the morning after blowing off her first day of classes, the thought of losing an entire semester forcing her out of bed. She will not let Ben Davies delay her graduation.

It's not even 7 a.m. when she logs onto the GSU website. Her goal is to find two Tuesday and Thursday classes that aren't full, since Ben usually doesn't go to campus on days he doesn't teach. She grabs a 9:30 Brit Lit class with an open slot, but none of the 11:00 a.m. classes she needs have any space. College Algebra is one of her last requirements, and the first period section is still open. Algebra at 8 a.m.? Death by Butter Knife would fill more quickly. It is the only math she needs to take, at least, so if she can survive it, she's done with equations forever. She registers for both classes, gets dressed, and forces a grumpy Sid to take a quick walk.

Nina's never been on campus so early, and the quad is emptier than she has ever seen it. The classroom, however, is almost full when she walks through the door. She takes a seat near the back and wishes she had gotten up early enough to buy some coffee. Scanning the other tired faces she sees a typical Georgia State blend: a few older students mixed in with a diverse group of people in their early twenties, the older ones dressed well enough to go to work after class, the younger ones wearing sweats, all staring at their phones. An anxious feeling starts to fill her chest as she begins to understand how big a mistake she made, thinking she could handle being around so many people in a room that looks so much like the one where she first met Ben.

Just as Nina stands up to make her escape the teacher walks in. A short woman with jet black hair pulled into a bun, she is holding a textbook in her left hand and a piece of chalk in her right, and talking at a rapid clip. "Welcome to College Algebra," she says, dropping the book onto her desk. "I'm Professor Dagmar." She starts writing an equation on the board. "The syllabus, including textbook requirements and grade breakdown, is online. Please review it before our next meeting." She turns to face the class. "Now, we begin. What is algebra?"

Nina sits back down and manages to stay for the entire class. When she makes it back outside, the quad is much more crowded than it had been an hour earlier. She takes a series of deep breaths, trying to shrink the balloon of tension in her chest. This is her first non-work outing into the real world since Ben broke up with her; maybe she should be satisfied with making it through one class, and blow off the first day of Brit Lit.

Sitting down on one of the concrete benches, Nina texts Connie to see if she is free to talk. The answer is an immediate phone call.

"You're up before noon, that's good news."

"I'll have you know I'm not only up," Nina says. "I just finished class."

"You went to class? Fantastic," Connie says. "Troy owes me ten bucks."

Troy and Connie were always making small bets, on everything from the exact arrival time of an Uber to college football games neither of them knew anything about. "And what exactly was the wager?"

"He said you were so bad off you'd skip the whole semester. I said you were too smart to let that asshole ruin everything."

Nina stretches. "I'm touched you're both so concerned."

"Easy money. You won't let your plans be fucked up by someone like Ben." As she says the name Connie grunts, then sighs.

"Was that a kick?"

"Yes. If this kid is a soccer player we're screwed. Adam's gonna have to learn the sports talk. Buy whistles and jockstraps."

"Oh, you clearly know all about all the sports stuff," Nina says, laughing. "This kid is gonna be in great hands." She stands up slowly. All she wants to do is go home, order some crappy food, and climb back into bed. "I've gotta head back in," she says. "I signed up for two classes, if that gets you even more money from Troy. Brit Lit awaits."

"I need to go pee, anyway," Connie says. "You didn't forget about Sunday, did you?"

"Sunday?" Nina closes her eyes for a second, trying to remember. What is supposed to happen Sunday, and how can she get out of it?

"Come on, Nina. I am not going to that place alone. Don't make me bring my mother."

As she reaches the door she remembers. "Buybuy BABY."

"Yes, yes, baby. Please?"

"Okay," Nina says. "I will go help you pick out whistles and jockstraps for this soccer player you are growing."

"Excellent. Now I'm hanging up so you don't hear me pee."

"A true friend," Nina says. She stretches, stands. Inhales, exhales. Ready, maybe, for the walk to the third floor and a hopefully distracting visit to the world of British Literature.

6 | Today Is That Tomorrow

Ben visited Georgia State the summer before starting his program to meet Dr. Reed and find a place to live. All the complexes close to campus were full or out of his price range, so he rented a small carriage house. Fully furnished, with a bedroom, living room, and small kitchen, the carriage house was set behind a large brick manor on East Rock Springs, a winding road lined with towering oak and maple trees that cut through one of Atlanta's old money neighborhoods.

It seemed like a great idea at first. He imagined the fifteen-minute drive from campus would create a healthy separation between school and the other parts of his life. The problem was he never developed any "other parts" of his life during his first three years in Atlanta. He was either on-campus or by himself in the carriage house, watching too many BBC detective shows and spending too much on DoorDash.

Then he met Nina. After only casually dating his first three years in Atlanta, Ben suddenly became part of one of those couples who saw each other four or five times a week and texted throughout the day. It was the most couple-like couple he'd ever been a part of, and he was surprised at how quickly he adapted. He got used to spending most nights at her place, especially when he didn't have to teach the next day. He loved waking up next to her, then walking somewhere in her neighborhood for a late breakfast.

Now that she's gone he's once again spending most of his time in the carriage house. It feels smaller than it did before. As he walks in to the kitchen to make his coffee the morning after the first day of the semester, he is reminded of the garbage compactor scene in *Star Wars*. Instead of trash, though, Ben feels himself being squeezed by an odd collection of lighthouse-related tchotchkes, not to mention the overstuffed couch and love seat, each covered in pillows embroidered with inspirational sayings: *Today is that tomorrow you were waiting for. Dreams are the way our hearts tell us what they need.* After more than four years, the place still smells like butterscotch and Lysol, just the way his grandmother's apartment used to.

He did spring for a nice coffee machine when he moved in, though, so his mood is quickly lifted, albeit chemically. He heads to the writing desk in the small bedroom, which he managed to turn into a good work station by hiding all the photos of golden retrievers and the cutesy mirror with "Do Not Be Afraid To Look Closely" etched in elaborate cursive along the frame. When seated at the desk he can look out into the back corner of the yard, carefully maintained by an elderly gardener and ignored by the children who live in the main house. In fact, the Maxwell children barely come outside at all; on the rare occasion they do, they turn into mute extras from *The Shining* as soon as they make eye contact.

Before he starts going through the notes and copies he made on yesterday's trip to the library, he checks his email and finds the best news he's had in two weeks: Fox Charles Brown confirming the time and place for his interview on Friday.

Brown, a photographer on the Macon club scene in the Sixties, took the shots used for Honeybird's posthumous live album, *One Last Time*. He's the first person who had direct contact with the band that Ben has managed to track down. The studio Honeybird used went out of business in the early Seventies. Willy Wilson, who managed the band and produced their two studio albums, has been dead for years; Ben can't find any surviving relatives, and since Wilson specialized in bands that never made it for one reason or another, he didn't leave behind much of a paper trail. Ed Harsch, who played organ and piano on some of the songs, died not long after Harlan and Nate. As far as Ben has able to figure out, "Cindy Songbird," credited with backing vocals on both albums, never recorded anything else. Darlene Honeybird, the lone surviving band member, has proven impossible to get in touch with, probably by design. Honeybird has a small but intense group of fans who use the internet to feed each other's obsessions, and making contact with Darlene is their holy grail. Posts on the Honeybirders Reddit thread make it clear that many of them are convinced Darlene knows "the truth" about the night of the fire. No wonder she's hiding. Interviewing Fox Brown will give Ben the chance to speak to someone who saw the band play live, and who knew Harlan personally. He writes back to thank him for the meeting, then reviews his list of questions for the interview.

He starts his Honeybird playlist for inspiration, and the first song that comes up is "Losing Control." It was Nina's favorite, so when Harlan sings, "You can't lose what you never owned," Ben's not thinking about Fox Brown, witness to history, but about Nina. He wonders, as he has done several times a day for two weeks, if he should call her mother to explain what's going on, but the one time Ben met Marion Alexander she made it clear she did not approve of him.

Nina's mother and grandmother were finishing dinner prep when he and Nina arrived. The four of them stood in the small kitchen as Marion Alexander called out commands for Nina and corrections for Ben ("That's not a paring knife, Ben—Nina, can you show him?"). He quickly decided that his best move was to say as little as possible, so he did a lot of smiling and nodding as Nina and her mother caught up on various family members he had never heard of. When they sat down to eat, Nina brought up his dissertation; Marion insisted the best music was made in the Sixties, and Nina told Ben she thought her mother would find Honeybird's story interesting. The topic just proved to be fertile ground for Marion's complaints.

"A rock band? That can be the topic for a dissertation?"

"Well, anything can be a topic for a dissertation—just depends how you handle it."

"And how are you going to handle a racist Southern band?"

"See, that's one of the interesting things about them," Ben said. "They were one of the first integrated rock bands of the time period, especially in the South."

"Doesn't mean they weren't racist."

"True, but for Macon—"

"They were from Macon? Awful city."

"Yes, before the Allmans—"

"Oh, God, you're not writing about the Allmans, are you?"

It was around this time he felt Nina's right foot running up and down his left leg. Ben was used to being the kind of boyfriend that impressed the parents of his girlfriends. He looked presentable, had a serious academic pursuit, spoke in complete sentences—why was Marion so determined to be angry at him? "No, this was before the Allmans. That's what makes them an interesting study."

"Please." Marion let out a loud sigh and shook her head. "You're not pushing some treacle about music being the thing that healed the racial divide, are you?"

"I'm not out to 'push' anything. I'm looking at what happened, and telling the story."

"The story? Like there can only be one?"

"There's lots of stories, of course. But you piece them together and—"

"And make up something that passes as history. Except the history you write will be changed by whoever comes along after you, which does make one wonder what value there is in the exercise at all."

"So if we can't get the complete story all at once we shouldn't even try?"

"That's not a question, just an excuse for all the mistakes you historians make."

"Can you pass me the bread, Ben?"

Ben had almost forgotten Nina's grandmother was there; she had maintained a steady silence since the meal had begun. She smiled when their eyes met, and he eagerly welcomed the chance to pass her the bread basket, and then to pass the wine to Nina when she asked. The two of them seemed to know just how to redirect Marion.

The mood lightened after that. For someone who sprinkled in a steady drizzle of complaints about modern capitalism, Marion was also a fan of good restaurants, and liked comparing notes with Ben and Nina about their favorite places to eat in town. The Beatles proved to be safe musical ground, and the debates about the pros and cons of *The White Album* were much less intense than their debate about the value of history.

Nina apologized as soon as they were back in his car. "Sorry she was so awful."

"Oh, she wasn't that bad. She just has . . . opinions. Lots of strong opinions."

"Um, yes. Yes, she does."

"It's good practice, defending my work."

"Marion Alexander can put you on the defensive, for sure. If I had more energy now, I could try and decide if she thinks you're too old for me, or if she's jealous because you're going for the Ph.D. she never had a chance to get." She rubbed the right side of her head with her hand. "I wish my grandmother hadn't been so quiet. I think this is one of those nights she 'forgot' to put in her hearing aids."

"Next time I'll forget to put mine in."

"I will say this," Nina continued, leaning back in her seat and dropping her hand from her head, "you held your own. She may not like you all that much, but I think she liked the way you hung in."

As she talked her left hand drifted over to his leg. Nina had a whole alphabet of physical moves—touching his arm when they strolled with Sid, rubbing her leg against his when they watched TV, leaning into him when they were in the kitchen together. "So she didn't like me, but respected me?"

Nina laughed. "Oh, I'm not sure she respected you. Grudgingly admired the way you didn't surrender? Will that do?"

"The way the Sioux may have grudgingly admired Custer?"

"Maybe not quite that much."

Ben tried not to let his ego feel too damaged. "That will do, I guess."

"And now it's over. She wanted to meet you, but we're done for a while."

"Thank God." Ben hesitated, then decided to ask about something he had noticed. "So, there are no pictures of your father?"

"No. Marion Alexander isn't one to hang on to the past."

Nina rarely mentioned her father. Ben wasn't sure if that was because she remembered so little, or because she did not want to talk about it. "How old were you, when he died?"

"Four."

"Do you remember him at all?"

"Not very much, to be honest. Fragments. Like, little bursts of images."

They were waiting for the light to change at Boulevard and Ponce de Leon Avenue. WRAS was on, the volume too low to hear more than the vague rumblings coming from the nighttime playlist. "Do you mind if I ask how—"

"Car accident. No other cars, no one else with him," she added quickly, as if used to anticipating the inevitable follow-up questions.

They sat in silence until the light changed and the car started moving again. "Is that when your grandmother moved in?"

"Yeah. I don't remember her ever not being there." She paused, before continuing in a softer voice. "I used to lay in bed, and I'd be sure, just positive, that the two of them were talking about Dad. That they had some secret information they wouldn't share with me. So I would sneak out of my room when I was supposed to be asleep and eavesdrop from the hallway."

Ben imagined a young Nina, hiding just out of sight, desperately trying to find out whatever she could about her missing father. He could feel the intense want, the desperate need to know. "And what did you learn?"

"That old people sure worried a lot about money, and spent a lot of time planning meals. And that neither one of them ever talked about Dad, as far as I could tell. It's like he never existed."

The image of Marion as a young, suddenly widowed mom allowed him to feel more sympathy for her. He laid his hand on top of Nina's, and they finished the last part of the trip in a comfortable silence. The plan had been for him to drop her off and go home, but as soon as he parked and looked over at her, he wanted to stay.

"So," she said, "this is when we pretend to say goodnight, but then you come in and stay. So let's skip the pretend part."

Remembering that moment, as Harlan sings "You can't lose what you have never owned," Ben thinks about the way Nina quickly learned to anticipate what he was going to say. Now that she is out of his life he misses that almost as much as he misses the physical contact. It felt good, to be with someone who knew him well enough to know what he was thinking and still wanted to be with him.

7 | How You Do It

When Nina gets home from her first day of classes, Sid is looking out the sliding screen doors. He turns around at the sound of her keys dropping on the table. Nina stares at him, not sure why she feels like picking a fight. Maybe she's just tired, or maybe it's the sight of the trash and dirty clothes still scattered around the room; she had this fantasy that the universe would reward her return to school with a magically clean apartment. Does she even have enough garbage bags for all this?

She sighs, puts her notebook down, and heads back into the kitchen to make some coffee. "You know, some dogs run to say hello." By the time she's poured in the grounds and water, he has wandered into the kitchen. "All these clips online of dogs knocking their owners down, they're so happy to be reunited."

"Hello," he says, before leaning his head down to take a few licks of water.

Nina hits start on the coffee maker, then bends down to root under the kitchen sink. She miraculously finds a roll of garbage bags. They're damp from the leaking disposal that Morris keeps promising to fix, but there should be enough for her to get rid of two weeks of Breakup Trash. This is what it has come to, she thinks, standing up and holding the wet roll as if it was the Sword of Excalibur: my life just got much better because I found some trash bags.

"Okay. How was your day, dear?" Sid says, walking by her on his way back to the living room.

"My first teacher must have had too much coffee and talked really, really quickly about algebra. My second teacher read off notes so old they crumbled as she turned the pages." She puts the garbage bags in the sink and reaches for a coffee mug. "Oh, and the whole time I was on campus I lived in fear of bumping into Ben. But other than all that, it was a great day."

He stops in the middle of the floor to lick his front left paw, then turns to look at her. "You get sarcastic when you're anxious. Do you want to talk about it?"

"About what's making me anxious?"

"Yes."

She opens the refrigerator to get the half-and-half. "Everything. Everything is making me anxious." She fixes her coffee and then turns to look at him. "What I really want to know is, did I fuck everything up?"

"Would you feel better if I told you something I cannot know for sure?"

"I would feel better if you just told me that Ben wasn't my last chance at finding someone."

He stares at her for a moment, then yawns, stretches, and stands back up. "We should not dwell in the past or dream of the future," he says. "We are here. In this moment."

Nina takes a sip of coffee as she watches him weave his way around discarded take-out containers on the floor. "I could use some help, in this moment, cleaning this place up. You could push trash into piles or something, right?"

Instead of answering her he jumps onto the futon. It should have been easier to train him once he started talking, but instead it became impossible for her to treat him like a dog. Maybe she should just work on teaching him better human manners—like not walking away in the middle of a conversation.

The first time Sid talked to her, Nina was asleep. She was dreaming that someone was whispering "I need to go out" in her ear, but she had an early class the next morning so she just rolled over. After the same voice repeated the same phrase she reluctantly opened her eyes and saw Sid standing on the bed, staring at her. When their eyes met he butted his head against hers. She didn't hear the words again, but he was certainly acting like a dog who needed to go outside.

Nina put on a hoodie and some sweatpants and got his leash. She hoped this was not going to become some new habit, especially on cold February nights. One of the best features of Sid was his easy maintenance. She never had to worry about him doing anything bad while she was out. She didn't have to feed him special food. She didn't have to get up in the middle of the night to walk him.

Luckily he peed almost as soon as they were out the door, and she was back in her bed in what seemed like seconds. Then, just as she was drifting back to sleep, she heard the voice again. "You should take me to the vet tomorrow. This body does not feel right."

Nina was awake. No one else was in the apartment. Who else could be talking to her? But a talking dog was impossible, of course. And even if the dog was somehow talking, would he really say "this body does not feel right"? She decided to assume it was all some sort of hallucination because she was so tired, then drifted back to sleep.

When she woke up the next morning, Sid was sitting on the bed and staring at her. She blew off her class and took him to Briarcliff Animal Hospital, where blood tests revealed a urinary tract infection. On the drive home she left the radio off, curious to see if he would talk again, but he just stared out the window, as he usually did on car rides. Maybe the whole thing was just an example of how closely human and pet had become connected; maybe she had become one of those "We each know what the other is thinking" dog owners.

There were no middle-of-the-night demands for walks after that. By the time Sid finished his medication Nina decided that the whole thing would make a funny story, if she had someone she could share it with. But she couldn't tell Ben; they had only been dating for a month, and she didn't want to seem like a crazy dog lady. Connie would try to believe her but would also worry, and warn her not to become too obsessed. "No guy wants to fight a fucking dog for your attention," she'd say, and she'd be right. Troy might understand, and probably have even crazier stories to tell about him and Carol, but he also might get worried and tell Connie. And then Connie would be mad Nina didn't tell her.

Then Sid talked again—this time in the middle of the afternoon.

Nina was washing dishes and on the phone with her mother when she noticed Sid watching her with a particular intensity. Announcing that she needed to take him for a walk served as a great way to end the call. She dried her hands and was reaching for his leash when she heard, very clearly, a voice call out to her.

"Thank you for taking me to the doctor."

Sid was sitting in front of the dining room table, just through the open doorway that connected the small kitchen to the main living space. His eyes tracked Nina as she walked over to him. It would be easier to try and ignore whatever was going on, but she wanted to see if she could get some answers. She sat down, crossed her legs, and looked right at him. "Okay. This time, I want to see how you do it."

Sid tilted his head, meeting her gaze.

"I want to see how you do it," she repeated. When he just continued to sit there, looking like a regular dog, Nina thought for a long second that she had imagined everything. That would be alarming, of course, but less so than really having a talking dog. In one scenario, her own life would be unsettled, and she would need to find a therapist; in the other, the rules of the universe would have to be rewritten.

She started counting backward from ten inside her head, planning to stand up when she reached zero. When she reached two she heard the voice again.

"Want to see how I do what?"

There was no doubt that time. His lower jaw had definitely moved at the same time she heard the voice. "Come on. You know what I mean."

He raised his eyebrows slightly, as if waiting to see if she had a treat.

"Oh, please, don't do the just-a-dog act. I need to know if this is happening, or if I'm going crazy."

"Even if it's happening, that does not mean you are not going crazy."

This was the moment she learned that a talking dog could also be a smart-ass. "Point well taken. So you can talk, and you're clever."

"I believe so."

The voice was a little deeper than she would have expected given his size, with a gravelly tone reminiscent of later period Lucille Ball, vocal cords drenched in cigarette smoke. "So how come you haven't talked before?" she asked. "Or did you talk to Denise? Is that why she got out of here so suddenly and left you behind? You talked to her and freaked her out?"

"No, I never spoke to Denise."

"Why not?"

"I never had anything to say. I only spoke to you because I needed some help."

She continued to stare at his jaw when he spoke. It barely moved, which may be why Sid's voice maintained a low, steady volume. "Why not just bark? Isn't that what dogs do?"

"Barking hurts my ears."

"Your ears?"

"The sharp pitch hurts to hear. This body is very frustrating."

That would explain why Nina could not remember him ever barking, while Troy's dog Carol seemed to yip every time she saw a shadow flicker. "What do you mean, 'this body is very frustrating'? You're a dog. What other body would you have?"

"I have not always had a dog's body."

"You used to have a different body?" Accepting that she was talking to a dog was one level of insanity. If he started talking about shapeshifting she was going to run out of the room.

"In previous lives, yes."

"Previous lives?"

"Yes."

That was when she began to really wish she was in a bad TV show. She would feel her forehead for some sort of raging fever, or perhaps pour a strong drink while the laugh track swelled, and everything would magically reset when they came back from commercial break. Instead all she could do was lean forward, put her head in her hands, and groan.

"And this is another reason why I don't talk unless I have to," Sid said.

"Because it sounds crazy?"

"It does not sound crazy to me. I have had many lifetimes to learn how to accept what is real. I have also learned, over many lifetimes, that this can be hard to hear. I choose my words and my audience carefully."

It's nice that he trusts me, she thought, but maybe it would have been easier if he didn't. "So how many—how many lives are we talking, here?"

"I don't know. I have lost count."

"More than five?'

"Oh, many more."

"More than ten?"

"You should move in bigger numbers, if you want to get to the answer."

More than ten? She decided to focus on the talking part first and stood up. "My phone," she said, spotting it on the dining room table.

"Calling the police?"

"No," she said, standing up to grab her phone. "I want to film you." She sat back down, swiping up for the camera. "I can run it in slo-mo, see how your mouth—"

"I won't talk while you're filming. And if you do it anyway, and it gets out, people will assume you just doctored the evidence—because I will never talk again."

Nina put the phone down, narrowed her eyes. "Why not?"

"I do not want to be anyone's sideshow."

"Oh, come on," she said. "I won't let you—"

"And I will not be anyone's lab experiment."

She stared at him. "Lab experiment?"

"Yes. If you had ever experienced being cut open while awake you would not ask me to risk having it happen again."

Nina wanted to believe the idea was ridiculous, but she knew that scared humans were capable of almost anything. It didn't make his demand of secrecy any easier to accept. "So I'm just supposed to believe all this without ever getting anyone else to look at the evidence with me?" she asked.

"Yes."

"But—"

"Yes."

It seemed unfair that Sid would be the only one she could be able to talk to about any of this. She put the phone down. "So why just me?"

"I have learned," he said, "that one person is the most I can trust. And I trust you." He stood up, and started moving toward the front door.

"What, you need to go out?"

"Yes, please."

"So why not just say so?" She stood up, wondering if the entire conversation had been the result of a mini-breakdown and the world would return to normal after a good night's sleep.

When Sid reached the front door he turned around and looked at her. "This body was not designed for verbal communication. My jaw gets quite sore, and my throat feels stretched out. So I try not to talk too much."

She grinned as she put on the leash. "Can I at least train you to use the toilet? So we can skip all this in and out, already?"

"My mind has one set of capabilities. My body has another."

She didn't think about what it would mean to share an apartment with Sid and Ben until the night before they were supposed to go look at the new place.

"So when we all live together, are you going to start talking to Ben, too?" They were sitting outside on her small balcony, where she felt safe talking to Sid when it was dark.

"What would I say to him?"

"I don't know."

"If I don't have anything to say, it's best not to speak. The fewer people I speak to, the better."

"Again with the secrecy. Don't you wanna be the world famous talking dog? We can get you on *Ellen*, I bet."

"The world is not ready to hear what I have to say."

She stared at him, marveling at the way his jaw barely seemed to move when he spoke. What might happen if Ellen DeGeneres discussed life and death, reincarnation, and the movement of souls between animals and people with this black furball? Would religions collapse, especially the monotheistic ones that promised a straight "one good life equals one great afterlife" plan? Would new religions emerge—the Cult of Sid? Most days, the world already seemed to be spinning off its axis; would forcing humanity to rethink everything from evolution to death be a fatal blow?

"Okay. Fair point. But what if I asked you to talk to him? Just once, and just Ben?"

"There's no guarantee he would share your discretion."

"I'm pretty sure he would."

"Pretty sure is not a guarantee." He turned to look at her. "Why would I risk that?"

"So he doesn't think I'm crazy."

"But how can I control what he thinks about you, or anything else?"

"Well, if I say I have a talking dog, he's gonna ask to hear it talk. And if you talk, he'll believe me."

"And potentially tell the world. Make history for once, instead of just reporting it."

"But if he heard you, he would believe you."

"Why can't he just believe you?"

"That's a lot to ask, isn't it?"

"Is it?" He started walking back into the apartment. Once again, Sid decided when the conversation would end. "Isn't that what people do when they're couples—believe each other?"

She knew he was right, philosophically, but she also knew it would be a big leap of faith for Ben to believe her. Nina still had trouble believing what was happening and she was the one Sid talked to. So she followed him into the apartment and decided she wouldn't tell Ben anything about her talking dog. Less than twenty-four hours later she would wonder why she ever changed her mind.

8 | He Will Get You Their

Ben heads down to Macon after his Friday class. The morning is clear and he's streaming a Jeff Tweedy solo album, but he still feels melancholic. Nina had insisted on going the last time he went to Macon, and even made a mix CD for the occasion, catching him up on Radiohead, Lydia Loveless, and Janelle Monae. They pulled off to visit a sausage place she had read about, where they ate too many weird samples and bought a T-shirt that said, "LET JESUS DRIVE AND HE WILL GET YOU THEIR." They spent the rest of the day throwing out random words and phrases that could be added after that possessive pronoun.

"Social Security numbers."

"Firstborn."

"Darkest nightmares."

"Cookies."

As Ben gets closer to Macon, he switches from Tweedy to *Waiting Here*, Honeybird's second album. The songs are a bit darker than those on the first, but also more advanced, musically and lyrically; the Honeybird of the first album could not have been confident and restrained enough to pull off "Losing Control." In some of the tracks Ben can hear the booze seeping into the guitar work. The leads are still soaring and cut even more sharply than they did on the first record, but they're also sloppier, sliding in and out of time more frequently. In spite of its flaws, it's a more mature and intense album than their debut, and every time Ben hears it he wonders what a third Honeybird record would have sounded like—if only they had lived long enough to make it.

He pulls into an empty parking space in front of Taste & See, the coffee shop Fox chose for their meeting. It has a standard hipster vibe, complete with leather couch, fireplace, and acoustic guitar music on the PA. Ben very quickly feels at home, glad to see so many people in a coffee shop not called Starbucks. As he wanders the lobby, though, he begins to notice the overt Christian angle. Flyers for worship meetings, posters of peaceful nature settings with religious quotes, and Bibles for the taking, stacked neatly next to the cream and sugar. Suddenly all the smiling people are a little more unnerving. He avoids making any prolonged eye contact, afraid that proselytization will be immediate and relentless.

Ben spots Fox as soon as he walks in: an older guy with thick glasses, a laptop under his arm, a big grin, and a wardrobe straight from a bad sixties movie, complete with tan vest and cowboy boots. He looks like one of those skinny senior citizens who can put away three burgers a day and never gain weight, thanks to the mysteries of metabolism. Ben waves and heads in his direction.

"Mr. Brown? Ben Davies."

"Everyone just calls me Foxy, man. Nice to meet you."

Ben was hoping that the "Fox C. Brown equals Foxy" jokes would be something he'd only have to suffer in emails, but Foxy looks serious. Ben pays for Foxy's triple cappuccino and muffin, and leads them to an overstuffed couch. Foxy is talking at such a rapid clip that Ben wonders if it's possible he's coked up. Maybe he just did so much coke earlier in his life that he feels the effects permanently.

"Man, I was so glad to get your email." Foxy sits down, places his laptop on the coffee table in front of the couch. "I think about that band a lot. Just tragic, man. A fucking tragic tragedy."

"Well, I can't thank you enough for meeting me. Not many people remember Honeybird—"

"Fucking tragic."

"—so to get to talk to someone who was there is just amazing."

"Oh, I was there, man. Foxy was there. Ask anything you want." He takes a big gulp of his cappuccino. "Got my grandfather's memory. That man remembered the moment he was born. Could describe the hair on the doctor's knuckles."

Ben nods, pretending the story makes perfect sense even as he wonders if it's not that Foxy did a lot of coke when he was younger, but that he's insane. "You mind if I tape this?" he asks, putting his digital recorder on the table.

"Go ahead, go ahead." Foxy opens the laptop, revealing a slide show cued up to begin. "I loved taking shots of these guys, man." He picks off a large piece of muffin and slides it into his mouth with two fingers, then taps the space bar to begin the slide show. "I worked this presentation up years ago, waiting for someone to come along and want to see Foxy's work."

The first few shots of Honeybird are familiar to Ben since they were used for *One Last Night*. The band played a big show in Macon at the end of the *Waiting Here* tour and had their engineer record the concert; after the fire, Capricorn Records put out a double album from that performance. By all accounts this was primarily done as a favor to Hank Honeybird, who used part of his biscuit fortune to bankroll the project. To everyone's surprise, the album generated great reviews and decent sales. In the early nineties Capricorn released a CD version with a few more photos from the same show, all taken by Foxy.

And they're all great, even the familiar shots more intense and vibrant in their full-screen versions. There are lots of pictures of Harlan, his hair swinging wildly, fingers caught in impossible positions on the guitar, looking as possessed as he often sounded. Darlene and Nate serve as human companions for Demon Harlan, their eyes locked on each other in most of the photos.

After that Macon performance—their last show, as it turned out—the photos move back in time. "These are the first shots I got of these guys," Foxy says, and they're exactly the kind of pictures Ben was hoping to find. The first few look as though they came from the same gig, taken at some tiny club Ben does not recognize from any of his other research. Their smooth faces and wide eyes remind Ben how young they were when they started. This Harlan has an uncertain look in his eyes, and Darlene seems to be frozen in place, staring down at her fingers. The only one resembling his future, confident self is Nate, grinning from ear to ear, arms in what seems to be constant motion.

"Where were these taken?"

"Green's, June of 1965. Hole in the wall that came and went real quickly, but those places got the Macon Sound off the ground, man." Foxy takes a swallow of coffee, laughs softly. "Shit, I was only there because I heard Hank Honeybird had a kid who played guitar. I had to see what the hell that was gonna be like."

Hank Honeybird. Ben had done some reading on Hank since his brief talk with Kuperman, and there was no doubt Hank was a big figure in Macon—literally and figuratively, at 6'4" and 250 pounds, with a thick head of black hair until the day he died. Hank started as a dishwasher without a high school diploma, opened two successful locations of Double H Biscuits before he turned thirty, and became a key powerbroker in Macon. If the Biscuit King had been content to stay local, he probably could have won a job as a state representative or mayor. But he had bigger dreams.

In 1956, Hank tried to use his political and financial capital to run for the U.S. Senate, after Walter George decided not to run for re-election. Looking at articles from the time, Ben had no idea why Hank Honeybird believed he could take on Herman Talmadge, a scion of one of Georgia's most powerful political families. Each Talmadge was more segregationist than the last, leaving no room to run to the right of Herman. But that was the only choice Hank Honeybird had; Georgia in 1956 was no place for a racial moderate. After getting steamrolled by Talmadge, Hank remained a force in local Macon politics, his endorsement for any local race as good as a victory. "And what was it like, seeing the band for the first time?"

"Man." Foxy shakes his head. "I watched these little kids get on stage, sure it was gonna be a disaster. Had no idea Hank's daughter was in the band, too—and an Afro-American on drums? Darlene looked like she was gonna faint, she was so nervous. But their first song began with Darlene and Nate playing like this fucking machine, you know, and then Harlan pulled this deep, bluesy sound out of his guitar. Started snapping pictures as soon as I realized what was happening."

Ben wonders if he should correct Foxy, and maybe casually point out that "Afro-American" hasn't been used since the early sixties, but doesn't want to start the interview with a confrontation. Besides, he reminds himself: that's the time period that shaped Foxy. Instead he focuses on the shot of Harlan, his back to the crowd and looking at Nate. While he can't see Harlan's face, Nate has a big smile. Darlene is in the far left of the shot, head down, feet frozen in place. "Do you remember what song they opened with?"

"'Heavy Heavy Hands.'"

"That's what they closed with, that last show in Macon, isn't it?"

Foxy nods. "Full fucking circle, man."

Ben scrolls through the rest of the photos, watching the trio quickly morph from scared kids into a confident band. The clubs in Macon get a little bigger, but the out-of-town photos from Atlanta and Charleston reveal much smaller crowds. In all the offstage photos Harlan and Nate always seem to be making each other laugh, and Darlene looks like she has a permanent glow around her. She's so well-framed in every shot that Ben wonders if Foxy had a crush on her.

Foxy maintains a running monologue as Ben looks at the pictures, summarizing the rise of Honeybird as if he was the fourth member of the band. He runs down the challenges of "our" small record label, and the preconceptions the rest of the country had about "our" southern sound. The slide show ends with a picture taken after that final show in Macon. The lights are up, a few stagehands can be seen milling around the edges of the frame, and the three members of Honeybird are covered in sweat and grinning. Standing in front of the drum kit, drinks in hand, they look like they have just conquered the world.

"Sure seems as though they genuinely liked each other."

"Oh, yeah, man. The camera can't make that shit up."

Ben turns to look at Foxy, who's licking muffin crumbs off his fingers. "Last show they played, right?"

"That was it. The fire hit two weeks later."

Ben shakes his head; seeing the photos has deepened the sense of loss. "Well, they're fantastic, all of them," he says after a short pause. He says it to boost Foxy's ego, and perhaps make negotiating for their use a little easier, but it is true that the pictures are even better than he'd hoped for.

Part of his brain is already writing more vivid descriptions of how the members interacted with each other, on and off stage.

"Thanks. I shot a lot of bands over the years, but always felt a special connection to these guys."

Ben leans back, still staring at the final shot. "Harlan does look a little skinny."

"That kid left it all on stage, every night, man. And never was much more than skin and bones. Whenever they came back from a tour he looked wiped out." Foxy grins, putting the rest of his muffin in his mouth. "Though I bet you're wondering about drugs."

Ben nods. "I gotta ask. Sounds like he indulged quite a bit."

"He was like his father in that way—big appetite. Wild Turkey, weed, women . . . Never seemed to get in the way of the music, though." Foxy shrugs. "But, hell. If you really wanna know, just ask Darlene."

Ben tries not to look too desperate. "I'd love to. I'm having a hard time tracking her down."

"Really?" Foxy's eyes widen. "You don't have much of a book without Darlene."

"I agree," Ben says, suddenly realizing Foxy could help gain Darlene's cooperation. Foxy wants his pictures published, and understands the book is much more likely to happen if Darlene is involved. "I can't track her down. It's like she's disappeared."

"Well." Foxy rubs his chin, nods as if agreeing with himself. "I'll talk to her. Tell her I met you and that you're here to do a serious book."

Ben thanks him, buses their table, then follows Foxy out the door. Downtown Macon is quiet: a few parked cars, an elderly couple crossing the main street, one teen on a skateboard.

Foxy's Dodge is right out front. Ben waits as Foxy puts in his laptop, stretches, then reaches into the well of the driver's door for a pack of Marlboros. "So you probably knew the scene back then as well as anyone," Ben says. "Think they would have been big, if it hadn't been for the fire?"

Foxy grins. "I loved that band, I did. But they were gonna have some challenges."

"Like what?"

"I mean, Darlene in the band was one thing, but Nate, too? Shit. Things might have been changing, but not that fast." He shakes out a cigarette. "But Harlan, man, he thought they could just roll into these Southern towns and get away with it."

"And did they?"

"Damned if they didn't. It helped that Hank Honeybird was just about one of the meanest assholes in the whole state. No one wanted to mess with his kid." Foxy lights his Marlboro, takes a puff. "Still, I know there were nights they were scared shitless. Darlene would admit it to me, you know, in private? Even if the guys never would. But Darlene and Nate knew to lay low when they got into whatever town they were playing, let Harlan do all the talking. The other two would sneak onto the stage when it was time to start, and as soon as they kicked into a song everyone just paid attention to the music." He pauses to take a drag, shrugs. "Like I said, I loved them. But aside from all that other shit, they would've had to deal with the Allmans, coming around the corner. They doubled that bluesy trio thing."

"But it was *One Last Night* that gave Capricorn Records the idea for *Fillmore East*, right? So Honeybird also made it possible for the Allmans to really get on the map?"

Foxy's laugh turns into a quick burst of a hacking cough. "Yep, yep. Timing, right? Life is fucking timing."

"And a fire that kills two-thirds of the band."

"Well," Foxy says with a grin. "They only found but one body, remember?"

Ben raises his eyebrows. "You think there's a chance Nate made it out?"

Foxy grins. "Oh, damn sight better than just a chance."

"Really?"

"Oh, yeah," Foxy continues, a wide grin spreading across his face. "That boy could run." He draws the last word out to three times its natural length. "I mean, they're all fast, but I once saw Nate race Harlan across a Waffle House parking lot, both of them high as kites, and it was like he was from some other planet—arms all swinging wildly, a black blur in the night." He winks. "Made sense to have a drummer like that for Harlan's music. Hell, rhythm and speed is what they have going for them, right?"

Ben swallows, trying to decide how to react. He settles for mumbling, "He was a great drummer." Ben knows what he should do: narrow his eyes and ask Foxy if he really meant to imply what he just implied. But the man standing in front of him, grinning at his own racist comment, has a stash of photos that will make his book much more marketable. And what change can he really bring to Foxy's worldview at this stage of his life? "And those are some great fucking pictures," he says, desperate to change the topic as quickly as he can. "I'm certainly gonna be in touch to work out the details, if you're really interested in licensing some of them."

"Indeed I am, my man, indeed I am. Been waiting for someone to ask."

Ben feels a little ashamed for not challenging Foxy more, but he needs the photos, and he needs Foxy to help track down Darlene. "And if you do get through to Darlene, send her my email, my cellphone, whatever she wants."

Foxy flashes a thumbs up as he gets into his car. "Imma call her on the way home, amigo."

On the drive back to Atlanta Ben plays *One Last Night*, start to finish. He knows from past trips that the record should match the length of the drive almost precisely, depending on traffic. If "Mr. Invisible" starts as he pulls out of town, then "Heavy Heavy Hands" will end just as he exits I-85.

He played *One Last Night* for Nina on their ride home from Macon. They were a little punch drunk after walking around for a few hours on a hot afternoon, still randomly shouting out ways to finish that T-shirt: "Jesus will get you their naked selfies!" "Secret recipes!" The longer they were in the car, the more attention they gave to the music. "Okay, this guy is no Thom Yorke," Nina said as they crested the hill and saw the skyline of Atlanta, "but he's not bad."

Ben tries not to spend the car ride home thinking about her. Instead, visualizes Honeybird as he listens to them play. Now that he has seen more pictures of the band, and from this final show in particular, he can imagine the performance more vividly.

And now that he has met Foxy he is more aware of the challenges the band must have faced. Ben is still feeling guilty that he did not call out Foxy's racism, but maybe all historians are doomed to feel some guilt. They can record and interpret as much of the past as they want, but will any of it really change what people think?

It's a question he wishes he could talk over with someone on the ride home.

9 | Miss See-o-bun

Troy and Carol are supposed to be coming over to take a long Sunday walk with Nina and Sid, but Troy cancels at the last minute. Nina's first instinct is to return to bed, but she knows she should go anyway. It's been less than a week since she started classes and actually cleaned her apartment, and she doesn't fully trust herself yet. She feels a bit like someone who just started a diet or stopped drinking, worried that she could backslide at any moment.

There's another reason she should go for a walk, even without Troy. Outside of B-6 Sid acts like an ordinary dog. As amazing as it is to think, "Yes, my dog really does talk to me," it is also nice to pretend he is just a regular dog. There is an accompanying tightness in her chest when she imagines that reality, though, because if he was just a regular dog she and Ben would be together now, planning their move. She's trying to take Sid's advice and stay in the present, but it's hard not to feel the past return when they walk by Tin Lizzy's. The hole-in-the-wall a block from her apartment has her favorite tacos in Atlanta, but it's where she and Ben had their last meal together. She can never go there again.

They had lunch before they went to look at D-14, the one bedroom apartment for rent in her building. They sat outside on a beautiful day, eating tacos and cheese dip and trading stories about recent phone calls with their mothers. Since Ben's mother lives in Seattle, Nina had not met her, just talked briefly to her on the phone. Connie told Nina this was a warning sign: "You need to move more slowly until you lay eyes on this woman. Buy the puppy without sizing up the breeding dog, and you can never be sure what you're gonna get." Nina refused to worry, though. They were happy when together. What else mattered?

After lunch, they had taken Sid for a quick walk before meeting Morris to get the keys. Ben had been in a good mood; he even played along when Morris asked to feel a historian's biceps. Nina had planned to drop Sid off at B-6 on their way to check out the new place, but Ben thought all three of them should go since they would all be living there together. Nina had worried that the apartment would feel even smaller with Sid along, but it turned out to feel bigger than she'd expected. Suddenly the idea of the two of them—the three of them—living together hadn't seemed impossible.

The front door opened into a small living room; a stove and sink were tucked behind a half wall off to the left, making it feel like a separate kitchen; and through an open doorway on the right wall she could see a small bedroom. Four rooms, 700 square feet? D-14 seemed palatial compared to her studio apartment.

Nina unleashed Sid when they walked in. "Morris says it can be ready start of the month," she said, watching Sid jump up on the only piece of furniture in the apartment, a battered green couch in the middle of the living room.

"This is the couch the last people didn't want?"

"Yes," Nina said. "Morris says he'll take it out if we don't like it, but maybe it's better than no couch at all?"

Ben looked at Sid, who was circle-dancing for a comfortable spot on the sofa. "And how do we feel about him sitting on it?"

Nina shrugged. "I figure his butt is cleaner than most things that have been on that cushion?"

"Fair point, fair point," Ben said, wandering over to look into the small bedroom. "The futon will fit in here for sure, so let's take that couch."

"A couch and a bed? Like, separate pieces of furniture?" Nina walked into the kitchen area, feeling very grown-up. She and Denise had stayed up that first night thinking they were adults, but this, this was real adulting—an apartment with more than one room and a boyfriend.

And a dog.

Ben walked back into the living room, riffing on the size of the shower, and what positions they'd have to assume for both of them to fit in there at the same time. Ben looked so happy, and Sid so peaceful. At that moment, Nina decided she was done with play relationships. Ben was going to see her in all of her moods, even on those days she would prefer not to be seen by anyone. Adult Nina could not begin this next stage of her most serious relationship by hiding something important from him. She needed to know that Ben could see all the parts of her and still stay with her.

"So, there's something I need to tell you. About Sid."

Ben looked at Sid and grinned. "What did you do now, Sid?"

"Well, it's more like . . ."

"Like what?"

She took a deep breath, and then just said it. She had never said it out loud before, to anyone. Even to herself. "More like he talks to me sometimes."

Nodding slowly, Ben turned to study Sid, who was curled into a ball on the couch. "Like, talks to with you his eyes? Seems to nod yes or no sometimes?"

"Um." She contemplated laughing the whole thing off, but Adult Nina forged ahead. "More than that."

"Oh." Ben turned from Sid to Nina. "Telepathically?"

"With his, uh, voice."

"Like, talks to you and you can hear him say words?"

"Yes."

Pause. "Huh."

The "huh" told Nina she had gone too far. She watched Ben's face as he processed and tried to think of what to say. The apartment seemed unnaturally quiet, like the whole world had decided to stop breathing at once so that everyone could hear what Ben said next.

"Really?"

"Really."

"Well." Ben started talking in a slower, more deliberate tone of voice. "So, can he say something now?"

She stared at Sid, but he was still curled up, head tucked out of sight. "I don't think he's going to."

"Why not?"

"Because I asked him earlier if he would, and he said no. He said he didn't have anything to say to you, and that you would just have to believe me." As she talked Ben refocused his gaze on Sid. Was he waiting for Sid to talk, or was he afraid to look at her? His silence was impossible to bear. "And you should probably say something, so I don't just start rambling."

"It's a lot, right? I mean, if I'm understanding correctly." He began to rub the back of his head with his right hand, still looking at Sid. "You and Sid have conversations. Conversations where you can literally hear him talking to you."

"Yes."

"But he won't talk to me."

"I don't think so, no."

"So why tell me at all?" He exhaled, shifted his weight, turned to look at her. "If the dog is never going to talk to me, why bring it up?"

"Truth is, I hadn't planned on telling you until the moment I told you. I was just going to keep it to myself." She was the one having trouble making eye contact now, but forced herself to look at him. Why did she think she'd be able to say this and not have things change? "But I want to do this right. If we're going to live together, you need to know it all. That sometimes the floss misses the trash can and I just leave it there until I clean the bathroom. That I have been known to run the dishwasher when it's only half-full. And I am not above streaming the Carpenters on Spotify."

"For the record, I know those things already. And none of them bother me. The Carpenters? That's a badge of honor."

"Right?" She latched on to the Carpenters, a sweet and buoyant lifeboat that could carry them to safety. "Just perfect."

"But this." He looked again at the dog. "This is not like those things."

"I know." She stared at Sid, wondering if he would come to her rescue and just say hello. "And I still don't believe it's happening, sometimes."

"But it is?"

"But it is."

"Do you want to talk to anyone?"

"You mean, like a therapist?"

He shrugged. "Maybe?"

Nina had thought about that, but by this point she had decided there was a fifty percent chance she was crazy. If Sid wasn't really talking to her, she was losing her grip on reality, but if the dog was talking to her she was sane. There were no halfway options. She hated the idea of exposing herself to a therapist, some complete stranger, without knowing if it was necessary. Especially when she felt so boring and average, except for this one part of her life.

"Not now," she said, after a short pause. "I mean, lots of people talk to their dogs, right? Mine just talks back. And it's not like I feel worse when I talk to him."

The silence that followed stretched out for what felt like several very long minutes. "I guess what I am trying to figure out," Ben finally said, "is what I'm supposed to do now."

The question made Nina feel optimistic for the first time since the conversation had begun. Asking what he was supposed to do meant he didn't think the situation was impossible. "I don't know if you have to do anything," she said quickly. "Everything will just continue the way it has been."

"So he'll still talk to you, just not when I'm around?"

"I assume so." She looked at Sid, who was pretending to sleep, acting as though he could not understand what they were saying. He had his reasons, she knew, but that didn't make it any less frustrating. If he would just say a single word, that would be enough for Ben to believe her. "He says that it's risky for more than one person to hear him talk. That when he's done it before—"

"Wait, so he has talked to other people?"

"Not in this body, but—" As soon as the phrase left her mouth, Nina knew she should not have said it. Insanity has a velocity, and she went from zero to sixty to a hundred rapidly. Stopping in the middle of the sentence didn't help.

"Some other body?"

There was only one answer, and she had to say it. "Yes."

Ben's arm reached for the couch again. "His body changes shape?"

"No," she said, going for an easy joke to see if it would help. "That'd be crazy."

"So—what? Reincarnation?"

"That's what he tells me."

"And you believe him?"

"I figure if I'm gonna accept a talking dog, I should believe him when he says he's been here a few times before, in other bodies?" She shrugged. "Maybe it makes more sense, in a way? Explains how it can be happening at all?"

"Nina." He continued to hold on to the back of the couch.

"It's a lot, huh?"

"It's a lot. A dog that talks? And has been reincarnated? I mean."

Another pause, and this one felt even more ominous. She had to ask the question she was most afraid to ask. "Is it too much?"

Ben paused, looking at Sid. "It may be," he finally said. "It may be too much."

The air felt as if it had died. This was the moment she knew this would be more than an awkward bump in their relationship. "Like, how much too much?"

He took his hand off the back of the couch and examined it, then walked over to Nina. For a moment it looked like he was going to hug her; instead he brushed his fingers gently against her cheek and said, "I'm sorry, I—I can't do this."

Sid looked at her as soon as the door shut behind Ben. "Does this mean that we're not keeping the couch?"

They return from their walk through Piedmont Park two hours later. Sid laps up most of the fresh water in his bowl and heads straight to bed. Nina watches him circling in a small spot against the wall.

"You know, I've always wondered why you do that first, instead of just laying down."

"I wonder, as well."

"But you're doing it now. Don't you know why?"

"Do you understand everything your body wants you to do?"

"Not at all."

"There are many things about this body I do not understand." He collapses quickly, his legs splayed out.

Nina heads over to the keyboard. She hasn't played the Kurzweil since Ben left. She picks up the headphones and wonders which song she should attempt first.

One thing her mother did right was make sure that music filled their house. Nina remembers records playing all weekend long, classical music on the radio during dinner. It was odd when she went to the house of a friend who didn't have music on. It felt so silent. Incomplete.

Her father made his presence felt through music, too, thanks to all the vinyl albums with "M.A." written in small, neat letters on the back. Nina thought those initials were the best part of the collection, rare tangible evidence of this person named Matt Alexander that she never got a chance to know.

"He hated writing on them," her mother said, when she noticed Nina running her finger over the initials, "but he had great taste in music and greedy roommates."

Nina was in third or fourth grade when her mother handed her an album with the photo of the top half of a Black woman's head on the cover. Her face was tilted slightly, like she was giving something or someone the once-over. *Nina Simone Sings the Blues*. "This is who your father and I named you after," her mother said, putting the needle down on the vinyl. The first song began with just a voice, a voice so deep and mysterious that it would have been scary if it hadn't been so beautiful. "She was powerful and righteous and strong," her mother said as they sat together, staring at the record player. "And her voice never lost its beauty. We wanted to make sure you had some inspiration, something to remind you to always make yourself heard."

Piano lessons started around that time. Every Tuesday afternoon she went to see Miss Siobhan, whose name she always mispronounced. "Shiv-awn, Shiv-awn," she mumbled under her breath as she slowly walked up the brick path, her mother's car already out of sight. As soon as the door opened and the imposing Miss Siobhan appeared, Nina would panic and say, in a loud, scratchy voice, the name she saw written in neat block letters every time she picked up her music folder: "Hello Miss See-o-bun." Her teacher would scowl, correct her, and the lesson would be off to a terrible start.

Nina loved the sound of the piano, loved the way her fingers felt on the keys, but she hated practicing. She was certain that she would never get it, that she could work hard and still fail to please Miss Siobhan—so why practice at all? It was a relief, when her mother stopped forcing her to take lessons after a year.

When she was a freshman in high school, Nina began to sit at the piano for no other reason than she wanted to. For the first time, playing was rewarding. When she stopped worrying about reading music the playing became her own. Maybe the distance between the dots on the page and the sound from the piano was too great, or maybe she had just been too lazy to learn a whole new language. She found it much more satisfying to slowly work her fingers around the keys, trying to find her own path to the right sound.

All these years later, one of the songs she'd been forced to learn with Miss Siobhan remains buried in her muscle memory. Why is there still space for "The Great Clock" in her brain? Maybe because it took weeks for her to make it through correctly. As she starts to play it, no less slowly and nervously than she played it on the baby grand that dominated Miss Siobhan's living room, another piano memory comes back to her: Ben's first visit to her apartment. She'd been so worried about making the place clean that she'd forgotten to cover the keyboard up. Naturally, it was one of the first things Ben noticed.

"Wait, you play piano?"

She blushed when he looked at her. An excited look appeared in his eyes at certain moments, and it always thrilled her. "Technically, yes, I do play. But I'm not any good."

"When did you start?" He ran his fingers gently across the keys.

"Third grade? My mother was determined that I live up to my namesake."

"Your namesake?"

"Nina Simone," she mumbled. Why was she so nervous about having him there? "My parents decided to shoot high."

"Well." He slid his hand off the keyboard and walked over to her. "So you can play piano and you're named after Miss Nina Simone. Will the surprises ever stop coming?"

"Surprises are good?"

"Surprises are—surprising."

"You academics, with the clever language."

He looked at the futon, folded up into a couch. "And that opens into a bed."

"It does."

"Interesting."

They hadn't slept together yet, but the kissing was more than good. She loved the way his hands could grip firmly and tenderly at the same time.

"So," he continued, "when do I get to hear you play?"

"Um, never."

"Why not? The neighbors can hear you play but I can't?"

"No one hears me play." She pointed to the headphones sitting on the edge of the keyboard. "I put those on."

"It's all a secret?"

"Yes. Secrets are good."

"Well, just know that I'm ready to hear the secret. Whenever you are ready to share it."

She never did play for him. He never asked again after that first time, either.

After she plays "The Great Clock" twice she stops, stretches her fingers. Ready to tackle something real, Nina puts her hands in position, settling on "Videotape" as a good song to start with. There's a lesson in all of these memories—there must be—but she will not look for it today. Today she just wants to play.

10 | What's the Difference Between?

School provides plenty of distractions to keep Ben from thinking about Nina, especially what, if anything, he could have done differently, and what he should be doing now. He's got forty-five freshmen with early-in-the-semester questions, a dissertation to finish, and an infinite supply of circular debates in the Cube Farm.

The weekends, though, are endless.

Most Saturday nights Ben would wait for Nina at B-6, while she worked the dinner shift at South City Kitchen. When she got home, he would warm up whatever food he'd ordered while she showered. She'd come out looking perfect, with still damp hair, those cute flannel pajama pants, and a baggy T-shirt. The two of them would eat a late dinner and watch whatever show they were bingeing, before spending the night wonderfully squished in that futon of hers.

They slept in late most Sundays. Nina let the other waitresses fight over the lucrative brunch service; she preferred the Sunday dinner shift, which she called "chill and quiet" and as "close to church" as she would ever get. After a cup of coffee they'd walk Sid, then wander to brunch. The lines were always long by then, but Ben never minded the wait. As they lingered on random sidewalks he and Nina would banter about the crumbling world, invent backstories for people in line, or play a few rounds of "What's the Difference Between?" It was the kind of routine that made him appreciate the beauty, and importance, of routine in a relationship. He misses it all.

What's the difference between tolerance and acceptance? Humor and comedy? Manners and etiquette?

He had dated Nina for a year, making it the most serious relationship he'd had since Amy, junior year of college. Looking back at that relationship now, he understands that it was just a college fling, dating with training wheels. He felt better when Amy was around than when he was alone, but they never fully incorporated each other into their lives. They almost always slept in their separate dorm rooms, kept groups of friends that didn't overlap much, and never visited each other's families.

Nina had been incorporated into his life. Since the breakup, Ben has needed to relearn just how slowly a Bachelor Sunday moves. Coffee, surf the *Times* online, start some laundry, then marvel at how little time has passed. The first Sunday of the spring semester is unexpectedly warm, at least, so he opens the front door as soon as he sees the Maxwells leave the main house. They wordlessly get into their enormous Lexus SUV, looking like they're embarking on a forced trip to somewhere unpleasant. Nina was always fascinated by the Maxwells, with their pulled-down shades and quiet house. More than once she had threatened to make up an excuse to knock on their door. "Cup of sugar? Wi-Fi trouble? Or should I just ask if they have any extra scotch?"

He decides to take advantage of their absence and the nice weather to work in the kitchen. He usually disables the Wi-Fi when it's time to work on his dissertation, but this morning he's too distracted. He opens a search window, wondering why didn't he think of asking Google for help earlier.

"What if someone believes their dog talks?"

The first results are too benign to be helpful: articles about canine empathy, ways to say "I love you" in dog language, and the importance of support animals. He adds a "really" to his search, and then a "literally," looking for that corner of the internet devoted to people who share Nina's problem. If there are other people who suffer her symptoms, though, they must keep it to themselves—or their psychiatrists.

He gets up from the table, stretches, pours more coffee, and returns, telling himself that her issue is beyond his limited abilities to do anything about. It's okay for him to be selfish and focus on graduating on schedule in order to begin his life. This means it's time to do some more research on Hank Honeybird, Harlan's racist father.

But first email. Then he'll turn off Wi-Fi.

This turns out to be one time when staying online longer than planned is a good thing. His most recent message was sent at 6:54 a.m. The name listed—"eybyrdhon"—means nothing to him, but the subject line is almost too good to be true: Foxy Said I Could Trust You. He hesitates before opening, as if he has sighted an impossible oasis, something that might disappear as soon as he reaches out to make sure it is real.

Dear Mr. Davies,

Foxy Brown informs me that you would like to talk about the band my brother and I were in. More importantly, he tells me that you are someone I can trust, and that perhaps I should take this chance to answer questions before my brain melts away. I am ignoring his rude comment but taking his advice.

Please let me know when you would like to schedule some time to talk.

Best,
Darlene Mansfield

After two years of searching, he has suddenly made contact with the lone surviving member of Honeybird. Ben spends half an hour writing and revising his reply. He limits himself to a single, focused paragraph, and manages to wait five minutes after he hits send before he refreshes his inbox to see if she has written back.

He finds a semi-edible apple and some cheddar cheese for lunch, then becomes antsy enough to finally start grading the in-class essays he has ignored for over a week. That, along with a walk, kills a few hours. He plays *Waiting Here* loudly and cleans his kitchen and bathroom. As he listens he pays special attention to Darlene's playing. She keeps the rhythms straightforward, with only a few flashy bass runs, and the bass and the kick drum are completely locked in—exactly what the songs and Harlan's guitar need. Every so often she unleashes an especially nice lick or counter-melody, but even then you only notice how much they add if you really listen closely.

Darlene has not replied to his email by the time he needs to face another post-Nina Sunday challenge. Ben has called his mother almost every Sunday night since he moved to Atlanta. He's hoping that she will start the conversation differently from the last two weeks, but is not surprised when she doesn't.

"So, have you heard from Nina yet?"

"No, Mom." More irritation than he had intended slips into his tone. He tries to be patient, remembering that after a single quick chat on the phone with Nina, his mother proclaimed her "the best one" he'd ever dated.

There's a pause, and then his mother quietly says, "Well, that's too bad. It sounded like she was good for you."

He winces because she is right. "She was," he says quietly. "We worked well, when we were dating. Once it came time to actually take the next step and move in together—that was too much. I don't think we'll ever talk again."

His mother must have heard the way his voice caught because she quickly moves the conversation onto firmer ground. Her new volunteer job at the library gets her out of the house a few mornings each week. This gives her a break from his stepfather, who took early retirement and now follows Ben's mother around, waiting for a task to be handed out. The irony is that when Ben was old enough to talk honestly with his mother about why her first marriage failed, she pointed to the fact that Ben's father had never been home. He traveled a lot for his job, and when he was in town, he worked long hours and went out for drinks with clients and coworkers. After that experience she wanted someone who would be around more often. The problem now? She has someone who is around more often.

"Tom just walked in. You want to say hello?"

"No, no, that's okay," he says, smiling to himself. His mother always offers to force his stepfather to come to the phone, and Ben always politely declines. "I need to look over this weekend's work before I turn in."

"Oh, your research! How is your guitar player? Have you talked to your brother yet?"

Ben swallows his sigh to keep it inaudible. His older brother plays guitar in an indie rock band, which somehow has their mother convinced that Dan is a crucial source for Ben's dissertation. "Not yet, Mom."

"I'm sure he'd love to talk to you, if you called him."

Ben promises to call Dan soon, then hangs up. The carriage house feels especially silent, allowing the echo of his mother's sad tone to linger. She never met Nina in person, and while he was disappointed at the time he's relieved now. His mother would have loved Nina if they had met—Nina with her big smile, easy laugh, sharp wit, lively green eyes. Nina was supposed to go home with him last month to Seattle over winter break. Embarrassing as it is to admit to himself now, he was looking forward to having a beautiful woman sitting next to him at the dinner table on Christmas Eve, someone for his mother to make a fuss over while his stepfather silently wondered how Ben had attracted such a catch. Nina did not have the money for a plane ticket, though, and resisted when Ben said he could just pay for hers.

"Why not? You'll love Seattle."

"I'm sure I would. And I'd love to meet your Mom."

"So?"

"So I feel weird, taking so much money from you."

"But, Nina, we're—"

"We're good," she said. "That's the thing. I don't want money to make shit weird."

Nina did meet Ben's father, though. He called one night to say that his flight out of Atlanta had been canceled so he was free for dinner. There was no discussion about how long Ben's father had been in town, or why he had been in town, just a last-minute offer of some time together. This was standard procedure for Ben's father and it drove Ben crazy. Still, he always said yes, just as his father knew he would. "Bocca Lupo at eight. My friends tell me it's the hottest place going right now." His father's voice, which was never warm in tone, sounded more detached on the phone.

Ben and Nina were at her place when his father called. Two hours later the three of them were laughing, sharing good wine, and enjoying several courses of fine Italian food. Ben saw how charmed Nina was by his father, and why not? The man was charming. When you were in the same room with him, and he had a desire to impress you, he was witty and engaged and full of funny stories. At the end of the night his father paid the bill, hugged Nina with what seemed like genuine affection, and issued lots of grandiose proclamations about seeing them both again very soon.

"He's fantastic," she said on the car ride home. "How come you never talk about him?"

He debated how much to tell her. They had been dating a few months at this point, just beginning to navigate that awkward period of transition from casual to maybe-sort-of-serious relationship. He never talked about his father because he only had memories of a man with a suitcase on his way out the door, or a man he was forced to spend a few hours with every other weekend, just so he could watch his older brother get all the attention. A man who took Ben's mother to court more than once in an attempt to reduce his alimony and child support payments—not out of any monetary hardship, but just so that he could claim a victory. Ben had no stories to share that made his father look good. What kind of warning sign would that send Nina? "Because that is probably the only time I will see him this year. And maybe for the next two years."

"No," she said. "He specifically mentioned he had to return to Atlanta—"

"Yup. And he won't call," Ben said.

And he didn't call again before Ben broke up with Nina. His lack of reliability was the most reliable aspect of his personality.

After dinner, Ben finishes his Sunday folding laundry while British people bake pies on his laptop. He checks his email one more time before going to bed. There's no way to know if the universe is rewarding him for dutifully calling his mother or folding his laundry the same day it was washed, but Darlene has written back. She wonders if he's free to talk one afternoon this week.

11 | buybuy

Nina would have calculated the odds of her walking around a mega-baby supply store with Connie as roughly equal to a messianic cult's end-of-the-world prediction coming true. Yet, here they are, strolling the aisles of buybuy BABY. Nina is on gun duty: she points the hand-held-scanner at the bar code of anything Connie decides to add to the registry for her baby shower and fires away.

"I keep hearing about the glowy happy stage of pregnancy. When does that start?" Connie is walking slowly, hand on her growing belly. "Thanks again for doing this. My mother offered to come, as if that would be any help at all."

After all these years Nina has still never actually met Connie's mother, who lives in a gated community a few hours north of Atlanta. Stories about Connie's mother have become so embedded into the mythology of their small group that Nina worries she might actually meet this woman after the baby is born; some characters maintain their power by staying offstage. "What about Adam? Didn't he want to be here for this?"

"Oh, God, no. The supplies, all the shit we're gonna have to get? This is the worst part for him." Connie points to a pack 'n play. "Scan that mofo."

Nina aims the laser gun at the bar code and pulls the trigger. She has to admit that this point-and-click consumerism is satisfying. "Bam."

"He didn't even want to register."

"Why not?"

Connie waves her hands as they turn down a new aisle of brightly colored boxes. "He has this idea that if we don't ask for anything, we won't get anything. But my thinking is, everyone's gonna buy us crap. Might as well be the crap we don't want the least."

"Isn't that the official 'buybuy BABY' slogan? 'The crap you don't want the least'?"

"Thing is, we need it. It's not like we can deal with this new human by wrapping it in paper towels and putting it to sleep on the couch." Connie nods at a play mat. "What the hell, let's get one of those."

Nina looks at the mat. She can't imagine its bright blues and oranges, and dangly giraffes and zebras, anywhere in Connie's house. She raises the scanner gun and clicks the trigger. "Done."

"I mean, he needs to grow the fuck up and accept the fact that we're gonna have a kid in four months. Everything is going to change. It's scary, but there's no going back now."

"It's scary for you, too?"

Connie shoots her one of her patented looks of disbelief, the kind of look you get when you suggest a movie or type of wine that you should know she cannot stand. "Of course it is."

Nina takes a closer look at Connie standing in the very brightly lit aisles, surrounded on either side by encroaching walls of baby supplies. Her belly is pushing against a loose orange shirt, and there are shadows at the edges of her eyes that Nina has not seen before. Could it be uncertainty, if not quite fully developed fright? "I thought you were excited to be a mother. How did you put it—'the chance to do the opposite of what my Mom did'?"

"Well. Yeah. That part will be fun." She raises her arms in a vaudevillian shrug and starts to move again, leading them down the aisle. "That doesn't mean it's not scary." Connie holds up a plastic placemat and points to the illustration on the packaging, which shows a young family out for dinner, the baby eating off the special placemat. "(a) This kid is too young to be going out, and (b) when we do take our kid out, he or she is using the same damn placemat we are." She tosses it back on the rack and breathes out. "So," she says, turning to Nina, "you ready to tell me the real reason you and Humbert Humbert broke up? For the record, I have been very patient."

Nina used to think Connie's nickname for Ben was too harsh, but now she's okay with it. "I told you. He freaked out when we were looking at the apartment."

Connie reaches the end of the aisle, exhales, rubs her belly, turns to her right. "Oh, come on. I knew he would fuck it up at some point, but that's not the whole story."

"But—"

"And if you don't want to tell your hormonal best friend, that's fine. I mean, I'll probably find some other reason to burst into tears in this suburban Wonka factory of brightly colored crap."

As much as she trusts Connie, Nina is not ready to say the words "talking dog" out loud again, never mind "talking dog with a side of reincarnation"—not after what happened last time. "We were standing there, in the living room, when he said 'I can't do this.'"

"You told me that part. And I believe it. So very wimpy white boy of him. But I still want to know why."

Nina pauses, trying to decide if she should lie to her best friend, or keep offering vague and incomplete answers. Before she says anything, though, Connie narrows her eyes and offers her own explanation.

"Jesus, he was fucking someone else, wasn't he?"

Nina hesitates, then nods. She doesn't like lying, especially to Connie. But when it's something the other person wants to believe—something she'll probably insist is true, no matter how much Nina denies it—is it really a lie? "Yup."

Connie points at a small, heavy duty trash can designed to hold diapers and/or nuclear waste. Nina aims and scans. "Cock. Roach. Another undergrad?"

"I didn't ask," she says. At least that's the truth.

"I knew it. They're all about power, his type. And now that you're older, now that he sees how together you are, it's too much."

Nina can't hide her surprise at that. "I'm together?" She laughs, shakes her head. "Have you met me?"

"Course. Look at you. Sharp-looking, getting your degree one brick at a time while supporting yourself, playing your piano all secret-like. You're a threat."

"I don't think he did any of this because I'm a threat."

"Trust me, you're a threat. Certainly too much for Humbert to handle." Connie leans back, groans. "Let's get out of here. This is enough shit for one baby."

They start slowly making their way back to the too-energetic clerk helping them set up the registry. "I don't know," Nina says. "Don't you want some cute maternity shirts? 'Adorableness Inside' or 'All I Wanted Was a Back Rub'?"

"Don't push it. I am entitled to nothing but supportive comments and actions until the baby has popped out and I'm back to my pre-maternity weight." They reach the clerk and Nina hands her the scan gun. As they wait for the clerk to print the registry, riffing about what the next wave of baby inventions might bring, Connie's phone begins to buzz in her handbag. When she takes it out and sees who it is, she sighs loudly and hits a button. "That's gonna be me someday, right?" She puts the phone back in her bag. "Driving this kid nuts with phone calls, or maybe just buzzing the chip we'll all have implanted in our heads by then."

"Yes," Nina says. "But don't worry. I suspect your offspring will quickly learn how to send all your chip buzzes straight to voicemail."

Connie takes the printout from the clerk, and they start walking to the front door. "And, back to my point, because I'm right. Ben backed off because you were too much for him to understand and that threatened him. He felt so threatened he went ahead and screwed someone else, to force you to dump him. That doesn't mean you did anything wrong. It just means you also have to keep leaning the fuck in. Become an even bigger threat."

Nina can agree with the part about Ben not understanding, but does not believe she is a threat to anyone, except maybe herself. She wishes she could tell Connie everything, because if you can't tell your best friend, who's left?

12 | Darlene Honeybird

Darlene Honeybird is now Darlene Mansfield. She has moved from Macon to Marietta, one of Atlanta's many Northeast suburbs, which became popular destinations for white homeowners fleeing downtown in the 1960s and 70s. Here's another example of the past not predicting the future, Ben thinks, as he recalls the wild-eyed bass player with out-of-control hair he saw in Foxy's pictures. He would never have imagined the woman in that photo living in a large suburban home, set at the top of a steep driveway, complete with a three-car garage.

Darlene's daughter, Anne, answers the door. She has her mother's red hair and expressive eyes, and leads Ben into a foyer with a vaulted ceiling and a sweeping staircase off to the left. He looks up to see two young boys leaning over the railing and watching him, one with a plastic bow and arrow aimed at Ben's head.

"It's okay," Anne says, shutting the door. "I don't think Toby will really try to shoot you."

"And even if he did he'd miss," says the boy without the arrow. He holds his hand up in front of his face when his brother turns to take aim at him.

"I won't miss from here."

"Yes, you will."

"Don't mind Romulus and Remus," Anne says with a sigh, leading Ben down a hallway off the foyer.

"Twins?" he asks, impressed with her historical reference.

"Yes, and they may kill me before they kill each other." When they reach the kitchen, she turns and points to an open doorway. "Mom has her own digs down here."

"Thank you," he says, his steps instantly muffled by the deep plush carpet on the stairs. Waiting for him at the bottom is a rail-thin woman with short gray hair, tortoise-shell glasses, and a skeptical look.

"Mr. Davies, I presume."

"Indeed."

"Step into my parlor," she says, waving him into a large sitting area. Against the wall to his left is a small kitchenette, with a sink, mini-fridge, and stovetop. To his right are two plush chairs, a circular coffee table between them. She sits in the chair on left, which he takes as his cue to sit in the other.

"Thanks again for meeting with me," he says. He takes his digital recorder out and places it on the coffee table. "Is it okay if I record this?"

Darlene nods, silently watching him angle the mic toward her, hit record, and settle back in his chair. Time suddenly stops moving. Even though this setup takes less than a minute, he feels as though she is judging his competence—and he is failing.

Ben takes his legal pad and a pen out of his messenger bag. He's been mapping out questions for almost a week and still feels underprepared. The fact that Darlene avoided talking about Honeybird for fifty years made him suspect she would not be an easy interview; her posture and tone of voice have convinced him he was right. "I thought we'd start with your father? Hank Honeybird—"

"Our father." Her hands are folded in her lap, the pointer finger of her right hand tapping a steady rhythm. "Why do you want to start there?"

Ben had not expected his opening question to be challenged. "Hank Honeybird was quite the force in Macon," he says, trying not to sound defensive. "I would imagine—"

"I am aware of who my father was, Mr. Davies. But if you are here to talk about Harlan, I am not sure our father is the place to begin." She points to the tea pot on the table between them. "Would you care for some?"

"No, thank you," Ben says, feeling a little too off-balance to trust himself with a hot drink. He suspects Darlene would have resisted whatever topic he started with, to test him. "I guess," he says, "that not talking about him could draw more attention than talking about him?"

She studies his face, then reaches down to pour herself some tea. "Would people learn a lot about you, Mr. Davies," she begins after taking a sip, "by studying your father?"

"My father?" He's impressed at how quickly she has turned the tables. Maybe this is what she needs before they can start talking: a sacrifice from him. "Probably not. We are very different people, I think."

She sips her tea. "Is he also an academic?"

"God, no. He's a businessman."

"What business?"

"Does it sound bad if I say I'm not entirely sure? He sells things to other businesses—software, marketing tools." He looks down, surprised to see he is doodling as he talks. "But I never understood any of that. I just knew that he traveled. A lot."

Darlene puts her teacup down. "There were many things our father did that I did not understand, either. The restaurant, making biscuits? That

I understood. I spent more than a few Saturday mornings working in one of his kitchens."

"Because you wanted to? Or you had to?"

"From the time I was in elementary school, it was assumed that I would take over the business someday."

"Not Harlan?"

"By the time he was in elementary school, it was understood that my brother would never run Double H Biscuits." A half-smile crosses her face. "Even though Daddy gave him a name that would befit such a purpose."

"What did you not understand then, the politics?"

"Yes." The smile vanishes. "I can still see flashes from that time, snapshots that are stuck in small corners of my brain. Picnics and barbecues, crowds of sweaty people. Walking around in dresses I would only wear once, in an attempt to make Hank Honeybird's tomboy daughter look like the ideal young lady. And all the while my mother's voice in my ear, quietly demanding I smile."

"And your father's voice?"

"Booming at all times, as if every communication needed to be shouted over the noise of a loud restaurant kitchen. Used at these rallies to say things I cannot repeat." She leans forward to pick up her teacup again. "I am sure you have read the press coverage already."

Ben nods. He wasn't going to ask her to repeat any of the awful language Hank Honeybird used in a desperate attempt to out race-bait his opponent, Herman Talmadge. "Talmadge was going to get the nomination unless he died, or got caught with a little boy in his bed. Everyone knew that."

"Everyone except Hank Honeybird."

He watches her take a sip of tea, the silence suddenly so complete that he suspects she is done talking about their father for now. All of his carefully prepared questions and segues need to be tossed aside, he decides, trying a new tactic to segue to the next topic. "I have to admit, the last thing I would want to do is be in a band with my brother."

"Really?" She sounds surprised for the first time. "Older or younger?"

"Older."

"Any other siblings?"

He shakes his head. "Just the two of us."

"Why don't you get along with him?"

She phrases the question in a way he never thought of it: he's always wondered why Dan doesn't get along with him, not the other way around. "I suppose," he says after a short pause, "that he is more like my father, and I am more like my mother." He shrugs. "And they got divorced."

"Interesting." She nods to herself. "Harlan and I did not take after either of our parents. It felt, in fact, as though we had been dropped on some alien landscape. We chose to not make our home on that landscape—instead we worked hard to escape, going out to the woods, playing in the barn. When we got older Harlan started to have other friends, of course, but he always let me tag along with him. If anyone gave him shit about it, he put them in their place."

"That's a good big brother."

She puts her hands in her lap. "Once he started hanging out in his room playing guitar, I made him try and teach me, so I wouldn't miss out on anything. He moved too fast, though. One day he was trying to form basic chords, and the next his fingers looked like they had never done anything but play guitar."

"Had he always wanted to play?"

"He listened to music quite often, quite loudly, and by the time he was twelve or thirteen, quite stoned. But he was perfectly happy just playing an old harmonica he'd found in the barn until Daddy gave him a guitar."

"Your father bought Harlan his first guitar?" Ben has always imagined that Hank Honeybird did not approve of his son being a long-haired rock guitarist.

"I suspect he did not pay for it. Most likely left behind by one of the tenants he evicted, and given to his ne'er-do-well son—probably to prevent him from playing that harmonica."

"How did Harlan react?"

"Surprised. It was not like my father to give presents except for birthdays and Christmas. And then, it was like he'd been waiting for just this moment. He would disappear into his room for hours, suddenly focused in a way he never had been before. It was the first thing he'd ever taken seriously." She pauses, shaking her head. "And I was so angry. That he got a gift but I did not, of course, but more than that. He had something to do that did not involve me. I demanded my turn with the new toy, but soon it was obvious that any time that guitar spent with me was wasted."

"But you became a very solid bass player."

She looks at him and raises her eyebrows. "I will accept that compliment because you didn't push it too far. 'Solid' is a fair assessment and the best I can hope for. When Harlan first brought home a bass and handed it to me I was terrified, given my failure with guitar. But he said, 'Only four strings, Little D. And just hit every time I stomp my foot.'" She grins, and the smile makes her look much younger. "That I could manage. And he was so good that no one paid attention to me."

The few articles he found about the band all praise, with good reason, Harlan's guitar prowess, but it's his songs that Ben wants to examine more closely. "When did Harlan start writing?"

The layer of restraint that had just begun to drift away slides back over her face. "My brother kept that side of himself a secret for a long time. It may be the one area of his life where he actually . . ." She pauses. "Where he seemed to be less than fully and completely confident."

"Why do you think that was?"

"I think we all keep parts of ourselves secret, even from the people we love the most." She looks like she is about to continue but then stops and folds her hands into her lap.

Ben senses she is forming more sentences in her head than she's saying out loud. "What was the first song of his you heard?"

"They weren't really songs at first, just chord patterns that we'd play through at practice. Those first few months we talked as much at practices as we played, with lots of breaks for Harlan to roll a joint. Every now and then we'd play a bad blues cover, dreaming that we could get a gig at Gus's Crab Shack someday." She shifts in her chair and makes brief eye contact. "But we kept coming back to one of those patterns, and slowly there started to be a shape to it. I had an uncle who developed his own photos, and he showed me how it worked once, how the picture slowly emerged from the dark. That's what this felt like. Like there had been a song hidden there the whole time, and we just had to see it."

"And what did you find, that first time?"

"'Mr. Invisible,'" she says, smiling as if remembering an old friend. "We wrote better songs over time, but that one has always been special to me, because it was our first. And as soon as we played it all the way through it sounded better than anything else we'd done. It was ours, a thing we had made, together. And I think for each of us, maybe for our own reasons, that was what made it so valuable."

As she starts talking about the music her posture relaxes again. She shares a few funny stories from Honeybird's first gigs, and then recaps the night their eventual manager Willy Wilson first saw them play. After the gig he wooed them with a steak dinner and bottles of expensive whiskey, and talked about putting Macon on the "goddamn map." Wilson also paid for, and produced, their first record, which sold just enough copies in the Southeast to fund a second. By this point Darlene is relaxed enough to share some memories of the band achieving some milestones: first time in the studio, first time they saw a picture of themselves in a newspaper, first time they held a copy of their record, first time they played outside of Macon.

"And you didn't have any trouble at the clubs?"

"Trouble, Mr. Davies?"

"Well, you did not look like most of the bands from the Southeast at that time."

"No. Or today, even, sadly."

"And you weren't worried?"

"I was terrified," she says. "Just terrified. Nate and Harlan weren't worried, though, and I was very aware that I was both the youngest in the band and the only girl. I knew that I could not admit how nervous I was. Luckily, nothing too horrible ever happened."

"Nothing too horrible?"

"A few close calls, usually in Alabama. And there was an awful night outside of Biloxi, some hole-in-the-wall that smelled of boiled peanuts and urine. The soundman warned us there had been talk of trouble, of some locals upset to hear there was a Black drummer. They used a different word, of course. We didn't let Nate out of the van until it was time for our set, and even then we unscrewed the one light that would have reached the drums."

"Why not just cancel?"

"We were young, and stubborn." She pauses and narrows her eyes, as if looking for something off in the distance. "And without ever saying it to each other, I think we also were convinced that we could change the South just by showing up and playing."

He writes down the phrase "Showing up and playing," which strikes him as a good chapter title. "And it worked? Nate hiding in the van?"

"We managed to get in and out without getting beaten up. It helped that there couldn't have been more than ten people in the place." She shakes her head, and turns to Ben. "Truth be told, I suspect Daddy's name helped protect us more than once. Most of the people who would be inclined to give people like Nate a hard time were, at the end of the day, cowards. Cowards who didn't want to make Hank Honeybird angry."

"More irony."

"Indeed." She offers another one of her rare smiles. "The most awkward moments came from people assuming Harlan and I were a couple."

"I hadn't even thought of that."

"Neither had we. But it did come in handy sometimes—most Southern men will leave another guy's girl alone. Unless they've had a few too many."

She yawns as she answers. If Ben needed any more incentive to pick the most important topic of those not covered yet, he now has it. "Okay. So, I do have to ask about these conspiracy theories, about the fire."

"Oh, Mr. Davies." Darlene rolls her eyes. "Just when I was thinking that this talk was going better than I had expected."

"Thank you," he says, "I'm glad to hear it. But the theories are out there. And the same way I had to ask about your father, I need to ask about this." He waits a moment, but her only response is to sigh and turn to face him. "Is there any doubt in your mind that Nate died in the fire?"

"None." Immediate, decisive.

"So why do you think his body was never found?"

"What year was this, Mr. Davies?"

He knows that she knows he knows the answer but tells her anyway. "1968."

"1968. How concerned do you think the good people of Macon were with finding the body of a Black man? How much effort would be spent poking through the smoking wreckage once the white boy had been found?"

"Fair point. But I would still think that—"

"The only people who cared were Nate's family, the poor and Black relatives of the man everyone decided must have been at fault." She shakes her head and exhales, an action that seems to cause her body to shrink further into her chair. "Not having Nate's body just made it all the easier to blame Nate. Tell everyone he must have started the fire and run away. Made a good excuse to turn Macon inside out, hunting a man everyone knew was dead."

Her tone makes it clear that she does not want to talk about this anymore, but Ben thinks he needs to ask one more time. The missing body provides oxygen for the Nate Is Alive conspiracies, and like the ghost of Hank Honeybird, the ghost of Nate Williams has a key role to play in the band's story. "Even if they weren't looking for his body, when they were cleaning the barn they would have found something?"

She looks at him with disappointment, like he has failed a simple test. "In my experience, we are most likely to find the things we are looking for."

"But—"

"Think of it this way, Mr. Davies. We have been talking for quite a while, but you, a presumably enlightened academic, have asked more questions about Nate's dead body than you have his drumming. The South has always made it easy for Black men to disappear."

It's hard to hear her criticism, but he also knows it's true. "To be honest," he says, hoping he does not sound too defensive, "it's difficult to find much information about Nate. I found an article where your father says he was sure 'Nate's family' knew where he was, but no specifics about who was in that family."

"It would be hard to find out much," she says, her tone softening. "He lived with his grandparents, who did the best they could do. But they were not the kind of family that would be detailed in public records."

"What happened to his parents?"

"All I knew is that they were not around, had never been around. Nate never seemed like he wanted to talk about it, so we didn't ask." She pauses. "Have you tracked down Toni yet?"

"Toni?"

"Nate's sister. She's the best one to talk to about all this."

"I didn't know he had a sister."

"She and I were the same age, each with big brothers we adored. That kept us pretty close, for a while."

"Are you still in touch?"

"Not as much as I'd like," she says. "But I can send her a note." She shifts in her chair and slowly begins to stand up. "I have devoted a lot of energy over the years to not remembering any of this. So I think I need to be done for today."

"I can't thank you enough for your time," Ben says, turning off the tape recorder. "And I'm sorry if this was too upsetting, or if I asked something I should not have."

"You asked about some things I have tried not to think about, but that is not your fault." She braces herself by placing her hand on the back of her chair. "The past is always there, even when I avoid looking at it."

Ben picks up his messenger bag. "So, if you don't mind—why did you agree to talk to me?"

Darlene smiles. "Now there is a good question." She slowly heads to the staircase, which he takes as his cue to follow her. "Foxy Brown was very good to all of us, and has never asked for many favors. He liked you, though, and thinks you could actually wind up publishing a book. He asked if I would help, so his pictures could be used."

For someone who is talking about this part of her life on the record for the first time, she is a natural. Ben got some useful information, and the book will already be much better because of her involvement, but he also suspects that she did not tell him anything she had not planned to tell him. He was going to wait to ask about another interview in a follow-up email but standing next to her at the bottom of the stairs he decides to ask now, while she is talking fondly of Foxy. "I do have some more questions, if you are willing to meet again?"

"I suspected you might, Mr. Davies." She rubs her neck as she talks. "Can we wait a few weeks?"

"That would be fine," he says.

She closes her eyes, exhales, nods. "Okay, then. I'm afraid I'm going to disappoint my mother and not walk you to the door. It's one of those days I prefer to hide in my cave."

Before he can thank her one more time she turns to walk back into the sitting area. Ben climbs the padded stairs and wonders how much Darlene actually revealed of herself today, and if he will ever get a chance to see any more.

FEBRUARY-MARCH

"Embrace nothing:
If you meet the Buddha, kill the Buddha.
If you meet your father, kill your father.
Only live your life as it is,
Not bound to anything."
—Gautama Siddhartha

13 | Robyn

After lying awake in bed for what seems like hours, unable to keep her mind from racing through everything that has happened since Sid started talking to her, Nina checks the time on her phone: 2:34 a.m. She angrily tosses the sheets aside and gets up, but it's not until she warms some milk in the microwave and walks back into the living room that Sid opens his eyes.

"I was worried you might be dead," she says, staring out the glass doors. It's been a long time since she was awake at this hour. The world seems especially dark and quiet.

"This body sleeps very soundly. But it is also acutely sensitive to changes in routine. Why are you awake now?"

"I wish I knew."

"So why don't you go back to sleep?"

His voice is more audible when the rest of the world is still. "It's not always that easy," she says. "All these years, you must have had a few sleepless nights."

"I don't need to remember those."

"You only remember what you need to, from one life to the next?"

"Why would I remember things I do not need to remember?"

Sid's logic is often as well-reasoned as it is annoying. She takes a sip of warm milk and thinks of her grandmother, who often has trouble sleeping. Many mornings Nina stumbled out to the kitchen and found her already hard at work, finishing some elaborate baking project or halfway through the knitting of a new scarf. "How many lives are we talking, anyway?"

"You have asked before. I still do not remember."

She watches a young couple walk stumble their way across the parking lot behind her building. Drunk? In love? Same thing? "Okay, then try this one," she says, turning to look at him. "What's the oldest memory you have?"

"Looking up at a Bodhi tree."

"Now that is interesting. And such a quick answer." A vague image comes to her mind: a tree with long branches stretching out, parallel to the ground, and lots of green leaves. "Do we have those in America?"

He stands up, stretches, then sits down on the bed. "The one I remember was not in America."

"Where was it?"

"Bihar."

"Bihar?"

"In what is now called India."

She's surprised. "I assumed you'd be reborn in the same country each time, but I guess once you open the reincarnation door, anything can go. Any country, animal, gender?"

"The modern world's obsession with gender always confuses me."

"So you have been women?"

"I have been in female bodies. But this first memory comes from a male body."

"Do you remember anything else? What was your name?"

"Siddhartha."

"Siddhartha?" She watches him as she finishes her milk, trying to process everything he's saying. What does it mean, she wonders, that she's accepted the talking dog part of her life and now is just struggling with the reincarnation aspect? "As in Siddhartha Gautama?"

"You have heard of him?"

"Sure." She heads into the kitchen, to put her empty mug into the sink. "In high school I had to read this book about him." She returns to the futon and sits down next to Sid. "He goes off in search of wisdom and enlightenment and becomes the Buddha." As she talks, Sid yawns, scratches his ears, and lays down next to her. He does not respond until she asks directly: "Are you saying you remember being that Siddhartha?"

"That is my oldest memory."

She lays back on the futon, legs bent, feet still touching the ground. That would mean Sid has been coming back in new bodies for over two thousand years. "Wow. I woke myself up because I was worried that I might really be crazy, and it seems like I was right." She turns her head to look at him. "I mean, are you really talking to me, now?"

"What do you think my answer should be?"

"Can you ever just answer the question without asking another question?"

"Is that what you want me to do?"

Was he this funny in previous lives? Probably. How could you survive walking the earth for so long without developing a sense of humor? "Do you like always speaking in questions?"

"I ask questions when I do not know the answer."

Staring up at the ceiling, trying to decide if those cracks near the moulding have always been there, she decides it's a good sign she's worried about losing her mind. If she had already lost her mind she wouldn't be worried, because she wouldn't realize what was happening. Right? "And Sid, really? Is your name always some variation of Siddhartha?"

"Siddhartha, Sid. These are just designations. We are not our names."

She sighs. "OK, we can have that discussion later. For now, if you are—were—that Siddhartha, the person with that 'designation,' then you became Buddha. Aren't you supposed to have all the answers to my questions? Not just more questions?"

"I don't think I'm here to do that for you."

She sits back up and starts scratching his ears. "So why are you here?"

"I think I am here to help."

"You were sent to me?"

He sits up and yawns, then licks his mouth. "Sent? By whom?"

"Whoever is in charge of the Reincarnation Machine. Someone has to be placing souls into bodies."

"I am more concerned with what I need to do than how I got here."

"But aren't you curious?"

"I accept that there are many questions we will never know the answer to."

"So you don't think about it."

"Did I say that?" Sid hops down off the futon and shakes his head, causing the tags on his collar to jingle. "I will admit that I wonder why I have never met anyone else who remembers inhabiting other bodies."

"Maybe they just don't talk about it?"

"Perhaps. Or they don't remember."

"Or maybe you were wrong about becoming enlightened?" The question is out before she realizes she may be insulting the Buddha.

"How can any of us be certain we are never wrong?"

A wave of sympathy for this tiny creature washes over her. If Sid really is the Buddha, then it must be frustrating to keep returning to this world. It makes the tone of annoyance that seeps into his voice at times almost forgivable. "Maybe you were right, but in a different way than you thought."

"A different way?"

"Maybe with enlightenment comes enhanced memory. Maybe we're all wandering more than once, but only the enlightened few can remember, from life to life." Nina wonders if that would mean that enlightenment is more of a curse than a reward, but she keeps that question to herself.

He stands up and heads for the kitchen. "Interesting. I shall think about it on our walk."

"Walk?" She is suddenly exhausted, and the idea of moving seems impossible.

"You woke up a creature with a tiny bladder. This is your reward."

Half an hour later they're back in bed. Sid's erratic snoring begins almost as soon as he lays down, but Nina still can't sleep. She wonders if her grandmother is up and reaches for her phone.

u awake

She hits send and puts the phone face down so that the light won't disturb Sid. After a few minutes with no reply, Nina rolls over onto her side, tilting her head slightly so she can stare out the sliding glass doors. The problem with this position is that it reminds her of falling asleep with Ben. When they both squeezed onto the futon, he would lay against the wall and wrap his arms around her, and she would be facing the same way she is now. The arrangement worked as long as they didn't mind being in constant contact with each other's bodies.

She didn't mind.

They had been dating for over a month when Nina decided it was time to talk about their romantic pasts on another sleepless night. "Andy Mueller," she said.

"Andy Mueller?"

"Andy Mueller." When they first started dating Ben was a reluctant hugger, but she quickly converted him. Feeling him in bed behind her, holding her tight, became one of her favorite sensations; his arms were stronger than she expected, and she loved feeling the slight paunch of his belly press against her back. She could never tell him that, of course, but she enjoyed having a secret spot on his body to seek out. "Andy was my first real love. Or, at least, what I thought was love at the time."

"When was this?"

"Second grade."

"You remember stuff from second grade?"

"Of course," she said, looking over her shoulder at him. "Don't you?"

"Mrs. Pinkham was my teacher." He shrugged. "But I only remember that because I was an eight-year-old boy, and we made lots of bad jokes about the name."

She turned back around, to look out the glass doors. "I still remember Andy. The way I felt all nervous inside whenever he walked into my sight."

"What did my rival look like?"

"Red hair. Thick glasses. Wore lots of corduroy and a dashing series of polo shirts that were a little tight in the belly."

He nuzzled her neck as she talked. "I can see your type hasn't changed."

"He was older, too, by a whole month." She took hold of his right hand, which was comfortably resting on her hip. "What about you? First crush?"

"Sherri Ferguson."

"Ooh, Sherri, baby. What grade?"

"Fifth? Sixth?"

She shifted her body, turning around to look at him. "What was she like?"

"Funny. Always making people laugh, always laughing. Unafraid to be loud. I was quiet, nervous whenever anyone even looked at me, so I thought she had some superpowers."

"How cute," she said, putting her hand on the back of his head. "Did you ask her out?"

"Oh, God no," he said. "I didn't date anyone until junior year."

"Why not?"

He shrugged. "Maybe that feeling of nervousness? Maybe fear of rejection? Or maybe it was just a result of having an older, much cooler brother, who always seemed to be dating several girls."

"How am I just finding out about this brother?" she asked. Ben's face had tensed slightly when he said "older, cooler brother," which made her suspect they didn't get along. "Are you guys close?"

"Not so much. But we never fought or anything either. Sort of feels like we're barely related."

"What does he do?"

"He plays guitar in an indie rock band. Travels in a van, puts out records, refuses to do anything else."

"Wow. Is he any good?"

Ben paused. "It's hard for me to say. He's always been my brother and he's always played."

"Do people come and see him?"

"If he were here, Dan would say that the two questions don't relate. That just because people come to see you doesn't mean that you are good—and vice versa."

She slides her hand from the back of his head to his shoulder. "Are you jealous of him?"

"For wandering the country in an old van?"

"For being this confident dude who always got the ladies."

Ben paused, nodded. "Yes," he said, quietly. "Not for the ladies part, but for the confidence part."

She remembers thinking it sounded like it was hard for him to admit that to her, or himself. After they were quiet for a second she smiled, raised her eyebrows and said, "So. Is he married?"

"He has a girlfriend we're all afraid is gonna realize she's too good for him. That doesn't mean you don't have a shot, though. He often multi-tasks." He leaned in to gently rub his forehead against hers, then pulled back to look at her. "Did you ever wish you had a brother or sister?"

"Yes. In fact, I pretended I had a sister when I was young. I used to walk around the house and talk to her."

"Talk to her?"

Nina hadn't planned on bringing up her imaginary sister with Ben but decided to go in all with the sharing. "Yes, talk to her."

"Did you name her?"

"Robyn," she said, impressed with his question. "With a y."

"Of course with a y. Was she older or younger?"

She'd forgotten until he asked. "Funny thing. At first she was older, but then when I got older, she became the little sister."

"And when did you stop talking to her?"

"Who says I stopped?"

He gave her a skeptical look, as if he wasn't quite sure she wasn't kidding.

"Of course I stopped. Maybe sixth grade?"

"Ah, the onset of puberty kills another imaginary friend."

Again she was impressed. She had never connected puberty to the silencing of Robyn, but it made sense. "Did you ever have an imaginary friend?"

"No. I was too nervous to think up something like that, to admit that's what I wanted. Even to myself. I like the way you went ahead and created what you needed."

Lying awake now, Nina realizes that Ben is still the only one who knows about Robyn. Telling the story out loud, and having him react the way he did, made her hope that those parts of herself that she had always kept hidden away were not as awful as they seemed. She liked the idea of Robyn's creation being a kind of bold and empowering act, not an act of desperation by a lonely girl.

Sid started talking to her not long after that night. She didn't share that with Ben at first. Now she knows she should not have shared it at all.

Nina tries to consciously slow her breathing. Maybe, if she just focuses on inhaling and exhaling slowly and evenly, and lays still, perfectly still, her brain will quiet itself. And then her body can fall asleep. Why do the dead and disappeared come to visit us in the middle of the night? Holding her eyes shut, breathing as slowly as she can, she answers her own question. Because that moment when we linger between being awake and being asleep, exposed and alone on the bridge, is when we are most vulnerable to attack.

14 | Heavy Heavy Hands

Duncan and his wife, Carrie, have Ben over for dinner a few times each semester. It's a win-win for Ben, because Carrie's a great cook and he never has to reciprocate. Duncan has been to the carriage house and knows it was not furnished with high energy young boys in mind. Their son, Ethan, has gone from four to almost ten in the time Ben has known them, and his noise and potential destruction levels have only increased as he's gotten older.

When Ben shows up for his first dinner of the spring semester, he's at their house without Nina for the first time since last summer. He can't decide if the silence between Carrie and Duncan is more profound than usual or if there's an extra layer of quiet draped over the table because Nina is not here. The long gaps force him to jump-start the conversation more than he wants. "So I'm thinking about taking up jogging," he says midway through the meal, after an awkward stretch of silent eating.

"Really? And what inspired this?" Carrie asks, eyebrows raised.

"I'm trying to grow up." It is an idea in his head, something he knows would be good for him to do, but all he has done so far is put some running shoes in his Zappos cart. "I've decided to stop taking certain things for granted."

"Like?"

"Like being in decentish health, and not having a gross belly."

"Bellies aren't gross," Ethan says, stabbing his fork into the middle of his lasagna. He's wearing an astronaut suit that he got for Christmas and only took off the helmet after much loud discussion. "Unless they're jiggly and wiggly."

"Exactly," Ben says with a sober nod. He always forgets how much Ethan listens—even when little kids seem to be off in their own world, a part of their brain remains tuned in to whatever the adults are saying. "I just need to make sure that my belly doesn't get jiggly or wiggly."

"Like Daddy's?"

Carrie laughs, and Ben shakes his head. "Um, I don't know anything about your father's belly," he says.

Duncan looks unimpressed with Ben's new exercise plan. "What's next, Mr. Cliché? A shiny new convertible to mark your mid-life crisis?"

"I'm only twenty-eight. It can't be a mid-life crisis."

"A mid-life crisis is just a particular kind of mental breakdown, and those can come at any age. Especially after a breakup." He's sitting next to Ethan and works on steering the boy's fork off from the side of the table and back toward his plate. "Besides, mathematically you could be at mid-life."

"And to think," Ben says, cutting into his lasagna, "there are sociologists trying to figure out why adult men don't have more friends."

"I can't imagine why not," Carrie says, playfully leaning into Ben. "But I was sorry it didn't work out with Nina. I always liked her a lot."

"Me, too. But Duncan was right. He told me it wasn't a good idea to date someone who had been a student."

"Never works out," Duncan said, reaching for his wine. "Never."

Carrie turns her fork to Ethan, points, makes the chewing motion with her mouth. "But last I heard," she says, turning back to Ben, "you guys were going to move in together."

"That was the plan," Ben said. "We were actually looking at an apartment together when we broke up."

"Dramatic."

"It always is with them young kids," Duncan says.

"She's twenty-four, for the record. Twenty-four is not young."

"Twenty-four is oldddddd," Ethan says, stabbing his lasagna again.

"So what happened?"

"Maybe it seemed too real, all of a sudden." Ben pauses, trying to think of an explanation that isn't complete but isn't a lie. "Something about standing there, thinking of actually moving in, just struck us both, I think, as just—not a great idea."

He looks over the table at Ethan, who has picked his helmet up from the ground and is putting it back on his head. Duncan glances at Ethan's barely touched dinner and then makes eye contact with Carrie, shrugging. She nods, and after two taps on the helmet from Duncan, Ethan takes off for the living room, where dozens of astronaut-related toys are waiting.

The adults quietly watch him launch into his world, the way adults tend to do whenever kids go off to play. Ben can't decide if he's jealous, wishing he could squat down in the middle of a floor with a bunch of cheap toys and sound so happy, or just exhausted, watching Ethan's endless energy at work. He grins as Ethan begins barking out official-sounding commands to the plastic figures under his command, then looks back at Duncan. "How did it go with Fletcher?" he asks, ready to stop talking about Nina. Duncan had a meeting with his advisor after their Friday class, but Ben left before he could get a recap.

"You know." Duncan takes a long sip of wine. "As it always does with the inscrutable Fletcher."

"You had a meeting with Fletcher?" Carrie asks, ripping off a piece of bread to soak up the last bits of her sauce.

"Yesterday."

The audible tension in their voices tells Ben he wasn't supposed to ask that question.

"So what did he say?" Carrie asks.

"He liked the edits of chapter four. He thinks that one may be done. Possibly."

"God forbid Fletcher come out and say anything concrete." Carrie puts her last piece of bread in her mouth and then reaches across the table to pick up Ethan's plate.

"He also assured me that the department does its best to make sure its Ph.D. students have all the time they need."

Carrie's and Ethan's plates are now stacked on top of each other, and she picks them up as she pushes her chair back. "And how much more time do you need?"

"I think one more year should do it."

"One more, one more. Will he be done before you, Ben?" She walks behind Ben's chair into the kitchen, separated by a half wall from the dining room table. "Or after?"

Ben feels like a flashlight has suddenly been pointed at his eyes. "Historians are terrible at predicting the future. You should know that by now."

"But you're making progress?"

"I had an interview last week with someone named Foxy. Is that progress?"

"Foxy? I didn't know you were writing about strippers."

"Self-assigned nickname of a skinny old man. Photographer who was on the Macon scene in the Sixties."

"That sounds fun. Stories about sex and drugs and rock and roll?" Carrie asks, starting to put plates in the dishwasher.

"The stories were good, but the photos are amazing."

"And how did it go with the sister?" Duncan asks.

Ben picks up his plate and the empty bread basket so that he can shuttle them into the kitchen. "We talked for a while," he says. "But she's very guarded. I'm hoping to get a chance to try again."

"Well, at least you got to talk to her," Duncan stands up slowly. "You twentieth-century guys have all these living sources who can talk to you."

Duncan loves to complain about how much worse medievalists have it in terms of sources, and Ben has grown tired of reminding Duncan that he chose his time period. "Don't give up. Maybe that 600-year-old monk who specialized in sacrilegious paintings is still alive, hiding in some retirement home. Florida," Ben says. "Maybe you get to take a nice road trip to Florida."

Carrie opens the dishwasher. "You're taking us, if you go to Florida."

Suddenly Ethan is in the kitchen, spaceman in hand. "We're going to see rockets in Florida? And Mickey?"

After chocolate cake from Alon's, Carrie tells Ethan it's time for bed. That is Ben's cue to leave; he can still hear Ethan screaming "One more liftoff, one more liftoff!" as he walks out to his car with Duncan.

Ben looks in the direction of the house. "Is it like that every night?"

"Since that fucking astronaut outfit came into our lives, yes." Duncan shakes his head. "Sometimes giving him what he really wants calms him down. Sometimes it's just the opposite."

"Write all this down for me, okay? In case I wind up having one of those?"

"My book wouldn't work for whatever kid you have. That's the catch."

"Mannnnn. No fair," Ben says, doing his best Ethan impersonation. He's happy to see Duncan almost smile. "And, hey, sorry if asking about Fletcher—"

"No worries," Duncan says. "Thing is, I'm not sure Carrie ever understood why I wanted to do this in the first place, you know? And now that it's taking even longer than I expected . . ."

"You'll finish," Ben says, even if Duncan looks so tired at this moment that he's not sure how it would happen.

"Of course." Duncan slaps him on the shoulder and heads back to the house. "We both will. You're lucky—you don't have someone breathing down your neck while you work. I need to finish before she kicks me out."

"You got this baby. Liftoff!"

"Liftoff," Duncan repeats, pausing to take a deep breath before he starts walking back to the house.

A distinct advantage of going to a social event where a young child lives is that things wrap up early. Ben is home before 9, so he decides he needs to work for at least an hour before finding some dumb show to stream. At this stage in his degree, if he is alone and awake he should be working. It feels like he has found the right story to tell, but he also needs to find a way to tell it. He's convinced that he can use Harlan Honeybird's story to talk about larger issues—racism, the Sixties, the role of the South's past in the South's present—but every time he tries to broaden the frame the images get fuzzy.

He talked to Dr. Reed about this during their first meeting of the semester. "I think the problem," she'd said, after letting Ben ramble about his concerns, "is that you are trying to tell the story before you know the story. You can't furnish the house before you build the walls."

Most of Dr. Reed's comments make more sense to Ben after he has thought about them for a while. This one clicks after dinner at Duncan's, while he is listening to Honeybird's debut album. Harlan Honeybird was only twenty-one at the time, but his voice already sounds world-weary, especially in "Heavy Heavy Hands," the closing track, and the album's best song:

> I never learned
> What not to say
> Maybe I just should
> Have hidden my eyes
> Then mumbled along
> With "thanks" and "alright"
>
> But the world shaped me up
> They made me understand
> When I felt the force of
> Their heavy heavy hands
>
> I'd like to pick you up
> Then hold you where you stand
> But I'm too weak to move
> These heavy heavy hands

Before he can develop a larger narrative, he has to figure out as much of Harlan's story as he can. Ben keeps thinking the real legacy of Honeybird lies in the songs: the songs support his argument that Honeybird was not just a decent bar band but an important musical turning point. Had he lived, Harlan Honeybird could have helped lead a new generation of Southern voices.

Ben starts the track again. Could Harlan be singing about his sister? Does he wish he could have done more to protect her, somehow? If so, protect her from what—the world? Their father? Darlene mentioned Hank Honeybird had a fierce temper, which is not surprising given Hank's disappointments and the way the world was changing around him. The white power structure remained in place, but the Civil Rights movement and key Supreme Court rulings created cracks in that structure. On top of that, his own children were making music with their Black friend.

The weight of the past could have been what was making Harlan's hands feel so heavy. The past his father wanted to hold on to was the same past Harlan was trying to move beyond. And what better example of the generational divide than a Southern man confessing to his own feelings of weakness, as a tentative first step toward building a new kind of strength?

Ben starts typing up these nascent ideas. He chooses to ignore the coincidence, buried in the back of his brain, that he's writing about someone strong enough to admit he is too weak to face certain challenges.

15 | Study Group Boy

Nina finds it funny that college students like to sit in the same seats every day. She used to choose a new spot each time a class met as a small act of rebellion, but it wasn't worth the tension of upsetting someone whose seat she had "taken."

It's no different in College Algebra. It's the last session before the midterm, and she's sitting in the same seat she's been in since opening day: at the end of the second row from the door, behind the white guy with dreads who never takes off his Beats and next to the guy in his fifties who lines three pencils up on his desk at the start of every class (a backup for his backup). To her right is an empty chair, filled every third class or so by a young blonde who surfs her phone whenever she manages to show up.

Nina has yet to talk to any of the other students, unless nodding a quiet "thanks" as you take the roll sheet from the person next to you counts. As she stands up to leave after the midterm review, she sees someone heading straight for her. It's the guy she calls "Asian Lenny Kravitz," thanks to his omnipresent leather jacket and fondness for sunglasses. He sits in the middle of the row along the windows, and she can smell the attitude off him from across the room. Up close his eyes have more depth than most dazed freshmen's, making him look closer to her age than eighteen.

"Study group," Lenny says, pointing at her.

"Excuse me?"

"Study group, this weekend. Gonna kill this midterm."

He is waiting at the end of her row. It wasn't what she expected him to say, but she's still not interested. "Thanks, but—"

"No, no, you're crucial," he says, following her out the door. "Crucial to the whole project."

"Crucial?" When they move into the hallway, he takes a few large steps to walk next to her. She turns to stare at him, impressed with his bravado, not to mention his shaggy haircut and confident smile. He clearly expects to get whatever he asks for. "You don't even know my name," Nina says, stopping in the middle of the hallway.

Lenny shrugs. "Why do I need to know your name? You come to every class, you pay attention, and you wore a Janelle Monae shirt more than once. All that tells me that you're crucial to the success of my newly formed study group."

"And who else is in this study group?"

"Me and you, for sure. I have solid 'maybes' from Front Row Housewife and Martin. Or Marshall. The Indian guy who looks like he should already be running some cool start-up or something?"

Nina has to give Lenny credit: she knows precisely which students he's talking about, and those are two of the students she's noticed paying close attention. "And why should any of us be in your study group?"

He's got his shades in his right hand, like a celebrity out for a walk who expects a crush of paparazzi to emerge from around the corner any moment. "It's in your own best interest, trust me. You're looking at the future of the music industry, but if I can't pass algebra, I can't graduate this semester." He holds his hands out. "And then the world will have to wait that much longer for my music. And, that's just . . ." Shudder, as if the horror of such a fate is beyond words. "Tragic."

The "future of the music industry" comment tells her the Lenny Kravitz vibe is intentional. Nina finds herself charmed by his ridiculous act in spite of herself. "The midterm is Tuesday."

"I know. So we need to get on this, right?"

It would be very easy to blame her busy work schedule and turn him down, but she hears a tiny voice asking what would happen if she didn't say no right away. "I have to get to my Brit Lit class."

"Oh. OK. Yeah, yeah, I feel ya." He slows down, conceding the race.

Nina stops and turns to face him directly. It's cruel, perhaps, but she smiles at his visible disappointment; he's even cuter when he drops the Super Confident look. "So maybe you should give me your number, in case I wind up with time to avert a great national tragedy."

"It's Howard, for the record." He grins. "But you can call me anything you want."

"Okay, Howard," she says, taking out her phone. He slowly calls out the numbers, and watches while she creates the new contact.

"Did you really label me 'Crazy Math Guy'?"

She nods. "Of course."

"And what should I label your number? If I am lucky enough to get it?"

"Nina."

His eyes widen. "Nina?"

"Nina."

"Goddamn. Nina like Simone is gonna save my algebraic ass."

Nina knows what she is supposed to do when she gets home from school. She is going to Connie's for dinner and then works double-shifts the rest of the week, so this is her best chance to do laundry. She also needs to clean the apartment, which has been regressing to the state of collapse it reached right after Ben broke up with her. And she knows Connie will be annoyed to find out that Nina didn't call her immediately after a not un-cute guy asked for her number. She is exhausted, though, so she sniffs her least dirty work outfit and decides it is clean enough, and sends Connie a text that says she has a Study Group Boy story to tell later.

And then she naps. She's still tired when she wakes up two hours later, and wonders if exhaustion is some stage of grief she had not gone through. She does manage to take Sid for a walk before she leaves. As she bends down to take off his leash he tilts his head and stares at her.

"Why don't you want to go to Connie's?"

Nina hangs up the leash. "We made these plans months ago. The last big hang before baby comes—Connie and Adam, Troy and Trent, and me and . . ."

"Ben."

"Yup." She changes his water, and begins to scoop out his dinner. "So tonight I return to being the fifth wheel. I enjoyed not being the fifth wheel."

"So why are you going?"

She thinks about that question on the drive over. The idea of disappointing Connie, who had made such a big deal of planning this last baby-free dinner, makes her more tired and sad than staying home alone, but maybe it's simpler than that. Maybe she just doesn't want Ben to ruin this night for her, even if it's possible that he may have already done so.

"You're early," Connie says when she opens the door. "Seven means eight. We have been over this before."

"Sorry," Nina says, "but you know my obsession with being on time. I even drove the last mile or two slowly, so I wouldn't get here early."

"And you know Troy and Trent's personalized interpretation of time. I should have told them five." She slowly walks away from the front door and collapses onto the overstuffed black couch that dominates their living room. "It's okay. Now I can sit down and tell you what still needs to be done."

"Perfect." Nina looks into the small kitchen off to the left. "But I don't want to steal Adam's job. Isn't he the one you're supposed to order around?"

"Of course. I sent him to Buford Highway for food. The thought of chopping and slicing and, quite frankly, standing for any period of time is just unthinkable right now."

"How many more weeks do you have?"

"Eight? Nine? A thousand?" She shifts on the couch, exhales.

"How are you sleeping?"

"In two-hour bursts, but I hear that's what happens when the kid gets here, so I guess it's good training." She points to the oak dining table. "Have pity on me and set the table."

"Of course, m'lady."

"And while you're in there working, you can tell me about Study Group Boy."

Nina moves into the dining room. "I'm impressed. I've been here for what, five minutes already? How did you wait so long before asking?"

"I'm practicing maternal patience." Shifts again, groans. "So he just asked you out of the blue? No classroom flirtation or anything?"

"No flirtation." Nina begins to organize a stack of plates and silverware piled chaotically in the middle of the table.

"Just how young is he?" Connie asks.

"He says he's a senior, so he's got to be twenty-two at least? Maybe a little older."

"Think he's interested?"

"In passing this class?" Nina finishes sorting the silverware and begins setting plates. "Yes, and so am I."

"You know what I mean," Connie says. "Is he interested in you?"

"I have the sense that he talks to all girls like he's interested. For now, I really think he's most concerned with graduating."

"But you're interested in him, aren't you?"

"It's too early to be interested in anyone. I was just about to move in with Ben."

"Two months is not 'just about.' Two months ago I could still see my feet when I stood up."

Nina starts laying out the silverware. Has it been two months? It still felt like two days. Time changes shape and size like some sort of science-fiction creature, and it makes her head hurt.

She has just finished setting the table when Adam comes through the garage door with a grunt, two white take-out bags in each hand.

"The Dumpling Man Cometh," he says putting the bags on the counter.

"My hero," Connie calls from the couch. "Whoever brings me a dumpling gets to name the baby."

Nina heads into the kitchen to help unpack the Chinese food, accepting an awkward hug from Adam. He and Connie have been married for more than five years, but Nina still struggles with what to say to Adam. When Connie first said she was dating a patent lawyer, Nina thought it was a joke, but maybe you have to know which crucial pieces you are missing before you can match up with someone who helps you find your balance.

Maybe a lack of self-awareness is the biggest reason so many people have a hard time finding the best possible partner. If that's the case, what does she not understand about herself yet?

The pairing did make sense for three minutes at Connie and Adam's wedding reception, when the two of them danced to Paula Abdul. Adam did his best not to trip over Connie as she sang along loudly to "Opposites Attract," staring at his new bride like he couldn't believe she existed, never mind that she had chosen him. For those three minutes Nina was jealous—not of Adam, for supplanting her as best friend, but of Connie, for finding someone who would look at her like that.

She and Adam dump the food into glass bowls and the three of them start eating without Troy and Trent. Connie and Adam are at opposite ends of the rectangular table, and Nina occupies a side spot by herself. She should start getting ready for her role as the Funny Aunt, Nina decides. Buy some goofy hats and t-shirts, brush up an old movies and musicals that she can force on Connie's kid. She also needs to remember to stop drinking any wine before she eats or she will be the Funny But Sad Aunt.

Her mood improves as they eat. Adam and Connie always like to order things super spicy, and she has missed that; Ben got the hiccups if he ate food that was too hot, but tonight there's enough spice to warm her forehead to the point of sweating. As they eat, Connie regales them with a fight she had with her mother over baby socks, and Adam is relaxed enough to share a story from work, something he rarely does.

Troy and Trent walk in as everyone is dishing out a second round of food.

"I can see we were missed," Trent says, dropping his coat on the couch.

"Please, please, don't get up on our account," Troy adds.

"Oh!" Nina says, feigning surprise. "How long have you guys been here?"

"So nice of you not to wait for us," Troy says, walking over to kiss Connie on the forehead.

"Like you would ever wait to eat dumplings," Connie says. "Now sit down. All this food needs to be gone, or I'll be sneaking out in the middle of the night to stuff my face."

And then the five of them are continuing the conversation they have been having for years. Nina has never thought of herself as part of a posse before, but she is hit with a sudden wave of gratitude as she understands that she is part of one now. The kid in school left out of all the other cliques is now in one. For the first time she understands that Ben might have been more than a little uncomfortable the few nights he joined the gang; if he was, she wishes he had just told her.

She wonders what else he never said.

16 | Actors and Assessors

"Tell me about the photographer," Dr. Reed says. "Will he let you use the photos?"

Sitting in Reed's office Ben shifts in his seat, uncomfortable as he recalls the end of his conversation with Foxy. "He will, and they're great. I think he's been waiting years for someone to ask."

"A firsthand account from this time period, and some good pictures? This sounds like a touchdown to me. So why do you look so unhappy?"

"It's that obvious?"

"Remember, Mr. Davies, I have conducted a few hundred interviews myself. I can usually read moods."

"Foxy was very helpful." He pauses, trying to find the most diplomatic phrase to use. "But at the end of our talk, he said some things that could be called racist."

"Well, in my experience," Dr. Reed says, "if the words can be called racist, that's because the words are racist."

"It just caught me off guard. Up until then he'd come across as a big believer in the band."

"And it's not possible he could be both?" She leans forward. "We're talking about the Deep South in the Sixties. Would it have been more unusual or less unusual for white men to be fans of loud guitars and also have racial prejudices against Black drummers?"

"I guess I was casting him as a music-loving hippie."

"And that type cannot be racist?"

"Point taken," he says, a little embarrassed at how naive he sounds.

"And his racism does not diminish his value as a source. People are complicated, even people who bear witness for us. More complicated people make for more complicated stories, but those are the stories more worth telling." She reaches into the bowl of butterscotch candies she keeps on her desk. "Sad, though. Another potentially valuable human, diminished by racism." She pauses to unwrap a candy and pop it into her mouth. "Now. What about the sister?"

Ben is impressed with how quickly she moves on to the next topic. Does it get easier as you get older to accept, and then dismiss, the uglier parts of humanity? "We talked for quite a while, but I sense she was only telling me the parts of the story she wanted me to hear."

"Ha!" Dr. Reed slaps the table and grins. "It's the song and dance we all perform, Mr. Davies. Everyone hides things from everyone else."

"So how do we get the information we need?"

"The solution is different in each conversation." She pauses for a moment, her mouth working the butterscotch. "Do you need to push a little bit when you sense her closing off? Or do you quietly wait and see if she is the kind of person who will talk to fill the silence?"

"How do you know which approach to take?"

"How indeed?" She shrugs. "There is no single approach, which is why talking to someone more than once can be so useful."

"She did agree to a second interview," Ben says. "And wrote to say she's trying to get Toni to come, too."

"Toni?"

"Sister of Nate, the drummer."

Dr. Reed's eyes widened. "Now, that would be fantastic. The closest thing to adding his voice, which needs to be heard." She leans back again. "And at some point you should probably find some journalists, maybe a music historian or two, to talk about how the music holds up, the band's legacy, etc."

Ben makes a note of this, and other ideas she has stirred up. Racists bearing witness. Everyone hides from everyone else. Look for Nate's voice.

"Find your focus, and the story may write itself: music and drugs, race and gender, a tragic barn fire and a missing body. It's all much more dramatic than one usually sees in a dissertation, so the challenge is placing this in historical context and convincing the rest of your panel this topic is capital-H History. That's why clearly placing Honeybird in the South, in the Sixties, is so important. The specifics that will make it universal. Turn down the background noise and focus on Harlan, Nate, and Darlene. What about the story of these three people will speak loudest to the rest of us, all these years later?"

When Ben gets back to the Cube Farm, Duncan is on the couch with Shelley. He motions for Ben to join them, but Ben doesn't want to get too comfortable. Every time he comes out of a meeting with Dr. Reed, he is acutely aware of just how much work he needs to do.

"Professor Davies. Just who we need to talk to."

"How can I help?" he says, stopping at his cubicle to put the copies of his midterm into his bag.

Shelley gives him a very serious look. "You can be the tiebreaker. For one month, the only music you can listen to is one double-album. *Tommy* or *The White Album*?"

Ben slides the messenger bag strap over his shoulder and takes a few steps in their direction. "First of all, it's unfair to put The Who against The Beatles. Though in my alternate universe, where they were just a power trio with Townshend on vocals, it's a closer call."

"Thank you," Shelley says, turning to Duncan with a triumphant grin. "Very well said."

Duncan shakes his head. "The question focuses on which album coheres better, and would stand up to repeated listenings. It has nothing to do with your jealousy of Roger Daltrey's range and golden locks."

"And, secondly," Ben continues, holding up two fingers, "the obvious answer is *Songs in the Key of Life*."

"Another historian refusing to answer a direct question," Duncan says. "How disappointing." He checks his watch. "Aren't you just out of a meeting with Reed? What pieces of wisdom did you collect today?"

"That I need to figure out what part of this story speaks loudest."

Shelley playfully slaps Duncan on the shoulder. "Is that your problem? You need to find the loudest part of your story?"

"I know all the parts of my story," Duncan says. "My problem is writing the story down."

Ben and Shelley look at each other and nod. "I think we can all agree this would all be a lot easier if we didn't have to write so much stuff down," Ben says, turning to leave.

He's not even out the door when his phone buzzes. *246 Decatur 8 pm res under my name.* He can't suppress groaning at the last minute notice, and his father's assumption that Ben will just go, and the fact that he knows he will just go. There are worse things, he supposes, than having a father who appears without warning and wants to buy his son a nice dinner. He could have had a father like Hank Honeybird, who took out his frustrations with the world on his kids.

Whatever disappointments Ben's father had with the world, he didn't make his children pay for them. One of the upsides of being an afterthought.

As soon as he sits down Ben can tell his father's mood is different from the last time he visited. When Ben was with Nina his father wore his Happy Salesman face and stood up to hug them both warmly; tonight, dark shadows circle his eyes, and a simple nod is his only greeting. When he's just with Ben, there's no deal to close.

"Get you a drink?" his father asks. A flick of the wrist magically summons a waiter. The staff at bars and restaurants know to keep their eyes on men like Robert Davies—big drinkers with short tempers and wallets pried open by deference.

"Just water," Ben says.

"And another of these for me, John."

John. Of course his father knows the waiter's name. "So, how long are you in town?" Ben asks, scanning the menu.

"Just tonight. Flying out to New York tomorrow to meet with a publisher, possible investors."

Ben has always found his father's job impossible to comprehend. He knows it involves selling services to large corporations, but sometimes it seems like the only thing he sells is the idea of selling. "Publisher?"

"We're talking multi-platform publishing. Books, but that's just for shelf space. Videos, podcasts, appearances—things need to be layered, now. Need to go where the eyes are."

"But what are you trying to get the eyes to see?" It's not the first time that Ben feels as though he's walked into the middle of a conversation his father is having with someone else.

"Only what I have been working on the last two years. Haven't you been listening?"

He puts down his menu. "Sorry, I guess I forgot."

They pause while their drinks are placed down, along with warm bread and a plate of olive oil. "Thanks, John." His father taps the menu on the table next to him. "I'm gonna start with the Caesar. Then the New York strip. Rare."

Ben's used to the impatient pace of dinners with his father, so he has his order ready. "The apple salad, please, and then the rigatoni."

"Actors and Assessors," his father says, as John walks away. Then he repeats more slowly, like he is driving home a point to a young child. "Actors. Assessors."

Ben nods, pretending to understand the reference. He takes a slice of warm bread and dips it in the olive oil.

"The world, Ben, the world. Two types of people: actors and assessors." His father takes a drink, studying his glass as he lowers it back to the table, as if judging whether or not it was worthy. "To succeed, we need to understand which category we belong to and what category the other guy belongs to." He swipes his hand through the air, knocking over an invisible army of incompetents who do not understand this truth. "When you have assessors trying to act, and actors trying to assess, then all you do is waste everyone's time."

Ben is trying to focus, but he's distracted by how good the bread is. He wonders if his father will want the other slice. "Like creators and consumers?"

"No, no. Actors. Action. Initiative. Actors generate new ideas, put things in motion. Assessors. Assessment. Check the results, measure the effects of what happened. Help the actors determine what still needs to be done." His father finishes the rest of his drink in a single swallow. "In the end, we are all consumers. This is about the most effective way to create the goods for that consumption. But not," he adds quickly, "just by studying the bottom line."

He looks to Ben for a reaction, but all Ben can do is nod.

"Take your brother," his father continues. "He's an actor. Not sure what his gross income was last year, but we can't use that as the only metric. His job is to create."

"Sure," Ben says, though he wonders if a "job" isn't something you need your girlfriend's income to pay for.

"You, you're an assessor."

Ben tries not to look disappointed. He's still not sure what these categories mean, but it sounds like the Actors are more important. "A critic?" he asks, but he can see by his father's face that his reaction is not the right one.

"Relax. You look like I kicked your puppy." His father rattles his empty glass, puts it down next to him on the table, and begins to scan the room—looking for his friend John the Waiter, no doubt. After he makes eye contact he turns his attention back to Ben. "It's not like one is better than the other. That's the whole point. The value is knowing what each should do. Lanes. Responsibilities. Historians? They should not act. They assess the actions of others."

"Huh." Ben has no idea what to say to any of this; any complaint he offers runs the risk of making him look more childish, and nothing he says will change his father's mind. Luckily the first course arrives, making it a natural time to change subjects.

"Nina couldn't make it?"

There was no reason for his father to already know about the breakup, but Ben is still caught off-guard by the question. "Nina and I broke up," he says quickly.

"Jesus, Ben. She looked like a good one."

"She was," he says, staring into his salad. Why does he feel like he's twelve years old again, confessing to his father that no, he would not be trying out for basketball or baseball or any of the ball teams? "Everything was great until we decided to move in together."

"Why would you screw up a good thing by moving in together?"

"We'd been dating almost a year, Dad. At some point—"

"Some point?" He starts on his Caesar. "I thought you were smarter than that."

Ben knows he should let it drop, that his father needs Ben to admit that he's wrong, but he doesn't want to. "I'm twenty-eight. If I've been dating someone for a year, and the two of us don't see any way to live together, what does that say about the relationship?"

His father's eyes have grown darker. "It says you have a relationship with a beautiful woman. And you keep her until you find the next one. You don't quit one job until you have a new one."

"Well, I never thought of it like that, I admit."

John shows up with another gin and tonic for his father, and wordlessly swaps out the new glass for the old. His father mercifully moves away from Ben's life and to a discussion of his current work struggles. Does his father drink like this every night, or just when he's in a fancy restaurant with a captive audience? Should Ben be worried? What if he's got the same misfiring gene that creates a desire for three drinks before the main course arrives?

"Still on track to finish on time?"

The question catches Ben off guard, coming in the middle of his father reciting a litany of reasons Hong Kong will soon supplant New York in importance. "What?"

"Going to finish before funding runs out?"

"Yes. Have readers for my comps lined up. Coursework done. Just need to finish the dissertation."

His father narrows his eyes as if straining to see something off in the distance. "Newspapers, right?"

"It was underground newspapers, yeah. I narrowed the focus to a band from the late Sixties."

"A band? That can be your topic?"

"Sure. It's history, right?"

"A band." His father pauses. "Call your brother. He knows all about that stuff."

Funny, Ben thinks. As much as his mother and father always talk about how different they are from each other, their conversations with him inevitably head down the same alleys. And they both seem to assume Ben's brother knows more than he does about everything, even Ben's dissertation topic. "I'll see him next week. He'll be in town for a show."

"We had dinner last month, in the city."

"How was he?"

"You know Dan. Ever the optimist." His father pushes his empty salad plate toward the center of the table. "Always one break away from some big turn in his life. Never anxious to take any of my monetizing suggestions. He needs to grow up and accept that part of being an actor is working to turn your actions into profit."

Ben is thankful he did not have to watch Dan and his father discussing "monetizing suggestions." "How was the show?"

"Oh, I didn't go."

Of course. The real shock would have been if his father had gone. "I like watching him." Ben gets this guilty feeling whenever he and his father get close to saying out loud what he suspects is their shared opinion about Dan's future—that he will someday soon be a washed-up, former musician, with no other useful skills. "He always seems happiest when he has a guitar in his hand."

"I've met lots of people who are happiest doing nothing," his father says, glancing around the table, no doubt wondering why his next course and new drink have not yet appeared. "Doesn't mean that the world is always going to reward them for it."

His salad is only half-finished, but Ben pushes his plate to the side. He should have thought of another compliment to offer Dan: how could he forget that Robert Davies was never that interested in anyone's happiness?

17 | Periods and Capitals and Everything

Nina had not planned to call Howard about his study group. He got bonus points for a sense of humor, the music angle didn't hurt, and he was perhaps even a little cute, with his shaggy hair and a nice tilt of the head when he talked, but it was not enough to add any more potential complications to her life.

Then Connie's dinner party kept her out late Thursday, and she worked double shifts Friday and Saturday. When she wakes up Sunday, she realizes it's suddenly the day before midterms week. She's not worried about BritLit, since she has her in-class essay on *The Canterbury Tales* all mapped out in her head, but Algebra looms large. There's a sharp stab of panic when she pulls out the study guide, one strong enough to prompt a text.

Hello. Is this Howard's Algebraic Ass?

She hits send, then arranges her study supplies on the dining table: notebook, textbook, pencils, calculator. If he doesn't respond in fifteen minutes she will just start studying on her own.

Luckily, she doesn't have to wait long.

please please please tell me this is nina
This is Nina.
periods and capitals and everything in a text bonus pointttts

She turns to Sid and reads the last message out loud. "So how harshly do I need to grade him on text grammar?"

"I have never figured out how anyone really says anything using that communication method."

When is this famous study group? she writes back.
u tell me u tell me
I can be ready in an hour.
bam, he writes back. *let me send the 411 to everyone else*
Where?
im old school waffle house is where ya study
That's adorable.
corner of piedmont and decatur in 90
Deal.

She closes the phone and starts to gather her study supplies. Sid stirs enough to ask, "Is it safe for you to go meet these people?"

"Oh, I hope so, Mom."

"Your tone makes it sound like my question was unnecessary. But how well do you even know this Howard?"

"Not well at all. But if this is all some elaborate plan to kidnap me, he has gone to a lot of trouble—signing up for this course and then waiting half a semester to make a move." Nina is almost giddy as she packs everything into her backpack. Anything is better than studying for Algebra alone, right? "And, if he is some sort of crazy killer, he should not have picked a Waffle House on a Sunday afternoon." When she's done packing up she turns to see if Sid has any response, but he has curled back up into a tight circle on the bed and seems to already be asleep again.

Waffle House is crowded, but Howard has magically commandeered a table. Front Row Housewife is actually named Linda, and Martin/Marshall is Tom. Nina never feels comfortable meeting new people, so she practiced her small talk on the train ride ("Born right here in Atlanta, actually." "I'm a sophomore, I think?" "English major! So, yeah, future substitute teacher.")

It turns out that Howard runs a very focused group, though; as soon as she sits down and says hello he passes around annotated copies of the study guide, each of the sample problems matched with its corresponding chapter. He assigns Linda and Tom questions from the first five chapters, says he and Nina will work on problems from the next five, and asks everyone to reconvene in forty-five minutes. She and Howard are able to talk through most of the problems, and it all seems less confusing than it did when she was trying to study on her own. Exactly forty-five minutes later each pair goes over the questions they thought were the trickiest, and ninety minutes after they started it's over.

Linda and Tom say quick goodbyes, leaving before Nina has even stood up. She looks at Howard and nods in their direction as they walk out the door. "If I didn't know better I'd say they were rushing off for some private time."

Howard stands up after Nina slides out of the booth. "Hey, I just want them here for study group. Whatever happens after that, man, I don't wanna know."

She stretches, puts her notebook into her backpack. He waits for her to lead the way out, which she thinks is sweet. "I gotta say," she says when they step outside, "that was really productive."

"I knew it would be," Howard says. "Same way I knew you'd come through. I wasn't gonna schedule anything until you sent your bat signal."

"Well, I'm glad I did." As she talks, she realizes it's the first time they're alone and not on campus.

"So," he says, looking around the tiny parking lot. "Did you drive?"

"MARTA is Smarta," she says.

"I'll just grab my bike and walk you." He half jogs over to a bike locked against the No Parking sign.

"One of those bike people, huh?"

"We're the worst, man."

"Making the rest of us feel bad and looking good while you do it."

"That's called a win-win." When the bike lock is off he stuffs it into his backpack. "Thing is," he continues, as they start walking to the MARTA station, "I've been scouting that classroom since Day One."

"Really?"

"Of course. I don't need to just pass this class, I need at least a B. I've spent a lot of time rebuilding my GPA, and don't want to Niagara it at the last minute."

"Niagara?"

"Fall over the edge, Simone. Keep up."

She can't decide how seriously she should take him, but that's also part of his appeal. "You just made that up, didn't you?"

"Words are like water, baby. Just let them flow. I put this class off as long as I possibly could. I knew the best way to get through it was to put together a damn good group."

"So you were scouting me?" Nina hears Connie's voice saying to step away from Stalker Dude, but she has to admit she's a little flattered by the idea.

"I was scouting everyone. Looking for people taking it seriously. People who want to learn this shit, for whatever reason."

"I looked serious?"

"Damn straight. I saw you in the back there, always on time and always writing stuff down and nodding when Dagmar explained something well. I knew I'd need you in my group."

"Well, I'm flattered. And a bit surprised."

"Why? You don't think you're serious?"

"I guess I never thought about myself in those terms—like, serious or not serious."

"Well, the world is divided into people who take life seriously and those who don't."

"But 'serious'? Like, no fooling around, no laughing? All doom and gloom?"

"No, no. Come on. You're talking to the foreman of the laugh factory here." He pushes his face into a much-too wide smile that makes her laugh. "I mean, serious, like, engaged. Here. Present."

It's one of the better compliments she has ever received, leaving her nothing to say in response. They walk the last half of the block in silence, but it doesn't feel awkward, and when they reach the entrance to MARTA he smiles again. "Thanks for coming, Simone. We're gonna kill this thing."

For a second she wonders if he's going to move in for an embrace. Instead he just holds his fist out for a quick bump. She taps her MARTA card, trying to decide if she's relieved or disappointed.

After she takes Sid for his walk, and then has some yogurt and a leftover slice of pizza for dinner, Nina settles down with her Mac to see what Netflix distractions she can find. Sid walks in to sit next to her after taking a long drink.

"That's a lot of water, old man. You're gonna need a walk soon, huh?"

"I'll give you fair warning." He licks his lips, scratches his right ear with his right hind leg. "You haven't talked about the study group."

"Howard said he chose me because he thought I was serious."

"You sound surprised."

"I am," she says, unable to decide if the endless sea of icons for shows and movies is inspiring or depressing. "In Algebra I have to work hard to stay awake. Maybe that's what he saw."

"I don't think so. He noticed you were present."

She looks up from the screen. "That's one of the words that he used."

"Then maybe I would like this Howard."

She's never thought about it before, so she asks. "Did you like Ben?"

"Did you?"

"Touché." She thinks for a moment, trying to think of the question in terms of the specific language parsing he is so fond of. "Did I like him, past tense? Yes. Very much."

"Do you like him present tense?"

Nina closes her eyes and imagines Ben in the room now. The apartment always felt better when he was here; it never felt crowded, even when the two of them shared the small space for an entire weekend. But then she remembers the way he looked at her just before he walked out, as if he was erasing everything they had said and done together. She opens her eyes and starts to scan the titles again. "No, I do not like him now."

"So what changed?"

"Can it be that we both changed?"

"That is how it works; we are all changing all the time. He must have changed in some way you did not like."

"Or maybe I changed in some way he did not like?" She thinks of her parents, and how they could have wound up as unhappy together as her mother says they were, just before he died. "Which means the challenge is to find a way to change together."

"And to accept that change is permanent."

Could it be that she is really settling on a random episode of *Friends*? All this talk of change has led to the bland comfort of Ross and Rachel and a craving for her grandmother's mashed potatoes. If she could hit a button and have those appear in front of her, she would.

She's finishing her second episode and debating a third when there's a knock on the door. She groans at the thought of having to stand up and wonders if she can just stay on the couch and wait it out. It could be Morris, though. A working garbage disposal would be worth the effort of moving.

It's not Morris or one of his hunky handymen. "I hoped I might find you at home," her mother says.

"Is everything OK?" Nina asks, as her mother brushes past her, paper bag in hand. "How's Grandma?"

"She's fine, fine." Her mother takes a bottle of wine out of the bag and holds it up triumphantly. "It just seemed like a nice night to have a drink on your deck."

Nina grabs two coffee mugs and follows her mother out to the balcony. She carefully places the mugs on the TV tray that serves as a coffee table, then pours a healthy shot of wine into each. Nina's mother raises her mug in a toast. "Happy Sunday," she says, before taking a long drink.

"Happy Sunday," Nina says. She takes a drink. "But come on, you have to admit this is kind of weird."

"What? A mother can't show up to surprise her daughter?"

"A mother can," Nina says. "But mine rarely does."

Her mother takes another sip of wine, turns to look at Nina. "You know what day it is today?"

"Sunday. We just toasted."

She shakes her head. "Smartass. I meant the date."

"Yes, I know what date it is." Nina turns to watch Sid, who has wandered on to the porch to join them and is sniffing at the edge of the railing. "And no, I didn't forget. Tomorrow is the anniversary."

Her mother's eyes widen. "Huh. Tomorrow?"

"Since the crash. Nineteen years tomorrow." She has trouble remembering her father's birthday, but she never forgets the date of his death.

"Then you don't know the date, darling."

Nina frowns. Is it possible she has missed the anniversary of the crash? Is that the last step taken before she completely forgets her father? "Wait. It's today?"

"I guess that explains why you didn't call."

"Shit." That news inspires her to take another long drink.

"And it's twenty, not nineteen."

"Twenty?" She can't believe she's lost count. It does explain why her mother has come to mark the occasion. "Whoa."

"Whoa, indeed."

For a moment the two of them sit in silence, drinking wine out of cheap coffee mugs and listening to the sounds of people walking across the parking lot. "Does it feel longer or shorter than that?" Nina asks.

Her mother shrugs. "Time doesn't seem to move, at least in this instance."

"I wish I remembered more," Nina says. "The funeral, at least. I wish I could remember saying goodbye."

Nina's mother smiles. "I will say this: he had a perfect fucking funeral." She closes her eyes. "Perfect day for it. No depressing rain, and no bright and ironic sun. Gray skies, with just enough chill in the air to allow everyone to leave their nice jackets on."

"It was outside?"

"Yes. His parents' backyard."

At rest, with her eyes closed, her mother is a different creature. Calmer. Younger. "I don't remember them," Nina says. "Dad's parents."

"Which is too bad," her mother says, sitting up straighter and opening her eyes. "They were his best attribute, I think."

"How come we never saw them? After?"

"They moved to one of those torture chambers out west. Phoenix? Tulsa? You did see them once or twice before they left. You don't remember?"

"Nope." She takes a drink, wonders what percentage of her life has already been forgotten. "How does it happen?"

Her mother turns to her. "How does what happen?"

"You were so unhappy, before the crash. You and Grandma make it sound like that last year with Dad was awful." Nina pauses, looking for a way to phrase her question. "So how did you go from being married to not staying in touch with his family after he died?"

"That's a fair question." She leans back in her chair. "It was hard for me—watching the man I fell in love with, a man convinced he could fix the world, turn into someone who could sit for hours holding the same can of beer, sometimes in the same clothes he'd had on the day before. Maybe I could have done more to try and help him? Maybe he needed more help than I could offer?" She takes a drink and shakes her head. "But I was tired, too. He had a hard time holding a job, those last few years, so I had to work full-time and take care of you. He'd resist any opening I gave him, so I stopped making much of an effort."

Nina wonders why her mother has never told her any of this before, but then again, she never asked before. "I just wish I could talk to him," she says, "just once more."

"So do I. I would like him to see what a beautiful daughter we created."

Nina is watching Sid, who is staring off the balcony into the parking lot behind her building. That might be one of the nicest things her mother has ever said to her; she's hoping Sid also heard it, so he can confirm later that she wasn't hallucinating.

"But," her mother continues after a short silence, "what I want most is a chance to ask him."

"Ask him what?"

"I just want to ask him why he left us."

Nina stops watching Sid and turns back to her mother. "What do you mean? It's not like he wanted to leave."

Pause. "Sometimes I wonder."

"What do you mean, you wonder?" It feels like her mother has suddenly changed radio stations. "It was an accident."

"That's what everyone says."

"But you don't think so?"

"Your father had driven that road many times." She closes her eyes. "He used to wake me up for his night-time drives. Sometimes to get some ridiculous thing he suddenly needed, like a candy bar, or a Mr. Pibb. Or maybe just to play a song—he always said Zeppelin only sounded good in a moving car. And I'd never want to go, but then I would, and then he'd always make me laugh. Then he stopped asking." Her mother opens her eyes, takes a long swallow of wine. "That's a hard turn to miss."

"You think he missed it on purpose?"

"I'm saying I don't know what to think."

"You've never said anything about this before."

"No. But we all have things we don't say, right?" Her mother drains her wine in a single swallow. "Okay, one more," she says, refilling her mug.

"So Dad killed himself?"

She sighs, shifting in her chair. "I don't know."

"That sure sounds like what you're saying."

"No. Your question implies he made a plan and carried that plan out. And I'm not sure he had the energy to do that. To be so decisive. It would be easier to just let the car miss that turn."

"Which is the same thing as thinking he killed himself."

"I think it's a more passive action. Like wanting something to happen, but not having the energy or the strength to do it yourself."

"So you just let it happen?"

"So you just let it happen."

Nina shuts the door behind her mother and walks over to Sid, who is perched in the far left corner of the futon, staring at her. "What?" she asks. "If you have a question you can just ask it, instead of giving me that stare."

"You look angry."

"Of course I'm angry. It sucks that he's not here and that I can't remember him. And to think that he might have left because of his own choice . . ." She stands in the middle of the living room unable to think of what to do next. Is "angry" the right word for whatever she's feeling? What does it mean, if her father did just let the accident happen, if he just let himself die? That life with her and her mother was so miserable it was not worth living? Or was he just crazy?

Did he hear voices in his head?

"Holding on to anger is like grasping a hot coal with the intent of throwing it at someone else; you are the one who gets burned."

"Which is why you just throw the coal, right? Then get some more and throw it again?"

After a long silence, Sid says, "This is where meditation would come in handy."

"I don't meditate."

"I know. This is where it would come in handy."

She stares at Sid, trying to decide if he is just a dog, some poor dog that a voice inside her head has attached itself to. If that's the case, what would happen if she just got rid of the dog—would the voice also go away?

But what if the voice has good advice? There are worse ideas than taking up meditation, after all. She walks closer to him and sits down on the floor, crossing her legs and straightening her back. "Okay. Now I just close my eyes and go, right?"

"No, you stay right where you are."

"Once again, I wonder why no one writes about how funny the Buddha was. Is." She closes her eyes. "I stay here and let my mind go blank."

"I'm not sure that's a worthy goal. Or even possible."

"What is the goal?"

"Not to erase the mind, but to still it. Become more aware, not less so."

She tries to focus on her breathing. Inhales, exhales. Instead of her mind clearing, though, she finds that remaining so still means that all of her thoughts find her more easily, a large flock of angry birds landing on a calm lake. And fighting for space in her brain are the sounds of her neighbors, and all the odd noises old buildings make. Is it always like this, she wonders? "It's very noisy," she says after a few minutes.

"The world does not stop just because we're sitting still."

"But how am I supposed to block all the noise? All my thoughts?"

"You don't. You listen. Listen to the sounds."

"And then what?"

"Listen some more. Find one sound to focus on. Befriend this sound."

"And the thoughts?"

"Don't fight them, but don't engage with them. Let them float by."

Nina fights the urge to stand up, fights off imagining how odd it would look to anyone who could see her sitting on the floor, being taught how to meditate by her dog. Instead she scans the sounds in her head, waiting for one to dominate. And there it is, courtesy of her Katy Perry-loving neighbor: "Last Friday Night," coming through loud and clear. Nina inhales, exhales, and befriends the distant sound of a pounding kick drum.

18 | His Demons

Dan Davies, Ben's older brother, tells everyone that he is a professional musician, and Ben supposes that is technically true since Dan has no other steady job. What Dan usually leaves out, though, is that when he's not on the road he works for a temp agency, and if it weren't for the kindness and patience of his long-suffering girlfriend, Emma, he would have been forced to give up music a long time ago. His band is in Atlanta as part of the tour for their third album, released on their third different indie label. The show is on the last day of classes before Spring Break, and even though all Ben wants to do is order some Thai food and stream something dumb before he spends his week "off" working on his dissertation and grading midterms, he heads off to watch his older brother chase a childhood dream.

Whenever Ben goes to East Atlanta Village, he thinks it is where he would have chosen to live, if he'd had more time to explore the city before moving. EAV has a couple of cool clubs with live music, a half dozen good-to-great restaurants, an excellent coffee shop, and more dreadlocks and tattoos in one block than he's spotted in five years in Morningside. It's also one of those rare in-town neighborhoods resisting, for now, the worst parts of gentrification. Then again, he enjoys walking down the tree-lined streets of his own neighborhood, staring at the houses of the wealthy, and not worrying about someone smashing his car windows. Maybe he's softer than he wants to admit?

Inside the club, Dan is still setting his stuff up on the stage. When they make eye contact, his big brother hops down from the stage to hug him.

"Bro!"

"Good to see you, man." Ben slowly pulls away from the extended embrace, and looks up at Dan. His older brother has always towered over him, and the heeled cowboy boots he's wearing make the height difference almost comical. "What the fuck—are you still growing?"

"High on life."

"And six-inch heels." Dan's hair is shorter than it has been in years, barely touching the top of his shoulders now, and he finally shaved off his goatee. Dan Davies just might be accepting the fact that he has crossed into his thirties.

"No Nina? She's too busy to meet her boyfriend's brother?"

Ben shrugs. If they had a different kind of relationship, he would have already told Dan he broke up with Nina, maybe in a lengthy email or a late-night phone call. He doesn't know that they'll ever have that kind of relationship. "Um, she's too busy for anything having to do with me these days."

"Oh, man." Dan pulls out his rarely used Concerned Older Brother Look. "That sucks."

The sudden pounding of a bass drum spares Ben from going into more detail.

"I gotta get to it," Dan says. "But we're in the middle slot. There's some kid with an acoustic on first, so we can grab a bite after soundcheck."

Before watching his brother at small rock clubs—first in the Seattle area and now in Atlanta—Ben had no idea how dull soundcheck was. All the inputs have to be tested one at a time, and inevitably there is a problem somewhere, some painful burst of feedback that causes the sound guy (always a guy) to start talking about numbers of various frequencies. Enduring this every night would drive Ben crazy, but Dan seems like he's in his natural element, bantering with the other musicians on stage.

He wonders if Dan would have the same reaction, watching Ben debate the minutiae of history and culture in the Cube Farm.

After a half-hour of line checks, the band finally runs through a song. Ben has to admit that it sounds better than the last time Dan was in Atlanta. All the musicians with him are new, unless the bass player is the same and just hasn't shaved in the last two years. Instead of a second guitarist there's now a female keyboardist. She has long legs, a confident stare, and a smoky voice that blends nicely with Dan's. The song itself isn't bad either, with a decent chorus. Still, it's hard for Ben to judge his brother's songs. He doesn't know if that's because it's hard to judge his own brother's work, or if it's because Dan's songs really don't seem that much better than anyone else's.

When the song ends Dan and the keyboardist share a look and a smile. Something about their eye contact makes it clear that Dan is either sleeping with her or trying to sleep with her. It's hard for him to believe now, but Ben used to be jealous of how much more like their father Dan was.

After soundcheck they head to the front patio of The Earl. The metal tables are covered in a sticky substance that is best not thought about, and a trail of cigarette butts has long since merged into the sidewalk. They each order a burger and an Amberjack and banter about how nice it is to be able to sit outside in March. When their beers come, the brothers clink wordlessly. After taking a long drink Dan leans back in his chair, exhales, and stares at Ben.

"So what happened with Nina? I was looking forward to meeting her. Last I heard from Mom, you guys were getting ready to move in together."

"I think that was our mistake. Should have just kept it more casual."

Dan takes another drink, his right leg tapping as he talks. "Well, I'm sorry, man. She looked hot in the pictures—you'll probably never get anyone that hot again."

"Yes, I am well aware of that," Ben says. "Thanks for your support."

"It's what big brothers are for, right?"

"Is that what they're for?"

Dan laughs, then begins to relay a long story about last night's show in Alabama, some dive that used tree trunks topped with stapled animal skins instead of bar stools. When their burgers arrive, Dan orders another Amberjack but Ben passes; the gene for copious drinking is something else his older brother inherited from their father. "Have you talked to Mom lately?" Dan asks, contemplating his burger.

Dan and their mother don't talk to each other for long stretches, but they both ask Ben, every chance they get, how the other is doing. As exhausting as it sometimes is to be the middleman, the idea of calling them out on their behavior is even more exhausting. "She's the same. That's part of her magic, right? Always the same?"

Dan nods, making a pool of ketchup in the middle of his fries. "Same as it ever was. Dad, too. And we'd be pissed if they changed too much."

Ben takes a bite of his burger. "Just saw him a few weeks ago."

"Really? Get a nice meal out of it?"

"You know it. Expensive Italian place."

"Good. I'll say this: the old man knows how to pick a restaurant."

"He kept going on about this new idea he has, using phrases like 'multiple platforms.'"

"The actor and assessor thing?"

"Yes." It hadn't occurred to him that his father would have told Dan, or if he had, that Dan would remember. Paying attention to other people's plans and ideas has never been a strength of his brother's.

"You know, I think he might be onto something with this one."

"Really?"

"Yeah, man. People like categories, being told it's A or B. No worrying about some complicated middle ground." Dan takes a long drink. "I've even talked about helping launch it."

"Launch what, exactly?"

"Launch the concept. Website, videos, maybe a podcast? There'll be a book, too, but something short and to the point. No one wants to read a fucking book." He looks up from his fries. "No offense."

Ben is surprised at how genuinely excited Dan sounds. "And what will you do?"

"I'll be there to talk about Actors. Our roles in the world, the ways to know if you are supposed to be an Actor, blah blah."

"Yes, the all-important actors." The words slip out before he thinks about it. Dan's knowing nod confirms what Ben suspected: he and their father talked about which son was the "actor" and which was the "assessor." He takes a sip of beer to keep from complaining about it. He knows it's ridiculous to still feel the way he did when he and Dan were younger and suffering through forced post-divorce visitation with their father. Inevitably their time would involve an activity that Dan excelled at but Ben found impossible—video games, or bowling, or a trip to the batting cage. Ben would get frustrated and complain; his father and brother would exchange looks of commiseration, or, even worse, just urge him to "try harder."

He tells himself he's older now, and can move past that. He decides to do the mature thing, and change the topic. "How's Emma, anyway? You get that lovely lady a ring yet?"

Dan doesn't fight when Ben offers to pay for dinner. When he heads back to get ready for the show, Ben wanders up and down Flat Shoals Road, the main drag of East Atlanta. The neighborhood has changed since the last time he was over this way. The restaurants have become more upscale, and a rash of condo construction has broken out. He almost sends Nina a text; she had predicted this would happen last time they went to The Earl, to see a band from Canada she loved. She hasn't reached out since the last time they talked, though, and he doesn't feel like he should be the first one to make a move.

They won't talk again. He's never put the idea into such clear and direct words in his head, but it's time.

He heads back to the club for the last few songs of the opener. College Kid with a Gibson sounds just as Ben imagined he would be, with a low gravelly voice that drops to a whisper during verses and swells to an uncomfortable kind of yowl for the choruses. There's some polite applause when he finishes his last song, and Ben throws in a few enthusiastic whistles.

After a short set change, the club lights dim and Dan leads His Demons onto the stage like a rock star. His smile radiates confidence, and his swagger makes it clear to everyone that he is the leader. He exchanges a quick nod with the rest of the band before turning to the crowd. "I am Dan Davies, and these are my Demons," he says with a sly smile, before issuing a loud four count.

The band is tight and confident. The crowd grows over the course of their set, and by the time Dan announces they have two songs left, there are 100 or so people in the small club. His older brother has always responded well to an audience. The cocky smile on his face grows as he leads the band through the closing songs: a new one that Ben suspects he will have a hard time remembering later, and, of course, "Glorious." The closest thing Dan Davies has to a hit, it has ended all of his shows since it was written, and probably will for as long as Dan keeps playing. And why not? Ben has to admit he always feels better after hearing a crowd sing along with that triumphant chorus: "Everything's gonna be glorious/It's all gonna be glorious."

As he watches Dan and his band take quick bows, basking in the enthusiastic applause, Ben wonders how his brother's life would have been different if he hadn't managed to write one great song. Dan probably would not have been signed by the cool indie label that put out his first record, and then dropped him when sales were disappointing. But maybe he would have written better songs, ironically, if he had not felt the pressure to write another one as good as "Glorious." Was it a curse to achieve above your natural ability?

After the set Ben helps them get their gear off stage. Dan Davies and His Demons manage to book extended tours every year or two but have never been able to afford roadies. Ben offers the usual rock club congrats to the guys in the band—great set, like that new one, you guys are tight—and turns down the offer of a post-show beer with Dan, who does not look surprised by the answer. "Yeah, you fucking academics," he says, walking with Ben out the back door. "Need to rest them big old brains."

"Hey, it's almost midnight," Ben says. They stop on the wooden landing outside the back door. "I don't stay up this late for just anyone."

They banter for a few minutes about the show. Ben is relieved he can honestly say it's one of the best sets he's seen Dan play. He keeps to himself his questions about how a band like this carves out a career in the modern landscape of YouTube and Spotify; he'll let their father be the one to offer unsolicited advice. The brothers talk about when they might see each other next and playfully debate whose turn it is to visit their mother.

Suddenly Dan puts his hands up, as if caught by surprise by someone with a gun. "Wait, wait, I'll see you this summer. When you come to New York for the filming."

"Filming?"

Dan shakes his head in disappointment. "Man. Dad didn't talk to you about it? I thought since he mentioned—"

"Nope." Ben has this sinking sensation he should have left before whatever news is coming next.

"I just think it's a cool idea, to have both his sons help launch this thing. There's a great fucking angle, right?"

"What angle?"

"The Actor son, the Assessor son. Perfect breakdown of how the system works."

"Ah," Ben says, trying not to sound frustrated. "The Assessor son."

"Yeah, Dad said he told you, broke everything down." Dan looks confused. "But it's not like one is better than the other. The world needs both. That's the beauty of the system."

Ben is tired, and beginning to feel worn down by the night in a way he had not felt just a few minutes ago. "So one category does all the stuff that the rest of us react to?"

"Well, yeah."

Ben shakes his head. Did his brother always discount him, and he just never noticed?

"But, I mean, it's not like you're out here, right? Not really. I mean, I'm the one out on that stage every night. You're writing about it—not living it."

Not every night, Ben thinks to himself, picturing those long stretches Dan is living in his girlfriend's house and bouncing from one temp job to another. But like most of the things he really thinks about his brother, or his father, or his mother, he keeps them to himself. Why does he do that, he wonders. Why not just tell them what he really thinks for once? "I'm tired, man," is what he says instead. "I can't plan summer yet."

"But you'll think about it, right?"

Ben nods noncommittally, offers one last hug goodbye, and walks down the steps to the parking lot.

Driving home, Ben feels the kind of exhaustion that settles into your bones after pulling an all-nighter before an exam. "Hotel California" comes on 97.1 and he turns the volume up. Not out of any special love for the song, but because the timing seems perfect. Dan was obsessed with that Eagles album in high school. He'd come home from school, slam his door, and turn his stereo up loud. All these years later, Ben can still hear the way the music sounded, pushing its way from Dan's room into his. He still knows all the words, can even sing along with the indulgent guitar lead at the end. In seven minutes, he will be that much closer to home.

He misses Nina the most when he is heading back to the carriage house, alone. He slept with her more than anyone else in his life. Thinking of it fills him with that particular kind of late-night melancholy, and the ache of her absence grows more intense. It's not just the sex he misses—sharing a bed with Nina was warm and exciting and intense, but also safe. He would never have guessed that such a perfect combination could exist. She seemed to fall asleep easily, rolling over and immediately starting to breathe deeply. Her breathing was a reassuring sound, a perfect way to transition from the waking world to the sleeping.

Other nights she would want to talk. This annoyed Ben at first, because she seemed most eager to talk on the nights when he was most tired, but he grew to love their late-night chats. There's probably a life lesson to be learned, if he thinks of all Nina's habits that he initially disliked but grew to love. He can hear her voice clearly now, even over the dueling guitar leads at the end of "Hotel California." It feels like he's walking out of his childhood bedroom and into Nina's apartment.

"So tell me how you got here, soon-to-be Dr. Davies."

"In this bed? I mean it's a funny story, actually. Professors aren't supposed to make a move on their undergrads, but—"

"No, not that one. Though that's a story I want to hear, too. Some other time."

"Which one? I mean, so many undergraduates, so little time."

"I mean, why did you want to spend, what, ten years of your life studying history?"

"Talk about your sexy bedroom conversations."

"Come on. I'm serious."

"It's a pretty boring story."

"Reminder: Ben Davies does not like talking about himself."

"I don't?"

"No. You always deflect questions that cut too close to home."

Lying in bed with his arm literally wrapped around her, almost naked, it was hard to imagine that he could be more revealing. Thinking about it, though, he conceded that his first instinct whenever she asked a question about his past or his family was to find a way to not answer. But that was his first instinct with everyone, not just Nina. What was different about Nina was the way she made him want to do better.

Ben turned his head to look into her eyes. In the middle of the night, there was just enough light from the parking lot behind Nina's building for him to see her face clearly when they lay in bed. "School was the only thing I was ever really good at. And when I got to college I also started enjoying it."

"But what is the 'it' that you enjoy?"

"Examining what has happened. Trying to decide what it means. And then telling people what I find. That turns out to be the fun part."

"Telling people, like, by teaching?"

"By teaching, but even more by writing. I got more and more excited about the writing part. I learned I could write down something that no one else thought of before."

"I can see that," she'd said, after staring at him for a long second. "I think that makes sense, for you."

"Well, thanks. I'm glad you approve."

He feels a sudden flush of fondness for Nina as he pulls into the driveway, remembering that conversation. Her approval felt so reassuring. For the second time in the same night he realizes how sad it is to put what has happened into words: he will never talk to her again. And remembering that conversation now, it also sounds like he's describing himself as an Assessor, and she is agreeing. So why does it bother him so much to hear his father and brother say it?

SPRING BREAK

"The core of Honeybird's sound is there from the opening track to their self-titled debut, released in June of 1967. 'Mr. Invisible' begins with Nate's rolls around the kit and Harlan's jagged strums—the random, un-self conscious sounds of a band preparing to flex its muscles. The song itself may not be as complicated in terms of production and arrangement as their strongest moments would be, but it is full of energy and many of the Honeybird trademarks. There's a solid groove, laid down by Nate and Darlene; some interplay between harmonica and lead guitar; and lyrics that underscore Harlan's desire to escape the situation he has been born into. Not only is it 'Time to be somewhere else,' it's time 'To be anyone else.' He knows that it is impossible, though. He knows that the son of Hank Honeybird will not be able to avoid the family name, that the past will always catch up to him."

—From Chapter 3 of *Screaming To Be Seen: Harlan Honeybird and the Struggle for a New South*, by Benjamin Davies. Draft, not for publication.

"It is on Honeybird's second album, *Waiting Here*, that Harlan really comes into his own as a songwriter. The requisite odes to drinking and women are still there, but there are fewer of them, and more songs like the thoughtful and complicated title track. Throughout these eight songs Harlan Honeybird wrestles with the concept of legacy, on an individual and a collective level. The son of a powerful white man, Harlan chooses to reject the power he has inherited, in order to avoid paying the same moral price previous generations paid. His songs highlight new paths that his generation may choose, in order to break the oppressive cycle that his father's generation had perpetuated.

"But even as he sings about making this choice, fronting a band that is the literal embodiment of this new approach, he is aware of the risks and challenges that will follow him. The album's sound reflects that tension, the midtempo songs drenched in an unavoidable tone of melancholy and loss. That sense of loss is made all the more intense because of what we know: Harlan Honeybird will not live long enough for us to learn if he is truly able to escape the pull of his past."

—From Chapter 4 of *Screaming To Be Seen: Harlan Honeybird and the Struggle for a New South*, by Benjamin Davies. Draft, not for publication.

19 | Skate Away

Nina has never experienced a typical college Spring Break. When she was eighteen or nineteen she wasn't in college. Then, once she started taking classes in her twenties, she needed to spend her break working extra shifts.

Last year she and Ben created their own holiday: Movies and Mochas. They went to see as many mainstream movies as they could—"The bigger, the dumber, the better!" Ben would say, rubbing his hands excitedly as they scanned the listings. The lines, the crowds, and expensive snacks were all part of the fun. Afterwards, they talked about what they had just seen over fancy coffee drinks. They pretended to be very pretentious critics who took these movies very seriously, name-dropping Jacques Lacan and examining "the male gaze." Nina felt like she finally had the high school boyfriend she had always wanted, and she got to take him back to her place at the end of the night. The week was such a success that she and Ben planned to do it again this year.

Now, Ben is gone. Connie is extra pregnant and extra grumpy. Troy is out of town. So Nina begins her "vacation" by cleaning the toilet. As she scrubs, she decides it is probably for the best that Howard is visiting his family in Charlotte. If he were around, she would be tempted to call him and risk hanging out more than they should. If they push their relationship too quickly, things might get awkward. Not only could that ruin whatever their relationship might become, it could jeopardize the study group and hurt her chances of acing the final. She'd been so prepared for the midterm it had been almost fun.

Howard and Tom had been waiting for her in the hallway after the test. "So?" Howard asked.

Nina smiled. "Nailed it."

Tom, who Nina could not remember ever smiling, looked practically giddy as he nodded. "Nailed. It."

"Damn straight," Howard said. "Same study group for the final, right?"

"I'm in," Nina said.

Tom fist-bumped them both before leaving. Howard looked at her and smiled. "So it's Tuesday," he said. "You know the city's best open mic happens on Tuesday, right?"

"I didn't know that, actually."

"Big Tex. Decatur."

"Well," Nina said, "with a name like Big Tex . . . "

"Wait—you've never been?"

"Nope."

"Oh, Nina, Nina. Let's do it. Tonight."

"Tonight?"

Her tentative response created a crack in his bravado. "Yeah, tonight," he repeated, in a softer voice.

"Sorry, I have to work."

"Oh."

It was a bit flattering to see him look so disappointed. "And that's a 'I really do have to work' line, not just a 'I'm only telling you I have to work so I don't have to go somewhere in public with you' line."

His face brightened. "I like that interpretation much better than the one my head was giving me."

She checked the calendar on her phone. "I am, however, off next Tuesday."

"Next Tuesday?" He shakes his head. "Spring Break, man. I am headed home tomorrow after my last test."

"Where's home?

"Charlotte."

"Charlotte? I have so much to learn."

"So much." He pointed to her phone. "So look at that calendar and find us another Tuesday?"

"First week in April?"

"First week in April. Bam."

Was this a date? She kept the question to herself. Enjoy the moment, Nina. "Are you gonna perform at this open mic?"

He looked horrified at the idea. "Uh, no. Not yet."

"The world isn't ready?" she asked, trying to anticipate the standard Howard approach.

"Oh, the world is ready. But I promised, promised myself that this semester would be all about school. And then I promised myself I would keep that promise. Soon as I graduate, I get to do other stuff, like hit the stage."

She sighed dramatically. "I guess I can wait. I just keep hearing this music is gonna change my life."

"One step at a time, Simone."

"OK," she said, heading for the stairs and her Brit Lit midterm. "One step at a time, Howard."

Nina finishes cleaning the toilet and the shower then heads into the kitchen. As she starts to work on the sink the water stops draining. She flicks the switch for the disposal on and off to confirm that it is not working. Again. When Nina moved in, Denise warned her that poor maintenance was built into the low rent, and that turned out to be a rare case of Denise being absolutely correct. Nina mumbles a curse under her breath as she twirls a wooden spoon into the drain, hoping to disperse the gurgling sludge.

"Is this a good time to mention the hundreds of years I survived without a garbage disposal?" Sid asks.

"No," Nina says, putting the spoon down and watching the last of the backed-up water drain away slowly. "No, but it is a great time to go for a walk."

On the way out she tells the hunky blond sitting in Morris's chair that her disposal is still broken. He's FaceTiming another well-muscled man in a tank-top but does write something on a Post-It and sticks it to the computer screen.

When Nina and Sid step outside she's surprised at the intensity of the sunlight. She's been so distracted by soap scum that she hasn't noticed how beautiful the day has become. It's just after twelve, so Crescent Avenue is filled with well-dressed people from the nearby office buildings, out for expensive lunches. It feels like all she sees are cute couples staring at each other and holding hands—the same way the radio plays nothing but sad songs about falling out of love every time you break up with someone.

Sid seems especially worn out after they return to the apartment. He takes a quick drink of water and shuffles over to the glass doors to take a nap. Watching him do his circle dance and then collapse makes her eye the futon, but she is determined not to sleep away her Spring Break. Boyfriend Walks Out, Woman Sleeps Away Her Free Time.

There, in the corner, is a better answer: her Roland keyboard. She pulls it away from the wall, positions the bench, and sits down. Then puts on her headphones and runs her fingers across the keys, pleased by the sound of the random notes drifting into her ears.

When her hands are loose, she decides to see if she can pick out the chords for a Joni Mitchell song that's been stuck in her head. The beginning of "River" should be pretty straight forward, with that sad riffing on "Jingle Bells," one of the few songs she remembers from her time with Miss Siobhan. Nina touches the keys tentatively at first, as if worried about buried mines. As she feels more certain about the dominant chords—F and C, just like that, maybe?—she strikes the keys a little harder, the sounds becoming sharper in her headphones.

After half an hour or so she feels like she is in the general vicinity of correct and decides she needs to listen to the song to see where she is still going wrong. She unplugs her headphones from the keyboard and plugs them into her phone. Laying down on the bed, she plays Joni's version, those opening chords so impossibly sweet and sad. Joni's voice has always sounded like a friend whispering to her and only her—a confession only Nina can hear. She whispers along with Joni; like going to the bathroom, audibly singing is something she does not feel comfortable doing in front of Sid. She can't even whisper the line about making her baby say goodbye, though. In a song full of moments of wonderful ache, that one hurts the worst. The best? She always imagined the skating away as just an escape, a departure, but nothing permanent. This time, when the song ends, she wonders if Joni wishes she could skate away, like, forever.

She hits stop as soon as she hears the first chords to "A Case of You." "Sid," she calls, sitting up. "Let's go for a ride."

He slowly raises his head and looks at her. "Now?"

"You know, some dogs literally salivate at the idea of a car ride."

"Is that supposed to make me feel better or worse?"

She stands up, stretches. "Let's go."

"Where are we going?"

"Old Briarcliff Road."

"Why?"

She picks up her wallet, phone, and keys. "That's where my father's car accident happened." She stands by the dining room table, growing impatient as Sid slowly stands up, stretches, and heads over to her. After avoiding the site for twenty years, she is suddenly anxious to see it as soon as possible. "And I've never been."

"There are lots of places you've never been."

"True."

"So why do you want to see this one now? What do you hope to find?"

They walk to the front door, and Nina takes down the leash to attach it to his collar. "I don't have hopes of finding anything in particular," she says. She stands back up and opens the front door. "I just want to see if I find anything at all."

20 | Don't Go, Darling

Most of Ben's students head off for a week at the beach, but the only trip he takes during Spring Break is to Marietta. He hoped that going in the middle of the morning would mean fewer SUVs and minivans on the road, but there may even be more than the last time he went to see Darlene.

This time she answers the door. "Mr. Davies," she says. "Welcome back."

He steps into the vast foyer, which is much quieter than it was on his last visit. "Thanks for making more time for me."

"I should thank you," Darlene says, closing the door behind him. "You were able to get Toni to the wilds of Marietta, something I have been unable to do for many years."

Ben turns to his left. Standing at the edge of the foyer, in front of a wide entrance to the living room, are two Black women, separated by a generation or two but sharing the same regal bearing. The older one must be Nate's sister; in her last email Darlene had written she thought Toni might come but also said that Ben should not be disappointed if she did not. "Nice to meet you," he says, walking over to them and holding out his hand. "Ben Davies."

"Toni Williams," she says, shaking his hand with what seems to be a bit of hesitation.

"Though you may be more familiar with her work as 'Cindy Songbird,'" Darlene says.

"Cindy Songbird?" Ben can't help but smile as a snippet of the backing vocals from "Waiting Here" drifts through his head. "I just want to say—"

Toni cuts him off, clearly unimpressed by the fact that he is so visibly impressed. "This is my granddaughter, Natalie Abrams."

"A pleasure," he says, turning to the younger woman. She's standing next to her grandmother with a skeptical look on her face, and he decides just to nod a greeting when she makes no move to unfold her arms.

"Let's go into the living room," Darlene says. "The kids are at school, and my daughter and her husband are at work."

Toni turns and slowly moves into the next room, holding her granddaughter's arm to steady herself. "I hope they warned the neighbors that Black people would be here. I don't want anyone to feel a need to call the police."

Darlene and Ben follow. He's careful to watch where he walks; there's almost more furniture than the room can bear, a collection of overstuffed couches, armchairs, and end tables. Generic portrait paintings cover the walls, and the pale white carpet is a thick shag. "Toni is not enamored of Marietta," Darlene explains as she and Ben reach the middle of the room.

"How you can live out here, surrounded by them." Toni settles onto the couch with the help of Natalie, who then sits next to her. "I just don't understand."

"Surrounded by who?" Ben asks.

"Republicans," Darlene says with a half-smile.

Ben grins, sitting down in one of the two large armchairs that face the couch. Darlene sits in the matching chair to his left. Toni and Natalie are directly across from them, separated by an enormous glass-topped coffee table.

"I hope I have not offended you," Toni says, eyeing Ben carefully.

"Well, Ms. Williams," Ben says, taking out his legal pad and tape recorder as he talks, "I can assure you that all the wild stories about leftists in academia—especially historians—are accurate." He holds up the digital recorder before he places it on the coffee table. "Is it okay if I record this?"

Toni nods.

"Thanks." Ben turns the recorder on and sits back in his chair, looking at his first page of questions. "And thanks again for your time. I thought we'd start with some basic questions about your family, what it was like for you and Nate—"

Darlene interrupts him by placing her hand on his arm. "Actually, Mr. Davies, Toni and Natalie are here to play you something, if that's OK."

"Of course," he says, looking up from his questions.

"We have a tape of one of our rehearsals. We thought you might want to hear it."

"Wow." It had never even occurred to Ben to ask if such recordings existed, given the time period. "That would be amazing."

"Darlene and I agreed many years ago that we'd only play it for someone if we both approved," Toni says, accepting a glass of water from Natalie. She takes a sip and hands it back. "She assures me that you will know what to do with this."

"Yes," Darlene says to Ben, when he looks in her direction. "So don't screw it up. Toni will never forgive me."

"I'll do my best." Ben shifts slightly in his chair for a more direct view of Natalie and Toni. "But this tape is from a practice? How did you record it?"

"Harlan became obsessed with being able to record ourselves whenever we wanted after he heard the tape of our homecoming show. So he decided we had to buy a reel-to-reel machine," Darlene says.

"Needed to all pitch in and get one just to shut him up," Toni adds.

"We'd come off the road with a little money and managed to squeeze a few drops of blood from Wilson Records. Harlan wanted to record our practices." She pauses, looks off in the distance. "Nothing worse than having some brilliant moment you can't recreate."

"And it was tough for Harlan to remember much, once he sobered up," Toni adds. She nods at Natalie, who is reaching for a remote on the coffee table. "Natalie is here to make sure all this works. I was not able to scare her away from the music industry entirely, I am sad to say."

"I'm an engineer," she says, turning to Ben and smiling for the first time. "Though I'm not sure Grandma will ever forgive me for any and all contact with the music industry."

"She won't," Toni says.

"Well, thanks for your help," Ben says.

"Don't thank me yet." Natalie is staring at the remote in her hand, shaking her head. "They gave me instructions before they left," she says, staring at an oversized black controller covered in multi-colored buttons, "but this has to be the least user-friendly thing I have ever seen." After a few moments of trying different sequences of button pressing, a loud click is heard from the receiver, stationed under the enormous flat-screen TV. The first sound is a steady hiss, and Natalie hits another button to pause the recording. "The amazing thing is, the tape still worked—once I found a machine that could play reel-to-reels. So I dumped it onto a hard drive before it self-destructed, then tried to make it sound as clean as possible. It's better than I expected, but there's still some background noise."

"I still can't believe that someone really wants to hear this," Toni says. "Never mind write a book about us."

"Toni's been spared contact from Honeybird obsessives," Darlene says. "Though I'm not sure any of them care as much about listening to the music as they do about inventing conspiracies."

"It's the world we live in," Toni says. Darlene quickly agrees, and soon the two of them are talking over each other about the changes in their lifetime, complaints issued in a kind of verbal shorthand that only develops between people who have known each other a long time. Ben catches Natalie's eyes, and she shakes her head and clears her throat.

"So what's on this tape? You need to set it up?"

"Just a band getting together to talk about new songs," Darlene says. "Trying to figure out what to do next."

"I think we should just hit start," Toni says, tapping Natalie on the shoulder.

Natalie hits play, and the hiss returns. Then there is a sound of a click, and the recording begins, in mid-sentence. "—unning now, I think," says a female voice. There's a giggle, then a pause. A different female voice, sounding more distant, calls out, "Stare at that thing a little longer. Just to make sure," and then several voices break out in loud laughter.

Darlene turns to Toni and raises her eyes. "Jesus. Listen to you."

"Listen to all of us. How young were we?'

"How stoned were we?"

"Pretty stoned." Toni turns to Natalie, who is sitting next to her on the couch with her eyes opened wide, as if in shock. "Not a word, baby girl. Do as I say, not as I do, and so on."

Harlan and Nate slowly take over the talking on the recording. Ben recognizes Harlan's voice from the stage banter on *One More Night*, and is surprised at how smoky and deep Nate's voice is. Everyone is talking about a party they'd been to the night before, with lots of references to people he's never heard of, and then suddenly there's a thunk, followed by the strike of a few piano keys.

"Piano?" Ben asks, turning to Darlene. There was some Hammond organ on the records, and a great piano track on "Heavy Heavy Hands," but those had been credited to Ed Harsch.

"There was an old upright in the barn," she says, staring at the stereo as she talks. "My grandmother's. Tuning was never great, but sometimes we worked out ideas that way."

"So what's cooking, what's cooking?" Harlan says, as he hits a few piano chords. After looking at Foxy's photos, Ben can imagine Harlan vividly. So tall he has to hunch over to play, long hair uncombed, eyes focused on the piano as he makes quick sudden stabs at the keys. The chords become more defined as he plays, slowly revealing the bare bones of a song. It's one Ben has never heard before. The women stop talking in the background on the recording, and he imagines their attention also being drawn to the chord sequence being played. It's one of those melodies that immediately sounds a little familiar—not because it is lifting from another song, but because it creates a feeling of nostalgia, of hearing a memory you didn't know you had.

"That's working for me already," says the young Darlene on the tape.

"And then there's the chorus, with a little stop at the end." The piano pauses for a few beats, then starts again. "I think I got a bridge, too," Harlan continues, starting a new series of chords. "Just a little something to set up the solo." That is, the voice has to be Harlan's, since it's the person playing piano, but it's the deeper voice, so Ben is suddenly very confused.

"Wait, wait." Ben holds up his hand and looks at Natalie, who picks up the remote and pauses the recording. He has been trying to figure out which female voice is Darlene's and which is Toni's, but now he is confused about the male voices, too. "I think I have people mixed up," he says, leaning forward. "I thought I recognized Harlan's voice from the live album, but he must have the deeper voice, the one talking through the song?"

"No, that's Nate," Toni says.

"But Nate didn't play piano or write songs."

"Sounds to me like he's doing both," says Natalie.

Ben is trying to process. Is this an unheard Honeybird song that happens to be the first one Nate wrote? But the way Harlan talked at the start of rehearsal, asking "What's cooking," made it sound like they were repeating a process they had gone through before—not like Nate is about to do something surprising and new.

The simplest answer is often correct.

He turns to Darlene. "So how many of your songs did Nate write?"

"All of them."

Ben pauses. Adding that one piece of information to the story changes everything he had imagined about how the band worked. "All of them?"

She nods. "Harlan wrote all his solos, and the three of us would work out the arrangements together, playing in that damn barn until things sounded right. But none of that would have ever happened without Nate's chord patterns."

"What about the lyrics and melodies?"

"Nate."

"Nate?" A long list of new questions is beginning to write itself. When he looks over to Toni she is tapping her granddaughter's arm impatiently.

"Start the tape, please," Toni says. "I haven't heard this damn song in fifty years, and now I need to hear that bridge."

The recording starts again. As Nate continues with the bridge the mood in the song switches. The volume drops and he repeats a series of chords, gradually building up the volume before returning to a more dramatic run-through of the verse. "And then I think a lead here. Big and dramatic, right—think you can do that, HB?" Nate asks. Harlan responds with a quiet "Uh-huh." Nate repeats the opening chords, playing soft with each pass. Then he stops, laughs, and says, "And then we have to figure out how to end it."

After a short pause, one of the female voices—Ben is still trying to tell them apart—says, "That's a hell of a thing there."

"You think so?"

"Double hell yes," repeats the female voice.

"I gotta admit, I was worried, y'all. Wasn't sure how it'd sound in a room with other people, you know? Not just me and my own head."

"It's a damn fine hell of a thing," the female voice repeats. It sounds more like Darlene than Toni. "You have a vocal melody yet?"

"Melody, most of the lyrics."

"Damn. What's it called?"

"'Don't Go, Darling.'"

"Ladies and gentlemen," Harlan says, "sounds like Honeybird is gonna have a damn love song on their next record."

"If we ever make another record," Nate says, and the room breaks into laughter.

"Oh, we'll make another fucking record, I guarantee you," Harlan says. "Even if we just might have to use this piece-of-shit tape deck."

The bravado, the confidence: it couldn't sound any sadder to Ben. At that moment Toni touches her granddaughter's shoulder again. "Can we stop there, please?"

Natalie pauses the recording. There is a long moment of silence. Ben blinks his eyes, the room slowly coming into focus. It feels as though the lights have just come up at the end of an intense movie.

"That's all I can stand for now, Mr. Davies," Toni finally says. She takes a deep breath, and reaches out her hand. Natalie passes her grandmother the glass of water and puts the remote down.

"I understand." He looks at Toni and then Darlene. "And I'm honored that you shared it with me."

"Remember, Darlene has vouched for you. So don't blow it for her."

He looks at Darlene, who seems hesitant to stop staring at the stereo. "I won't."

Toni takes a long drink and then nods. "Good. Then Natalie will work her magic and send that recording to you, and you can have it." She exchanges a look with Darlene. "You can hear the whole damn thing."

"Yes," Darlene says. "The whole thing."

"Thank you," he says. He gives Natalie his email address. "You don't happen to remember the date, do you? Even the approximate month, so that when I cite it I—"

"Yes," Darlene says quietly. "August 17, 1968."

"August 17?"

"Yes."

"Wait." He pauses to make sure his memory is correct. "So, this practice is the same day as—" He stops himself from finishing the question he suspects they do not want to hear.

"Yes. The fire is that night."

"Wow." Ben listened to the tape as a historian, selfishly measuring it in terms of its value for his book, but they'd heard the sounds of their brothers, who would both be dead just a few hours later. "I didn't know. I'm sorry."

"You have committed no crime, Mr. Davies." Toni looks over at Ben. "It was good to hear his voice again. But that's all I can listen to today." She shakes her head, leans back on the couch. "I know you have questions, and I will do my best to answer someday, but I think I need to take a break now."

Ben nods, knowing that he cannot insist Toni continue. At the same time, she is the most direct line to Nate, and he worries that he may never get a chance to talk to her again. He is trying to think of what to say when Natalie catches his eye.

"I was thinking that I could help Grandma answer some questions by email, if that would be okay?"

"Of course," Ben says. It would be better to interview Toni in person, of course, to gauge her tone of voice and watch her reactions to different topics, but Natalie's offer is at least a chance to ask more questions after he finishes reviewing the practice. There's a weight to the air in the room now, and he knows it's time for him to go. He puts his legal pad back in his bag and stands up. "I can't thank you both enough for sharing this with me."

"Just be fair to them," Darlene says, not looking at him.

"Yes, both of them," Toni adds.

"I will," Ben says, watching what seems to be an entire conversation pass between the two women in a single look. Two women, two brothers, two very different families, across fifty years of history.

21 | Where the Fire Goes

Nina drives to the place where her father died with Sid beside her in the front seat, hyper-aware of the way her chest feels as it rises and falls. When they pass the Fox 5 building, set back from the road on their right, she slows the car. Old Briarcliff is the next turn. It's the last turn her father successfully completed.

"You seem tense," Sid says.

"You dogs, and your famous sense of emotional intuition."

"Sarcasm. You adopt that tone when you are nervous."

Nina turns on her right indicator and steers onto Old Briarcliff. The road slopes downward as it curves to the left. She feels like she is piloting a submarine, diving below the surface. She glances quickly in the rearview mirror, to make sure that there is no one in a hurry behind her.

"Do you know where . . ."

"Just past the stop sign," she says quietly, finishing Sid's question.

Old Briarcliff Road splits off Briarcliff at a northeast angle, then dead ends at a three-way stop after less than a mile. Continuing straight at the stop sign leads to a one-lane bridge that connects to the back parking lot of a strip mall; turning right leads to Old Briarcliff Way, which soon crosses Clifton Road and changes names.

Her father ran off the road at that split, straight into a ravine. His Chevy hit a tree, and he probably died upon impact. No one knew where he'd been headed because he'd left the house sometime between 11 p.m., when Nina's mother remembered falling asleep, and 1 a.m., when his car was found. If he'd been driving slower or wearing a seat belt, the story could have had a much different ending.

Nina has always imagined the one-lane bridge as something out of a Western movie, with a covered roof and slats that look as though they will fall off at any moment. Idling at the stop sign, she's surprised that it's paved, and not all that narrow.

"This is where it happened?" Sid asks.

"This is where it happened."

Her father must have been going too fast. Maybe he was distracted, and went through the stop sign without noticing? Or maybe he changed his mind about which way he wanted to go and couldn't adjust quickly enough? According to her mother, the police think some time passed before anyone came along and discovered the accident site. Cellphones were less common, so the first person on the scene had to drive to a gas station to call 911.

A sleek-looking BMW comes down the hill to Nina's right. She waves the driver through.

How fast would her father have to be going to miss that turn? A part of Nina wishes she could hover above the site that night twenty years ago. The position of the car might tell her if he had tried to correct his course once he realized what was happening, or if he just let it happen, just let himself slide across the frozen ice and fall into the river.

A honk from behind causes her to blink, refocus her eyes. When she looks in the rearview mirror she sees a very uptight woman in an SUV waving her hands. Nina continues straight, driving more carefully than Matt Alexander had.

Nina's most vivid memory of her father is a bus ride. She doesn't know if it's a real memory, or just a compilation of fragments her mind stitched together. She has thought about it so many times it's beginning to blur around the edges, a photo held too often.

The bus is crowded, with so many people standing in the aisles that the whole world sways every time there's a curve or a turn. Nina is standing in front of the folding doors on the side of the bus, staring out the windows. Her father is behind her, one arm draped around her neck, the top of his chest crowning the back of her head. The flannel of his shirt tickles her cheek. She can feel the stubble of his chin rubbing against the top of her head, and smell cigarette smoke buried in his shirt sleeve.

Nina's mother became annoyed when asked about this memory. "Do you think these lips could ever kiss someone who smoked? And I would never have let your father take you on a bus. He was too scatter-brained. I'd have been worried he would lose you." As far as her mother was concerned, the entire memory is a creation of Nina's overactive imagination, probably fueled by the hours of TV her grandmother let her watch.

Buried in that brief bit of memory, though, is such warmth, such a sense of security, that Nina knows it is true, even if some of the details are wrong. Just remembering he was there with her, even once, always makes her feel safer. What if he was the one person strong enough to listen to her talk about Sid? What if the one person who would have believed her died twenty years ago?

It's certainly never occurred to Nina to talk to her mother about Sid. Of course, as freaked out as her mother would be if Nina did tell her, Nina also knows that she would be disappointed or angry (or both) if she discovered her daughter had a talking dog and didn't tell her. Marion Alexander harbors the illusion that she and her daughter share all details of their lives, the way two besties would. Nina, however, has always been more inclined to talk to her grandmother.

Grandma was there every day when Nina came home from school. She would sit down at the kitchen table, with a glass of milk and whatever homemade treat Grandma had made, relieved to finally unleash all the questions that built up inside her during the school day. They came out in rapid bursts between bites of her snack and were often about the whole concept of school: Why did she have to remember things that didn't matter? Why did she have to be so quiet in class? Why couldn't she stay home and play? Her grandmother would patiently answer as she sewed, or worked on dinner, or scrubbed the stove until it sparkled.

Sometimes Nina would sneak in questions about her father. "Why did he have to die?"

"We all die, Nina."

"But why did he die that night?"

"Only God knows."

"Why wasn't Mommy in the car, too?"

"She had to stay home with you."

"Why didn't I just stay with Grandma?"

"I was at my own house."

"You have another house?"

"Grandma used to have her own house."

"But why did Daddy's car crash?"

"Finish your snack."

On the other side of the one-lane bridge, the road widens, then twists its way up a hill. After a final curve to the left, she winds up in the back corner of a strip mall parking lot. The anchor store is a run-down Kroger that she only went into once, with Connie and some friends when she was still in high school and they needed a late-night candy bar fix.

Nina pulls into a space and leaves the car running. It's colder than usual for March, so she wants the heat to stay on. She closes her eyes and leans her head back. She's looking for a word to describe the sensation growing inside her chest accurately. Is it panic, or anxiety, or just grief? She does not remember ever grieving for her father. She was so young that she may not have understood how to grieve fully.

"Do you want to talk about it?" Sid asks after a few moments of silence.

"Not yet."

As much as it annoys her, the person she really wants to talk to is Ben. She wants to tell him she's finally visited the accident site. He'd been surprised to hear she'd never been.

"You've never gone? Really?"

They'd been talking while prepping dinner at her tiny kitchen counter. "Why would I go?"

"To see where it happened. To obtain a concrete image."

"Oh, perfect. To have a clear image of where my father met his demise. Excellent."

"What I mean," Ben had explained, "is that a concrete image might offer more resolution, more closure, than whatever your brain works up on its own."

"You historians, and your fascination with old battlefields."

"We don't look at the past to wallow in it," he'd said, eyes focused on the cutting board. "We look at the past so we can be done with it."

Nina opens her eyes and scans the large parking lot. Ben assured her she'd have more closure after seeing the site, but she only has more questions. "Let's go home," she says to Sid.

When they reach the three-way stop at the bottom of the hill she doesn't linger. She's looked at the past once, and now she needs to move on. She suspects it will be the last time she'll drive down Old Briarcliff.

Sid stares straight ahead from his position in the passenger seat next to her. Even after talking to him for months, Nina rarely knows what he is thinking. Is the Buddha part of Sid contemplating eternity? Or is the dog part of Sid staring outside and thinking about food?

Right now, thinking about her father, she is hoping it is the former. After she finishes the tricky left-hand turn on to Briarcliff she asks, "So what really happens when we die?"

"Why would you want to know that?"

"Doesn't everyone want to know that?"

He turns to look at her. "Shouldn't we be more concerned with how to live, not how to die?"

"Oy. Now you're killing me." She raises her hand. "And no, no jokes about how you're trying to help me live, not trying to help me die. Can you drop the existential shaman act for a moment?"

"I have an act?"

She imagines legions of devoted Buddhists praying for the chance to have a conversation with the Enlightened One. How would they react when they found out he was a wise-ass? "Okay, try this," she says. "What do you remember about the process? About leaving one body and then arriving in another?"

"I was somewhere else. Now I am here."

"You don't remember an in-between time?"

"No."

"But you're the Buddha."

"I have memories of that life, yes. But that does not mean that is who I am. And now I am living this life."

Briarcliff is more clogged than it was on their ride over, so Nina turns down a side street to weave through the Highlands. "What do you think will happen next time?"

"Why think about that which I cannot know?"

"Back to a human body? Maybe a cat?"

"You think that after this life I will return in a cat's body? And here I thought we were friends."

"How come the history books don't talk about your sense of humor?" She grins at him while they wait at a light. "Okay, so how about this: what body do you hope to arrive in, next time?"

"You really are ready for this poor dog to die."

"'All conditioned things are impermanent.'"

"Is that one of mine?"

"Some website says it is."

"Is the Internet ever wrong?"

She makes a disappointed sound and shakes her head. "Your questions are usually more complex."

"Now who is being funny?"

"I am not ready for you to die." The light turns green, and they begin to move again. "Of course. But I don't believe you never wonder about what might happen to your soul next."

"Consciousness."

"That's your goal?"

"That's the term. My consciousness is what I carry with me."

"And you never wonder what will happen to it next?"

"I am working toward Nirvana. That is my goal."

"But didn't you already achieve it?"

"While I hoped my journey would be complete by now, I can feel my soul getting closer."

"Does it make you angry to not be there yet?"

"Why would it make me angry?"

"It would make me angry." They're driving by the park off Virginia Avenue, the one with that sad plaque in memory of a family killed when a tree fell on their car. Just stopped in traffic on a rainy day and a tree falls on you. If that's not just random, if there's really some sort of consciousness directing such evil events, Nina does not want to know. "If I were the Buddha, I would feel like I'd done enough to get off this mortal coil, earned some Nirvana, already."

"The past is gone, and I cannot predict the future. I am here, now, so my mind, my mind must remain here."

She wonders if he still believes all of this after all these years. If he did, would that represent a genuine commitment to his beliefs, or would it mean that he was the crazy one, not her? "So, where do you go when that journey is complete? Next time, or the time after, or thirty more lives later—where will you go?"

"Where will I go when I am released from samsara?"

She knows she read that term while dabbling in Buddhism research, but after a pause she says, "I admit I don't remember what that is."

"The endless return to this world. When I wake up, and I am still here, I know that my work is not yet complete."

"So every night when you go to sleep, you expect to die?"

"There are those who believe we do die, every night. When we wake up in the morning we know that our journey is not over yet."

"Okay," she says, slowing down as the street narrows. "Where will you go when you are released from samsara?"

"Where does the fire go?"

She pauses. "Where does the fire go?"

"When the fire burns out, where does it go? It was here, right in front of us, burning so brightly—where is it now?"

"Is that a deep way of saying you don't know?"

"Or a different way of phrasing the question?"

Nina wonders if these circular discussions are making her any smarter. She pulls into the back lot of her apartment building. What would she and Ben have talked about if they'd gone to the accident site together? "I don't think that's an easy turn to miss accidentally," she says softly.

"Just because things are not easy does not mean they do not happen," Sid says.

She turns the car off and turns to look at him. "I'll never know, right?"

"I think it is much easier to count the things you may someday learn than to count all the things you will never know."

22 | Don't Go, Darlene

When he stops at one of the half dozen Starbucks between Darlene's house and the highway, Ben is happy to see an MP3 of the Honeybird practice tape in his inbox. He uses the free Wi-Fi to download it, and by the time he gets his latte, he has queued up the recording for his drive home.

He starts from the beginning, anxious to hear everything again with the voices attached to the right people. Knowing Nate is at the piano completely reorients the scene in his mind. On this listen Ben imagines everyone sitting around Nate at the piano; he's the one that the rest of them need. The song is even more moving the second time he hears it, in spite of still clearly being a work in progress. Maybe because it is so clearly a work in progress? There can be a fragile quality to a demo version of a song that sometimes get lost in the finished recording.

He's in a thick stream of cars heading South on 75 when the recording passes the point where Toni made them stop. Ben hears Harlan tuning up the acoustic, Darlene and Toni talking quietly in the background. Their lack of formal training is evident when Nate starts to talk Harlan through the basic structure, attempting to translate some of the trickier chords from piano to guitar. "And then this one, I don't know what the hell this is," Nate says when he hits one of the chords in the bridge. "Like, I just kind of moved my fingers around until it made sense."

"Uh, if you don't know what it is, then I sure as fuck don't." The two laugh as Harlan tries out a few variations. "I think this is close enough for horseshoes," Harlan finally says, strumming the chord he settles on. "Let's just try to make it through this thing from the beginning."

The two of them run the song down from the top. Darlene and Toni stop talking, and Ben can hear a nice natural echo in the room; they could have recorded their next album in that barn and had great results. "You might as well start singing something," Harlan says, and after a few bars Nate begins to add a mumbled melody. His voice is hesitant and quiet, but also has a deep, round tone.

When they hit what sounds like the chorus, the mumbles turn into words, and Nate's voice grows more confident. The directness of the words, and the chords, and the sound of Nate's singing, hit hard.

Now you're close
So please don't go

After a second chorus and verse, they stumble through the bridge, a series of repeated eighth notes that grows louder and louder. Then Harlan starts scatting an impossible-sounding guitar solo, and goes on for so long that Nate begins to laugh. "I don't know how to end it," he says, struggling to be heard over Harlan; eventually Toni calls out, "Okay, okay, we get it already."

"So, yeah, that's the idea," Nate says. "We'll need to find an ending. Maybe fade-out?"

"I like the idea of fading out," Darlene says.

"Man, fade-outs are always so unsatisfying," Harlan says. "It's like drinking a six-pack and not getting a buzz."

"Um, only one person in this room that could be true for," says Toni. More laughter.

"I mean, I want to know when we hit that climax."

"This one's about love, not fucking," Darlene says.

"I keep telling you, all songs are about fucking," Harlan says, laughing.

"Not this one," Darlene says.

"Darlene's right," Toni says. "I think my brother wrote a goddamn love song."

"So love fades out?" Nate asks quietly.

"No, no," Darlene says. "Love is there before the song starts and keeps going after the song ends. So maybe we fade in and we fade out."

"This is too deep for me, y'all. I mean, we're not even stoned yet." Harlan starts strumming again.

Toni says she has to get home to check on their grandmother, Harlan insists on going to grab some weed, and everyone talks at once for a few minutes before Darlene's voice cuts through clearly. "I'll come by in a bit," she says, and then a door shuts.

The silence that follows is so prolonged that Ben begins to wonder if the reel-to-reel ran out. No one's mentioned the machine in a long time—did they forget about it? Then Nate plays the piano again.

"How long do you think he's gonna be gone?" Darlene asks.

"You kidding? First he needs to remember what he went into the house for. Then he needs to find the weed, get the supplies, and then, then he's got to smoke a tester." Laughter. "It's gonna be a while."

There's another long pause, interrupted only by sounds of quiet shuffling. Then he hears Darlene say, "We should stop. What if he comes right back?"

"When has Harlan ever come right back? Anywhere?"

More silence.

The traffic has turned into a single, slow-moving mass of unhappy cars. Ben's eyes are on the Mini Cooper in front of him but his brain is floating around the inside of the Harlan family barn, studying Darlene and Nate. Two people alone, periods of silence, worried about someone coming back: they were making out? He wonders if he should stop listening, but Toni and Darlene both made a point of saying he could hear everything.

After some more quiet shuffling noises Nate starts to play the chords again. "I want you to hear the real song," he says.

"The real song?"

"I want you to hear the real words."

He plays the opening sequence through once and then starts singing. His voice sounds fuller than it did when Harlan was in the room. More confident.

> Only thing I knew for sure
> No one can know me
> Sitting on my heavy hands
> Let life pass by me
>
> Just hiding here in plain sight
> No one can see me
> I really thought I was right
> Until you found me
>
> Now you're close
> So please don't go
>
> Only thing we know for sure
> No one can know us
> But we don't even see them
> Too far below us
>
> Now you're close
> So please don't go
>
> I need to say it out loud
> Gotta tell somebody
> Gotta let you know,
> Oh, I gotta let you know
> I need to say it, say it, say it
>
> Please don't go, Darlene

Darlene don't go
Don't go, don't go
Don't go, Darlene

The final chord sequence grows softer as he plays it, and there's a long silence. Off in the distance there is a random shout, followed by a crashing sound, and Ben imagines a drunken Harlan causing some sort of commotion. The next voice on the tape is Darlene's, sounding more subdued than she had earlier. "I thought it was 'Don't Go, Darling.'"

"Well, that's what the world will have to hear. Right? 'Cause they can't hear the truth." Random piano notes, quiet. "But I wanted you to hear it." Followed by more silence.

He feels like he's spying, but Ben can't stop listening.

"I hoped that was what the song was about," Darlene starts saying, her voice so hushed he has to strain to hear. "As soon as you started playing. I closed my eyes, and I imagined you were singing to me."

"Of course I was singing to you. Who else, who else would I ever sing to?"

More intense kissing sounds, broken by the sudden sound of laughter. "What?" Darlene asks.

"That fucking tape."

"It's still going?"

"Still going."

"Think it recorded us?"

"That's what this thing does. Record shit. So, yeah."

"Fuck."

Sounds of someone walking closer to the machine. "Doesn't mean anyone needs to hear it. We'll just stop it, and then later we can—"

Click.

23 | What Do You Want Me to Say

Nina went back to her mother's for dinner the Sunday after she moved out, unintentionally starting a tradition that continued the first few years she lived in Midtown. By the time she was dating Ben the Sunday dinners had slowed down to once or twice a month; her mother's lack of fondness for Ben made it easy to stop completely.

Nina deployed a series of excuses to keep from restarting the tradition after the breakup. It's not that she dislikes going home. Her mother has lived in the same house for more than thirty years and there's something reassuring about being so familiar with a place in the world. It's a place where the quirks all make perfect sense to Nina. Of course you have to pull the hall closet door up slightly to open it. No, the outlet next to the sink has never worked. Still, Nina wasn't ready for all the talking, all the energy required to answer questions about the way her life was going.

As she lets herself in the back door for her first Sunday dinner in months, Nina smiles at the sight of her grandmother standing at the stove, stirring a large pot of chicken stew. "Hello, hello," Nina says. It's hard not to have a brief flash of worry when she hugs her grandmother, who seems so much smaller and thinner every time she visits. Her grandmother smells the same, though: Peppermint and cocoa butter. "You made my favorite," Nina says.

"It is my favorite, that's all."

"Of course." Nina walks over to help her mother set the table.

"You look so tired," her mother says after a quick hug. "Isn't this Spring Break?"

"Yeah, but I've been working extra shifts."

Her mother narrows her eyes, silverware in hand. "Why? Do you need more money? Is there—"

"Everything is fine," Nina says. She retrieves the bread basket from the kitchen island and places it in the center of the table. "I'm just thinking about taking a class in the summer, maybe three in the fall instead of two. So I need to start working extra shifts when I can."

"Planning ahead? Jesus. What's gonna happen if you start acting like a full-time grown-up?"

"I can't imagine."

The three of them finish dinner prep—glasses of water filled and placed out, wine put on the table, stew ladled into bowls. Her mother changes the Pandora station from Billie Holiday to Mozart, and Nina smiles to herself. Her mother has played classical music at dinnertime for as long as Nina can remember, because she read somewhere that it was good for brain development.

When they sit down to eat, her mother and grandmother start catching her up on the various neighbors who have come, gone, fought, and made up over the past few months. It's not until the three of them each get a second serving that her mother asks about Ben. "So," she says, refilling everyone's wine, "have you have you heard from the historian?"

Nina looks at her grandmother and rolls her eyes. "I don't expect that to ever happen, Mom."

Her mother takes another piece of bread and uses it to point at Nina as she continues. "Trust me. You need to watch out for the dead cat bounce. Just when you think he's out of the game, he'll jump up at you off the concrete."

"You never did like Ben."

"I'm glad you didn't ask it as a question. Because, no, I didn't."

Nina tears a piece of bread in half and dunks it in the stew. "Because he was older? That would be inconsistent, you know, since Dad was—"

"It's not the age, Nina. It's the power imbalance."

"What power imbalance?"

"He was your teacher."

"Was."

"If the power structure begins with such an imbalance, it can never be recalibrated."

"Wait—what happened to the woman who worked so hard to fight the power?" Nina raises her eyebrows in mock horror and turns to her grandmother. "That was Mom, right?"

"You have no idea," her grandmother says. "Every night she made it home safely I thanked Saint Teresa."

"The power structure. The social power structure." Now her mother's spoon is a pointer. "That's what we fought. But a woman should never have to battle an imbalance of power in her personal relationships."

"So if Ben hadn't been my teacher at some point, you would have been okay?"

Her mother puts her spoon down, shrugs. "Probably not. But I knew I couldn't do anything about it."

"See!"

"I'll always be honest with you, Nina. For better and for worse. Even when you would rather I lie." Nina's mother wipes the edge of her soup bowl with her piece of bread. "Vanessa Fazio," she says, turning to Nina's grandmother.

"That one."

Nina is confused. "Who is Vanessa Fazio?"

"When you were in third grade," Nina's mother starts, pausing to take a sip of wine, "there was this girl in the neighborhood that you really wanted to be friends with. You kept asking me to talk to her mother and have her over for a playdate. I kept saying no, because I knew the girl and her mother and didn't like either one of them."

"An awful girl," her grandmother says. "Awful."

"Grandma." Nina holds her hand to her chest, a southern belle who suffered a profanity. "I don't think I've ever heard you say anyone was awful."

"Kissinger. Awful." Her grandmother swallows a spoon full of stew. "And that Fazio girl."

Nina shakes her head. "I don't remember any of this."

"But I do," Nina's mother says, pushing her empty bowl to the side. "Every day you asked, and every time I tried to get you to give it up, you dug your heels in more. The girl's mother called a few times offering to have you over there, but I refused to let you go to that house."

"Why didn't you like them?"

"The father was a work friend of your fathers, so we wound up at their place for some terrible party years before you were born. The layers of pretension in that house—the forced smiles, the bragging about consumption, the subtle way the husband and wife sliced at each other all night. With parents like that, this little girl had to be awful." Her mother shrugs. "But you wouldn't shut up about Vanessa, so I finally gave in one day and set the thing up. Vanessa came over, all lacy frills and attitude, and thirty minutes into the playdate you begged me to send her home."

"How come I don't remember this?"

"You were eight, nine? Aren't you listening? The moral of the story was clear to me."

"Don't trust little girls named Vanessa?"

"Yes. But I also learned forbidding something just made you more determined."

Nina nods. "You never did say 'no' to any of the guys who wanted to ask me out."

"She wanted to," her grandmother says. "Believe me."

"But Vanessa Fazio also taught me that I could trust you to see through the bad ones. I just needed to give you a chance to do it."

"So you didn't think it would work out with Ben?"

"No. I worried when it lasted longer than I thought it would, but I figured that just meant the sex was good."

When she was younger, Nina thought her mother made blunt comments about sex to be shocking, but as she has grown older she wonders if it's just an awkward attempt to show she cares. Maybe her mother wasn't torturing her, when she made Nina and her friend Suzy Lockwood practice putting condoms on bananas? All the while maintaining a running commentary in a no-nonsense voice: "Number one dodge: 'I don't have any with me.' Number two dodge: 'How do I even put this crazy thing on?' So you bring your own and put it on him." Nina finishes her wine and smiles. "So is that what kept you and Dad together," she asks. "The sex?"

Marion Alexander doesn't look surprised too often, and she recovers quickly. "The sex brought us together," she says. "Stubbornness kept us together."

The three of them stand up, almost in unison, and start to clear the table. Nina could dodge the question, but decides to go ahead and just bring up the subject the two of them never discuss. "I went to the accident site."

"What accident site?"

"Dad's."

"Oh. That." Nina's mother looks into the cupboard to the right of the stove, takes out a container for the leftover stew. "Grandma made extra stew for you to take home."

Nina hugs her grandmother, who is bringing in the empty wine glasses. "Thank you, Grandma." She turns back to look at her mother. "But 'Oh, that'? That's all you have to say?"

"What do you want me to say?"

"I don't know." Nina opens the dishwasher and begins to load the bowls. "I'd never been there before."

"Well, it doesn't make sense for many people to use that road, that's for sure." Nina's mother puts the top on the glass container and slides it to the side. "But that's what your father liked. The quiet."

"Where was he going that night?"

Her mother turns around. "I have no idea. I have never known. And after hours of thinking about it, and wondering why—after years of putting myself through that—I woke up one morning and just accepted the fact that I will never know."

Nina waits for her mother to continue, to offer some big revelation. Instead, she just walks the empty stewpot over to the sink. "But you were married to him."

Her mother turns the water on, then pours some dish soap onto a sponge. "If you think being married to someone means that you magically know everything that person is thinking, then you will be very disappointed if you ever do get married."

"I don't think you know everything about them," Nina says. "But the big stuff? Like whether or not they may have wanted to kill themselves? That stuff, yes."

"The biggest stuff is easiest to hide," her grandmother says quietly.

"Your father," Nina's mother continues, turning the faucet off and then beginning to scrub the pot, "liked to say he contained multitudes. But as he got older, it seemed like each of those multitudes was some variation of a man who was happiest when he was alone. He used to wake me up to drag me along on those rides, but that stopped." She raises a soapy hand, scratches her nose. "In fact, I'd have been worried if he did wake me up to say goodbye. That would have seemed more unusual. I was used to finding him in bed next to me in the morning, clothes still on. When the phone woke me up, and he was not there? I knew something was wrong."

"Do you think he missed the turn on purpose?"

Nina's mother sighs. "Again, I am not sure what you want me to say. That your father may have been too stoned to notice what he was doing? That he may have been too depressed to understand what he was doing?"

"So why did you tell me at all? Why not just let me keep being sure it was some awful accident?"

"Because I think you are old enough to know everything I know." Nina's mother dumps the dirty water out of the pot. "And everything I don't know."

Nina turns to her grandmother, who is gathering silverware from the table. "What do you think, Grandma?"

Her grandmother answers after a slight pause. "I think that he was a happy young man who grew sadder each time I saw him." She takes a few steps toward Nina and when she is close enough hands the spoons and knives to her. "And we will never know what happened that night."

The three of them continue cleaning, the Mozart sounding louder now that the talking has stopped. Nina tries to imagine what it must have been like for her mother, living with someone who grew more sad and solitary as time passed. Someone prone to wandering off, a feral cat you had to trust would find his way home. Until the night he didn't come home, and you had to accept that you would never know what trail he had been following when he met his end.

24 | Home of Historic Rock

Ben spends the rest of his Spring Break reviewing his research. Everything he thought he understood about Honeybird—the individuals, their relationships, the music, and the meaning of their songs—needs to be revised.

When he forces himself to reread his analysis of the songs on Honeybird's first album, he is embarrassed to see how wrong he was. He filtered the lyrics through his certainty that the songwriter was a young, white southerner who rejected his position of privilege. Now Ben knows the real voice in those songs belonged to a twenty-year-old Black man who had started school before the *Brown v. Board of Education* ruling, living in a state where it was illegal for him to marry the woman he loved. As a fan of the band, Ben is excited to be able to make so many new interpretations. As a graduate student who has already written long chapters about each of the band's records, he is exhausted just thinking of the work ahead of him.

Ben will have to do the same thing for their second album, *Waiting Here*. In his first analysis, he argued that the chorus of the title track—"Now all the doors are locked/But who has the key/And who built these walls/Closing in on me"—was Harlan giving voice to a generation of new southerners, a generation who felt trapped by the sins of their past. He even wrote a whole paragraph about what he assumed was a shout-out to the legacy of Hank Honeybird: "No one ever sees/my father's son." Nate, writing as a Black man in the South in the mid-sixties, had a different set of doors and walls blocking his way—a much more impervious group of obstacles.

On Friday he heads to campus to meet with Dr. Reed. He emailed her a recap of his meeting with Darlene and Toni, as well as the MP3 of the practice. As soon as he steps through the door she begins talking, waving a sheet of paper. "You were right. Your book will be about the songs, and the real identity of the writer of those songs. With a love story, on top of that. These developments have made your work even more relevant. And more marketable, which is always a good thing."

When he sits down she hands him the paper. One side has a list of university and independent presses, and the other is filled with handwritten notes.

"Those presses are some good possible matches, and the notes are for your book proposal," Dr. Reed says. "You should start working on that right away. Already shopping a book for publication when you're on the job market is a huge plus." She pauses, and then narrows her gaze. "Now. Can I ask why you're so unhappy? You should look like a Leakey who has just found the bones of a fully formed foot."

His initial instinct is to insist he's fine, but he decides that if anyone might understand what's bothering him, it's her. "It's not that I'm unhappy." He pauses, looking for the right word. "I'm disappointed, I guess."

"Disappointed?" She raises her eyebrows. "In a story like this?"

"Disappointed in me, not the story," he explains. "I've spent years studying this time, getting to know Macon, and the Honeybird family. Listened to the music again and again, examining the meaning of the band and Harlan's songs. None of it was correct. I missed it all."

"New data, new information, creates the chance for deeper, fuller interpretations. Don't be afraid to absorb and adapt. It's one of our most important functions, as historians and writers."

"But I was so proud of it, so convinced I had found something important to say. And now I have to hear the songs in a new way."

She shakes her head. "'Have to hear?' Rephrase that. You now have an opportunity to hear the songs in a new way, having absorbed some new information. You have an opportunity to tell a more interesting and important story. A more honest story." She leans forward as if moving in for her closing argument. "But that's not what's bothering you. It's Harlan. You've grown too fond of him."

Too fond? Had he crossed the line from a healthy interest to a blind love? "I don't know if that's true," he says, aware of how weak his objection sounds even as he says it.

"And that fondness makes you protective, which is understandable," Dr. Reed continues. "But don't let that keep you from finding the real story."

"The real story?"

"Yes. It may have started as Harlan's story, but it's bigger than that now, right? Now you also have the story of a Black voice being silenced. Your work can allow that voice to be heard."

The phrase sounds wrong to Ben. "I don't think it's really that Nate's voice was 'silenced,'" he says. "People got to hear the songs, after all. Listening to everything again and knowing who wrote the songs, it's kind of like the truth was out in the open."

"His voice was there, but no one knew it was his voice." She shrugs, leans back. "Okay, then. Appropriated."

Ben had convinced himself that Harlan was trying to move away from the belief system of his father's generation. Now it seems he just used his power in different ways. Was that because there was no other choice or because he did not look hard enough to see an alternative?

Ben goes to the Cube Farm after his meeting with Reed. He expects it to be deserted since it is the last day of Spring Break, but Shelley is there, sitting on the back couch. As he unpacks his laptop and notes he smiles at her. "Hard at work?" Her MacBook is open and in her lap, but she's staring at the screen with an expression somewhere between blank and sleeping.

"That's what I tell myself," Shelley says. "I mean, I get bonus points for coming here during Spring Break, right?"

"I tell myself that, too," Ben says as he opens his laptop. "I also worry that it makes us like the kids who went to the library during lunch."

Shelley makes a look of faux worry, her eyebrows arching up over the black rims of her glasses. "Um. Was that not the cool thing to do?"

"No, no, of course it was." Ben opens chapter three of his dissertation, his old analysis of Honeybird's debut album ready to be deleted and replaced. "I guess this is where we pretend to not want to interrupt each other, but secretly hope to be interrupted?"

"Then we should definitely interrupt each other," Shelley says. "Please."

Ben walks over to sit down at the other end of the couch. "A crucial part of writing is the time you talk about writing."

"Yes. It turns out that I have grown dependent on bullshitting with fellow grad students as a warm-up to getting any actual work done."

"Then you have mastered the first lesson of grad school."

"So," Shelley says, staring back down at her computer screen, "how far along were you on your dissertation at the end of your second year?"

"Oh, man. Not far. I wasted the first year on a topic that didn't pan out. I've felt behind schedule ever since."

"And now you have one year of funding left?"

"Uno mas."

"Can you do it?"

"I have to," Ben says. "I'll be writing all summer, but I need to finish. So I have to keep to the schedule—which is why I'm here today."

"I have lists of shit to do. Is that a schedule?"

"It's a solid first step," Ben says. "The next part is setting deadlines."

"Well, I can make deadlines just fine," she says, closing her laptop and sliding it between the right side of her body and the arm of the couch. "Do I have to keep them, too?"

Ben nods. "Sadly, yes." He points at her laptop. "But I bet you're further along than you think."

"Oh, you would lose that bet, my friend. I'm still researching female abolitionists and female punk icons—and even money says you know which category I spend more time on."

"And once you have these two columns of research filled out?"

"Then I try to see if I can mash them together. And hope I have something worth saying."

"Something worth saying." Ben repeats the phrase slowly. "That's what keeps us all going, I guess. The chance that we might find something to say."

"I just need to make connections between strong brave women that worked to bring about change. But trying to get there makes my head hurt."

"It seems like those connections should exist. Trying to carve out a role for women in the male sphere and all that?"

"That's always been my hunch," Shelley says. She turns slightly to her side, so she is looking at Ben more directly. "But I feel like there are all these racial landmines that are just gonna blow up on me."

"I can see that," Ben says. "You don't want to come across as, like, trivializing the abolition movement by comparing it to female-driven guitar rock in the Seventies."

"Argggh." Shelley puts her head in her hands. "That is exactly the issue I have been worried about these last few weeks. Why didn't I see it as quickly as you did?"

"I'm not saying it's a dealbreaker." Ben wonders if he should comfort her, maybe pat her back? But he doesn't want to be seen as patronizing, or worse, so he keeps his distance. "You go into the writing aware of the issue and then bend over backward to explain it in the intro. Besides," he adds, trying to lighten the mood again, "it's not like being discussed at the same level as female rock icons is a bad thing, right?"

"Now, that's true," she says, straightening up.

He shrugs. "So just focus on that. Certainly a timely issue, right? Women in rock, and what happens when they get 'too loud'?"

"It's where I want to go, I'm telling you. Pollant thinks the abolition angle can work—women struggling to get 'heard' through their centuries, blahdy blah. And Duncan thinks I'm crazy to pass up hitting two markets with one book."

"All fair points." Ben pauses. "But you just wanna rock."

"I just wanna rock. You get it. Of course you would, with your dead guitarist."

"Well, I get the wanting to rock part, sure. All historians do," he says, trying not to laugh as he continues, "it's why we're here."

"Georgia State: Home of Rock."

"That's what my brochure said." Ben grins. "My problem is trying to make it not just, like, rock, musically, but rock historically."

"Georgia State: Home of Historic Rock."

Ready to keep things light, Ben begins to riff on that idea, describing famous musicians as historians and vice versa. The whole conversation lasts almost an hour, before Shelley checks the time on her phone and sighs. Dr. Pollant prefers to have their progress meetings via Skype, even if she is across the hall in her office. She also wants Shelley to be somewhere she is assured not to be interrupted, so Shelley goes home to take the calls.

After she leaves, he's alone in the Cube Farm. It's what he hoped for, but it feels melancholic. He enjoyed talking with Shelley, and it may have been the first time the two of them spoke without other people around. He's always thought she was attractive, with her thick-framed indie musician glasses and sharp sense of humor, but hadn't allowed himself to think of her as anything other than a fellow grad student. He had been dating Nina, for one, and it also seemed like it would be very complicated to get involved with someone in the Cube Farm. What would happen when you broke up?

He opens iTunes and hits shuffle on his "Writing Playlist," fifty or so songs that all are upbeat and not too complicated. It wasn't just his first private conversation with Shelley alone; it was the first one-on-one conversation he'd had with any woman—other than Dr. Reed—since his break-up with Nina. And he'd survived. Maybe he wouldn't be alone forever?

APRIL

"Men leave their children all the time and the world celebrates them for it. Buddha left and Odysseus left and no one gave a shit about their sons. They set out on their noble journeys to do whatever the hell they wanted to do and thousands of years later we're still singing about it."
—Ann Patchett

25 | Cynophilist

When Nina arrives at Big Tex Cantina, Howard is waiting for her at the front door. He's wearing a different leather jacket, light brown and body-hugging. Jesus, she realizes, he's not just decent-looking. He's hot.

"I don't think we'll have to fight for a table," Howard says as he holds the door open for her. To the left of the entrance is a corner booth with six or seven middle-aged people. A lanky teen, wearing a beret and a serious look, holds up the right wall. Otherwise, a half dozen tables remain empty in front of the small stage. The restaurant's main dining room and bar are behind them, and it sounds like a much bigger crowd is in there.

"Well, we are early," she says, sitting down at the table closest to the entrance. An eager waitress appears to take their drink order, and Nina realizes she forgot to carefully plan her choice. Is Howard a drinker? Recovering alcoholic? She smiles and orders a ginger ale, relieved when he says, "The same for me."

"Confession," he says after the waitress walks away. "I'm early everywhere."

"Oh, are we at the confession stage already?"

He looks at his watch. "We have a few minutes before they get started, so yes: confession time."

"First one's easy, then. I am also always early."

"Life is timing, right?" He pauses, grins.

She nods. A Nineties song plays over the PA—Third Eye Blind? Matchbox 20? What's the difference between those two bands, anyway? Before she can decide if that topic can generate enough banter to keep things from getting awkward, Howard clears his throat.

"So, Nina."

"So, Howard."

"Where are you with God?"

She wonders if he's ever going to stop surprising her with sudden changes in direction. She hopes not. "From confessions to God, huh?"

He shrugs. "We could make small talk, I guess, about traffic getting here, or Algebra, or whatever. But I'd rather get to some interesting stuff before the music starts."

"Interesting stuff—I like that idea." She pauses, trying to think of an appropriate answer. Think like Sid, she tells herself. Answer Howard's question with a question. "But what do you mean, 'where am I with God?' Like, from God's point of view?"

"Well, if you have access to that inside information, I'd love to hear it." He pauses as the server sets giant plastic tumblers of ginger ale in front of them. "But for now, I'm more curious about where things stand from your point of view."

A year ago, this would have been an easy question to answer. Nina assumed that God, if he or she or it even existed, thought about her as much as she thought about God, which was not much at all. Living with Sid changed that. If she isn't crazy, Sid's existence says something about whether or not there is a God. If life is just a weird genetic fluke, the fact that a dog talks is an odd, but not impossible, mutation. A consciousness that has been reincarnated many times, in different types of bodies, indicates that living creatures do have some sort of soul.

"My position is evolving," she finally says.

"Evolving?"

"When I was younger, my atheist mother took the whole idea off the table for me. Then, the way some religious kids rebel by announcing they don't believe in God? I rebelled in high school. I told my mom Van Morrison had convinced me there was a God."

"He can do that," Howard says. "How did your mother react?"

"She said never take drunken Irishmen seriously, even if they sing well."

"Fair point." He grins. "Sounds like your mother has a sharp sense of humor, but we'll pick that up during Crazy Family discussion."

"We'll need more than a few minutes for that one."

Howard nods soberly. "Of course. But we're not done with God yet. After the high school rebellion? Where is this evolving position today?"

"What's the clockmaker analogy? Like, if there is a God, he or she or it just gave us the clock and went home. It's up to us to wind the damn thing, make sure it keeps running." She could stop there, but she decides to include some of her more recent, Sid-inspired thoughts. "But I have also been leaving myself open to the possibility that there are things I do not understand, can never understand. Maybe that's the space where God could be?" She shrugs.

Howard thinks for a moment. "I like that answer," he says. "Not thinking too much about it, day to day, but also leaving open the possibility."

Nina watches the emcee head for the microphone with a list of performers in hand, and is relieved when Howard turns his attention to the stage; the place is so small and the crowd so sparse that talking through the acts would make her feel awful. And if he knows to be quiet at an event like this, he might also be the kind of guy who knows not to talk during movies.

The emcee thanks everyone for coming out, pushes some drink specials, and introduces the first act: an older man older with thinning hair and a battered acoustic guitar that looks like it has many stories to tell. He checks the mic a few times and tells an awkward joke before starting to play. His strumming is stilted at first, but his voice has a sweet tone. When he sings about a dog that ran away when he was a kid, his guitar playing evens out. At the end of the song he holds a few long, deep notes that are quite affecting. The small crowd applauds enthusiastically and the performer melts with visible relief, bowing his head ever so slightly.

Before Nina can ask Howard what he thought, the performer starts playing again. His charm begins to fade when he starts singing another number about a dog—this time, his grandfather's border collie. The applause is a little less enthusiastic when he finishes, and soon drowned out by "Heart-Shaped Box" on the PA. Nina turns to Howard, anxious to debrief but also worried about coming off as too negative. She settles for saying, "So."

"So, indeed," he says.

"Should we comment after each act, or just let the whole thing wash over us and debrief at the end?"

"I've come twice before, but always by myself. Never needed a game plan before."

A young, surfer-dude type is walking up to the emcee. "Looks like there's not much time between each act," Nina says. "How about just one word for each?"

"Perfect." Howard takes a drink of his soda and nods. "I'll go first: Cynophilist."

She raises her eyebrows. "Um?"

"Someone who likes dogs."

"Oh, that's good. You're setting the bar high, huh?"

"How else would you want it set?"

The second performer is introduced. Nina has just a few seconds to come up with a respectable word choice and settles for "Earnest." Howard smiles in agreement, and they both turn their attention back to the stage. Over the next ten or so performers, they keep their comments to one word each.

"California."

"Lifeguard."

"Pacing."

"Arrangement?" ("A question?" "As in, did you even try to work out an arrangement for this one?")

"Emo."

"Almost."

"Davidcassidy."

"That's two words," Nina says, though she has to admit it certainly fits the twenty-something whose songs both featured "love" in their choruses.

"Not if I say it real quick," Howard says. "What's your word?"

"Skin," she says, watching Davidcassidy get hugged by the three young women who had moved to the front table for his songs.

After the emcee announces a fifteen-minute break, "Magic Man" begins to play over the PA. Nina turns to look at Howard, and he raises his eyebrows and puts a ten-dollar bill on the table. "Ninety minutes of this is usually enough for me."

Nina stands up and follows him to the door. She wonders if two sodas cost ten dollars or if he's just a big tipper, which would be a definite plus. She also wonders if the whole night is over; she's fine ending the Open Mic portion, but she's ready for the Howard part of the night to keep going.

"I have a final one-word comment," Howard says when they step outside. "Icecream."

"Okay, that one is one word," she agrees.

"Perfect. To Jeni's we go."

As they walk they start bantering about the open mic. Nina likes that Howard focuses on something each act did well. He even finds a way to point how good the chorus could have been in the second song by "Davidcassidy." "He went right to the edge," Howard says, holding his thumb and forefinger close together, "but he never figured out a way to resolve that last line. So the whole thing kind of dripped onto the floor."

"Well, you sure talk like a musician." They're waiting for the light to change so they can cross Commerce Drive. "But you keep dodging whenever I ask when you're gonna get on that stage."

"Need to get through this semester," he says. "Eyes on the prize. Get my degree."

"But you play, what, sousaphone? Washboard?" She grins. "We talking country, opera?"

The light changes and he tells his music origin story. Got his first guitar when he was six, wrote his first song at ten, conservative parents who hated the whole idea of "wasting" so much time on music. "I mean, I'm not talking full 110 percent Asian Stereotype. Maybe 90 percent." Getting a business degree is his escape hatch, a parting present to his parents before he goes off to see what he really wants to do with his life. It's also an escape hatch that could turn into a trap; if his final GPA is over 3.5 he gets a cash bonus—but below 3.5, and he has to go work for the family nursery for a year.

They're passing the courthouse and the eternal flame lit for casualties of war. It always seems a little sad to her, that the flame is off the square by itself. Does the fire burn if no one sees it? "What's your answer to the God question, anyway?" she asks.

"Me? I am also evolving."

They walk a few steps in silence, and she wonders if that will be his full answer. Just as he opens the door to Jeni's, though, he adds, "But I have never been able to imagine how all this could be possible without someone or something to thank for it."

His words bump around inside her head as they switch from talking about God to tasting ice cream, each having a few samples before deciding on their flavors.

"A Savannah Buttermint kind of girl, eh?"

"We're the smartest people at the party," she says. "Though the Darkest Chocolate does indicate a fondness for extremes that I can appreciate."

She asks to pay since he paid for the soda and is pleased when he does not put up a fight. They head outside with their cones and slowly wander over to one of the benches near the enormous steel globe on the square.

"Thing is," he says, before stopping to work at the melty edges of his cone.

"Thing is—what?"

"It's silly," he says, "but it does tie back to the God question." He takes another lick of his cone, then turns to her. "I can remember, as a kid, thinking that everything was alive."

She pauses, wondering just how much that "everything" is supposed to cover. "Like, everything in nature?"

"Everything. Period."

For the first time, Nina tries to imagine a young Howard. Chubby cheeks, for sure, and a kind of mischievous grin present at all times. A happy kid, probably—but also probably a pain in the ass at times. "Chairs? Tables? Win—"

He cuts her off. "Floors, walls, spoons."

"Spoons?"

"I mean, we shouldn't just start listing stuff because we'd be here a while. All of it. Anything I could see, I decided it had to be alive."

"Interesting kid."

"I had my moments."

"What inspired this?"

He has made it down to the cone and takes his first bite. "My stuffed bear."

"You had a stuffed bear?"

"Of course," he says, eyes wide. "Didn't you?"

"Of course," Nina says. "A stuffed panda. Peter."

"Oh. A panda?"

His voice is so dubious she laughs. "What, you're the one person in the world who doesn't like pandas?"

"They're cute and all, sure," he says. "But there's some debate, man. Could be a bear, could be a raccoon." He grins. "My bear was Tommy. Kind of a nondescript brown thing, plastic eyes, patchy fur. I can't remember much about life before I hit school, you know, but I can remember Tommy. And I was sure he had to be alive."

"Seems fair enough," she says. "Even though I never thought about Peter being alive or dead."

"Because you assumed he was alive, I bet."

"Of course."

"See? I figured if he was alive, then all the stuffed animals my brothers had, they had to be alive, too. Only logical."

"Indeed."

"See where this is heading?"

"Now I see."

"If stuffed animals could be alive, other toys had to be alive, and if stuff made out of wood and plastic could be alive, then—well, why not everything else?"

Nina stares at the remaining portion of her cone, plotting her end game. One wrong move, and she could wind up with ice cream on her shirt. "I'm trying to imagine how thinking that way would have affected a young me," she says before taking a bite. "Would I be more happy or more afraid?"

"Afraid?"

"Yeah. Would I be afraid to touch anything, afraid I was going to hurt it? If I bumped into a chair, would the chair feel pain?"

"Oh, I see. Yeah, I just mumbled 'sorry' a lot, real quietly."

"That's cute."

He puts the last bit of cone into his mouth with a dramatic flourish, chews. "Oh, young Howard was very fucking cute."

They lapse into a natural silence, and Nina surveys the night scene as she finishes her cone. Decatur is uncomfortably crowded with packs of free-range toddlers on the weekends, but tonight, only a handful of couples of various ages aimlessly stroll. "So how did it affect you?"

"I felt less alone."

"So did you feel more alone when you got older and understood everything wasn't alive?"

"Don't we all feel more alone as we get older?"

"'Life does not alternate between aloneness and participation, but embraces them both.' Or something like that."

He raises his eyebrows as the two of them stand up. They slowly walk across the square, tossing their napkins into the trash as they walk by. "That sounds Buddhist, friend."

"I think so? I read it in some book review in the *Times*."

"So, what, you bring out your Buddhist bits for the Asian guy?"

She wonders for a split second if she has really offended him, but then he starts to smile. "Of course. Next, I'm going to ask about the real story behind General Tso's chicken."

"Ancient Chinese Secret," he says.

"Damn." She shrugs. "I have been reading a little on Buddhism. Dabbling."

"Like, *Buddhism for Dummies* dabbling?"

"Man," she says, laughing, "it's that obvious?"

"Yeah, but it's cool. I mean, there are much worse things to dabble in, right?"

"Probably," she says. "All part of the evolution, I guess?"

They grow quiet as they approach the parking lot. Being with Howard has been very comfortable, but inside the growing silence Nina has room to worry that beginning another relationship too quickly would doom it. And when (or if?) she does start a new relationship, with Howard or anyone else, she'll have to figure out what to say about Sid. Or not say about Sid. If someone thinks their dog talks to them, how open and honest can they ever truly be?

She decides she has to say something, even if she is not sure exactly what she will say.

"We spent so much time on God and ice cream that we never got to the 'weird family' discussion," she starts as they get closer to her Honda, "or the 'people we used to date' discussion."

"Well, I was hoping there'd be more discussions, like, down the road," he says.

"Me, too." She leans her against her car. "But I just want to say something now, even though it might be weird, because I don't want things to be more weird later."

"Uh-oh." Howard raises his eyebrows. "You're married? Or vegan? Out on parole?"

"So vegan is worse than being married, but better than being out on parole?"

"Sounds about right."

"Well, none of those, at least not yet. But," she continues, trying not to flash back to standing with Ben in the apartment, slowly drowning as she reached for the right words, "I was in a relationship that just went sideways in January."

"January," he repeats. "Was it serious?"

"Yeah," she says, aware of an anxious sensation in her chest. Is it just thinking about Ben causing that reaction, or talking about Ben with Howard? "We were planning to move in together. So. Yeah."

"That must have been rough," he says.

"It was." She puts her right hand up in a stop motion, anxious not to scare him off. "But it's over. Done. I'm not bringing this up now, because I still want to see him, or anything like that. I just need to move . . . slowly."

"I get it," he says quietly. "Though I have to admit I have thought of kissing you. More than once."

Nina feels a blush bloom on her cheeks. "I might have thought of that, too," she says quietly.

"But I had a relationship that went sideways last year. Maybe even like, flipping at the Daytona 500 upside down ways. Thing is," he continues, staring down at the parking lot, "I didn't handle it well. At all. I blamed her for everything, so I got angry, and hurt, and then more angry. I said dumb things, did dumb things, and then my grades got fucked. So then I blamed her for that, too."

She waits for a second, to make sure he's done. "How fucked?"

He looks up at her again, shakes his head. "Well, let's just say that my GPA fell below that magic point my parents set."

"That point separating you from the nursery?"

"Yup. Eventually, I realized that maybe it wasn't all her fault, that maybe most of it was mine. And that screwed me up, too. Like, how could I have been so wrong?"

Nina nods. "That I can relate to."

"I saw it all wrong. I treated her wrong. And I spent the summer rebooting." He stands up straighter. "What I told you before, about not playing out or anything until the semester ends? I mean, I told myself nothing else but school until I graduate. Not even dating."

"Sounds like a good plan. No one wants to repeat senior year."

"Oh, I'm gonna finish. Closing in on a 4.0 for the semester."

"Getting back over that magic point for your parents?"

"Oh, yes. It's close, but I'm over." He runs his finger along the hood of her car. "But I wanted to hang out with you. A lot. So, I told myself, tell myself, as long as we don't kiss, it's not like, a date date."

She pauses. The parking lot is mostly empty, and the night suddenly feels much quieter. "So maybe just hanging out is a good idea both of us."

"Okay," he says, holding out his hand. "Then for now we'll just hang out."

She shakes his hand. It's warm. His grip feels warm and familiar, and it takes a little bit of effort to separate her palm from his. "We'll just hang out." She opens the car door, and turns to him before she gets in. "So, when is your last final, exactly?"

26 | She Had This Dog

Ben has just left the Georgia State library when his mother's name appears on his caller ID. She rarely calls during the week so he's worried about hearing some awful news, but it turns out she's just trying to get a phone number for Emma, Dan's girlfriend. Ben doesn't have one, but sends along an email address, then continues his walk to the parking deck.

He's crossing Courtland Street, listening to his mother describe her plan to fly Dan and Emma out to California so they can "catch up," when her tone changes. "You know, I haven't heard Nina's name in a while."

The comment catches him by surprise; his mother has not asked about Nina for weeks. "Why would you expect to hear her name?"

"I know you said it was all over, but I really thought you two might work it out."

"That's not gonna happen."

"Why not? Sometimes people—"

"Trust me."

"You never did tell me what happened. Did she see someone else? Because you could let that go, darling. It's not like the old days. I mean, your father—"

"That wasn't it, Mom," he says quickly, not anxious to hear another list of his father's sins. Is she so concerned about Nina because she thinks so little of his chances of finding anyone else? "She didn't cheat. I didn't cheat."

"So what was it?"

He reaches Piedmont just as the light changes and takes a deep breath. He's never told anyone the real reason for the breakup. Maybe if he tells his mother the truth, she will move on. "Well. She had this dog."

"The dog? Pets can be hard, and I know it's not your thing, but is that reason enough?"

"She said the dog talked to her."

"Oh." There's a pause, and he can hear his mother's brain spinning, trying to process. "Talked to her how? Tail wagging and eye contact?"

The light changes, and he begins to cross. "I never actually saw—"

"You know, I had a friend once, who used to sit there, and look at her cat, and swear that she and the cat were having a conversation."

He glances at the parking deck, just a few more feet away, and reminds himself to be patient. "No. Not like that."

"Oh."

"Actual words."

"Actual words?"

"That's what she said."

"Oh." Pause. "Did you hear the dog talk?"

"No, Mom." He starts walking up the ramp to his car. "Because it's impossible."

Another pause. "Well, what did you say? When she told you?"

What did he say? It's hard to remember the exact words. The whole conversation is like a crime scene he has not wanted to return to, an event whose outcome no amount of close examination can change. "I don't really remember. I mean, it took me a while to even figure out what she meant."

"But how did this lead to breaking up? Did the dog tell her to do it, or something?"

"I broke up with her."

"Because of the dog? Because—"

"She didn't just say the dog talked to her. The dog told her he had been reincarnated."

It sounds like his mother takes a drink during her next pause. Most likely water or tea, but when they make the comedy film of his life the camera will cut to the mother character downing a shot of scotch. "Reincarnated? Like Shirley MacLaine?"

"Maybe he had been Shirley MacLaine. I didn't ask for a list of former lives."

"Oh."

Another pause, and he can visualize her face as she works through the news. It's a lot to take in, but at least he won't have to talk about it again. "So you can see, I just couldn't keep going."

"But why not?"

The question catches him by surprise. "A talking, reincarnated dog?"

"I grant you, it's not a situation I would call ideal. But it's not as bad as Scientology, which I always thought would be a dealbreaker."

"Scientology?"

"With the n-grams or whatever they are? Or Mormonism, with gold tablets? I always wondered if I could date a Mormon."

"I don't know—"

"How long did she say this had been going on?"

"The dog talking?" Ben tries to remember if he had even asked. Would it make any difference? "She just said 'for a while.'"

"So you were dating her, and the dog was already talking?"

"Yes, but I didn't know it."

"Why does knowing change anything? You were happy before you knew. Just pretend she never told you."

He reaches the car, puts his messenger bag on the hood and opens the flap so that he can get his keys. "How could I do that?"

"Relationships are compromise, Ben. Nothing but compromise."

"But a talking, reincarnated dog?"

"The reincarnation part doesn't bother me."

"Doesn't bother you?" He unlocks the driver's door. "Really?"

"It's out there, I know, but I don't pretend to understand how any of this works. Your father was a Catholic, after all."

Now Ben's even more confused. If there's one thing he thought his mother and father had in common, it was Catholicism. "But you're Catholic, too?"

"I converted for our wedding."

He opens the front door to put his bag inside, then leans against the side of the car. "You weren't Catholic before Dad?"

"No, Presbyterian. But it was important to him to get married in a church, so I converted."

"But after the divorce? You kept making us go to mass every Sunday."

"I'd converted. It was a pain in the ass, and I wasn't about to lose all that hard work just because your father was bad at marriage."

All those wasted Sundays at church. If she didn't want to be there, and he and Dan didn't want to be there, why did they go? "There's a difference between being Catholic and thinking your dog is talking to you."

"My father would disagree with you. The idea that millions of people took their orders from some old Italian man—that was nuts. You're the historian. You know we didn't have a Catholic president until JFK."

"That's true. But still not the same. A talking dog is—"

"Is what? Harder to believe than religion? That's one thing Tom will get on the phone to talk about, if you want him not to shut up."

"Not necessary," he says. "How could I live with someone who thought all that? In a year or so I'll probably have to leave Atlanta, to find a job. What if she's really not well?"

"She was the same Nina you—you, my lone wolf son—were going to move in with."

Lone wolf: is that what his mother thinks of him? "But hearing voices? Isn't that a red flag?"

"It's a lot, I know." His mother sighs. "But we all have red flags. I'm not saying it would have worked out. I'm just surprised that you didn't try. Didn't you want to understand why she believed that? What was going on in her life, that this is what she thought? Wouldn't you want to know if she really isn't well, and needs help?"

Those last questions are the ones that linger in his mind on his ride home. Should he have tried to understand? If he could go back and try again, would he have anything else to say to Nina? The fact that he can't think of a different way to respond after three months could mean that there's nothing else he could have said or done. Or, that he still isn't smart enough to figure it out.

27 | Buddhism for Dummies

"So when are we going to talk about Howard?"

Nina struggles to keep the phone between her shoulder and chin as she slips on the black Nikes she never unties, her official Sid Walking Shoes. "Do we have to?"

Connie groans. "Of course we have to. I am pinned to my couch with an ever-expanding creature growing in my stomach. I will be here for the next four weeks, or maybe longer. Maybe forever if said creature refuses to leave. Meanwhile you, my oldest friend, get to walk around in the universe. And you have been spending time with a cute Asian man."

"But—"

"More than a week ago, your honor, the defendant confessed that the aforementioned date attended an open mic and ate expensive ice cream, and I only have gotten stray texts about this."

"But that's the only time we went anywhere, I promise." She moves toward the front door, and Sid follows. "And I need to get outside to meet Troy."

"If he's supposed to be there now, you still have half an hour."

"No, he was supposed to be here half an hour ago." Nina bends down to attach the leash to Sid's collar.

"Well, then, just talk to me until he gets here. Please. You are all that stands between me and actually watching *Downton Abbey*."

"You buried the lede," Nina says. She shuts the door behind her and begins to summarize the night with Howard. She nods hello to Morris and the three young men circling his desk. Morris gives her a big smile and makes some weird hand gestures and a grinding noise—promising, again, that a new garbage disposal will be hers soon. She flashes him a thumbs up, wondering why getting a disposal is turning out to be as hard as attaining Nirvana.

When she steps outside she sees Troy and Carol waiting. Before she hangs up she promises to call and finish the Howard story later.

"Howard story?" Troy asks, eyes wide. "Do I get a Howard story, too?"

As she and Troy start their walk she summarizes the date night. This time she makes it to the end, and Troy wants to know why there wasn't a kiss.

"I mean, it doesn't have to be tongue, at this point. But a little something-something?"

"I'm not ready yet, with or without tongue."

"When will you be ready?"

"I don't know. But I promise to tell you all about my make-out sessions, when they resume."

Troy accepts that answer, and then begins to catch her up on his world. Everything seems to be going well: "Eat Your Art Out" has scheduled some live tapings, and there may even be a performance in New York. His voice sounds flatter than usual, though, and his shoulders slump in a way that Troy's shoulders never do. They stop walking so Carol and Sid can investigate what must be an especially fragrant bush, and Nina tries to decide if she should risk digging deeper than their usual level of banter to see what's wrong.

"Do you think they love us?" Troy asks.

Nina watches the two dogs rubbing their noses against the ground. "Dogs love all humans. It's their default. They also love sniffing butts and eating trash to see what happens."

Carol pulls away from the bush and rubs against Troy's leg as she walks past, as if on cue. "I know they love us as dispensers of food. But some dogs can love individual humans, really love them, like those dogs tackling soldiers returning home from active duty. But I'm asking about these two, here. Do you think they love us?"

They've reached the far side of the public pool in the center of Piedmont Park, which marks the halfway point of their route. She chooses to answer his question with one of her own. "Work is going great, and you look fabulous—so what's wrong?"

"What makes you think something's wrong? Just because I wonder if our dogs have formed a healthy and natural bond with us?"

"Come on, Troy," she says, dropping her voice to a softer, more sober tone than she normally uses when they talk. "You haven't been dialed up to your usual ten these last few weeks and have canceled more times than your Frazzled Gay Card allows. And this morning you seem almost—melancholic." They walk silently for a few seconds, matching Carol and Sid's slow amble.

"I'm nervous," he finally answers. "The one time I told someone, he laughed."

"Well," Nina says, "I can promise you I won't laugh."

"Really?" He looks at her. They have stopped so that Carol can sniff an empty bag of chips. Sid watches her closely, as if waiting for a scouting report.

"Really."

"I want to be a father," Troy says after a quiet moment. "I want to adopt a kid."

Nina reaches out to grab his shoulder. "Why would I ever laugh at that? It's the best idea I've heard all week. All month."

The dogs finish examining the Lay's bag, and everyone begins to move again. "It doesn't make you want to laugh?"

"No," she says. "Not at all." It's true that she would not have thought of Troy as a father if he had not said it, but as soon as he did say it, the idea seemed perfect. How great would it be to have a dad who was funny, loved Top 40 radio and Marvel movies, and made perfect milkshakes and pancakes? She would have loved a dad like that. "And I don't think Trent should have."

"He apologized. Said I caught him by surprise."

She weaves her left arm around his right as they walk back through the entrance to the park. "I'm guessing Trent doesn't want the same thing?"

"No. He doesn't know 'where we'd keep it.'"

"That does sound like Trent."

"But I mean, he didn't want a dog either," Troy continues, turning his head and lowering his voice. "And now he's the one making sure we only buy organic dog food."

The light changes. They cross Piedmont, fighting the flow of people who have just gotten off work. When they reach 12th Street, Nina asks, "Do you think Trent might change his mind?"

"Do I want him to, if that was his first reaction?"

This time Sid is the one who has stopped, so he can carefully investigate a phone pole. Carol wanders over to see what smells so good, and Nina watches Troy watching them.

"It's hard to explain how much it hurt, to have him laugh at that moment."

"I can't imagine," she says. The truth is she can imagine quite well, so well that she wonders if she should tell Troy how a big revelation ended her time with Ben. It could sound like she was trying to change the topic from Troy to her, though—not to mention what she'd say when he asked what her big secret was. "And if he doesn't change his mind?"

"I can accept it, I think," he says, after a short pause. "I mean, it's not like we ever talked about this beforehand. I didn't want kids before. Maybe I'll go back to not wanting kids?"

"But you look sad, thinking about it."

"I'm sad he laughed. And I'm sad that I'm having such a hard time moving past it."

They reach the corner of 12th and Peachtree. Nina steps over to push the crosswalk button, and then turns back to Troy. "Can I get Buddhist on you for a second?"

"Buddhist? Really?"

"I've been reading *Buddhism for Dummies*. So obviously I'm an expert."

"Well, in that case, of course."

"There's a saying—something along the lines of, 'Holding on to anger is like holding a hot coal so you can throw it at someone else; you are the one who gets burned.'" The light changes and they start to walk again. "Or this one: 'Forgive others not because they deserve it, but because you deserve peace.'" As she talks, she watches to see if Sid is listening.

Troy shrugs. "Listen, I can appreciate a good Buddhist line now and then, especially all that stuff about being in the moment, but he loses me with the Runaway Dad thing. Though I fully concede that could be thanks to my own Daddy issues."

"Who among us doesn't have those?"

Troy stops to stare at Carol, who seems to be trying to decide whether or not she wants to lick a damp stain on the ground. "Well, Carol doesn't. How much harder could a baby be?" He holds up a finger before Nina can answer. "And that was rhetorical, friend. Rhetorical."

They cross Crescent, their walk almost over. She's glad that she doesn't have a shift tonight; she can have an early dinner and fall asleep reading *Lord Jim*. "What do you mean, Runaway Dad?"

"You're the one dabbling in Buddhism. You don't know about the family he left behind?"

"No."

"A wife and a son."

They walk in silence for the last half-block. "I didn't know you were a studier of the Buddha," Nina says when they reach her apartment building.

"Just a studier of crappy dads. I mean, once I was old enough to understand not everyone's dad disappeared shortly after birth, I began to look at other cases."

"Like the Buddha."

"Like the Buddha. Talk about living in the moment, right? So in the moment that you forget about the kid who was there, like, the moment before?"

They confirm plans for their next walk and hug goodbye. As Nina watches Troy and Carol fade from sight, she realizes that she hadn't known before today that his father left him at such an early age. Is that one of the reasons they got along so well: disappearing dads? She watches Sid as they head back into the building. Did he really walk away from his child? If so, how has he lived with himself for all these hundreds of years?

28 | Magic Candles

For their next interview Darlene asks to meet at the Rookery, a burger joint in the heart of downtown Macon. Ben walks past a dense cluster of families and senior citizens waiting at the hostess stand, then climbs the dark staircase in the back of the restaurant. Darlene is waiting in the last booth of seats pushed against the wall of the narrow balcony.

"Welcome to my hiding spot, Mr. Davies. And thank you for driving to Macon."

"No problem," Ben says, sitting down. "Though I was surprised you suggested it."

"I have not been back since my mother died in 1998. But there were some things I needed to take care of in person. This seemed like an appropriate spot for our conversation."

As she talks, a waitress places a milkshake in front of Darlene, then turns to Ben. "What can I get you, darling?"

Darlene points to her shake. "This is the Jimmy Carter, which I highly recommend."

"Peanuts?" he guesses.

"Banana ice cream, peanut butter, and, of course, a strip of bacon." She breaks a piece off and holds it up as evidence before popping it into her mouth.

"How can I say no?"

"It's one of the few things in Macon I miss," Darlene says as the waitress walks away.

Ben takes out his digital recorder and holds it up. "Do you mind?"

"Not as long as you don't mind if I start on my shake before yours arrives." She takes a sip, smiles.

"So when did you move away?" Ben asks, hitting record.

"I should have left right after the fire. I wanted to. But my mother was a mess." Darlene picks the bacon up, dips it into the shake, and takes a bite. "She wandered the house sobbing. Fell asleep every night on my brother's unmade bed. My father, meanwhile, left every morning in a rage, determined to find answers that did not exist. Neither one of them could help the other, which was, I believe, the story of their marriage." She shrugs, sighs. "My mother had no one else to turn to, so I stayed."

"For how long?"

"Long enough to work with Willie to put the live record together and to help my mother organize Harlan's things. Then I left."

"Where did you go?"

"I had no destination in mind. I just knew I had to leave Macon." She laughs softly, using her straw to stir her shake. "Made it all the way to Atlanta, where I stopped for a night to stay with a friend. Wound up marrying her roommate and having children. Not quite the dramatic path I had imagined my life taking."

For a moment, they sit there in silence. Ben resists the urge to start asking all the questions he has from listening to that practice tape, reminding himself that sometimes the most important thing to do when interviewing someone is not say anything.

"But that's the end of the Honeybird story," she finally says, leaning back in the booth. "You must have questions about the beginning."

His shake arrives, and Darlene begins to talk before he even asks a question. In a voice just loud enough to be heard over the classic rock blaring through the Rookery, she tells a story about two children born to homes with abusive authority figures (her father and Nate's grandfather). They begin to play music together, these two loners who each suddenly have a friend who understands them. The barn they use as a practice space becomes what they consider their real home. They hang out there, playing music and listening to records—on weekends, after school, and as many days in the summer as they can manage. Harlan doesn't come around as frequently, thanks to his tendency to sleep away most of the afternoon. This gives Darlene and Nate time to create a sanctuary from the terrifying world outside.

Darlene's voice sounds calmer, more at peace, as she shares the story. Her monologue wakes up memories of Ben's own teen years—how isolated he felt, how amazing it would have been to find someone to share that isolation with.

She goes on to describe the night Honeybird recorded the practice tape, the way she felt when Nate played "Don't Go, Darlene." From the first time she heard that chorus, she felt like he was singing to her, and only her. She stops suddenly to address Ben for the first time in almost fifteen minutes. "Are you a religious person, Mr. Davies?"

The question catches him off guard. "No," he says quietly.

She leans forward, examining his face. "I was not either," she says, after a moment of study. "But my years with the band made me realize that religion does not have to involve a church or a temple, or even a God. If being religious means accepting that there are powers and forces we cannot understand, only appreciate, then I became a believer playing music." She sits back again and nods, as if having answered a question she had been silently considering. "The whole band became religious, in the sense that we thought music really would save us. When you first asked if we were worried on the road? As scared as I was at times, I really believed that if we—the three of us in that band—believed we were safe, nothing else would matter."

"And that faith did save you."

"For a while. But Toni warned me," she continues, pushing her empty mug to the side. "She always told me it would not end well."

"So Toni knew about you and Nate, but Harlan didn't?"

"Toni was not one to miss clues. She called Nate out when he came home after our first kiss. She knew he'd been doing something with someone." She starts playing with her napkin as she speaks, folding it into a series of smaller and smaller triangles. "My brother, though, was never one to see the forest when there were pretty trees to look at. He was thinking about music and girls and weed, and not always in that order."

"He never wondered what the two of you did with all that time alone?"

"To be honest, I just don't think it ever occurred to him. Harlan would have sooner believed aliens had landed than accept that Nate and I were a couple. I was forever his little sister, ten years old and struggling to keep up with him."

"So when that practice tape was recorded, he didn't know you were a couple?"

"No. But if we'd kept recording, you would have heard for yourself how he reacted to finding out."

Ben thinks back to the end of the recording. "So after you and Nate turned the tape machine off, Harlan walked in on you?"

"Yes." She places the now triangle-shaped napkin in the center of the table and moves her hands away. "We weren't doing anything untoward, Mr. Davies, I assure you. Just sitting side by side on the piano bench, talking."

"And that was enough?"

Staring at her hands, Darlene nods. "I have this memory of laughing just as Harlan walked in. The kind of laugh you share with a romantic partner—the result of an inside joke, perhaps, or some flirty comment of Nate's. My brother saw me with this super happy grin, eyes locked on Nate's face, and I could tell he figured it out."

"Whoa," Ben says. "How did you feel, when that happened?"

"In those first moments? Relieved. I don't think I understood until then just how hard it had been to carry that secret around. How heavy a weight."

"How did you think Harlan would react?"

She returns to fidgeting with the napkin. "He always said he'd have to approve of any of my boyfriends, but he loved Nate like a brother. And now I loved Nate. I thought it would all work out perfectly." She shakes her head. "I was so young. I can see that now."

"So he didn't approve?"

Darlene closes her eyes. "I can still see him standing there. Bottle of whiskey in one hand, two joints in the other." She exhales slowly and opens her eyes. "And angry. So angry that he looked like our father. I'd never imagined such a thing possible."

Ben tries to imagine a stoned Harlan walking in on his sister and his best friend. His Black best friend. "What did he say?"

"He called us selfish," Darlene continues. "Said we'd get so lovey-dovey that we wouldn't want to practice or anything else. Or we'd break up and that would be the end of the band."

"I mean, things can change when you have a couple in the band. Fleetwood Mac, right?"

Darlene laughs softly. "Does that make me Stevie Nicks? Because I'm not sure that comparison holds, Mr. Davies."

"Well," he says, "it can create tension?"

"It can. But we told him we'd been a couple for a year and things had been fine." She shakes her head. "I thought he'd be reassured, hearing that, but it just made him angrier."

"Because it had been so long?"

"Yes. We kept talking about how long we'd been doing this, thinking it would make him feel better, but he just kept getting angrier. And he had a point: if anyone found out, getting booked into clubs in the South would be the least of our worries."

After a moment, Ben phrases his next question carefully. "Was Nate's race a problem for Harlan?"

"I don't want to say it," Darlene says in a slower cadence. "But I have always thought that if Nate had been white, Harlan would not have been so angry." She pauses, sits upright. "I think Nate's friendship was one of the great joys of his life. But when it came to a Black man dating his sister? I think it bothered him. And I think it bothered him that it bothered him."

Ben can see how hard this is for Darlene to relive, but he needs to hear the rest of the story. "And the fire was that night?"

"That night."

"Did you guys have a chance to work things out?"

"No. Harlan stormed out. His last words to me were an ultimatum: Nate and I needed to decide if we wanted to fuck each other or play in the band with each other. After he left, I ran to see if Toni was still up, so I could tell her what had happened. Nate followed me."

Ben pauses, working the logistics out in his head. "But if the fire is that night, how did the tape—"

"Nate took it, on our way out. He was angry at Harlan—those two, always more alike than they wanted to admit. Stomping around Toni's room saying he would quit the band if he had to. That if that was the choice, he'd quit the band." She pauses, shakes her head. "At some point he threw the reel-to-reel on Toni's bed, and said that 'Don't Go' would be the first song in our new band."

"Would you guys have done that? Left the band?"

She shrugs. "I don't know, but I really didn't think it would come to that. I thought Harlan just needed time. Time to understand that Nate and I were the same people, that we were all the same family we had become." She shrugs. "So I told Nate he had to go find Harlan and check on him. I thought if we both went it would just make Harlan angrier, but hoped that if it was just the two of them they could remember everything they had been through together. The son of a failed politician who ran on fueling white anger, and the great-grandson of a slave, making something new, together?"

Ben has never thought of the friendship in these stark terms, but she's right.

"On his way out the door, Nate said he wished Harlan had never learned the truth, that we had just denied everything. That as painful as it was to keep everything a secret, telling the truth was worse." Darlene leans back in the booth, looking much older than when she had started telling her story. "And that's the last thing he said to me. Less than two hours later the barn was on fire."

Their booth grows quiet. In the distance, Mick Jagger mourns "Angie" over the restaurant's PA. "So," he continues softly, "how did they wind up back in the barn?"

Darlene shrugs. "No one knows. Maybe Harlan went back there, and that's where Nate found him. Or maybe they went out there together."

"You think they talked it out?"

Just as he asks the question the waitress shows up with the check, dropping it on the table without even making eye contact.

"The answer to that depends on my mood," Darlene says. "On my darkest days, I see the two of them getting in some horrific fight. A fight I have caused. Then someone knocks over a lamp, starts a fire."

"A lamp? Like one of those old gas lanterns?"

Darlene nods. "We kept blowing fuses in the barn. Harlan set up half a dozen of those old lanterns so we could unplug everything but our amps and the PA. Made for a better mood, too. We called them our 'magic candles.' We kept saying that was what we'd call the next album."

"Good album name."

"If those two got in some ridiculous fight, they could have knocked one over. And if they were too busy fighting and didn't notice, that barn would go up in minutes."

"What do you imagine if you're in a better mood?"

She smiles. "In a better mood? Then I imagine that they smoked a joint and calmed down. Started listening to music. Then one of them dropped the joint, or left it burning when they fell asleep." Darlene pauses, shrugs. "Of course, even in that version they still wind up burning to death. That's the one part of the story I can't change."

Ben pauses. "Do you agree with Nate, then? Do you wish you guys had managed to keep your secret?"

"I'm not convinced Nate really believed that. I think he said it because he was angry and frustrated."

They have been here a long time, and he hasn't even asked about the songwriting yet. "I know that you must be tired. And I hate to ask for more of your time, but—"

"The songs, the songs."

"Yes," he says, nodding. "The songs."

She picks up her handbag. "Can we talk about the songs as we walk around the block? I need to move my legs before getting back in the car."

29 | Dog Dreams and Human Dreams

It's late afternoon by the time they get back from their walk with Troy. Sid sits by his bowl patiently, watching Nina go the pantry for his food, almost like a regular dog. Regular dogs get more excited about the miracle of another meal, though, and don't ask about their owner's love life. "So when do I get to meet Howard?"

"Oh, I don't think that ever needs to happen."

"Why not?"

"Do you remember how it worked out with the last boyfriend of mine you met?"

"So he's your boyfriend?"

She picks up his bowl and carries it over to the pantry. "I am not ready to use that term," she says, opening the door and reaching into the dog food bag for the scoop she leaves there. "I may never use that term again."

"Why not?"

She fills his bowl, closes the pantry door, and turns to look at him. "Because I have conversations with my dog—who was the Buddha in a past life. Which is either proof of reincarnation, among other miracles, or--" She stops and puts the bowl down in front of him.

"Or?"

"Or proof I am losing my mind. As the daughter of someone who may have intentionally driven his car off the road, to his death, that seems like a definite possibility."

He sniffs his food. "Thank you for feeding me," he says, before he leans down to take his first bite.

As unnerving as it is to wonder if she is losing her mind, it is nice to have a dog that thanks her for each meal. "You're welcome." She walks over to the sink to wash her hands so that she can start on her dinner. "Did you ever give Denise dating advice?"

"I never had anything to say to Denise. And the only boyfriend I met was Roland."

"He's the one who gave you to Denise?"

"Yes. He found me in the pound. He didn't look long—I think he just took the first small black dog he could find."

She turns around and leans against the sink as she dries her hands. "Roland went to the pound? That's a sweeter move than I expected from him." Sid returns to eating, and she heads over to the fridge to inventory her leftovers. "What was life in the pound like?"

He chews for several long moments before answering. "It was a good test for my meditative skills. And that is all I will say on the matter."

Nina spots some carrots, half an onion, and some chicken broth. Soup. She can pour it over leftover rice. By the time she gathers her ingredients, Sid has finished his dinner and sits by the side of his bowl, his tongue looking for stray bits of food in the hair around his mouth. "Is what Troy said true?" she asks, taking out the cutting board and clearing an area of the counter for prep. "About your family?"

"I have been a part of many families." He moves to his water bowl.

She begins to slice the carrots carefully. "Siddhartha had a son. How could you just leave him?"

At first, he does not answer; the only sounds in the kitchen are her chopping and the gentle lap of water. Nina does not look at him as she waits for her answer. Finally he says, "Did Siddhartha Gautama have to separate from his family when he left on his journey? Yes."

"You're talking as if it was someone else. But it was you."

"I was in that body, yes."

"So it was you?"

"My soul is mine."

She looks over her shoulder. He is on the edge of the carpet, watching her. "So why did you leave them?"

"It was a long time ago."

"That's not an answer."

"I didn't say it was."

She turns to face him. "Were you always like this when asked a question? Maybe your wife threw you out."

"Your question is imperfect."

"Meaning?"

"You make it sound as though I had a choice. I did not have a choice. There were things I needed to do. To do them meant leaving my family behind."

"You say it so casually."

"That does not mean it was easy."

"Why couldn't they come along while you searched for enlightenment?"

"I knew that I had to be alone for my search."

Nina turns her attention back to the onion on the cutting board. "How could you—how could he—do that?"

"Suffering is universal. Ending suffering would be a universal good for everyone, including the boy."

She looks over her shoulder again. "So increasing your son's suffering was worth it in order to end his suffering?"

He tilts his head at an angle. "People cause their own suffering when they want things they cannot have."

"But he could have had you."

"How could he, when I had my own journey to make?"

"But your son also had a journey." She takes two steps toward him, wondering why he does not seem to understand how important this is to her. "One that may have been more fulfilling if you were around."

"His journey was his own."

Nina remembers a quote, maybe from that Buddhism book? Or was it in an episode of Black Mirror? She finishes cutting the onion and turns the fire on under the pan. "Did you really say, 'If you meet your father, kill your father'?"

"I have said lots of things. What I cannot control is what people hear."

"Were you trying to justify your absence by saying fathers were unimportant?"

"Is that what you think the line means?"

"It's one of the meanings," she says. "I mean, I don't think you meant to literally kill. But that we must move on from our parents and their ideas of who we are, to be our own selves."

"We are always moving. We should keep our mind, and thoughts, with us, in the present."

She pauses, wondering where to take the conversation next. "How much do you remember about the night you left?"

"I have lived many, many lives. I do not remember all the details of each life."

"But leaving a child behind?" Her voice is rising, even as she tries to contain it. "That would be more than a detail, yes?"

"Why are you so angry about something that happened hundreds of years ago?"

"Why do you think?"

He stares at her silently for a moment. "The loss of your own father has nothing to do with these events."

"I am not sure about that." Nina drizzles olive oil into the skillet. "The Buddha can understand a lot, but I don't think you can understand what it's like to have your father choose to leave your life." She watches the oil, waiting for it to dance in the pan. "Maybe this is why you are here," she continues when the oil starts to come to life. "Maybe this is some sort of penance."

"Penance for what?"

"For abandoning your family?" Nina slides the onions into the pan. There are few things more satisfying than the sound of that sizzle.

"Even if I was worthy of penance—a condition I am not saying I agree with—who would be in charge of such assignments?"

"Maybe whoever keeps putting your soul into new bodies." She stirs the onions. "Have you interacted with other people whose fathers are missing, for one reason or another? Maybe that's the common thread between your various reincarnations."

"I cannot remember all of my bodies."

"So it's possible."

"Of course it is possible. But how many people do you know who also fit that description?"

Nina is trying to remember what Denise's relationship was with her father. The boyfriend who gave her Sid was old enough to be her father; maybe that was a clue. The onions are beginning to glisten, so she slides the carrots in. "What about Troy's question about Carol? Does she love him?"

"Do you really think I have conversations with a dog?"

She has to laugh at that. After adjusting the flame, she wipes her hands on the dishtowel and turns back to Sid. "No, that would be crazy."

"But love is not what you say. Love is what you do."

"So Carol shows her love by her actions?"

"I cannot speak for Carol."

She turns around to stir the vegetables, enjoying the way the colors become more intense as they caramelize. "Okay, so speak for yourself. Leaving your family—what does that show?"

"Not all actions are intended to deliver a message to others."

Nina opens the refrigerator to look for the stock and the rice. "Convenient. We never need to be held accountable for our actions, then."

"We hold ourselves to account. You want me to feel my current life is a punishment, but I do not feel this. If that is true, I accept it: I am responsible for my own actions. As you are responsible for your actions, and for your inaction."

She closes the fridge and turns around. "My inaction?"

"You need to stop waiting."

"Waiting? For what?"

"More like for whom. For your father. For Ben. For anyone else."

She shakes her head. "You think I am just waiting for them?"

"Wanting. Waiting. Is there a difference?" He turns and begins to walk over to the sliding glass doors. "You have just begun to find your own path. It is not time to turn around."

Nina walks back to the stovetop. Conversations always seem to end on Sid's terms, not hers. She doesn't know what she expected him to say; all she knows is that he did not say it.

They don't talk the rest of the night, not even before or after the final walk. Later she lays in bed, unable to sleep, unsure if she is angry or disappointed. Not only did he abandon a child, but even now, hundreds of years later, he is unable to admit that what he did was wrong.

Shifting from side to side, unable to sleep, she feels like she is fourteen again, the sound of a slamming door still echoing in her room, the closing punctuation mark to some argument with her mother or grandmother. Or both. Nothing felt more unjust to Teen Nina than having the two older women in the house unite to work against her wishes.

She wonders if Sid is asleep or just pretending. Can dogs pretend to sleep, even when they are inhabited by the Buddha? Which part of him wins at night—does he dream dog dreams or human dreams? Or do the fragments of two thousand years drift through all of his dreams?

30 | Mr. Invisible

Ben steps outside and blinks slowly. After the poorly lit balcony of the Rookery, the sun and heat seem especially oppressive. Darlene turns to her right, and he follows her down Cherry Street.

They walk in a comfortable silence, but Ben knows he needs to get her talking again. He decides to take the most direct approach. "So," he starts, turning on the tape recorder in his hand, "did Nate ever get mad about the songs?"

"I know how it looks," she says, shifting the shoulder straps of her bag. "Fifty years later I see how bad it looks. But you have to understand, when we first started it was just us, playing Otis Redding songs and smoking weed. Making our own private world." They reach the end of the block. Darlene stares into the distance before turning right. "Then one day Nate started banging on the piano while we were waiting for Harlan. God, the hours we spent waiting for my brother to get out of bed or have one last joint." She stops and gently presses her left hand on Ben's arm. "I didn't know the piano was even in tune, didn't know he could play at all, never mind so beautifully. It was like—like watching Clark Kent rip off his shirt, his secret powers revealed." She releases his arm, and they start walking again.

"He never told you guys he played piano?"

"No. Of course, we never asked. Why would we? We thought we knew everything there was to know about Nate. He and Harlan had been hanging out for as long as I could remember. Nate's grandfather did odd jobs for our father, and the boys quickly grew tight."

"Was it easier for them to be friends when they were younger?"

"Yes. The older they got the harder it was for Daddy. He couldn't write it off to Harlan just being young and not knowing what he was doing. And it was much harder to have a Black teenager in his house than a young Black boy. So the two of them started hanging out more in the barn. Easier to escape Daddy. Easier to smoke weed. They moved the record player out there, and Harlan's amp. Then one day there was a drum set. I don't think Nate had ever played drums before, but it didn't take him long to figure it out."

It's early evening now. The sidewalk is crowded with that odd mixture of people who head out for early dinners—senior citizens, people with young kids—and men and women in business attire, just leaving work. "How did the songwriting work?"

"At first, it was just Nate playing some different chord patterns on the piano. The three of us sort of mixed and matched. We put a sequence together, then started banging out ideas for our parts, trying to remember what we'd come up with."

"Did Nate have lyrics, too?"

She shakes her head. "Once we had the music all worked out enough that it felt like a song, that first time, Nate and Harlan dared each other to go home and write some words."

"And Nate's were better?"

"Nate's were done, so yeah, they were much better." Darlene laughs. "Harlan smoked a joint and fell asleep in the barn without writing a word. I think he knew Nate would come through. The next day he showed up with the words for 'Mr. Invisible.'"

"Were the other songs written the same way? Just general chords, and then—"

"We tried it that way again, but none of them worked as well," Darlene says. "Then Nate started sitting down at the piano and running things through for Harlan and me. Just the way you hear on that tape."

The sequence of events sounds believable to Ben. And yet. "But didn't Nate want to get writing credit?"

"Credit from whom, Mr. Davies? When all this happened it was just the three of us playing in the barn. And even when we started playing gigs, the crowds at the first few were very small. It wasn't like people were asking Harlan about chord structure or the meaning behind 'his' lyrics. We were just happy they were enjoying it."

"When was the first time the issue did come up?"

"When we signed a contract. I mean, I'm sure Harlan had received a few compliments about 'his' songwriting by then. He was growing more—confident, I guess, is the word—in accepting those compliments." She stops in front of a bench. "My car is here. Shall we sit for a few minutes? I will have to go soon. I want to start driving before it gets dark."

"Of course," he says, holding an arm out to help steady her as she sits.

Once settled, Darlene begins to talk in the same even tone she'd used during her monologue in the Rookery. This time she talks about Nate. He needed to escape a grandfather with a well-grounded fear of what Southern society would do to a young Black man with a defiant streak and strong arms, a fear so intense that the grandfather decided he had to break that defiance. When Nate found his place in the band, behind the drums, he was so happy that he did not care, at least at first, about getting credit. "Then

Willie came along and put us in a studio before we even signed a contract. None of us knew anything about making records. We just assumed it would all work out. When the record was done, we got handed something to sign."

"Did anyone look it over for you?"

"Daddy. He didn't understand rock bands, but he sure knew about contracts. Daddy made sure the songwriting royalties went to Harlan, but we didn't know since we never made any royalties. We thought we had credited it fairly, more or less, on the record."

"'Songs by Honeybird'?"

"'Songs by Honeybird.' We meant the three of us, but everyone just assumed that Harlan was the writer, since he was the singer and the guitarist."

"And the white male?"

"And the white male." She sighs. "It wasn't until the live record that Harlan alone was listed as the songwriter."

"Was that the label's idea?"

"No, Daddy's. He was executor. He insisted on Harlan getting full songwriting credit so he could squeeze out every dime. I didn't fight him. I put that album together for the three of us. It was when we'd all been our best, and I desperately needed it to exist. But then it started to do well, and that led to people talking about Harlan's songs more than they ever had before."

"Well," he says, trying to decide how hard he can push her on this point, "there were a few reviews of the first albums in the South, especially in some of the underground papers. And a few of those singled out Harlan's songwriting."

"Yes, but remember this was before news from all over the world showed up on your phone. A lot of those we never knew about, and the articles we did see, we didn't talk about in much detail. We'd just pronounce the writer brilliant or full of shit, then move on."

"But those were Nate's songs." He pauses, but she doesn't respond. "And in the first article I ever read about the band, Harlan was asked about the way he wrote songs—and answered like he was the one who wrote all the songs."

She is staring down at her hands. "I loved them both, Mr. Davies. And I watched for years as my brother struggled to escape the shadow of our father, trying to find his own way. I could see how he never thought he was good enough—until the band." She turns to face him. "I saw him beginning to believe the story, to believe the songs were his. And maybe he had to believe that to sing them the way he did."

Ben wants to challenge that answer, because many people perform songs well without taking credit that is not theirs. At the same time, he is trying to understand how hard it must have been for her to find a way to do the right thing for both of the men she loved. "How did Nate feel about all this?"

"Frustrated." She looks away again, staring at some point off in the distance. "He was proud of those songs and angry that he was not getting credit. He was also very aware of how much he could and could not ask for from the world. Of how he could be denied things, even if they were his." She exhales. "So we let people talk about Harlan's songs, let Harlan talk about how he wrote his songs, and pretended it wasn't a lie. A lie that I blamed the record company for, and Harlan for, and even Nate for going along with it—but then I understood that the only person whose actions I could have controlled, the only person who I could have made stand up for the truth, was me."

"So why didn't you say anything?"

"I was afraid, of course," she says quietly, still looking down.

"What's the worst that would have happened, if people found out that Nate wrote the songs?"

"So many bad things could have happened after that. That's what made it so terrifying. If I stood up for Nate, would people wonder why I was so concerned with him getting credit? Would I run the risk of revealing to Harlan, to everyone else, just how close Nate and I were? My father would not have stood for that, as you well know. And even if I was able to still keep that part of the story secret, would Daddy have made us break up the band? It was one thing to have Nate in the band, as 'just the drummer,' but for Hank Honeybird's son to sing songs written by a Black man?" She turns back to Ben. "Or would Harlan have taken out his own embarrassment on Nate?"

Imagining everything from the perspective of a nervous nineteen-year-old, Ben could see how all those fears could be overwhelming. "And, to be fair, something else I need to remember is how young you were. All of you."

"At the time I could not imagine ever being any older, but yes, I can see now how young we all were. That is not an excuse, of course. Just part of the explanation." Still looking at Ben, she narrows her eyes slightly. "To be honest, I also thought anyone who really listened to the words would figure it out. Harlan sang them well, don't get me wrong. But it was obvious to me that those were Nate's words. It's one of the reasons I was uneasy at our first meeting. I was sure you knew, and I would have to explain."

"I missed it," Ben says, shaking his head. It's still hard to believe how completely he had misunderstood the lyrics he had been so proud of interpreting. "The clues were there. Songs about being trapped, songs about wishing he was invisible, songs about not having control. But I had a story in my head, and could make the songs fit that story."

They sit in silence for a moment. The shadows of the evening have grown longer. Ben wonders how Darlene has lived with everything that happened for so long.

Darlene checks her watch, then turns to Ben. "Foxy tells me you're gonna use some of his pictures."

"Lots of them, I hope," Ben says.

"He also says," she continues, "that if you manage to turn all this into a book, a real book that gets into stores and not just something that sits on the shelf of your office, that it could lead to the albums being reissued."

"It wouldn't surprise me."

"I would like that," she says. "I have been keeping the tapes with me, all these years. It would be nice to do something with them. And it would be nice to finally give Nate the credit he deserves."

"'Songs by Nate Williams'?"

"'Songs by Nate Williams.'" She flexes her fingers, and then rubs her hands together. "I confess, I was only going to tell you enough to have a few quotes for the book. You know, as a favor to Foxy. But then I wondered if I could use this project as an excuse for Toni to meet you, to come see me. And she did, on the condition that anyone who writes about the band agrees to tell the whole story."

"Which explains why I got to hear the practice tape. But," he adds quietly, "you could have edited the recording."

"You mean stopped it before Nate and I gave ourselves away? That would not have been the full story." Her voice catches. She clears her throat, continues. "Toni thought it important for people to know her brother had been loved. She wants everything to finally come out, and so do I." She stops fidgeting with her hands and reaches out to touch Ben's shoulder. "But you have stopped asking about his body. I did expect you to be more determined."

He tilts his head and studies her face before responding. Is she teasing him? Or is Nate going to walk out from behind a tree and introduce himself? "Okay, then I'll ask again. How can you be so sure that Nate is dead, even though they never found his body?"

She pulls her hand away from his shoulder, places it back into her lap. "Because they did find his body."

"They did?" Nate dying in the fire with Harlan had always been the most likely scenario. So why does Ben feel so sad to have it confirmed?

"They did."

"When?"

"Not long after they found Harlan's."

"I mean—when did you find out?"

"As soon as it happened. I believe my father's words were, 'Found the bastard.'"

Ben sits up straighter, any stirrings of grief erased by anger. "So you've known this whole time, and didn't say anything?" A man walks by talking loudly on his cellphone, loosening his tie with his free hand. Ben stares straight ahead, wondering how someone can carry a secret like that around for so long. "Who else knew?" he asks, turning back to her.

"Just a handful of the local firefighters who were going through the rubble." She closes her eyes and continues. "I stood out there through the night as they searched, hoping Harlan and Nate would emerge out of the ashes, somehow. From some hidden bunker, or hole in the ground." She opens her eyes. "If I had not been there, I have no doubt my father would never have told me about Nate."

"Why didn't he want people to know Nate's body had also been found?"

"Oh, Mr. Davies." She smiles for the first time in a while. "Don't historians need to be able to think like the people they are studying?"

She's right. As soon as he dares to imagine being Hank Honeybird the answer is obvious. "As long as there was a chance Nate was alive, your father had a scapegoat."

"Yes. And a way to deny Nate's grandparents the chance to mourn, to bury their grandson."

"So the firefighters didn't say anything?"

"They were all local, people who'd known Daddy for years. When Hank Honeybird told them to make it look like the body had never been found, that's just what they did. I suspect it was not the first time they had kept quiet about something for my father."

That sounds believable to Ben. Hank Honeybird may never have become a senator, but he remained an influential figure in Macon until his death. "And you never said anything?"

"No, and I am aware that people will have questions about that. 'She said she loved them both—how could she do that to Nate, to his family? To his sister, who was supposed to be her best friend?'" She sighs. "And the answer will make them mad: money."

"Money?" Ben's too surprised at the answer to be angry.

"My father threatened to cut me out of his will if I said anything. At that point I was planning to leave Macon as soon as Harlan's funeral was over and never go back, so I didn't care about the Honeybird biscuit fortune." She pauses, shakes her head. "It is more than a little funny, isn't it? A man who worked so hard to be remembered as tough is most famous for his fluffy biscuits."

"History really is ironic. We keep saying it because it's true."

"But then I thought about Toni, and their grandparents, and how they would need money. I couldn't help them if I got disowned. So I decided to go along with his demands." She shifts on the bench. "Understand, I did not think I would have to keep the secret for long. I thought we would get through Harlan's funeral and then everyone would assume Nate was dead, too. But my father worked hard to keep alive this idea that Nate was out there, and that he must have had something to hide, since he ran away."

"Was it hard to talk to Toni without telling her?"

"Of course. But I'd lost my brother and my boyfriend. I couldn't lose my best friend, too. I knew how angry she would be, and I couldn't risk it." She turns his way, a determined look in her eyes. "So I focused on helping Nate's family as much as I could. I thought of that last Honeybird show, the one we'd recorded, and how if it even sold a few hundred copies that would be more money?"

"And it sold a lot more than that."

"I had no idea that would happen."

"It must have been satisfying, on the one hand? To have some validation?"

"Of course," she says. "But also so sad, that Nate and Harlan were not there to see it."

"And all the songwriting royalties went to Harlan's estate, so you had to keep the secret about Nate to get your share?"

"Yes—a share I gave to Toni. She had stopped talking to me by then, so I was afraid she would return the checks, but she didn't."

"Why did she stop talking to you?"

"Remember, nothing gets past Toni. She became convinced that my father knew what had happened to Nate, and she wanted me to ask him. She even began to demand that I arrange for the two of us to talk to him."

"And you didn't want to risk that."

"I couldn't. Of course, keeping the secret cost me her friendship, anyway."

"How long was it before you guys talked again?"

Darlene sighs. "Years. Even then it was a slow thaw. Christmas cards, birthday cards, and then finally emails."

Ben wonders what would have happened if it had not been for the fire. Would the band have kept making music? Could Darlene and Nate have somehow overcome the daunting odds to stay together? "What did Toni say when she found out?"

Darlene seems to wince. "I'll let you know when it happens."

"You never told her?"

"I was afraid that if I told her while Daddy was alive, she would go demand to know where Nate's body went. And then Daddy would know she knew, and I'd never have any money to send her. I just thought that when he died, it would be easier."

"And after your father died?"

She shakes her head, stretches. "That stubborn old man lived so long. Much longer than Mama, who never did recover after the fire. By then I was married, divorced, and had a teenage daughter of my own. Toni and I had moved from emails to phone calls, and I did not want to risk losing her again. So I thought, I thought maybe we could just let this secret stay buried."

As hard as it is for him to imagine keeping this a secret for so long, Ben has to concede that each choice probably made sense at the time. "So why dig it up now?"

"A secret like that, Mr. Davies, does more than eat you alive. I feel like these secrets have been conducting experiments on me for fifty years. And it has to stop."

She stands up and Ben knows that the interview is over. He will not see Darlene Honeybird again. "Thank you for trusting me," he says.

"Maybe I needed to tell a stranger, in order to be able to say the words out loud," she says, slowly heading toward her car. "But the truth is out now. And I feel some peace, now, knowing that."

He follows, carrying her bag. After she opens the door he holds it open for her and hands her the bag, which she bends down to lay on the passenger seat. Standing back up, car keys in hand, she looks to her left, to her right, then smiles. "I enjoyed that shake," she says.

"So did I."

"Good." She nods to herself, as if answering a question only she heard. "I do not think I will be coming back to Macon, though," she says. With what looks like a great deal of effort she slowly sits down in the car seat, slips the keys in the ignition. "No. I will not be back."

31 | New Garb Disposle

The semester is almost over when Nina has one of those truly awful waitressing shifts. It's the kind of night where it feels like the customers are collaborating against her, each table choosing to display a different example of Worst Customer Behavior. The last two-top refuses to leave until the lights are turned on to Obnoxious Setting, so it's almost midnight by the time she makes it back to B-6.

The apartment feels especially empty as Nina steps inside, and at first she blames it on Ben. His absence hits her hardest on Saturday nights, since he was usually waiting for her to get home from work, delicious take-out and funny stories ready to go. After she puts down her phone and keys and glances around the apartment, though, she does not see Sid. While he has never been the "Run to say hello" dog, the kind of dog that acted as though the miracle of your return would cause him to explode with excitement, he could always be found on the futon or stretched out in front of the sliding glass doors. And he is in neither place.

She calls his name casually, not panicked. Not even nervous. One minute passes. Then two. Nina tells herself that Sid is just hanging out in a new spot, and she is not seeing him where he is. Not seeing someone where they are? Maybe she has become a Buddhist, after all.

She's surprised at how many possible hiding spots she finds for a fifteen-pound dog once she starts looking. Under the bed, of course, where she finds no dog but several items she did not even know had gone missing: one black glove, one slotted spoon, and two T-shirts, so dirty that she leaves them where they are. There's also enough space between the bookshelf and the wall for Sid to hide in if he curled into a tight ball, but he is not there, either. She even looks in the bathroom, a room she can't remember ever seeing him enter.

He has not crawled into the shower.

Nina returns to the living room and stands completely still. It occurs to her that she has never been in this apartment alone. Sid was here when she moved in with Denise, and has been in the apartment with her ever since. Maybe that is why she is not more worried; it is impossible to imagine that he is not here, somewhere.

She knows she has moved far beyond the grasping at straws stage when she starts opening the doors under the kitchen sink. No Sid, but a clue: a piece of the pipe under the sink is newly-installed shiny. She stands up and sees a yellow post-it note on the sink faucet, with a barely legible message: "New Garb Disposle!"

Morris. After asking him for almost two years, Nina finally has a new garbage disposal. And whatever pretty boy he sent to do the job probably left the fucking door open. That would explain how Sid could have wandered out, but why would he?

She looks at the clock on the microwave: 11:57. Was Morris still awake? There's an after-hours phone number she's never used, and she pulls it up on her phone without hitting the call button. Instead she decides to walk the floor first—how far could he have gone? Maybe he wandered out and when he came back, the door was closed. Maybe he's waiting somewhere safe for her to come home. The way a child would, if taught properly.

Nina steps out in the hall, leaving the front door ajar. Not an ideal thing to do, she knows, hearing her mother's indignant shock at the idea of essentially inviting the world to come and steal all of her stuff, but if Sid is out there wandering around, she wants him to be able to get back inside.

A walk up and down the hallway of her floor reveals no traces. He isn't just hiding in the stairwell. She checks the second and third floors and even the basement—maybe he wanted to go to the floor with the least amount of people? She looks between washers and dryers and then dashes back to her apartment.

The door is not open any wider than it had been when she left on her search, so she knows Sid has not pushed his way in. The room feels so different without him. Can air be changed by someone's absence?

Nina calls Morris. He picks up after the first ring, and starts talking excitedly about the new garbage disposal. When she cuts him off to ask about the dog, his tone changes.

"I swear, darling. I didn't see your doggie. I wouldn't let no doggie out." Shuffling sounds. "Tommy Tom, did you see a doggie when you put in the disposal?" Mumbling, and then Morris is back on the phone to confirm that no, no one saw no doggie when they put in the disposal.

Her chest fills with a tense, cold panic. So Sid snuck out quietly to avoid being seen? Since she asked Sid about the family he abandoned he has seemed quieter than usual. Did she destroy another relationship by saying something she should not have?

She decides to start another floor-by-floor search. She bumps into a male couple leaning against the door of D-14, unable to keep their hands off each other. There must be a panicked look in her eyes, because the men stop fumbling with their keys to ask what's wrong. She's surprised that they seem to know her and Sid, and even ask what happened to the cute guy they used to see her with—but they have not seen Sid.

She begins to imagine her search as it would be depicted in a foreign film. Fellow apartment dwellers, who have been carving out existences in isolation from each other, brought together by the hunt for a young tenant's lost dog. Of course, if it's a French movie, there's no guarantee they will find the dog, dead or alive. Perhaps just a final, distant, fuzzy, shot of what could be her dog—or not—walking down a city street, alone, as the credits roll. The American remake will give her a gun and a hunky male co-star, and make sure there is a happy ending.

Thirty minutes later, Nina's back in the apartment. Still no Sid. She feels like she needs to call someone for help. It should be Connie, who usually is still awake at this hour and loves to take control in a crisis. She's due in a few weeks, though, and has been complaining about falling asleep by nine every night. Troy would step up if Nina ever needed him to; she still remembers how quickly he made it to her place when she called him the day Ben broke up with her. But Troy has his own domestic drama to deal with.

Ben would have been an excellent choice to call. And if he'd been waiting for her to get home from work, either here or in their new apartment, Sid never would have gotten out. That means she has one more thing to blame Ben for.

Her mother? Her mother wants to be the one Nina will call, but having her come over to help look right now would just add to the stress.

12:39.

That means there's only one name on the list, but it's a name that should not really be on the list. It's too early in their relationship to call Howard in a time of crisis. And didn't she just mentally mock American culture, writing the movie of this crisis in a way that made her heroine call a man for help? She compromises by sending a text, which is a much less overt and intrusive way of reaching out for help. He would have set his notifications to silent if he'd gone to sleep, right?

so my dog is missing

Howard calls immediately. "What do you mean, missing?"

"I mean, I came home, and he's gone."

"Couldn't he be hiding somewhere? Animals do that, right?"

"If you'd seen my apartment, you'd know I can look through the whole place in just a few minutes."

"If this weren't such a serious type thing, you know, I'd make a joke about how it's time I come and see your place."

"Thank you for being serious."

"It's one of my middle names."

"One of them?"

"I have seven or eight."

There's a silence, and she notices the background noise on his end of the line. Is he at a party? A game—is there some sort of sports thing happening tonight?

"This is me bantering, to distract you," he says. "Is it working?"

"I shouldn't have called. You have better things to do than worry about my dog."

"Nina."

"Howard."

"I can assure you, seriously, in all seriousness, I want to do whatever I can to help."

He is so good at bantering that she sometimes forgets how sincere he can be, too.

"Like, right now," he continues, "what are you doing?"

She blinks, focuses. "I am standing in the middle of my apartment, wondering what to do."

"Come on, think like a cop show. The first few hours in any missing persons case are crucial. We need whiteboards and bad coffee and dramatic music."

"Not sure my apartment can fit a whiteboard."

"Well, we need to make flyers at least, right?"

"Flyers?"

"Yeah. So we can hang them up. Post them online."

"Right." She tries not to get too optimistic, but it feels better to have a plan. Something to do. "So I need a picture?"

"Maybe two. Like a close-up, and then one that shows his size. I'll be right over and we'll go print these damn things and hang 'em up."

As much as she hoped he would come over, it never occurred to her that he would. "Howard."

"Resistance is futile."

"Thank you."

"Let's find this damn dog."

She hangs up and heads to the table. She has just opened her laptop to look at pictures, grateful to have a task, when her phone rings again. "Change your mind?"

"The time has come to spit it out, Nina. No more secrets. Lyft needs to know where you live."

While she's waiting for Howard to come over, Nina picks the best picture of Sid she can find, and quickly posts it to Facebook and Instagram. She lays out a quick flyer, but when she looks for a 24-hour copy store she realizes that they'll have to drive to get to one. She feels this need to stay close in case Sid is still nearby. That's when she remembers her mother forcing her old color printer on her. By the time Howard buzzes to be let in, she's dragged the printer from the back of the pantry and started making copies.

Howard's focus impresses her. "Night owls," he explains, after she comments on how alert he is. "Always good to have a few of us on call, you know? Because we get shit done while everyone else sleeps."

He insists they go right out to start hanging up flyers with packing tape. They hit as many of the busier intersections as they can. Saturday night means plenty of drunk yuppies around to ooh and ahh over the picture of the cute dog and offer sympathy, but no one has seen Sid. They work for over an hour, and when the flyers are gone Howard suggests they check around the back of the apartment building. When that turns into another dead end, Nina finally says they need to stop for the night.

2:33.

For the first time, Nina is beginning to understand that Sid may be gone for good. Howard follows her in, and after she drops her phone and the packing tape on the table, he makes eye contact. "Sorry," he says. "I was hoping for a midnight miracle."

"Me, too," she says. Howard has gone above and beyond to help, and she suddenly feels the need to play hostess in return. "Want some warm milk?"

"Warm milk?" Eyebrow raise. "Really?"

"Yeah, really. My grandma has a terrible time sleeping, so she used to have a cup every night. And I'd sit with her."

"So I'm grandma in this scenario?"

"Exactly. Can I call you Nana?"

"No." He grins. "No, you can't. But sure, I'll take some warm milk."

"Excellent." She gets a pot and measures out two mugs of milk, just the way her grandmother did. As she warms the milk he asks polite questions about the apartment—how long she has been there, what the neighborhood's like. He's sharing an apartment in Cabbagetown, after two years in the dorms and a stretch of couch-surfing among friends.

"So, I have to ask," she says, carefully pouring the milk between two mugs, "when I called it sounded like there was a party going on. How much did I ruin your night?"

"No party. Just Everett, my sports junkie roomie. You heard ESPN turned up so loud it can be heard from any room in the apartment."

They sit at the kitchen table. Howard breaks an awkward silence by making exaggerated blowing noises on the surface of the milk and taking his first sip. "Ah," he says with a sigh. "There's a taste I haven't had since I was . . . five?"

"Did your grandma do this for you, too?"

"You mean my apoe?"

"Is that what you call her?"

"Yeah. Well, called. She died when I was young."

Nina lets the milk linger at the back of her throat for before swallowing, the way she used to watch her grandmother do. The same way most people assumed she had a dad, especially when she was younger, she has always assumed everyone has a special grandma.

He takes another sip. "So, are you one of those always-had-a-dog people?"

"Not at all. Sid's my first."

"We had a dog when I was a kid. Molly."

"Molly? Please tell me she was a Golden Retriever."

"Border Collie."

"Close enough."

"Man, I loved that dog. Like, me and my brother were always fighting about who Molly loved more, but we all knew it was me."

"Of course." Nina takes her first sip. "And now you're gonna tell me she ran away, but came back?"

"Oh. That would be a good story to tell now, right?"

"It's not the story you're gonna tell?"

"Nah. If I'd thought of it, I would have just made that story up." He shrugs. "Molly lived to be, like, fifteen or something crazy. Fell asleep one night and never woke up."

"Okay." She smiles. "Not the story I was hoping to hear, but still a good story."

"Thanks. It was supposed to be an 'I get what it's like to feel connected to an animal' story."

"Sid is my only one of those stories. I never had an animal before."

"No? Not even a hamster or cat? Goldfish?"

"No. My mother didn't like the idea of caging someone against their will."

Howard laughs. "Really?"

"Really."

"Man. So, I guess, like, visits to the zoo and stuff were out?"

"If we'd ever gone, it would have been to protest."

"Is your Mom still that intense?"

Nina nods. "Can be, yeah."

"Damn. So if and when I meet her, I need to be on my toes?"

"And then some." She's smiling despite how bad she feels every time she looks at the futon and sees Sid is still not there. Maybe it's because she's so happy and sad and tired, all at the same time, that she decides she should not wait until the semester ends to tell Howard how weird she is. He can leave while the leaving is good; it will hurt less to get rejected sooner rather than later.

"The thing is. About this dog." Nina pauses.

"Wait, there is no dog?" His eyes grow wide. "Is this like some trick ending?"

"No, no," she says. "But this dog is different."

"Well, they're all different, right? Snowflakes, people, dogs?"

"Fair point." Inhale, exhale. "I talk to him."

Howard shrugs. "I'd be more worried if you didn't talk to your dog."

She pauses to take a sip of milk, and for a second, almost takes the out that he offers. "I mean, we talk to each other. He talks back."

Howard looks at her closely. "So you talk to each other?"

"Yeah."

"Like—words?"

She nods, and in a flash sees him holding out his hands in surrender and then walking out. "Like words." She studies his face for any sort of reaction, but it remains inexpressive as he takes a slow sip of milk. Her nerves have just about convinced her to try to laugh the whole thing off as a joke when he looks at her and smiles.

"Did he have anything smart to say?"

A wave of relief passes through her chest. He may still think she's crazy, of course, but that is a pretty good follow-up question. "He could be kind of a pain in the ass, to be honest."

Howard shrugs. "I guess if you're gonna have a talking dog, you want him to have some personality, right?"

"Oh, he has it. But, I mean, it's also helpful to talk to him, sometimes." She finishes the rest of her milk, in disbelief that Howard is taking the news this well. Unless he's just humoring her and plotting his escape.

"Well, we need to find him then, so I can meet him."

"I—I mean, I don't know that he'll talk to you."

"Why would he?" Howard says. He finishes his milk and puts his mug down next to hers, so close they almost touch. "He hasn't even met me yet. Need to build up some trust."

She allows herself to make extended eye contact with him for the first time since confessing. "I have to say, I am kind of impressed with your reaction."

"What, you expected me to bolt for the door?"

"Maybe not bolt. Casually stroll?"

"Please." He closes his eyes, yawns. "I hope you have more faith in me than that. You didn't run when I told you I used to think everything was alive, right?"

"Not yet, anyway." She closes her eyes in relief. The motion also makes her aware of just how exhausted she is. "I could fall asleep right in this chair."

"I think I just did." He has his phone in his hand. "And I don't know why a damn Lyft costs so much more at this time of night."

"Tax for scary people who need a lift at 3 a.m.?"

"But where's my harmless Asian discount?"

She smiles again, stretches. "You could just sleep here. In a completely not-yet-graduated, just-hanging-out, totally platonic fashion."

"I should fight you and insist I just go home, but I am so tired." He puts his phone down, yawns, nods. "Yeah. I'm just gonna lay down on that floor, if that's okay with you."

"Of course." She stands up, stretches. "I even have an extra toothbrush."

"Because lots of men sleep on your floor?"

"Ha. No," she says, slowly making her way to the bathroom. "Just a slight obsession with clean teeth and a fondness for using a new toothbrush as soon as the old one feels gunky."

When she gets back to the living room, Howard is pointing at the keyboard in the corner. "So you been holding out on me, Simone?"

"Just a hobby," she says, blushing.

"Um." He turns to her. "So we do open mic on the same night, right?"

"Oh, no, no." She hands him a toothbrush. "The only people who have ever heard me play are my old piano teacher and my dog."

"Then it's time." He moves his right hand toward her, pinky held out. "Pinky promise. We do it together. In May, after finals."

"May? No way." He looks so confident and serious that she finds herself imagining this could be possible. "What if I really suck?"

"Then you better practice." He wiggles the pinky. "Come on. I gotta get you to sign off now, when you're tired and sad and shit."

"Exploiting the grieving dog owner?"

"Damn straight. Distraction in action."

Before she can let herself think about it anymore she completes the pinky promise, then quickly pulls her finger away. He gives a satisfied nod and takes the toothbrush.

By the time she has washed the pot and the cups and taken one last look in the hallway before locking the door, Howard is out of the bathroom and curled up in a ball on the floor—no pillow, no blanket. She pulls an extra comforter from the end of her bed and gently drapes it over him. It's a good sign, she decides, that he can fall asleep so quickly. His mind must be untroubled.

Or he feels safe.

After placing the blanket on him she stares for a few long seconds, trying to figure out if he's really asleep or just pretending. She decides it doesn't matter, that he is at least determined to have her think he's sleeping, so she looks up, yawns, stretches. Then stares at the glass doors leading to the balcony.

The balcony. The one spot she never checked. She couldn't think of any way Sid could get out there without her knowing. Maybe he'd been sleeping when she left for work? She quietly walks over to the glass door, unlocks it, and slides it open. Once she steps outside it only takes a moment to realize that no one is there. No last-minute miracle.

Nina sits down in one of the chairs. A quick scan of her Facebook and Instagram postings reveals a few likes and random comments, but no Sid sightings. She stares at the photo of Sid on her Instagram feed for a few seconds, wondering if there is an answer to be found there. Was he really who he said he was?

"Is" he who he said he was, she corrects herself. No past tense, yet.

She swipes the app closed and opens iMessage. *You awake?*

Her grandmother's response is immediate. *ofc*

What you doing?

not sleeping

Netflix?

british ppl bad teeth makin pies

Hope no soggy bottoms

lol

Nina can see her grandmother, in her favorite chair, watching the TV with the volume down and captions on. *Gma?*

nina?

Was my dad crazy? She hits send, pauses, then adds, *Like really crazy?*

For a few seconds there is no response, and Nina wonders if she has asked one question too many. The dots finally appear, though—then disappear, the answer started then erased, before appearing again.

no but he was troubled noones fault some have a hard time with the world he loved u

Thanks

yw

xo

xo

Nina closes the phone and walks over to the railing of her small balcony, scanning her eyes as far off into the horizon as she can. Lights, people, sound, the ever-expanding universe. Sid is out there somewhere. Is she better off or worse off having found him only to lose him? Now that she knows what the universe is capable of, now that she can imagine new ways the world can amaze and surprise her, how will she navigate it alone?

32 | The Sparrow

I know that it has taken me a long time to get back to you, Mr. Davies, and I am sorry about that. While I have a long list of reasons that have delayed my response, it is also true that for a few days I just did not open your email. I understand that the past is a world you must visit, but for me . . . For me, it is a place that I spend a lot of time avoiding.

[Pause, distant sound of another voice.] He knows I'm recording this instead of typing it, honey. He's not an imbecile. [Distant sound of another voice.] Mr. Davies, Natalie is very concerned that you understand that this recording is in lieu of writing my responses down for you. My arthritis has been bothering me today, and I did not want to keep you waiting any longer.

I should also confess I do not even have your questions in front of me.

[Pause, sound of drinking.] I do remember you asked about our childhood. Funny thing is, I remember more about Nate as a child than I do myself. He was my big brother—not just because he was older than me, but because he always loomed so large in my world. He was always there, towering above me. Even when I grew to within an inch of his height, much to his own disbelief, he still towered above me. He was a presence. A force. I am aware that I am his sister, so you may wonder if my opinion is to be trusted. But I suspect Darlene will tell you the same thing.

I think this is why Darlene and I got along so well, from the moment we met. We both had these big brothers that we loved, these boys so like each other that they seemed as much brothers as friends. Brothers who had both decided they needed to protect their little sisters from the dangers of the world. And I can see my granddaughter scowling at me, as I say this, but today's women are on much more equal footing and thus much more able to take care of themselves than I was in the Macon of the 1950s. I started to go to school in the pre-Brown South, Mr. Davies. It wasn't a different world; it was a different universe.

And one that was slow to change. *Brown* did not change my world instantly, other than making the white people even angrier.

Living in that world is what kept me worried about Nate. Worried about him my whole life. I worried about him not being able to keep quiet when he was supposed to. I worried about him looking at someone in a way he was not supposed to. I worried about him failing high school because he never wanted to go, and then what would he do? I worried about Vietnam, because it sure seemed like a place they'd send Black men to.

He kept saying that there was nothing to worry about, that he knew how to keep his head down, and that was true. It drove Nate crazy, I know, to have to follow the code, but he did it. He did it because he was smart, and even when he was angry he knew what he had to do. But I still worried, about everything. So when he started to hang out with Harlan? I won't lie. I did not trust the Honeybirds. How could I, knowing what my grandmother said about Hank Honeybird? The way she made the sign of the cross any time anyone said his name? To be honest, I only think she let Nate hang out with Harlan because she was too nervous to forbid it. She was afraid of making that family mad.

And because Nate would have done it anyway. When there was something he really wanted to do, he could be as stubborn as a man ever born.

I fully expected it to stop when they got older, too. Young boys of a different color like that, playing? That's one thing. But teenage boys, white and Black, together in Macon, at that time? That was another thing.

When I saw them make music together, I understood. That was the first time I saw Harlan treat Nate as an equal, as if he was his own brother. When Nate told me he was gonna be in a band with the Honeybird boy, I could not imagine it. Could not. I could have sooner imagined he'd had a second head that I'd never seen. I mean, drums? I'd heard him banging on our grandmother's piano, but never for long—soon as he knew someone was listening he'd stop. He told me Harlan bought him a drum set, and I said I needed to know two things about that: What was Harlan gonna expect in return? And when did Nate learn to play the damn drums? Nate said playing the drums made a lot more sense than school ever did, and that Harlan didn't ask for anything, other than Nate not show off too much.

And, good Lord, the idea that Harlan was gonna do the singing? I'd never heard him string together more than two words. One of those white boys who had everything handed to him without ever having to work for anything. How could he be bothered to learn how to play a guitar?

But Nate kept asking me to just come see for myself, kept telling me that they were actually getting good. Then he told me that Harlan's sister was playing bass and that, that I had to see. One of my girlfriends was supposed to come with me, but her parents told her there was no way she was going to that Honeybird house. I told Nate I'd be there so I went, all by myself, no idea what to expect. But the sound, the sound the three of them made? So loud, so confident. Nate never looked happier, and Harlan? Turns out he never said much because his voice was made to sing.

They were playing when I walked in and kept going for another half hour or so. That's when Darlene came over, and we talked for the first time. And now you can understand just how much my life changed, this one day. First time seeing Nate play. First time meeting Darlene, who would become a sister to me. Oh, and yes, first time I smoked pot—don't make that face, Natalie. I know that none of this is really a surprise to you.

I just started showing up at that barn most days after school. I was always good at school, always did well and went every day, even though Nate sure didn't. Those first months they were just doing old blues songs. Or maybe some weird version of a Beatles song. Nate even had them work up on of our grandmother's favorite gospel songs: "I sing because I'm happy, I sing because I'm free."

I was shocked when they said they'd written a song of their own. Must have worked it up while I was at school or work—I had a job by then, mother's helper after school. Always said I wouldn't take care of some rich white woman's kids, but we needed the money, so there it is. Anyway, that song, the one about being invisible. I just couldn't believe it. Kept asking them who really wrote it, and they all just laughed, and we smoked a little, and they played it again, and they kept saying it was them, it was them. "It's our song, Toni."

It wasn't until later that Nate told me he'd written it. And I just wanted to kill him, for not telling me earlier, for not letting me know all that was inside him. But when I asked why they didn't just say that when they were playing it, he said the song belongs to the band now. But I could tell he was proud. "How did that one sound?" he'd ask me every time the band worked up a new song. I mean, how did it sound? Amazing. Each one of those pieces of Nate came out as beautiful jewels. Those songs were pieces of my brother that he'd kept hidden from everyone, maybe even from himself.

And then the record came out, with "Songs by Honeybird" in giant letters. Everyone assumed Harlan Fucking Honeybird shaped those jewels, of course. Had to be the white guy.

Darlene and I were close enough by then for me to get mad at her, to let her know I was angry. How could they do it? How could they keep from telling everyone who wrote the songs? She said that wasn't it. Tried to explain how they each did something to make the songs sound the way they did, but she knew it was bullshit. It wasn't like a lot of people paid attention, especially at first, but that name, in the Southeast, got them some attention. Some interviews. And every time that lie was told that lie grew. That's the only way lies stay alive: because people tell them.

It was our first real fight—our only fight, until the end. I was so mad, so mad that they were all going to play along like that. I had learned to swallow injustice, to breathe it in like air, but having it fed to me by Darlene, my first white friend? It was too much to bear. Nate was the one that calmed me down, of course. Nate said he had never thought anyone else would ever get to hear his songs. Said now that they could be heard, that was enough for him. He said if it was enough for him, it needed to be enough for me. He reminded me that every time the three of them went on the stage in some small club in the South they were making a statement, and he said that would have to be enough for now. Promised that they'd talk more about the songwriting down the road. Down the road.

[Pause, sound of glass being picked up and put down.]

I didn't get mad when I found out about Darlene and Nate, though. I'd been at those practices, in the barn in July and August, watching her watch Nate when he took his shirt off because he got so hot playing. And you know I was worried, more worried than I'd been about anything before: not about the way she looked at him, Mr. Davies, because I had grown to love Darlene—even after the mess with the songs, I still loved her, like a sister, so I knew that she could be good for Nate. No, I was sure worried about people coming in and seeing the way she looked at him. Because her looking at him like that could have gotten him killed. So I was not surprised. I was not angry. I was terrified.

Maybe I should have tried to stop it, before it even started. But he was happy. Happier than I'd ever seen him before. Doesn't mean I didn't try to talk him out of it, didn't ask him what the hell he was thinking. He said he loved her, said they would be safe. He said they knew they'd have to leave Macon, leave the South, but Darlene couldn't do it yet. That the band was keeping her brother alive.

I mean, the irony of that.

So, much as I know it bothered him, I don't think he stayed angry about the songs. He knew he wrote them, Darlene knew, and Harlan knew. And that was all that mattered, because he was young and in love for the first time in his life. I'd tell him I was worried it was gonna get him killed, and he'd tell me he would never be in love like this with anyone else.

Turns out we were both right.

[Background noise, sound of tape being shut off.]

33 | Lost Dogs and Newborn Kittens

When the knocking on the door wakes her up, Nina feels a surge of relief. She imagines that some neighbor has found Sid. When their eyes lock he will give her a slightly annoyed look—annoyed because his adventure ended too quickly, perhaps, or because she didn't prevent him from going on an adventure. And she will be so happy to see him she won't even get annoyed at his annoyed look.

Nina swings her legs off the futon and is surprised when her right foot bumps into Howard's back. How had she managed to forget that he stayed over? Talk about your exciting first nights together. She starts to apologize before realizing that he's slept right through the kick.

First lesson of the day: Howard is a heavy sleeper.

The knocking returns as Nina walks to the front door. She is greeted not by an annoyed Sid, but by an annoyed Connie.

"Again, I remind you," she says, pushing past Nina and into the kitchen. "I am the first call when shit goes down." She turns to face Nina. "The first."

"You're clocking in at 800 pounds and live half an hour away," Nina says. "No offense, but you're not a lot of good in a dog search."

"And that means I have to find out from Instagram? I'm here now, right?"

"You are. And it's so, so early."

"Well, give the demon child credit for that," Connie says, pointing at her belly. "This kid had better start sleeping in once they're here. That's all I can say."

Nina watches as Connie's unbuttoned windbreaker falls open. She is enormous. "How many demon children are you carrying, exactly?"

"Twelve." She exhales. "And they are always moving."

"You didn't have to come out here, you know?"

"Your dog is gone. This is crisis time, right?"

"I didn't think you even liked him," Nina says. "Or dogs in general."

"Oh, I don't. But I know he meant a lot to you." Connie steps forward and hugs her for several long seconds. "But how did this dog get out?" she asks when she leans back. "He never wants to even move, far as I can tell."

"I don't know. I came home and he was gone."

"Out an open window?"

"An open door. I think it was Morris."

"Morris? The guy with the teeth? And by that I mean, without the teeth?"

"The apartment manager, yeah. They came in to do some work yesterday and must have left the door open."

"Oh, Nina. I'm so sorry." She shakes her head. "And I'm also so fucking tired from standing. Why are we still standing?"

As Nina watches Connie turn and head into the living room, she remembers: there's a man on her floor.

"There's a man on your floor," Connie says, just as Nina thinks it.

"Yup."

"Is he a hostage? Do we need to tie him up?"

Nina walks over and stands next to Connie, both of them staring down at Howard. He's curled into a sort of ball on his side, the blanket she gave him half on and half off. She's relieved that he fell asleep with his clothes on. "I'm beginning to think he's just gonna sleep forever, so maybe we don't need to."

Connie looks at her. "This is Howard?"

"This is Howard." Nina leans her head against Connie's shoulder. As the adrenaline rush of waking up wears off, the exhaustion creeps in. And sadness. "He came over last night to help look."

"That is too fucking sweet."

"Yup."

Howard is finally reacting to their voices, and slowly stirs. He rolls onto his back, stretching out the arm he had been using as a pillow.

"He's like a newborn kitten," Connie says, slowly settling into one of the chairs at the dining table.

"Morning, Starshine," Nina says to Howard. He blinks a few times, slowly sitting up. "I hope you enjoyed the finest thin carpeting 60 West 12th Street has to offer."

"Morning." He rubs his face, looks at Nina. "What time is it?"

"It's almost eight."

He nods like that was the answer he was expecting. "And hey, I'm Howard," he says, offering Connie a tired wave.

"You better be. After all the Howard stories I've heard, if there's another man on her floor she has a lot of explaining to do."

Howard stands up, stretches. "Howard stories?"

"Mostly good, don't worry," Connie says. "She didn't tell me you were twelve, though."

"Ah, that's just my Asian babyface thing," he says, rubbing his cheek. "I turn fourteen next month."

"You told me you were fifteen!"

Howard asks, through another yawn, "Any Sid updates? Any hits from those flyers?"

"I just woke up. Was gonna log in and check."

"I'll get my phone," he says, heading over to the kitchen table, where he left it. "We can double team."

"I'll help Nina wade through that stuff," Connie says, phone already in hand. "I need you to get us some coffee."

"Coffee, of course." How had she forgotten? Nina walks back into the kitchen. "I can make us some."

"Oh, I need a big latte and some sort of perfect pastry," Connie says, leaning back in her chair. "Your cute friend can get us some."

"Cute?"

"Oh, you're fucking adorable," Connie says. "And if you bring back a latte from Highland Bakery and a perfect pastry, you'll be even cuter."

He nods as he rubs his eyes. "Yeah, I can do that, I can do that." Yawns again, shakes his head, then looks at Connie. "So. What is the perfect pastry?"

"That's your test, young warrior."

"A test? On it." Howard picks up his wallet and phone. "I'll be right back with the largest lattes they can make and a perfect pastry."

"I have faith." Nina bows in his direction.

"I don't have faith in anything," Connie says, beginning to scroll her phone. "But maybe you can prove me wrong."

After Howard leaves, Nina brings her Mac over to the table and sits down next to Connie. "You want Insta or Facebook?"

"I'm checking comments on your Insta."

Nina goes to her Facebook page and is surprised to find thirty-seven new responses to her post about her search for Sid. She feels a sudden burst of optimism, even though she knows most of the comments will be commiserating reactions. Maybe one is from somebody who has actually seen Sid? For the first time since she moved in, she wishes she was virtual friends with more of her neighbors.

"You're getting shares and reposts," Connie says. "Which means lots of randos talking about how cute the mutt is, but it also might lead to some real news."

"Same here," Nina says, turning to look at Connie. "And I'm impressed that you haven't said anything."

"About the hot Asian guy who slept on your floor last night? I hadn't even noticed."

"Good."

She continues scrolling. "If I had noticed, I would have said he seemed sweet enough, and he gets bonus points for coming over to help you look for Sid."

"Nothing else happened. If you were wondering."

"Well, he was sound asleep in his clothes. So if something had happened, it must have been pretty weird." Connie lowers her phone and looks at Nina. "Is he gay?"

"No." Nina pauses. "I mean, I don't think so? I told him I wasn't in a hurry to rush into something, and he's also coming off a bad break-up. He made a vow of chastity until the semester is over, so he can make sure he graduates, and that's a good thing, right? Really wants to graduate?"

"Could be." Connie turns back to her phone, right thumb scrolling. "Or he's gay."

Nina follows the reposts, the tight knot of worry in her stomach growing larger with each dead end. She tells herself that any soul that has existed for a couple of thousand years knows how to survive a night outside. And if Sid is dead, somewhere, he is also—not dead? What would he come back as next time? And what will she do, without him to talk to?

Nina and Connie keep scrolling through posts and comments until Howard returns. He impresses Connie with his speed and his pastry choices: two kinds of muffins, two kinds of croissants, and what he calls a "bonus danish."

"That's five things for the three of us?"

"They're all huge, so that seemed like a pretty good ratio," he says. "If they'd been smaller, I would have gotten more."

Connie takes the chocolate croissant in one hand and her latte in the other and looks toward Nina. "Not bad," she says. "You can keep him around for a while."

Howard bows. The three of them sit down around Nina's table, brainstorming over pastries and coffee. Where could Sid have gone? How far away could he have gotten, really? Maybe someone just picked him up and carried him off?

"It's still most likely he never left the building," Howard says, crumpling up his muffin wrapper. "I mean, it's one thing to get outside your apartment door. But he would have had to time it just right to get out of the building without someone noticing."

"He is a tiny thing," Connie says, eyeing the stray bits of leftovers from their feast. "It's possible no one saw him slither by."

"But it's also possible he just found some hiding spot," Howard says.

"And it's possible I missed something last night, running around," Nina says. She suggests taking another look around the building with Howard, while Connie stays in the apartment and runs through social media one more time.

It feels different to walk around the building with Howard. They run into more people than they did last night, but none of them saw Sid roaming around. After searching each floor and checking the parking lot, they take a final walk around the block. There is still no sign of Sid anywhere other than the flyers they hung up last night. When they walk back into the apartment an hour later, they wake up Connie, who has fallen asleep with her hands on her enormous belly.

"Any sign of him?" she asks, slowly standing up.

"Nope." Nina stares down at the food and water bowls. It's much too early to pick them up, but she can suddenly imagine that time coming. And then what? Would she give them away, or just put them in a closet somewhere, on the one in a million chance he turns up again? It has happened before; you read about these dogs that disappear and turn up suddenly after several years.

"The good news is, I didn't pee on your chair. The bad news is, I need to run to your bathroom now, then go home so I can fall asleep for my second nap."

"Yeah, I need to hit it, too," Howard says as Connie slowly walks away. "Maybe catch some real sleep, and then knock out this fucking astronomy." He helps her gather the trash from their pastry feast, then pulls out his phone. "Why didn't you take astronomy, too? I need a good study group."

"I'll just take your notes when you're done," she says. She is almost overcome with gratitude, standing next to him. Not only did he stay for nearly twelve hours, looking for a dog he had never seen, but she told him about the talking part—and he still stayed. "I don't know how to thank you."

He looks up from his Lyft app. "You know why I came, right?"

"You love dogs?"

"Nah. Not really."

"Superman complex?"

"A little. But this time? This time I came because I know if I had called you at some crazy hour with some sort of crisis, you'd do whatever you could to help."

"As if I'd even answer the phone," she says, annoyed at herself for deflecting instead of accepting the compliment.

He looks back down to check Lyft. "Damn. I got played again."

Connie is walking back to them just as he says that. "It's so confusing when you're so young, I know," she says, tapping his shoulder. "But you can pick a damn pastry." She reaches out her right pointer finger and closes his app with a swipe. "So I'll give you a ride home."

Nina is trying to process how physically intimate Connie is being—tapping his shoulder? Swiping his phone? Was she ever that at ease around Ben? "That's nice of you," she says, "But don't scare him, please."

"Scary? Am I scary, Howard?"

Howard looks over to Nina. "The answer is no, right?"

"Right." She hugs Connie goodbye, and then, as Howard is passing her on his way to the door, she reaches over to give him one, too. She doesn't hold him too tightly, or for too long. They have both been wearing the same clothes for two days, and Connie is watching. "Thanks again," she says.

She promises to update both of them with any news, and then she is alone, having a dialogue only with herself as she tidies up. The apartment has never felt this quiet. A few months ago she imagined living with Ben and Sid. Now both of them are gone, the latest additions to the list of men in her life who disappeared, fates unknown.

34 | Back to the Batting Cage

At the final meeting of the semester with Dr. Reed, Ben asks the question that has been bothering him for weeks. "Is it weird to get angry at the subject you are researching? Especially when they've been dead for fifty years?"

Dr. Reed leans back. Her right hand begins to tap on the arm of her chair, which Ben has learned is a sign that she considers the question a good one. "It is one of the stages of grief, Mr. Davies."

"So I am grieving who I thought Harlan was?"

"Perhaps." Tap, tap. "Who did you think he was?"

"I thought he was the son of a die-hard segregationist who was going to use music to create a new, integrated South. He was still growing, as a songwriter and a musician, when he died in a tragic fire. I thought he was someone who may not have achieved his goal, but at least he laid the groundwork for those who came after him."

She shrugs, a poker-faced negotiator waiting to see what else is going to be offered. "And I think all that could be true. Or, at least most of it."

"Except the songwriting."

"Yes, the songwriting. Though one could argue that Harlan's guitar made Nate's songs more complete."

He scratches his head, looking for the right words. "But I argued that he wrote songs about the struggle of one generation trying to overcome the sins of another."

"And instead?"

"Instead he was taking credit for songs his best friend wrote about being Black in that system."

She leans forward again, clasping her hands and placing them on the desk in front of her. "Isn't one possible explanation for that—explanation, not excuse—the fact that he was trapped in the same system as his Black best friend? You can give him credit for what he managed to do while still pointing out his human failings. He did lead an integrated band in the South and was managing to get that band some attention."

"But—"

"But did not push the boundaries further. Maybe he could have. But he didn't." She unclasps her hands, holds them open. "And you wanted him to, you wish he had. But the evidence has led you to a new understanding. You have just pulled the camera back a little further, and shown that Harlan is part of an even bigger story. A more important story."

Ben wants to believe her. He also knows that he is not supposed to let his own feelings play too large a role in shaping his work. And yet he still feels angry. "What's the next stage of grief?"

"Bargaining. Then depression. I'd skip those and move straight to acceptance so that you can finish a draft this summer. Revise over the fall, defend in spring. You can still finish on time."

"You make it sound like such a straightforward path."

"It is. So stay on it."

"I will."

As he answers, she nods, checks her watch, and then does something she has never done during one of their meetings: she hits a remote control next to her phone, silencing the music. "There are two more issues to discuss."

"Okay," he says, worried about what she needs to talk about without music.

"First, and I do ask you to keep this quiet for now, Dr. Kuperman had a stroke Wednesday." She holds up her right hand as if to block the expected follow-up question. "He is still with us, but I do not expect him back on campus any time soon. I know the three of us were supposed to meet next week to talk about Hank Honeybird, but, well, that won't be happening."

"That's awful," Ben says. The two of them fall silent, and it's easily the quietest time he has ever shared with Dr. Reed. It's hard to imagine the 8th floor without Kuperman's booming laugh or blaring jazz music.

"It is a hard time for all of us, as you can imagine. He has been on the other side of that wall for twenty years." She sighs. "Which brings me to the second piece of news. This will be my last semester at Georgia State. In fact, it will be my last semester at any university." She opens her eyes wide. "As hard as it is for me to say, in a few weeks, I will no longer be a full-time academic."

Her tone of voice is casual, but Ben has to struggle to keep his face neutral. His first reaction is selfish: You couldn't have waited until I was done? "Wow."

"Wow, indeed. I am sorry I did not tell you earlier, but the few people who did know were sworn to secrecy. I was determined not to suffer through a Goodbye Tour." She reaches for a butterscotch. "But fear not," she continues. "I will still be your advisor and shepherd your dissertation through its final stages."

He doesn't even try to keep his relief hidden. "Fantastic," he says.

"To mark the end of my time here, I am turning my annual May Day Celebration into a sort of—well, not retirement party, because I don't like to think of myself as 'retired.' Let's call it a 'Goodbye To GSU' party. And I was hoping some of my advisees, past and present, could be there. I did want to give you a heads up before the email arrives and you get word of my retirement that way."

Reed's May Day parties have been the source of Cube Farm speculation for years, since no grad students ever got invited. Faculty members who did attend kept details to themselves. "I'd be honored."

"Excellent. You're going to be my last graduate student, Mr. Davies. Don't drop the ball."

After their meeting, Ben heads over to the Cube Farm to grab his bag and a stack of in-class essays, the last grading he needs to finish before finals. Duncan is there, as he seems to be most of the time these last few weeks, but does not even notice Ben.

"Deep in thought, Professor?"

"Always." Duncan looks at his watch and yawns. "But I have been sitting here pretending to be productive long enough. I need to go pick up Ethan." He stretches, stands up. "How did it go with Dr. Reed?"

Ben picks up his laptop bag and stuffs the stack of essays in the side pocket. "I just need to spend every waking moment this summer writing, and I should be on track to finish next year."

"You're zooming along, brother." Duncan stands up slowly. "Congrats. You will officially beat me in the Dissertation Duel."

"It's not a contest."

"Of course it is. And we're all trying to beat the money clock."

Ben watches Duncan put his laptop into his bag. It's always hard for him to know if he should push for a deeper discussion with Duncan about any of this. "Have you heard from Fletcher yet?"

Duncan nods. "End of semester, end of funding. He's gonna try to get me a section to teach in the fall for adjunct pay, but no promises."

"Man. Sorry."

"Fuck it." Duncan slides the strap of his bag across his shoulder and steps toward Ben. "Maybe it's what I need, right? Force me to finish."

Ben picks up his bag, and the two of them start walking for the door. "What did Carrie say?"

Duncan raises his eyebrows before pushing the door to the Cube Farm open. "Carrie? I'll let you know when I tell her."

"You haven't told her?"

"Not yet." He shrugs, and for a few long seconds they walk in silence. "Trust me," he continues when they reach the bank of elevators. "If you ever date someone long enough to figure shit out, you'll learn that the way information is released—the timing and phrasing of all information—is crucial."

"Well, at least Fletcher will be around next year."

"Wait." Duncan hits the down button and turns around. "The rumors about Reed are true?"

"You heard rumors and didn't tell me?" Ben raises his eyebrows. "What the fuck?"

"Well, I didn't hear them—Shelley did, from her mysterious advisor. And since I've never even seen the guy, I wasn't sure how much to trust it."

The doors to the elevator open. "Well, it's true," Ben says, following Duncan onto the elevator. "Retiring at the end of the semester."

"So soon? She must really hate all her doctoral candidates."

"Yes, that's exactly what she told me."

The campus becomes a ghost town on Friday afternoons, especially when the weather is nice, so they make it from the eighth floor to the first without having to stop. "I did get an invite to her May Day Celebration, at least," Ben says, when they step outside.

"What? You're gonna go to the infamous May Day party?"

Ben is pleased to be the one with surprising news this time. "Yup. She's inviting some advisees this year. Wanna be my guest?"

"Yes, please. I'll tell Carrie I need the night off."

They walk down the stairs leading to Courtland, where Duncan heads toward MARTA and Ben walks to the parking deck. After making plans for lunch on Wednesday, they head in different directions. In a week they'll teach their last class of the semester, and in two weeks they'll be handing in final grades. If Duncan doesn't get a section to teach next semester, will Ben even see him at all? Will there be anyone left on campus for him to talk to?

When Ben gets home, he's happy to see that the transcription of Honeybird's practice tape he outsourced has already been finished and emailed to him. He stays up late reading it, blocking out key sections to work into the dissertation. As a reward he sleeps in the following day, which means he's just making coffee when his phone rings. The name on the caller ID worries him. "Dan?"

"You sound surprised."

"Well, I can't think of the last time you called me at nine a.m. Did someone die?"

"Um, no. All parental units alive and accounted for. I think."

"Phew." Ben hits start on the coffee maker.

"Though you now have me realizing that, yeah, one of these days, one of us will be calling with some awful news." There's a pause, and it sounds like Dan is unwrapping something. "So less than a minute into this call and I'm thinking about death. Thanks for that."

"It's what I do." As he talks, Dan starts to make chewing sounds. "And now I'm thinking about food."

"You're welcome. That's a classic Drake's coffee cake you hear me devouring."

The cereal he has just poured into a bowl suddenly looks a little less enticing. "Where you calling from? Rome? Paris? Gotta be somewhere a few hours later than where I am."

"Upstate NY, baby. Emma hates sleeping in, and when I'm home, I adapt to her schedule. Love is sacrifice."

"How long are you off the road?"

"Nothing booked until the Fall. Need to knock out some recording. Need to figure out what the fuck happens next."

Ben listens to the coffee maker slowing down: almost ready. He's never heard Dan express any sort of uncertainty about his career, not since he got his first guitar at nine. "Up early and engaging in existential questioning? Is this the same Dan Davies I have known literally my entire life?"

"The one and only."

"Wow."

"I've always been introspective, man. It's just I usually do it, like, in a song. Instead of in an early morning phone call."

"This doesn't mean that I need to start sharing my feelings now, does it?"

"Oh, God no. Remember, musicians are all about themselves."

"Phew."

"But that does bring me to why I called."

"It wasn't just to say hello?" Ben pours the coffee into his travel mug.

"I mean, sure. Hello, Ben."

"Hello, Dan."

"And hey! Long as I have you on the phone."

Ben laughs. "Damnit, I knew there was something else."

"It's about this idea of Dad's."

"God. The Actor/Assessor thing?" He fills his travel mug with coffee and puts the top on. "I really don't want to have anything to do with it, man."

"I know you have your issues with Dad."

"It's not that."

"It isn't? Because I have issues with Dad, so if you don't, let me know your secret."

Ben exhales slowly. Is this actually going to be a long and honest discussion with his older brother? "Okay. Yes. I have my issues with Dad."

"That doesn't mean this isn't a good idea."

"And that doesn't mean I have to be involved." He moves to stare out his kitchen window. The Maxwell kids are sitting in the back seat of the car, but the parents aren't out. "At all."

"No, but I want you to be involved." The sound of more unwrapping. "And it works much better if both sons are talked about."

"Dan—"

"I'm just gonna lay it out. I need to be involved. It would help me to have all these platforms playing clips of my music. I mean, the royalty checks from 'Glorious' get smaller and smaller."

"Hey, at least they're still coming, right? And you can wave them at Emma and tell her your love for her keeps paying—literally—with those checks."

Dan laughs. "Man, I can share the secret with my own brother, right? That song's not about Emma."

"Really?" Ben is caught by surprise. "'Then I heard your voice calling out to me,' and that stuff about climbing aboard the future bus? That wasn't for Emma?"

"No, but she thinks it was, so shhhhh."

"So who—"

Dan is chewing again. "It was my guitar, man. Once I found the guitar, that's when this shitshow called life made any sense to me."

Ben shakes his head. He would never say it out loud, in so many words, but he did not think Dan's songwriting was complex enough to hold multiple readings. "And here I thought I'd figured you out."

"Oh, come on, man. That's how art works, right? We all bring our own stories to it, etc. and so forth and all that." Dan pauses to burp. "But that was, like, ten years ago. There's new stuff in the works, and I want people to hear it. You were at the show—this is the best band I've ever had."

"It did sound great," Ben says, still staring at the Mercedes SUV. Where are the parents? Inside, fighting? Or are the weird kids playing some sort of silent game? At that age, he and Dan could never have sat so still in a car without their parents to keep the peace.

"Radio's dead, and I'm not some smooth-faced and snotty teen from England, so YouTube's out. I need a fucking angle, Ben, and this could be it."

This is the bluntest he has ever heard Dan be about the state of his career. "Dan. You're killing me."

"So let's live and let die, man. Just say yes. We'll do it after your semester ends. Trip to New York on Dad. How bad can it be?"

"How bad can it be? I can think of many ways." He wants to bring up the batting cage debacle, Dan and his father watching him flail, screaming out incomprehensible tips between their bouts of laughter, but is afraid of how petty he will sound. Dan talked him into trying that, too, probably by saying "how bad could it be?" Two hours of being loudly criticized by his father bad, that's how bad. "Just imagine the set up from my point of view, man. You rocking out on some stage, being all Mr. Actor, and me what? Looking like a boring professor? Holding a clipboard and a pencil and 'assessing'?"

"No rocking out, I promise. Clips of us talking, maybe cool shots of NYC, and yeah, maybe later some clips of my music can be put in there. And some plugging of your work, too. It's pretty impressive to get a Ph.D., right?"

"So, yeah. Rock star brother, and look, guy in tweed jacket with elbow patches!"

Dan laughs. "Man, Dad was right. You're upset with all this."

It drives him crazy, that he's the one accused of behaving improperly. "We're different people, and I totally get that."

"But you don't like that I'm an Actor and you're not."

"You make it sound like it's an actual thing." The Maxwell parents have finally come out, and he can feel the tension from across the driveway. He turns away before awkward eye contact is made. "It's just a schtick Dad has invented to make some more money," he says, moving to the kitchen table.

"I'm last to give him credit, man. But in this case, I think you're wrong."

Ben hopes his silence is answer enough to force Dan to change topics. It's not.

"And even if he's not onto something, even if you're right, what can it hurt? Come film a couple of fucking videos to help me out."

"It's not that I don't want to help you out. It's that I don't want to spend a couple of days listening to Dad order me around like a fucking movie director."

"So you do it for me. Not for him."

Ben pours some milk over his Oat Squares and takes a bite. Standing up and eating cereal in the kitchen as he fights with Dan: it really is just like the old days. "You do sound like him now, you know. Trying to close some deal."

"Oh, low blow."

"Sorry, correction. He'd be much better at closing the deal."

That gets a laugh, at least. "Fair point." Dan calls out in the distance to someone in a muffled voice. "Okay, I gotta go. Emma's getting ready to leave for work, and she's on about something." Pause. "Can we at least settle for not saying no today? For all those brother bonding memories we may or may not even have?"

Ben takes another bite of cereal. His brother has never been one to accept an answer he didn't like. If he keeps saying no Dan will just call back later to try again. "Okay, okay. I can give a very tentative not saying no. Yet."

"Then I'm hanging up before that changes, brother."

And with that, the line is dead, and Ben is once again alone.

MAY

"Too often enlightenment is understood as some new state of consciousness that is achieved, as though it is an object to be obtained, or something to strive for, outside of ourselves. Yet the Buddha saw that his grasping mind was the problem. He had gotten reality upside down."
—Yonguey Mingyur Rinpoche

"No one wanted this show to end: not the band, not the fans. Harlan could feel this, as he and his loyal rhythm section pushed 'Heavy Heavy Hands' past the ten-minute mark, his solo continuing to find new peaks and valleys. When they finally hit that last chord, they held that sound as long as they could, urged on by a packed theater of loyal fans. The only solace to be found, when the lights came on? Now Honeybird could go home, take a deep breath, and then hurry up and make a new record. Macon can't wait."
—"You Can Go Home Again," *Macon Telegraph*, August 4, 1968

35 | May Day

After another study group meeting the day before the final in Algebra—same Waffle House, same booth, everyone sitting in the same place, because Howard is superstitious that way—the test itself is wonderfully anticlimactic. Nina finds Howard and Tom standing in the hallway, just as they were after the midterm. When Tom moves in for an awkward hug, she responds with the best Bro Pat she can muster. He was the king of wacky mnemonics, so he has earned a hug. One.

"So when's your last exam?" Howard asks when they are alone.

Nina takes out her phone to check her calendar. The end of the semester approaches, which means their first official date is getting closer. "I know it's Friday," she says, scrolling to her calendar, "but can't remember the time . . . 8:00 a.m. Oy."

"And then you're done: bam. Signed up for any summer classes?"

"Not yet. But I will do it. I took a vow."

"Vows are good."

"I've heard," she says, smiling. Anticipating their first kiss is better than some of the actual kisses she's had, so she doesn't mind waiting a little longer.

"My last one's Monday. By 10:30 I'm done."

"By 10:30 Monday you'll be a college graduate, you mean."

"If I pass Astronomy, yes. If I don't, you have to take that in the summer with me."

"Then pass that fucking test, okay?"

"Okay."

It's hard to talk as they make their way down the crowded stairs, the air drunk with students who have survived another final exam, but once they are back on the ground floor, heading to the quad, she asks him a question she cannot believe she has not asked before. "So, um, what happens next?"

"For Howard?"

"For Howard. He's not going to start talking about himself in the third person after he graduates, is he?"

"Never. Shoot him if he does, please."

"Not a fan of guns," she says. "I could start riffing on other forms of painful punishment, but we shouldn't start that kind of discussion until after your last final, right?"

"Probably a good idea," he says. "Though I was thinking we could just do something low-key tonight, even, since Algebra's done? Maybe just dinner? If it's under ten bucks a head it's not a date, is what I read. Somewhere."

She smiles. "I think that might be true. But unfortunately I have plans with Troy tonight."

He stops walking, narrows his eyes. "Um, who is this Troy? Should I be worried?"

"Nothing to worry about. This Troy has been living with this Trent for three years now, and I do not think he is looking to change teams."

He mimics wiping his forehead in relief. "Good, because I need these hands for my guitar. Need to get them back in playing shape—I have a pinky promise about open mic night. In May."

The thought of playing for Howard always makes her feel uneasy—not just because she worries that he will think she can't play well, but because it reminds her of the pinky promise. Which reminds her of the night Sid disappeared. "Show-and-tell time soon, huh?"

"For both of us. And I have a plan for that, too." He pulls out his phone to check the time. "But I gotta jet to the library and deal with astronomy now. When are we gonna celebrate the end of my college career?"

"Monday, after your last final?"

"Okay, but I'mma text you before that."

"Deal."

When Nina gets back to her apartment, it's time for the end-of-semester ritual she began after her first college class. It was a freshman comp course, and though she was surprised at how demanding the grad student in charge of the class was, she managed to pull off an A. When she came home after taking the final, she wasn't sure what to do with her overstuffed notebook. She didn't want to clutter her apartment with papers she would never look at again, but she wanted to preserve some record of what she had done. She decided to keep three items that summed up the class: her first attempt at a five-paragraph essay, which had an earned a depressing C+; the revision, with its beautiful red-inked A; and the final paper, on the significance of space in *The Office*. For every class since she has limited herself to three artifacts stored in a binder optimistically labeled "Nina Gets Her Degree." For Algebra, the choices are easy. The syllabus, on which she had scrawled "I'M DOOMED;" the copy of the midterm study guide that she and Howard had marked up together; and the midterm itself, with its glowing 94.

She puts the rest of the papers in the recycling bin and feels an immense sense of satisfaction. Something about surviving this semester makes the idea that she will get her college degree seem much more real. Three more years? Could she maybe do it in two if she pushed herself? What she really wants to do to celebrate is order Thai food and stream some cheery French movie—not go to a big party with lots of strangers. Troy hasn't seemed himself since he told her the adoption story, though, and she doesn't want to be one more person letting him down.

Actually, what she really wants to do is talk to Sid. She wants to hear him make wise-ass comments and dodge her questions with questions of her own. She wants to pretend to be annoyed at having to take him out one more time before she leaves and maybe even make a joke about how many thousands of years it takes to become toilet trained. Most of all, what she wants is to ask him why he left. She can't blame Morris or whatever hunky assistant he had work on the sink—they may have left the door open, but Sid chose to walk through it. Why? Was he mad at the way she got mad at him for abandoning his son? That didn't seem very Buddha-like, or Sid-like. (What's the difference between Buddha and Sid?) What she preferred to think, what she hoped he would say if he were able to explain, was that he left because she was ready—that whatever need had caused him to appear in her life had been resolved. Even if she wasn't sure she believed it, she would like to hear him say it.

She opens the refrigerator, looking for lunch. Troy has promised fantastic food at this party, so she doesn't want to eat too much. That's a good thing, because there's not much to tempt her—just a container of dead lettuce, two eggs, and a single taco of forgotten origins. And one slice of chocolate cake, which moves to the freezer. That's not something she wants to eat; she just wants to preserve it as long as she can. It's tangible proof of the most surprising part of Sid's disappearance: that Marion Alexander, of all people, was so understanding. Nina texted her mother the day after Sid disappeared, to explain why she could not make Sunday dinner. Two hours later Nina's mother and grandmother were at her apartment with a pot of chicken stew and a cake.

"A cake?" Nina had asked, as confused as she was touched.

"Dogs are hard," her grandmother said, taking the cover off the cake carrier. "But it is chocolate."

If Nina squinted, she could see a face of some kind on the cake; what she could see very clearly was Sid's name, spelled out in Red Hots candies. "You guys," she said. "I didn't think you even liked dogs."

"Who doesn't like dogs?" her mother said, already starting to clean out Nina's refrigerator.

"But you never let us have any pets," Nina said, watching her grandmother clear a spot on the counter for the cake. She knew she should be embarrassed at her messy apartment, or the dirty clothes she was wearing, or the way her eyes were watering, but they did not seem to care, and she did not have the energy to care.

"Oh, Nina," her mother said, holding an old yogurt container. "Pets die. I was just trying to spare you more death." Her mother sniffed the yogurt, shook her head, and walked it over to the trash. "But you loved Sid, so we loved him. That means we celebrate his life."

"But he could still come back," Nina had protested, but even as she said the words she understood it was less and less likely.

"Of course. And then we'll throw another party."

"With cake," her grandmother said, nodding.

"And music," Nina's mother said, walking over to the stereo. "How come there's no music playing?"

Watching her grandmother busy herself in the kitchen, and her mother try to figure out the remote for her stereo, she realized that they have been showing her what to do her whole life—they had taught her how to cook, to appreciate art, to be alone. And now they would help her learn how to grieve.

Every time Ben rings Duncan's doorbell, there is an explosion of noise: Ethan shouts out "doorbell" and runs loudly from wherever he was in the house to the front door, and then Duncan or Carrie start screaming at Ethan to be careful. So it feels very, very wrong when he comes to pick Duncan up for Reed's party, rings the doorbell, and only hears silence from inside the house.

Ben has just convinced himself he should go ahead and ring again when the front door opens slowly. Ethan is wearing a much too large Atlanta United Jersey and holding a video game controller.

"Is your Dad home?"

Ethan turns away without saying a word, which Ben interprets as an invitation to come inside. When he steps into the living room, the house seems in a special kind of disrepair and chaos, with stray shoes and dirty socks strewn across the floor, dirty dishes covering the coffee table. What's most unnerving is how loud the silence is. There's no TV or radio blaring. No raised voices urging someone to do something or stop doing something else. It's as quiet as his carriage house, and that's something Ben would never have thought possible.

When Duncan eventually walks into the living room he looks exhausted and not dressed for a public gathering of any kind. His Metallica T-shirt has noticeable rips, and the left leg of his baggy gray sweatpants is covered in multi-colored splotches. "Hey man," he says, scratching his head.

"Looking good," Ben says, trying to lighten the oppressive mood. "I knew you were excited to finally get invited to this party—but you didn't need to buy a new fancy outfit."

"I need them to see the best side of me, of course." He shrugs. "So, yeah, sorry I forgot to text. I'm not going, as you may have guessed."

"Making me go stag?"

"Sorry, brother. Things kind of blew up here."

"I can see that," Ben says, looking around the living room. "I can't believe Carrie is letting you get away with this mess."

"Carrie has, um, stepped out for a while."

Ben processes the words and chooses the most optimistic meaning. "So when does she get back? We can be fashionably late."

Duncan shakes his head, glances out the front window. "I don't see that happening any time soon, to be honest."

"Oh. Okay."

"She was a little angry when she left." Duncan looks over his shoulder into the dining room and then motions for Ben to head outside. "I'm letting Ethan binge on PS4."

He follows Duncan onto the front porch, and the two of them lean against the railing. It's one of the better Atlanta evenings, not yet too muggy and damp. Ben waits for Duncan to say something, but he just quietly stares at a crumpled and deflated soccer ball on the floor of the porch. "What happened? You told her about no more funding?"

Duncan looks up. "I hadn't planned to. I was gonna wait until the right time. Kept hoping some miracle would bail me out—like, maybe I'd pick up a class at GSU and a class at Perimeter and have something to offer."

"But she found out anyway?"

"Yeah, when she dug around my email."

"Oh, man. That doesn't sound like good news. For anyone."

"Yeah. And I wish the worst she'd found was an email from Fletcher explaining why I couldn't get more funding."

"There's worse?"

Duncan reaches his foot out to drag the flattened soccer ball closer to him. "Stuff she thought was worse," he says, grinding the ball as he talks.

Ben studies Duncan's face for more clues: what could be worse?

"Harmless, really," Duncan continues. "Just some flirting by email. Chats that could look different than they were."

That could be worse. "Chats with who?"

"Shelley."

Ben takes a moment to remember scenes of Duncan and Shelley on the couch in the Cube Farm. "How far back does this stuff go?"

Duncan is looking back through the screen door as he talks. Inside, the house is still eerily silent. "I don't remember, really. Couple of months? And it's not like we ever, you know, talked about what each other was wearing or anything."

"What did you talk about?"

"You sound as schoolmarmish as Carrie." There's an edge to his voice now. "School, life. What we could do to be happier people."

Ben tries not to let the schoolmarmish comment sting. "So why was Carrie so upset?"

"I don't know."

Studying Duncan's face, Ben has an epiphany he probably should have had a long time ago: Duncan lies easily. "Come on. You know why."

"I don't think she liked me talking about her with Shelley." He rubs his head as he answers, his voice softer.

"You and Shelley talked about Carrie?"

"Of course. It's a big part of my life, right?"

"What were you thinking?"

"I was thinking it was good to talk to someone about this. It's hard."

"What's hard?"

"Marriage. Shelley gets it."

"She gets it? She's what, twenty-two?"

"Twenty-three. But she was married for a year. You didn't know that, did you?"

"No." Information is coming too fast for him to keep up with it. Shelley had a previous marriage? And she and Duncan have been chatting online? He knows that everyone's private life is more complicated than most people ever see, but he's always prided himself on noticing the big stuff. What else has he been missing?

"She got married right out of high school, to some loser she thought she was in love with. Lasted less than a year. So, yeah, she has some insights." He shrugs again, pressing down against the soccer ball with his bare right foot. "Carrie can be hard."

"But why not talk to Carrie about whatever you talked to Shelley about?"

"You've so never been married." The edge is back in his voice.

"No, but—"

"Because that's not how it works. There are things you can't say to your spouse. Just can't."

"But you can say them to Shelley?"

"Yes. She was married before; she's in the same grad program. We have a language."

"And she's cute." He intends it to be a question, but it comes out as a statement.

"That doesn't hurt, man, of course not. I'm human. And the physical side of life with Carrie has disappeared these last few years."

Ben is very aware of the sound of his breathing as he tries not to imagine Carrie and Duncan not having sex. He starts to say something and then stops, and the look on his face seems to make Duncan angry.

"Don't give me that stare, man."

"What stare?"

"That 'how could you do this?' stare. You're not in the trenches."

"I wasn't—"

"You were. It's harder than it looks, man. But maybe you know that? You broke up rather than move in with someone."

Ben wants to point out that Duncan never liked the idea of Ben dating Nina, so it doesn't seem fair to criticize him for breaking up with her. He could also finally tell Duncan the reason for the breakup. What better time than now, when they are being all honest with each other? Instead, he decides to ignore any anger Duncan feels now and shift from questions about why Duncan did what he did to questions about what can be done. "How did Carrie find all this out?"

"She was up late working, and her laptop crashed. So she used mine."

"And went to your email?"

Duncan shrugs, looking over his shoulder through the screen door again before turning back to Ben. "I mean, she knows the password to my laptop, and I don't log out of my email—it's not like I was acting like a man with something to hide."

"So why did she look?"

"She said she had a feeling. Says I've been acting differently. I figure if I have been acting any different, it's because I'm a little less stressed, talking to Shelley."

"And then she left?"

"I came out for breakfast this morning and she dumped all this on me. Said she was going to her fucking sister's house, and I can just imagine what that one's gonna say. Probably has a divorce lawyer camped out in the guest room, waiting for this day."

"And Ethan?"

"She said I could suck it up and be the one who has to do everything for a change."

"Is Mommy home yet?"

Ethan's voice catches Ben off-guard, and from the look on Duncan's face, he hadn't seen the boy walk up to the other side of the door, either.

"Not yet, buddy," Duncan says, his voice coated in that too-happy-to-be-natural tone.

"Why not?"

"Well, I told you, she needed to—"

Ethan unleashes a piercing scream and runs off. In the distance, there is the sound of glass breaking.

"That's my sign." Duncan takes a deep breath, stands up, and puts a hand on the door. "Sorry I'm in a shitty mood. Sorry to miss the party. And sorry about anything else the world needs me to be sorry for, okay? Tell the world I apologize for everything. Even the shit that isn't my fault."

Ben can't think of another thing to say, so he just nods. He stays until Duncan goes back in the house, using a fake, cheery voice to call out, "Where's my little man?"

Troy said he was picking her up at 8 p.m. for real, and when Nina walks out the front door of the apartment building two minutes early, he is already in a Lyft, waiting. On time and looking great, a nice-fitting shirt lit up by his smile.

"Thanks for coming," he says, leaning over to give her one of those awkward seated hugs. "You look fabulous." He sits back and points to the attractive man in the driver's seat, tight blue button-down barely containing his shoulder muscles. "This is William, who has me wishing I was the kind of person who could hire a driver for everything."

"Hello, William," Nina says, buckling in. "I do have to wonder, though, who is throwing the kind of party that inspires you to be on time."

"Maddie Graves. She sifts through all the podcasts in the South for Public Radio International, looking for the best stuff. She throws a party every year on May Day."

"Ah," Nina says. "Is she a fan of 'Eat Your Art Out'?"

Troy nods. "There's talk of it being pitched to Midwest stations this summer."

"That's great," Nina says, grabbing his left arm. "Because someday I want you to be one of those funny guests on 'Wait Wait.'"

"A man can dream," he says.

William is driving them in the direction of the Highlands. "So why couldn't Trent make it?" she asks. "NPR loves the gays. You would have stolen the night."

"Trust me, we would have. But he was vomiting all day Sunday, and I am not going to risk him infecting these people I need to impress."

She watches him watching out the window as the car turns off Ponce onto Moreland. "How is Life with Trent these days?"

"It's okay. Good, even," Troy says, turning back to look at her. "I mean, I had to decide if I wanted to be with Trent and without a kid, or try to find a way to have a kid on my own?"

"And the winner was Trent?"

"For now." He shrugs. "I feel better that it's out, that I don't have to keep dealing with this thought trapped inside my head? And okay, his reaction wasn't the best, but you know, he also didn't run away screaming." Troy smiles. "He didn't even actually say no. I mean, he didn't say yes, either, but he didn't say no."

She rests her hand on top of his. "Listen to you, Mr. Calm and Chill Troy."

"I'm just trying to live in the moment, like your hero, the Buddha."

"Oh, I don't know if I'd call him my hero," she says. Remembering Sid is still hard, can still make the inside of her chest clench. "But it is nice to try to live in the moment."

They begin to wind through the back streets of Little Five Points. "And the food will be good? Because I did not eat all afternoon, so I could eat all night."

"This is my first actual invite to said party," Troy says, "though I have heard tell of carving stations, dessert bars, and more good wine than normally seen anywhere outside of Paris."

"Dessert bars and people who will never see me again," Nina says. "That's a combination I like."

"Feel no shame," Troy says. "And you can keep going back to get more for me, too, since I will see them again."

"And here we are," William says, slowing down in front of a two-story house, the white of its bricks and the dark black of its shutters looking freshly painted.

"You didn't say we had to go back to the fifties for this party," Nina says, caught off-guard by the enormous white columns lining the front porch. "And by that I mean the 1850s. Was I supposed to wear my hoop skirt?"

"Think of it as a sort of ironic statement about the New South," Troy says. He steps out of the car after her and offers her his right arm to hold on to. "A new generation of misfits and outcasts, partying on the remnants of the ruined Old South."

Ben has to park several blocks away from Dr. Reed's house, and it's his least favorite kind of parking: parallel, in a spot that's smaller than it appears at first, on a narrow side street. After he turns the car off he sits for several long minutes, decompressing from the stress of the parking and adjusting to the news from Duncan. He's always treated Ben like a younger brother, which made sense because Duncan was further along in the program. Now it turns out Duncan is just as screwed up as Ben.

He forces himself to get out of the car. Ben hates showing up late for parties; it makes him feel like he's back in the high school cafeteria, trying to navigate between cliques that formed when he wasn't looking. The house is larger than he expected—two-story, white, with beautiful brickwork on the sidewalk and front patio, and large white columns that give the place an antebellum feel that seems out of place in Little Five. Either Reed's history books somehow led to bigger royalty checks than he imagined possible, or she married someone who makes a lot of money.

Ben puts on the most casual, "Hey, happy to be at another party!" smile he can manage and opens the heavy wooden door. He enters a wide hallway; ahead of him are clumps of people, drinking and laughing and clearly in the middle of conversations that would be awkward to force himself into. He hopes to quickly find someone else from the department, some friendly soul that he can latch on to, but his initial scan comes up empty. As he makes his way into the house he distracts himself by looking at the photos lining the left side of the hallway. Black-and-white shots, all in professional-looking frames, all of people—sometimes just one person, sometimes a couple or a group. He has this feeling he should recognize some faces, but aside from a photo of what seems to be Muhammad Ali (really?) standing next to what may be a younger Dr. Reed, he doesn't.

The wall of photos opens into a large sitting room. His flight instinct engages with so many people present, but he sees a table with alcohol and well-dressed bartenders in one of the corners and decides that is a good place to start. He's glad he has some wine in him before he bumps into Dr. Fletcher, who is suddenly standing too closely, wearing his standard dark sport coat and white dress shirt.

"Salutations, Ben."

"Hey, Dr. Fletcher." They exchange an awkward handshake, each being careful to maintain control of their drinks.

"Enjoying the party?"

"Just got here," Ben says, taking another sip of wine. "Nice house."

"Yes, these old in-town homes cannot be beat. And the decorations, of course, are perfection. But what else would you expect from Maddie?"

"Maddie?"

Just as Ben asks the question Dr. Fletcher turns to accept the embrace of a tall Black woman, her stylish gray dreadlocks long enough to brush against Fletcher's coat as they hug. "This young man was just asking who you were," Dr. Fletcher says, pointing at Ben. "Ben Davies, this is the one and only Maddie Graves."

"A pleasure," Ben says, wondering if he is supposed to know who Maddie Graves is as he shakes her hand.

"Ah, Mr. Davies. With the dead guitarist?"

Ben nods. "That's me."

"Well, Barbara has talked quite a bit about your work," she continues. "I hope that your final product is as impressive as she expects it to be."

"Me, too," Ben says. Making small talk with Maddie and Dr. Fletcher, Ben learns that Maddie is a programming executive of some kind with Public Radio International. Ben resists the urge to mimic that radio voice saying "PRI" after so many of his favorite podcasts, though he does confess he feels sort of like he is meeting a rock star.

"If you don't mind," Maddie says to Dr. Fletcher, after they all refill their drinks, "I am going to steal Mr. Davies away to give him a tour."

Ben says goodbye to Fletcher and follows Maddie back into the main hall. He's hoping that he's doing a decent job of hiding his relief at escaping Fletcher, but he needn't have worried; as soon as they are out of earshot, Maddie exhales loudly. "That angry little man corners me every year. I wish Barbara did not have to invite him."

Ben nods in agreement and listens as Maddie points out interesting features about the house, which the two have shared for over twenty years. He is impressed by Maddie and the beautiful home but even more impressed by how Reed managed to keep so much of her private life private.

At the back of the first floor is an open dining area, crowded with people carrying full plates of food while jazz music plays softly in the background. A long buffet table dominates the center of the room. Stations of food line the left and right walls; a man in a tuxedo is carving various hunks of meat at one station, while a woman in a tall white chef's hat makes omelettes at another. Finally, of course, there is a long bar with three young hipsters fixing drinks.

"I'd suggest starting with the curry. Maddie makes it herself, and it's always one of the first things to disappear."

Ben turns and smiles at Dr. Reed, who has seemingly appeared from nowhere to stand by Maddie's side. "Thanks for the tip," he says, "and thanks for the invite. This is quite the party."

"All these people coming to say goodbye," Dr. Reed says. "It makes me worry that I really am heading out to pasture."

"Some of these people are here to see me," Maddie says. "I'm the one who still has a job."

They head over to the buffet together, and Ben is glad that he decided to come, even without Duncan. Walking with the two of them through the crowded room, selecting delicious-looking food, bantering about the world collapsing around them (again) and what academia may or may not be able to do to help—it all feels like a flash-forward into a possible future version of himself: Dr. Ben Davies, confidently moving through the world with other people who think Big Ideas.

Plates full, they slowly weave their way through the crowd. Ben is listening to Dr. Reed and Maddie debate where they can eat with the fewest interruptions, when he has to come to a full stop. Over by the curry, standing next to Troy, smiling and laughing, is Nina.

Nina.

Her hair's longer, touching her shoulders now. Her eyes seem especially alive, and the light purple blouse makes her skin glow. Had Ben never seen her before, he is certain that she is the first person in this entire crowd he would have noticed, really noticed. Seeing her is simultaneously a relief (she didn't collapse after their break-up) and a cause for concern (how could she look so great after their break-up?).

He's impressed with how calmly he excuses himself, saying that he has seen someone he needs to say hello to, promising to come back. And then he heads straight for the back door, which leads, he hopes, to a safe escape.

As she and Troy work their way down the large buffet table, Nina concedes that the food all looks as good as promised.

"Can you still eat after chomping down all those mini-crab cakes?" he asks. "Should I see if we can get some to-go bags?"

She is trying to think of a polite and funny way to let him know that she has noticed he has engaged the casual head swivel to check out the other attendees but decides not to say anything; he is here for work, after all, and needs to schmooze. Just as she's decided to forgive him, though, his head freezes and he stops moving down the table, preventing her from reaching the samosas. "Okay, friend," she says giving him a nudge with her elbow. "I've been lax about the way you're prowling for someone more important to talk to, but you need to keep the food train moving, at least."

He turns to her, nods with his head across the room. "Did you see him?"

Nina looks in that direction, just in time to see Ben headed for the back door. Quickly. Did he see her and run? Really? "What is he doing here?"

"No idea," Troy says. "And I'd go beat him up, but I can't make a scene at a PRI party."

She had worried about what she would do or say if she ran into him on campus, but she never thought about what to do if they bumped into each other somewhere else—never mind what to do if he ran away. "No need," she says. For a moment she debates letting him run and hide, which would be a fitting epilogue to their relationship, but she decides that this time she will not let him off so easily. She turns to head for the door. "I can do it."

"Nina."

She looks back, smiles. "Fear not," she says. "I'm not going to make a scene. Just going to make him quietly uncomfortable."

She carries her plate to the doors at the back of the room and pushes them open to casually step outside, just another guest looking for some fresh air. The backyard is bigger than she expected. There's a large brick patio with two metal tables, with five or six people at each, talking loudly over the chaotic sharing of food and wine. Off to her left lies a thicket of bushes, to her right a small pond, complete with some of those floating white flowers. A backyard big enough for a pond in the heart of Little Five. Who would have guessed?

He's sitting on the far end of the low brick wall that circles the pond, balancing a plate of food in his lap. Now that he is here in front of her, Nina feels more nostalgia than she had expected, surprisingly eager to find out how he's been. She sits down next to him, placing her drink on the wall and balancing her plate carefully in her lap. When she's settled she takes a bite of the curry. "I gotta say," she begins, "I didn't know what to expect from this party. But sitting next to you, eating some kick-ass curry, was not on the shortlist."

"It is kick-ass curry," he says, nodding. "And no, this was not on my shortlist of possibilities, either."

Her taste of the pesto dish is just as satisfying. After a sip of her drink, she turns to Ben and waits for him to make direct eye contact. "I want to ask why you're here, so we can try and work out the weird math that led to this moment. But maybe it's more fun if we don't know."

"Could be," he says, turning back to his plate. "It's certainly a surprise, to see you."

She waits for him to look at her again, but he keeps his attention focused on his plate. He's nervous, which is surprising. She expected to be the nervous one, the one who would try to duck any sort of meeting. "Did you really just turn and leave the room when you saw me?"

"Um. Yes."

She grins. "I have seen you naked, you know. Many times. So there's not much left to hide."

"I wasn't hiding, so much as . . ."

"As what? Running away?" That does make him look her way, and she smiles to let him know she is not going to stab him angrily with her knife. "That would make a good 'What's the Difference Between,' wouldn't it? What's the difference between hiding and running away?"

"No, that's not it, either. Not running away."

"So what was it?"

He pauses. "Just trying not to make you uncomfortable."

"Ah, how kind of you, to make my discomfort your excuse." She wipes up some of the curry with an exquisite dinner roll. It seems a waste to spend this conversation, which probably will be the last one they ever have, just making him feel bad—even if that would feel good and be wholly justified. "So how are things with your guitarist?"

He puts down his plate and picks up his glass. "Well, things have gotten interesting."

"Interesting?" She waits for a second, and then presses when he doesn't continue. "Come on—don't make me wait for the book or movie. What did you find out about the fire? Was it the Klan? Vengeful lover? The drummer, after all, who you found hiding in some small Midwestern town?"

He tells her a better story than she expected: no mysterious cause for the fire or magically alive drummer, but a forbidden love, a secret songwriter, an old practice tape that proves everything. As he gets into the story the tone of his voice sharpens and clarifies, his whole body relaxes, and his eyes brighten, and she remembers that she first fell for him watching him talk about history. He gains a confidence he lacks during his daily life.

"What a great story," she says as he wraps up. Both their plates are empty now.

He shrugs. "Yes, it's a great story. At the same time, it's made me more than a little angry."

"Angry?" She studies his face, which is lit on his left side by the cool electric tiki torches along the garden's far wall. If they'd stayed together, would she be able to tell just by looking at him why he would be upset by these developments?

And then she gets it. His guitarist.

"Oh. This means that Harlan took credit for someone else's songs," Nina says.

Ben takes the last sip of wine from his glass. "Yup."

The dominoes keep falling over in her head as she thinks about it. "And not just someone else's songs—his best friend's songs. His Black best friend."

"Yup again," Ben says. "That's all true, and it's all a drag."

They sit next to each other in silence for a few minutes after that, and she remembers how comfortable she used to feel, being quiet with him. "But," she starts slowly, "fuck him, right? Turns out it's not his story."

"Sure it is," Ben says. "He's the one with the crazy segregationist father, the family past he has to overcome. Who throws off his father's segregationist views to lead a new kind of band in a new kind of South. Who would use his integrated band to bring literal and figurative harmony."

"It's the drummer's story," she says, surprised he doesn't see it. "It's Nate's story."

"Nate's story?" Ben says. "But Harlan had the famous father, the past he was trying to overcome. He was the one with access to an old form of power, choosing to reject it." He shakes his head as he talks. "The Honeybird name had power in Macon."

"Yes, but that's only part of the story." She picks up her glass, takes a drink.

He pauses, remembering his last conversation with Dr. Reed. "That's what Reed says. Harlan has to be placed inside a larger story now."

"Well, she's right. And the larger story is Nate's—Harlan fits into Nate's story, not the other way around. You kept telling me the songs were this huge part of the band's importance, right? Well, Nate wrote them. Nate was the voice of the New South, turns out. And sure, Harlan went a different route than his old man and seemed more at ease in an integrated world, but he also didn't mind taking credit for his best friend's work. So maybe there was some more of his old man in him than you want to admit."

"But the sources," Ben says. "There are so many more sources about the Honeybirds, than Nate or his family."

"You have the songs," she says. "And interviews with the bass player. And you even talked to the drummer's sister, didn't you?"

Ben nods, takes a drink. If she's right, he's missed the obvious frame his dissertation needs. Harlan doesn't need to be centered in some larger story of the South. Nate is the center. Without his songs the band never would have made any records, and Harlan is just the underachieving son of a segregationist. It's Nate's story—and an even better story than the one he had planned on writing.

He can see Nina watching him work through all of this. She wears that look of victory he saw after most Scrabble games, or when a restaurant she picked turned out to be great after he was leery. She seems more focused, more confident. Is she different, or does she just seem different because he hasn't seen her in so long? Everyone's different than they were five months ago, but is she any more different than she would have been if they hadn't broken up? "You're right," he says. "Even when I was adjusting to the story being bigger than Harlan, I was still filtering it through him."

"Imagine that. The white guy thinks it's all about the white guy." She smiles with satisfaction, takes a drink. "I think I'd get an A for my argument."

"Oh, for sure." The longer they talk, the less nervous he feels. Even her dig about his white male gaze makes him melancholic, reminding him of how sharp her mind is, and how much he has missed her.

Which is when he remembers the dog.

"So how is Sid?" he asks, wishing his wine glass would refill itself.

"Sid?"

"Yes."

"Well." Nina pauses and empties her glass. "I lost Sid a few weeks ago."

"Lost him?" How old was the dog? Ben can't remember.

"Yeah. I mean, I came home and he was gone."

As much as he sometimes wished that dog had never lived with Nina, that is not the ending he wanted. "He got out? How? From what I remember, it was hard to get him to move much at all."

"My guess is the guy Morris sent to work on the sink let him out."

"Wait—you got that fucking garbage disposal fixed?"

"A brand new one, baby."

"Amazing. But lost Sid at the same time? That's awful."

"Oh, come on. You were never the biggest fan."

"Fair point." He starts to continue but stops himself, wondering how to phrase what he needs to say next. Is this why he's avoiding contacting her? Knowing he'd have to apologize? "And I'm sorry. For how I reacted."

That grin again. "You mean when you literally walked out on me?"

"Yes. That was . . ."

"Shitty?"

"Shitty."

"Apology reluctantly accepted. It was a lot to put on you."

"But I could have done better. Should have." He closes his eyes, hoping to think of brilliant new words to add, some combination of phrases that makes his reaction, and the months of silence, forgivable. Nothing comes to mind. When he looks back at her again he sees Troy walking up behind Nina.

"I have more wine," Troy says, holding out a glass for Nina.

"How sweet," she says, taking it and smiling.

Ben can only imagine how Troy feels about him, so he tries the lighthearted approach. "None for me?"

"Oh, I thought of things to give you, trust me. But I decided to behave." Troy turns to Nina. "Are you okay? Do you need an escort out?"

"No," she says. She takes a sip of wine. "It's fine. And we're almost done here."

When Troy leaves Nina turns back to Ben. "I really am going to get up and walk away soon," she says. "I just wanted to thank you before I left. I finally did something you suggested I do a while ago."

"Really? What?"

"I went to the crash site."

He whistles. "Your father's crash site?"

"Yes," she says, telling him what her mother said about the accident, and what she saw and didn't see when she went to look.

"Do you think it was an accident?"

She shrugs. "Sometimes I'm convinced one way, then I'm convinced the other. And I know it doesn't make a difference, really? That either way, he's gone." Her face begins to feel a little warm—that's just the wine, right?

She's not going to suddenly cry about this for the first time in front of Ben. She is not. "But if he let it happen or chose for it to happen? To leave us—me—behind?" She avoids his eyes as she finishes; the last thing she wants is for him to reach out and physically offer comfort.

"I know you know this," Ben says after a pause. "But if he really let that happen, that's on him. It had nothing to do with you."

"I know that, intellectually," she says. "But it's hard, to think I wasn't reason enough for him to stick around."

"But even if you hadn't only been four years old, it still would be on him. The only person who could have changed that decision was him. And it just might have been too hard for him to do."

"I am glad I went," she says. "It was easier to just assume it was some horrible accident, but I'm learning not to settle for easy. Going there, visiting that place, forced me to . . ." She pauses, looking for the words. "Maybe it forced me to see how angry I was at him, for not being here? For whatever reason."

"Could be. That would mean we're both angry at dead men."

"Fucking dead white men, right?"

"Maybe they did the best they can?"

"You think?"

"Some men are too weak to do what they should, so they just do what they can," he says.

"So I have to just forgive all these weak men?"

Ben nods slowly, even though he is on that list, too. "Forgive and accept, maybe? Accept the fact that they are not as strong as you?"

"Jesus," she says, shaking her head. "If they're not as strong as me, then they're fucked."

"Oh, you're strong," he says.

"Crazy strong?"

"In all the best ways."

"I hope you're right." She looks over her shoulder, as if sensing that Troy is waiting for her by the door leading back into the house. "Crazy enough to perform at my first open mic this month."

"What?" It's the most surprising thing he has heard all night. She never even wanted to play piano for him, never mind in front of a room full of strangers. "When?"

"I just promised someone I'd do it in May. I'll make it as late in May as I can."

He tries, and fails, not to wonder who the someone is she has promised. "It sounds like a great idea to me."

"We'll see. I need songs first. Most people do originals, and it turns out I've never written one of those."

"You have a few weeks, right? And I know you can write." He feels a blush come across his cheeks as he remembers flirting with her in class.

"From no songs to two in a few weeks? Not sure about that."

"You have to do two? Maybe one original and one cover?"

She smiles. "Maybe I can work up a Taylor song. 'I Knew You Were Trouble'?"

"Just what I was thinking."

Nina picks up her plate and the two empty wine glasses, then stands up. "I'm gonna go back to my Gay Date." She bows slightly. "Thanks for an unexpected and interesting interaction."

"Well put," he says, returning the half-bow from his seated position. "You do have a way with words." He makes her smile with that, and he's glad that she chased him down. This was a much better ending than the one they had before, another reminder that closure should never be undervalued.

That idea makes him think of how hard it must be for Darlene and Toni, denied a chance for closure with people they had been close to. And that reminds him of that practice tape.

"Nina," he calls, standing up. She turns to him, a quizzical look on her face, as if to ask, Why would you blow a decent ending? "For the open mic—how about a song that no one's ever heard? That you could make your own?"

36 | National Burger Day

Ben arrives a half-hour early at the Starbucks Natalie selected for their meeting, so he takes out his Mac and checks in for tomorrow's flight. He dreads walking onto set of the "Actors & Assessors" launch video, but that dread is eased by the business class seat his father purchased and the three weeks at a Chelsea Airbnb negotiated as part of his involvement. Honeybird never made it to New York, but their story—the first draft, anyway—will hopefully be finished there.

After he gets his boarding pass he looks over his email. Toni wrote, asking him to let her know when he gets the release from Natalie and apologizing again for the delay in the second part of her recorded answers. He had given up on getting any more information from her, after two follow-ups went unanswered. But when Nina expressed interest in covering "Don't Go, Darlene," he felt like he had to ask permission, even though only a few people would hear Nina's version. Toni wrote back the next day to say she loved the idea of someone singing Nate's songs and attached an MP3 with another forty-minutes of stories about their childhood.

There's also an email from Duncan. They were going to get together one more time before Ben left for New York, but it never happened. They've only seen each other once since the failed May Day party run, and it felt like they'd been through the male equivalent of an ill-advised one-night stand: one friend seeing the other at an especially vulnerable moment. Ben knows that Carrie is back, and in the new email Duncan refers to "minute progress in the Reykjavik negotiations," but Ben has resisted asking for details about Carrie's mood, or Shelley, or how much progress Duncan has made on his dissertation. Callous as it sounds, he just needs to finish his own work and hit the job market in the spring.

It is beginning to feel like time to leave Atlanta.

Nina calls Connie when she gets to Big Tex. They've been talking several times a day since Sarah was born, and Nina wants to have the evening check-in now, so she doesn't find a series of messages after she plays. "How's the world's best mom?" she asks, watching Howard walk up with his guitar. He'd dropped her off at the front door with her keyboard. Didn't ask; just did it. His natural sweetness is something she has to stop being suspicious of and just accept.

"I don't know who that is, but can you ask her to call me? Because I'm lying on my bed, surrounded by what seems like a lifetime of dirty clothes. There's a pretty strong scent of puke in the air, and sweet Jesus, *The Golden Girls* is on TV, for some reason."

"Is that why you're whispering? Don't want to miss a good Estelle Getty quip?"

Howard raises his eyebrows, mouths, "Estelle Getty?"

"No, I can't find the fucking remote. Sarah is asleep next to me, and I know her pop-up timer will go off any second. So I'm not moving. Trying to make the silence last as long as possible."

"See? Super Mom!"

Snort. "Tell me of the real world. Are you going out with Howard again? Or gonna just skip straight to the hot Asian sex?"

"Oh, we'll have hot sex," Nina says, just to watch Howard duck his head and blush. "But we're gonna go grab dinner first. It's National Burger Day, you know."

"Man, have a kid, and you lose out on all the big holidays. Will you take pictures for me?"

"Of the sex or the burgers?"

"Sex got me into this mess. Shots of clean tables and cute waiters, please."

"Of course," Nina says, but her answer is drowned out by a sharp, sudden cry from Sarah. Connie offers a quick goodbye, and just before the line goes silent Nina hears a soft and reassuring, "It's okay, baby, it's okay." Once again she marvels at witnessing this side of her friend. Had this calm and nurturing Connie always been there, just overshadowed by the other, louder Connies?

And if Nina ever has a kid, what secret part of herself will emerge? Hopefully not an anxious and sharp-edged Nina, reminiscent of her mother, but a calm and centered Nina, more like the maternal side of Connie.

She hangs up and turns to Howard. "If she ever finds out you played in public and didn't tell her, she's going to kill you," he says.

"But I didn't tell anyone."

"'I'm not anyone,'" he says, in his ever-improving impersonation of Connie.

"Then we'd better not let her find out."

"Secrets? Mmmm, mmmm, my baby's got a secret."

"Nice reference," she says, holding the door open for him, "but I'm still not wearing a Madonna wig. Ever."

Big Tex is just as she remembers it from their previous visit; it even looks as though the same people are in the corner booth, and the performer who was first the last time they came is tuning up his guitar. The familiarity is reassuring, calming. The whole car ride, she wished she was the kind of person who could have a couple of beers to relax and still be able to remember how to play the songs. Luckily routine can be just as calming, so once they have added their instruments to the small stack to the right of the stage, she quietly asks Howard if he would mind getting her a ginger ale. He smiles. "Your usual. Of course."

She watches him walk away, order the drinks with a smile from a waitress, and then check in with the emcee. Confident. In control. Like he does this all the time, though she knows that this is his first public performance since a friend's party, almost two years ago.

Nina thought he was joking when he suggested, as the semester ended, that they reveal their musical skills, or lack thereof, at the same time. "We each learn the same song, get together, play it. Bam. You show yours, I show mine." After a long dinner and a second glass of rosé she understood he was serious, and agreed to his crazy experiment. When he said the test song should be "I'm So Tired" she protested that there was no piano. He told her just to work out the chords so she could play along. "Trust me. It's perfect," he insisted. "Two minutes long, slow as fuck, and I'll even sing it," he said.

A week later he showed up at B-6 with his guitar and they played it together. They botched the count-in on the first attempt, and she had to stifle a laugh when he started to sing—not because his voice was funny, but because she was so relieved it sounded so warm and deep—but then she had two of her best minutes of the last few months. They didn't even need to talk about it afterward; he'd just grinned, kissed her on the forehead, and then asked, "So what songs we gonna do at the open mic?"

Natalie walks in right at seven-thirty. "Thanks for coming out this way," she says when he stands to greet her. "This week is crazy at work."

"Thank you for meeting me again."

Natalie settles into the overstuffed chair next to his and politely declines his offer of a drink. "Grandma says to apologize again for taking so long," she says, reaching into her large handbag and taking out an envelope.

"Thank you," Ben says. He didn't think he needed a release from Toni, but Reed kept telling him he would feel better if he got one, that sometimes people feel differently when secrets they willingly revealed to one person are out in the world. Aside from finishing his negotiations with Foxy for photo rights, he now has all the clearances he needs for the dissertation. He takes the envelope and slides it into his laptop bag. "And thank your grandmother for me, please."

"I will." She hesitates and then adds, with her first smile since arriving, "I think she's ready for the story to come out. Even though it's been hard to relive everything."

Ben nods. "I will tell the story as well as I can, I promise."

"Grandma thinks you can," she says, reaching back into her handbag, "and thought you should have this."

She hands him an ancient-looking spiral-bound notebook, its bright yellow cover filled with random doodles of hearts, a few birds, and a tall tree with lots of scraggly branches in the bottom right corner. In the center, hidden amidst the drawings, the name Toni Williams is written in a flowery script.

"Says she came home from school one day and couldn't find it anywhere. Turns out Nate had taken it, said he needed some paper. And then he never gave it back."

Ben carefully flips the pages as Natalie talks. Random notes on the American Revolution are interrupted by a new handwriting halfway through. Lyrics, with lots of scratched out words and questions. The first page is labeled "Tired Tired Hands," and is clearly a very rough draft of what became "Heavy Heavy Hands." The switch from tired to heavy was smart, creating a more interesting, more unexpected, image. Looking ahead, treating the brittle pages as carefully as he can, Ben sees that the rest of the book is filled with lyrics, most of them featuring lots of crossed-out words and changes, the kind of editing trail a historian dreams of finding. "This is just, I mean." He carefully closes the notebook and turns back to Natalie. "It's incredible. Can I keep it long enough to make copies?"

"It's for you, Mr. Davies," Natalie says. "Grandma says it hasn't been hers since the day Nate took it."

He looks down at the notebook, and then back to Natalie. "I really have nothing to say."

When she stands up to say goodbye, he also rises. He watches her leave and then sits back down, still holding Nate's notebook. It feels odd, to be holding such a direct link to such a very different time. Just a few minutes ago he had been sitting with Natalie and no one around them had given them a second look. That certainly would not have been the reaction if Darlene and Nate had been sitting closely together in Atlanta fifty years ago.

He's still flipping carefully through the notebook when the alarm on his phone goes off. If Big Tex is on schedule, Nina is about to play Nate's song.

"Ladies and gentleman, 'Study Group.'"

Nina stares at the keyboard, trying to create a calm and still universe for herself by studying the shape of the keys, the way the flats fit into the whole notes. After they're introduced she turns to Howard. His smile is as confident and wide as it was the first time he walked over to her after class; it calms her enough to allow her to scan the crowd. Maybe a dozen people, including the emcee and other performers impatiently looking at their watches, waiting for their turn to play.

"Thanks for coming," Howard says, giving his guitar a strum. "We're gonna start with a fifty-year-old unreleased song from a band you've never heard of." He waits for the polite laughter, smiles when it arrives. "Because that's how we roll." He turns to Nina and points at the microphone angled in front of her keyboard. "You should go ahead and say hello to the good people," he says. "Make sure that thing works."

She doesn't sing until the second song, but it does make sense to at least test the mic, so she quietly says, "Hello to the good people," trying not to be alarmed at the way her voice sounds in the PA.

There's more polite laughter, and as it dies down Howard's right hand begins to strum. They agreed he should start "Don't Go, Darlene," because when Nina gets nervous she speeds up. After two rounds of the chords, she starts playing and he begins to sing.

> Only thing I knew for sure
> No one can know me
> Sitting on my heavy hands
> Let life pass by me
>
> Just hiding here in plain sight
> No one can see me
> I really thought I was alright
> Until you found me

It was odd for Ben to suggest that she and Howard play some unrecorded Honeybird song, but Nina was curious enough to ask him to send it. Then she loved it so much that she forwarded it to Howard, and he thought it was "about damn time people heard this." Which meant they'd just had to write one song before their end of May self-imposed deadline.

> Now you're close
> So please don't go

At first she worries they're playing too slow, but a few seconds later she's afraid they're playing too fast. The only way she can keep playing at all is by watching her fingers hit the notes. The bridge manages to pull her out of her head and fully into the song, and then the slide into the outro catches her by surprise: it's over already?

As they hit their final chord her eyes find Howard's, just in time to be looking at him while they hear the applause. It's at least as loud as it was for the girl who sang about stabbing her mother to death, and Nina considers that a win.

"Thanks, everyone," Howard says, quietly checking his tuning. "That's an old love song written by Nate Williams, and we thought it was about time people heard it. So thanks for listening. But I told Nina," he continues, turning to look at her, "we had to write one of our own, for the proper Study Group experience. And she said?"

Again he is forcing her to talk, but he is also setting her up for easy return shots. "You're fucking crazy," she says into the mic. More polite laughter, and then he gives a nod to let her know it's time to start.

Howard starts this one, too. She listens closely to his voice, which sets the tempo since there is not much guitar at the beginning. When it's time for her to come in she closes her eyes, making the crowd disappear and the music easier to see, trusting her fingers to find the right keys. Howard told her he had something that could work for their original song, but needed help finishing it. She suspected a trick, of course, that he could finish on his own easily enough but wanted to prove wrong her insistence that she could not write a song, ever.

He played it for her in B-6, sitting on the futon, shirtless, leaning against the wall, completely calm. She was worried about what to say if she didn't like the song, but luckily didn't have to figure that out. His voice sounded even better singing his own words.

> I'm turning off the doors
> Locking all the lights
> Just to be certain
> I do it more than twice
> Cutting all the knots
> Fixing what is right
> And just to be certain
> Shutting both my eyes

It was one of those songs that felt like someone had been spying on her, it seemed such a part of her life already. There was no chorus yet, so Howard told her she needed to write one, and hummed a little melody that could work. After worrying about her assignment for days, convinced she would let him down, the answer came one night after a long work shift. Tired, feeling a bit sad and lonely, and annoyed at herself for feeling sad and lonely, she missed Sid more than she had since the night he disappeared. That was when she understood that she would always miss him, and that waiting for that feeling to go away would make her as unhappy as waiting for him to come back. Knowing his food bowl and leash were still hidden in the pantry only made her feel even sadder, but keeping some tangible artifacts close felt necessary, at least for now.

So she grabbed a container of cold leftover Dan Dan noodles from the fridge and headed to the balcony, remembering the night she and Howard wandered around the apartment building, looking for Sid. Nina wanted to believe that he wasn't wandering Midtown as a lost dog, but that his soul had moved on, that he had finally achieved Nirvana and was freed from the cycle of life and death. Even so, she still wished that he had stayed with her. She knew it was selfish, to wish his transcendence be delayed so that he could spend more time with her. But she was a work in progress and not ready for Nirvana yet. That meant a little selfishness was forgivable, right?

> Morning comes and I have not left
> Another day I'm not done yet
> Long is samsara
> Samsara is long

Nina called Howard to sing her idea, as softly as she could get away with. She told him he could hate it, her feelings wouldn't be hurt if he thought it was too sad. He loved it, though—or said he did, anyway. "The best lyrics can mean different things to different people, Simone, and I don't think it's sad. Like, samsara is that time we're here, trying to get things right. And this says we have a lot of time to do that, to try to get it right. That's a good thing, isn't it?"

Howard said that he hears her voice singing every time he plays the song, and that it won't sound finished until she sings it. She refused to take on lead vocals the first time she performed in public, but agreed to join him for the lines "Long is samsara/Samsara is long." His voice sounds so confident and clear that she's afraid when her voice will ruin the effect. When he starts the series of chords that transition into the chorus, though, he turns to give her a slight nod, and she decides she can try. After taking one last breath, she leans forward, her lips as close to the microphone as she can bear to move them. The first syllable is a little scratchy, but at least she comes in at the right spot. She even manages to sing the word "samsara" clearly.

Time seems to accelerate during the second half of the song. Suddenly she is singing the chorus again, and while it's impossible to know how her voice sounds to anyone else, inside her head it sounds like her, it sounds just as she hoped her voice could sound. For one perfect moment that is satisfaction enough. As they run the chords down one last time for the outro, she forces herself to focus her gaze, first at Howard, who looks so comfortable in the world, and then out into the crowd. The same number of people seem to be watching as when they started, but she doesn't recognize any of the faces. Has the audience turned over, or was she so nervous earlier she could not see clearly? When they reach the final chord, her fingers float as they leave the keyboard, freed from a gravitational pull she did not notice until it was gone. She closes her eyes so she can hear the music more clearly, listening as it slowly drifts into the air, completing its journey to wherever the fire goes when it has burned out.

Acknowledgements

Songs by Honeybird has traveled an especially long and winding road to publication. Once again, I could not have done this without a large and supportive cast of friends.

My invaluable writing group—Susan Rebecca White, Sheri Joseph, Beth Gylys, and Jessica Handler—patiently read most of the failed earlier attempt at this novel, as well as sections from the reboot; their advice over the years has made me a better writer and a better reader in more ways than I can measure. Jessica also came with me to Big Tex for open mic night research, and provided many great one word reactions, some of which I just went ahead and stole.

Alison Law was line editor extraordinaire, helping me hunt down excess semi-colons and break up some of those longer and windier sentences.

Lunches with Daren Wang served as support group meetings and brain-storming sessions. Without Daren's help I might still be looking for a title, and might not have ever realized the key role a broken garbage disposal could play.

Bob Fenster read multiple drafts of the novel, offering insightful comments and displaying an eagle eye for typos. My other beta-testers were Marsha Cornelius, David Epstein, Tricia Brock Madden, Craig Dorfman, Richard Fulco, and Pam Dittmer, all of whom provided crucial feedback.

There would be no soundtrack without Jeff Jensen, who gave voice to Harlan, and Jonny Daly, who was the perfect producer, engineer, and mix master. A project like this only works if everybody is all in on the concept, and they both went above and beyond. The same goes for all the Honeybird co-writers, including Jeff and Jonny, as well as Bob Fenster and Chuck Walston. Thanks to Lee Kennedy for his bass work, Bill Shaouy for his keyboard magic, and Bill Phillips for bringing those crucial horns to "Waiting Here." Steve Gorman and Sven Pipien were the perfect rhythm section for "Heavy Heavy Hands," which was engineered by Marty Kearns (who also provided some fantastic piano playing). Amanda Motes Glass and Laura Seebol sang beautifully with Harlan, and C. G. Brown provided Nate with the voice he deserved. Finally, Kris Hauch and Kim Ware proved the perfect choices to provide music for the two non-Honeybird tracks, and Joel Boyea's mastering finished things off just right.

I'm also lucky to have skilled visual artists to call on. Michael Hunter designed the CD Booklet, and Sarah Marks created a cool logo for Honeybird and a unique version of the Samsara Wheel. Anne Richmond Boston asked me a whole bunch of perceptive questions about the book, and then designed the perfect cover.

This book wouldn't even be in your hands without the support and enthusiasm of Mark Doyon and Wampus Multimedia. I've had the chance to release music and books with a wide range of companies, big and small, and nothing makes an artist feel better than trusting their work to people who understand what you are trying to do.

Finally, and most importantly, thanks and love to Bruce & Olivia & Teagan, who have made my life richer than I ever dreamed it could be.

Notes on Research

Writing this book required me to learn more about Buddhism and Macon. To learn more about Siddhartha Gautama, I started with Karen Armstrong's *Buddha*. For more about the philosophy and ideas of Buddhism, I used the same book as Nina—*Buddhism for Dummies*. I also read *In Love With the World: A Monk's Journey Through the Bardos of Living and Dying*, by Yongey Mingyur Rinpoche and Helen Tworkov, which helped me gain a better understanding about the Buddhist frame of mind.

To learn more about Macon's racial and musical past, I started with *Street Singers, Soul Shakers, Rebels with a Cause: Music from Macon*, by Candice Dyer, which was full of valuable quotes from the time period, as well as lots of great pictures and thoughtful analysis. *Macon Black and White: An Unutterable Separation in the American Century*, by Andrew M. Manis, provided a thorough and readable overview of the city's political history. Dr. Manis and Dr. Robert Burnham were also kind enough to talk to me on phone about this project, and helped me get a better understanding on what life may have been like for Darlene, Harlan, and Nate during this time period.

www.ingramcontent.com/pod-product-compliance
Lightning Source LLC
LaVergne TN
LVHW021151180125
801621LV00001B/58